Savage
Oaks

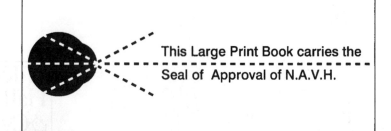

This Large Print Book carries the
Seal of Approval of N.A.V.H.

Savage Oaks

JULIE ELLIS

G.K. Hall & Co. • Thorndike, Maine

Library of Congress Cataloging-in-Publication Data

Ellis, Julie, 1933–
    Savage oaks : a novel / by Julie Ellis.
       p.   cm.
   ISBN 0-7838-9158-X (lg. print : hc : alk. paper)
   1. New Orleans (La.) — Fiction. 2. Savannah (Ga.) — Fiction.
 3. Plantation life — Fiction. 4. Large type books. I. Title.
PS3555.L597 S26 2000
 813′.54—dc21   00-044941

*For Maurice and Mabel Silberman,
and, of course,
Nancy and Gillian and Janet*

With grateful acknowledgment of able research assistance provided by Aline H. Morris and Rose Lambert and staff of the Louisiana State Museum in New Orleans; Lilla M. Hawes, Director, Georgia Historical Society in Savannah; the Steamship Historical Society of America (Staten Island Office), the Genealogy and History rooms of the New York Public Library; and the Mid-Manhattan and Epiphany branches of the New York Public Library.

One

The early October sun shone on the vast green woods of poplars, chestnuts, and live oaks that stretched for three leagues behind the Convent where Suzanne Duprée had lived since she was three, and lent a golden glow to the Seine, which flowed beside the property. Pheasants and partridges fed fearlessly along the path where Suzanne often rode.

Her luminous amber eyes swept appreciatively about the familiar view as she tossed back her long, tawny hair from the oval of her face. Why must she waste such a glorious day in the classroom?

Once she had enjoyed her studies because they alleviated the loneliness that was so much a part of her life. But now she inwardly rebelled at this confinement. Ever since Cecile had left the Convent to be married, Suzanne had felt an intensified loneliness, a new restlessness.

"It's no use, Napoleon," she sighed, tugging at the reins. "We must go back to the Convent."

Napoleon whinnied in protest, but he obeyed. Dear Napoleon. Suzanne leaned forward to caress his silken neck as he galloped towards their destination.

As she rode, the breeze whipping through her hair, Suzanne allowed her mind to race back through the years. How tenaciously she had clung to her little-girl fantasies about Maman and Papa! In that secretive little world she had been so confident that one day Maman and Papa would appear at the Convent at the edge of Paris to swoop her up and take her away with them. Even now she clung to the precious shadowed memory of a young woman with a lilting laugh and a man who tucked her into bed each night. Always she was frustrated that the memories were faceless; but she could see, even now, the intricately designed ring that Papa always wore. She had loved to sit on his lap and twirl the ring on his finger. Not until she was ten did she accept the truth, that Maman and Papa had died in a steamboat accident on the Mississippi River.

The other students who came to study at the renowned Convent from all over Europe had families and homes to which to go during school holidays. But Suzanne remained at the Convent, desolate and shamed. Only three times in all those years had she had a visitor. And each time it was Mr. Gilbert Mauriac of New Orleans, in the United States, her guardian and a dear friend of Papa's. Each month she dutifully wrote to "Uncle Gilbert," as she called him.

Why did Uncle Gilbert always evade her questions about Maman and Papa? She had been too shy at their last meeting to press him, and it was simple to avoid what she asked in letters. Could it be true that she was left afloat in the world with no uncles, no aunts, no cousins?

The last time Uncle Gilbert had come to Paris was three years ago, in 1852, when she was fourteen. He had taken her to *Trois Frères Provençaux* for a dinner that she had talked about with such enthusiasm that the Sisters had reproached her. After dinner they had attended a performance of a Molière play at the Comédie-Française. And when he discovered her passionate interest in what was happening in the world, he had arranged for the Paris and London newspapers to be delivered to her regularly, and at intervals he sent batches of New Orleans and New York newspapers to her.

Suzanne's thoughts shifted to her closest friend, Cecile, whose magnificent wedding had taken place three weeks ago today. It was Cecile who had brought her out of her shyness, coaxed from her the high spirits that she had guiltily kept locked within her lest they offend the Sisters. Cecile's parents, the Comte and Comtesse de Mirabeau had sent Cecile to the Convent because morals were shockingly lax in Paris and Cecile was too venturesome for their comfort. It was Cecile who had persuaded the Sisters to allow the two girls to ride each morning in the woods.

"They allow this," Cecile confided with ribald amusement when the arrangements were consummated, "not because it is so fashionable, but to give us exercise that will keep us less inclined to think wicked thoughts."

"Cecile, you talk sinfully," Suzanne had laughingly reproached, but she adored to hear Cecile's earthy confidence about the notables — and the demimonde, a term invented by Alexandre Dumas *fils* in his play that opened at the Gymnase Theatre in March.

Cecile always listened solemnly while she talked about Florence Nightingale, who had gone fearlessly to the Crimea to nurse the wounded, and about Anne McDowell and Lucy Stone and Lucretia Mott, who were fighting for women's rights in the United States. What a shock it had been when Cecile told Suzanne she was to be married!

"Cecile, who?" she had clamored in disbelief. Cecile knew no young men.

"I met him when I was last home. Just once," she conceded with candor. "His parents have made the arrangements with Maman and Papa. Suzanne, it is that way in France." Cecile shrugged philosophically, but her eyes avoided Suzanne's. Only last week Cecile swore she would never marry a man she did not love. Cecile wanted to run away from the Convent with her so they might join Miss Nightingale in the Crimea.

"Oh, Cecile, I'll miss you." Suzanne had felt suddenly desolate.

But the most exciting time in her life had been the week before Cecile's wedding, when she stayed at the imposing de Mirabeau mansion on the Faubourg-St.-Germain. The vast rooms were lavishly furnished with the finest antiques and elaborate wall hangings. There were monumental fireplaces and marvelously paneled ceilings. At first she had felt ill-at-ease in the lavish *chambre* that was to be hers for the week. After the austere whitewashed room at the Convent it was almost overwhelming. But quickly Cecile had swept her up into the festivities. She awoke that first morning to find Cecile at her bedside, impatient to show her Paris. . . .

"Up, Suzanne!" Cecile ordered ebulliently. "Maman is taking us today to see Monsieur Worth about your gown for the wedding. And afterwards she is taking us to luncheon at Magny's in the Latin Quarter!"

Quickly Suzanne dressed, then Cecile and she presented themselves to the Comtesse with their girlish anticipation well hidden by the required demeanor. They drove in the de Mirabeau landau along the wide boulevards noisy with the clatter of carriage wheels and the resounding ring of horseshoes. Landaus, coupes, victorias and phaetons hurried to their destinations, viewed by the throngs that lined the walks on either side. Singers, jugglers, magicians, organists with colorfully garbed monkeys competed for the attention of pedestrians.

"*À la coque!*" called the egg merchants. "*À la*

barque!" coaxed the oystermen.

Driving along the Rue de Richelieu, Suzanne felt part of herself caught up in the convivial spirit of the occasion, yet deep within herself she was painfully aware that she was alone in the world, with neither mother nor father to nurture her through such a momentous event.

The de Mirabeau landau stopped before the house of Gagelin, where Monsieur Worth was said to create masterpieces for ladies who could afford his services. Suzanne had expected that her gown, a gift from the Comtesse, would come from the new department store, Le Louvre, which had been opened earlier this year; but the Comtesse insisted on an original design from the great Monsieur Worth.

In a dream Suzanne stood patiently while Monsieur Worth himself draped fabrics about her small, fragilely slender form.

"Seventeen yards of velvet for the skirt," Cecile whispered impishly when Monsieur Worth left them alone for a few moments. "So much that there is not enough for the top."

Suzanne worriedly inspected her reflection in the tall mirror opposite. This was a stranger staring at her, in yards of pale yellow velvet, trimmed with bands of matching velvet, with a train of Brussels lace, which she must learn to manage before the wedding.

When at last they left Gagelin, the Comtesse took them, as promised, to Magny's, where a table had been reserved for luncheon.

"Maman," Cecile whispered, wide-eyed as they followed the maitre d' to their table, "is that not Mme. Sand sitting there?"

"You are not to look," the Comtesse ordered sternly, but both Cecile and Suzanne gazed in fascination at the woman clad in male attire, who was talking animatedly with three gentlemen.

"George Sand, who wrote *Indiana*?" Suzanne was awestruck. Secretively, wickedly, she had bought books by Mme. Sand, which condemned man's cruelty, social prejudices, and conventional morality, and hid them under her mattress in her room at the Convent.

"The writer," the Comtesse confirmed with disapproval. But as they were seated, she covertly inspected the objectionable table. "There are the de Goncourt brothers and M. Turgenev with her," the Comtesse conceded with reluctant approval.

The Comtesse, knowledgeable about the sumptuous fare at Magny's, ordered for them the *pieds de mouton à la poulette*. After serious consultation with the wine steward, she chose a bottle of Château Lafite 1847. After the bland, modest food of the Convent, this was an incredible feast to Suzanne.

Each day and evening seemed to surpass the previous one in the splendor of the diversion devised by the Comtesse. They visited the Guignol on the chestnut-lined Champs-Élysées and attended an Offenbach operetta. Suzanne was entranced by the night scenes of Paris, the rattle

13

of the night omnibuses ablaze with colored lights blending with the sounds of the street criers selling flowers and soap and mussels. *"Fleurissez vos amours,"* the flower girls urged exuberantly.

There were dinner parties in Cecile's honor in great houses on the Rue St. Honoré on the Right Bank and the Faubourg-St.-Germain on the Left Bank. One afternoon, like all fashionable Parisians, Suzanne, Cecile, and the Comtesse visited the colorful Garden of the Tuileries, where at least twice a week the military band of the Garde Impérial presented a concert. Suzanne was delighted by the sunlit panorama that spread before them. The ladies wore billowing crinolines; the gentlemen were in tophats, frock coats and light trousers. Here and there was a colorful uniform. Children elegantly dressed in the latest fashions and accompanied by their governesses played with hoops and balloons.

"Look at all the glengarries and Scottish tartans," Cecile whispered as they paused to admire a trio of winsome children. "Anything remotely English is much admired."

"When the Empress is in residence at the Tuileries, she sometimes strolls here," the Comtesse confided. "She's beautiful, but she wears too much paint on her face."

Everywhere there was an air of elegance, Suzanne thought. Rarely would the working class be represented here. She knew, unhappily, about the slums that infested Paris. Near Rue Montmartre there were rows of decaying houses with open sewers running in front of them, and in the vicinity of Rue Saint-Denis workers crowded into miserable little hovels to make artificial flowers and tawdry jewelry. Even in the space between the great Louvre museum and the Tuileries there were slums.

"Come," the Comtesse said when they were weary of walking. "Let us go to Tortoni's for ice cream."

The following afternoon the Comtesse escorted Suzanne and Cecile to the Bois de Boulogne, the great park and woods on the edge of Paris, for a drive around the lake. This was a spectacle for which Paris was famous. All along the Avenue de l'Impératrice, which led into the park, they saw the gentlemen with their ladies in elegant riding habits. Around the lake rode gleaming carriages drawn by purebred English horses.

Suzanne was enthralled by the splendor on every side. Flowers, sweeping expanses of lawns, waterfalls and winding streams vied for her admiration.

"There are over two thousand acres here," the Comtesse told Suzanne. "Four hundred thousand trees have been planted. It reminds me much of Hyde Park in London."

"Papa says the Emperor himself and the Duc de Morny ride here," Cecile said blithely. "I myself have seen the Empress here in her carriage. Before and after her were grooms wearing royal livery and an equerry on horseback surrounded the carriage. Her gowns are the most lavish in all of France!" Cecile pantomimed eloquently. "My cousin Jean tells me that when Eugénie's hairdresser arrives at the palace to do her hair, he must wear knee breeches and a sword."

"Eugénie thinks only of fashion," the Comtesse said with disdain. "And Louis Napoleon thinks only of women."

With breathtaking suddenness the day of the wedding arrived, and Suzanne stood before the awe-inspiring gothic cathedral of Notre-Dame, where Cecile was to be married. Her eyes swept upwards, admiring the glorious towers, the rose window, the spires. With Cecile's cousins she walked slowly down the four-storied nave, remembering that here Mary Queen of Scots was married to the Dauphin, and Henry VI was crowned King of France in 1431. Here Napoleon I seized the crown from the Pope and crowned himself Emperor in 1804.

Suzanne trembled, dazzled by the splendor of the Cathedral, the colorful costumes of the clergy, the bright hues of the military uniforms. The jewels of the beautifully gowned ladies reflected the myriad candles that illuminated the cathedral for the wedding.

With Cecile's cousins, she sat in a heavy, ornate pew and completely lost herself to the impressive nuptial Mass. As she listened, she remembered, uncomfortable with recall, how she had asked Uncle Gilbert, when he was last in Paris, if she had been born a Catholic, not truly

expecting a negative reply. It was a wicked th'
to ask, when Mère Angélique had been so devoted to her. Uncle Gilbert had said, after a few
moments of thought, that her parents had been
Protestants. After that she had felt less obligated
to consider becoming a novice, as she knew Mère
Angélique prayed she would.

She had no call to take the veil. The obsessive
need in her life was to penetrate the frustrating
wall of mystery about her parentage. As the
beautiful voices of the choir filled the cathedral,
Suzanne silently vowed to dedicate herself to discovering every small detail about her mother and
father. She would seek out people who had
known Maman and Papa. She would talk to
them. Maman and Papa would become alive in
her mind.

If anyone saw the tears that spilled over, Suzanne
reassured herself, they would believe that she was
overcome by the drama of the nuptial Mass.

Suddenly now a doe sprinted across the riding
path. Suzanne's reverie was splintered as Napoleon reared slightly. No more of this, she rebuked
herself. She must not be late for her class.

Soon the château rose into view. It had been
willed to the Order sixty years ago by a French
Comtesse who had spent her declining years in a
convent, with the stipulation that a school be organized for well-born young ladies. Suzanne circled around the château to come to a halt before
the gatekeeper's cottage, where she would leave
the roan. Who would believe this imposing struc-

ture had been built in the fifteenth century? It was the hard white *pierre de Boulay,* of which it was constructed, that provided the château with this aura of eternal youth.

Twelve hundred workmen had labored for ten years to bring the château to completion. Large and frequent windows pierced the substantial walls, allowing sunlight to flood the interior. The buildup of towers, gables, and dormers was highlighted by the *donjon* at the southeast corner of the château, and chimneys stood like protective towers against the blue of the sky. The château stood at the end of a courtyard. The main building rose to four stories, with low wings at each side.

Despite her deep affection for Mère Angélique and the Sisters, Suzanne felt herself encased in loneliness. Only when she rode in the woods — and now, alas, without Cecile beside her — was she able to obliterate from her consciousness the bitter knowledge that she was, in truth, totally alone in the world.

Suzanne dismounted, walking with lithe grace to the low wing of the château that housed the classrooms. As she crossed the threshold into the classroom, the teaching Sister smiled gently and beckoned to Suzanne.

"Mère Angélique wishes to see you in her apartment," the Sister said softly. "Go to her now."

Suzanne's eyes widened with astonishment. She whispered a polite assent and whirled on her heels, forgetting the Sisters' rules about walking, not running, within the château. Why did Mère Angélique call her to her private apartment? Was Mère Angélique, whom she adored, angry with her? Was she being too impulsive again, speaking out too freely in class? That she had learned from Cecile. Yet she was glad for this release.

Breathlessly she arrived at Mère Angélique's apartment, remembering how each Christmas, when she had frequently been the only child remaining in the dormitory, Mère Angélique had entertained her at a small party for just the two of them. She remembered the time when she was so ill with pneumonia, and Mère Angélique had sat with her through two whole nights. Was Mère Angélique going to talk to her about becoming a novice when she completed her education? *She couldn't.*

Suzanne knocked uneasily at Mère Angélique's door. A Sister pulled it wide, beckoned her inside. Mère Angélique sat on the small sofa where she consulted on emergencies with the Prioress or Vicaress.

"Suzanne, come sit beside me. We'll have tea." Mère Angélique smiled reassuringly, but suddenly Suzanne's heart was pounding. Only on momentous occasions was a student invited to have tea with Mère Angélique. Why were her eyes so sad today?

Obediently Suzanne sat beside Mère Angélique, alarm growing within her. The last student to have tea with Mère Angélique was there to be told that her mother had died. *What could be in store for her?*

"Suzanne, *ma chérie,* I have received a letter from M. Mauriac," she began slowly.

"He's not ill?" Suzanne broke in fearfully. Uncle Gilbert was her only link to her mother and father, to her roots.

"No, M. Mauriac is quite well," Mère Angélique soothed. "But he wishes you to return to New Orleans. You are to live on the — the — " Mère Angélique reached for the letter, scanned it anxiously. "On the plantation Tintagel," she read triumphantly. This was the plantation Uncle Gilbert had bought for her four years ago with funds from her estate. "He tells me it is very beautiful there."

Again Suzanne saw the infinite sadness in Mère Angélique's eyes, but now she comprehended. She was to leave the Convent, to put an ocean between Mère Angélique and herself! She had dreamt extravagantly of leaving the Convent and moving into the world she knew only from newspapers and books. But now that the moment was here she was beset by doubts.

"When?" Suzanne stammered.

"Tomorrow. M. Mauriac has made the arrangements."

"Why am I to go to Louisiana?" Suzanne asked bewilderedly. Mère Angélique had not said that her studies were finished.

"M. Mauriac has not set forth a reason, but he would not take this step unless it was important."

There was a faint reprimand in her voice that Suzanne would question his decision. "He knows, Suzanne, that you are ready to take your place in the outside world. Both M. Mauriac and I are proud of the way you have progressed in your studies. I doubt that there is a young lady in the whole of Louisiana who has been schooled so extensively."

"Must it be tomorrow?" Suzanne was trembling. It was so unlike Uncle Gilbert to be so peremptory.

"M. Mauriac has been specific," Mère Angélique said firmly. "I have already sent to Paris for a large portmanteau for you and have communicated with Mme. Vauban, who will accompany you to New Orleans, where her sister lives. She will deliver you directly into M. Mauriac's hands, and then she will go to visit with her sister for a month. You are to take only what you need with you for the trip. Your books and the rest of your wardrobe will be sent in a trunk by a later boat." Mère Angélique was talking with compulsive quickness, her voice unsteady.

"But tomorrow?" Suzanne reiterated. Her eyes clung to Mère Angélique's face. This was so unreal.

"Suzanne, it is better this way," Mère Angélique said tenderly. She forced a smile as the Sister arrived to serve them tea. "You will write me often and tell me how you are?"

"Regularly," Suzanne promised, tears stinging her eyes.

The day sped by with terrifying swiftness. The

other students were wildly curious about Suzanne's sudden departure. To them this was a glorious adventure. Everyone wished to help. But far into the night, Suzanne lay sleepless, staring at the ceiling, trying to remember everything Uncle Gilbert had told her about Tintagel.

"It adjoins Savage Oaks," he had said to her. "Savage Oaks is one of the showplaces of the South. A truly great plantation," he added with infinite respect.

She had talked with Cecile about Tintagel, which, of course, took its name from the Arthurian legends. It was at Tintagel in Cornwall that King Arthur was said to have had a castle. Laughingly she had corrected Cecile's pronunciation of Tintagel.

"No, no, Cecile!" she had reproached. "That's not the way you say it. First you say 'tin,' then emphasize the 'tag,' remembering that the 'g' sounds like the 'g' in 'badge.' Tin*taj*el."

"Oh, Suzanne, you will someday be a teacher," Cecile had mocked.

In the morning. forcing back tears, Suzanne said goodbye to Mère Angélique and the Sisters, while Mme. Vauban waited in the carriage. They would take the railroad in Paris to the port of Calais, and then would proceed by boat to England, where their destination would be Liverpool. Uncle Gilbert distrusted the packet ships that sailed from Le Havre to New York. Instead they would travel by a luxurious Collins liner to New York, and from there by train, coach, and ship to New Orleans.

Once in Louisiana she would seek out people who had known Maman and Papa. She would search for surviving relatives. She had made a vow in the Cathedral of Notre-Dame. *Nothing must stand in her way.*

Two

Savage Oaks was built in the grand style by Jonathan Savage, late of Cornwall, England, in the early days of the nineteenth century, not long after the United States bought Louisiana from Napoleon for four cents an acre. The stately white plastered brick mansion sat on a slight incline with a magnificent view of the Mississippi, behind a wide expanse of gardens that had been coaxed into a spectacular beauty through the years. The broad front gallery was two stories in height, supported by six fluted Doric columns. Over the large recessed doorway hung a graceful wrought-iron balcony. Now, in mid-October, the first camellias promised to blossom shortly under the outstretched limbs of tall, moss-draped live oaks. In their seasons dogwood, azaleas, magnolias, Cherokee roses and wisteria lent their fragrances to the river-scented air.

Handsome, dark-haired, dark-eyed Keith Savage scowled as he rode towards the house and spied the carriage out front. Gilbert Mauriac's carriage. A house servant had come to the mill to tell him of Mauriac's arrival.

"Mornin', Mist' Keith." The Mauriac coachman twisted about in his seat to greet him cheerfully.

"Good-morning, Sebastien."

Impatiently Keith dismounted, gave the reins to the small slave, who darted forward eagerly to take them. This was not the time of year for anyone to come calling, with the grinding season launched. Every hand on the plantation — man, woman, and child — was working eighteen hours a day, Keith along with them.

He mounted the steps with his jaw set, knowing Gilbert Mauriac had not come on a social call. He remembered Mauriac's compassion when the New Orleans attorney-banker sat with him after they had buried his father eight months ago, and told him the devastating facts about Savage Oaks' financial situation.

"Your father was fighting for survival, Keith," Mauriac had said gently. "Three bad seasons and a lot of equipment that had to be replaced put him heavily in debt to the bank. Come to the office in a week or so," he suggested diplomatically, "and I'll show you the figures."

Mauriac knew how fragile their hold was on Savage Oaks. But it was still inconceivable to Keith that Savage Oaks could go into the hands of the bank.

He reached for the door, pulled it open, strode into the wide hall, past the graceful, mahogany-

railed semicircular stairway and over a scattering
of priceless Persian rugs, to the library. His father
had been so proud of the library with its English
walnut paneling and book-laden shelves, its antique furnishings brought from England and
France. The Italian prints that hung on one wall
had been a sixteenth birthday gift from his
grandparents to his mother. The rosewood piano
that sat in a corner of the room had been his
father's wedding present to his mother.

From the open door Keith saw the slight, dis-
tinguished figure of Gilbert Mauriac, still handsome at forty-one, standing beside the carrara
marble mantel, his patrician face somber.

"I'm sorry to have taken so long, Sir," Keith
apologized perfunctorily, steeling himself for
what Mauriac must be here to say. That the bank
was displeased with the slowness with which he
was meeting his obligations. "We're into the
grinding season." Mauriac knew this was the
time when every sugar planter abandoned all socializing.

"I'm sorry to have called you away from the
mill, Keith." Mauriac smiled, but his eyes were
opaque. "How are Jane and Phillip?"

"They're both well, thank you." His sister,
Jane, ten years his senior and a surrogate mother
since he was four, knew about their financial difficulties. He saw the anxiety in her eyes, though
she never probed. Phillip, his younger brother,
nineteen and headstrong, knew nothing, though
he had been home from Princeton — at the col-

26

lege's request — for almost a year. Phillip lived in a world of his own. "Please sit down, Mr. Mauriac." Keith gestured him to one of the pair of gold velvet-covered chairs that flanked the fireplace.

Despite the pleasantness of the morning, Keith's hands were perspiring. He knew he was far past due on his bank notes. Even if the price of sugar went up by January, when the grinding would be finished, he would be able to reduce the loan by a painfully small amount. There was the overhead at the plantation to worry about until the next year's crop was ground and marketed, plus replacement machinery that was essential. Papa died of a heart attack brought on by his fear of losing Savage Oaks; he was convinced of that. Every year a plantation here or there went under to the bankers. Yet what could he say to Gilbert Mauriac that would make the bank less impatient to close out his loan?

"Keith, I realize how hard you've been working," Mauriac said slowly, searching for words.

"It's necessary," Keith dismissed this brusquely. If it had not been so urgent, he would never have given up reading law in Judge Campbell's office in Washington, which Senator Slidell had gone to such pains to arrange for him. He had worked twelve hours a day in that law office, he recalled with pride, not even coming home for the hot months when so many people deserted Washington.

"Keith, I know what you're going through,"

Mauriac said unhappily. "I know what Savage Oaks means to you. I wasn't just your father's banker and attorney. I was his friend. That's why I've fought so hard with the bank to give you time to pay off the notes. But now — " He spread his hands in a gesture of futility. "They don't see how you're going to be able to cope with such a massive debt."

"Mr. Mauriac, I need more time." Keith felt color flood his sun-bronzed face as he struggled to retain his composure.

"They'll give you more time only if there is definite indication of your acquiring new assets. Beyond the sugar crop," he added. His eyes probed Keith's. "Keith, I've known your family too long to mask the seriousness of the situation. You'll have to come up with fresh assets quickly, or the bank will take over Savage Oaks." He hesitated, seeing the color drain from Keith's face. Then he spoke slowly, cautiously, "There is a way to save Savage Oaks. A route not uncommon in the Deep South." He leaned back in his chair with an air of carefully choosing his words. "I know of a young lady. Pretty, intelligent, exquisitely educated in a convent on the outskirts of Paris. She's an orphan, my ward." Keith stared at him with astonishment. He had never once heard Mr. Mauriac speak of a ward. "Suzanne's inheritance could pay off the bank. It could provide funds for restoring Savage Oaks to its earlier grandeur."

"Mr. Mauriac, what are you trying to say?" Keith was stiff with rejection.

"I'm discussing an arranged marriage. Suzanne is very young, only seventeen; but she could become the perfect mistress for Savage Oaks, though I realize that Jane will always manage the household," he soothed diplomatically. "Also, Suzanne owns Tintagel." Keith was startled by this revelation; he had understood that Mauriac bought Tintagel for an absentee planter. So he had bought it for his ward! "That would add another thousand acres to Savage Oaks."

"Mr. Mauriac, I could never enter into an arranged marriage," Keith said with cold deliberation. "I've always considered the custom degrading to both parties."

"Keith, you have no other choice," Mauriac reminded forcefully. "You must be rational. I can hold off the bank for another two or three weeks. A month at the most. Suzanne will be arriving from Paris in ten days. I'll arrange a meeting. She's lovely. You'll see for yourself. Make your decision after you've seen her."

"I don't see how I can do this, Sir," Keith said tightly, but even as he spoke, he knew that Gilbert Mauriac was right. He could not give Savage Oaks over to the bank. "You said she was raised in a convent. I'm not Catholic," he hedged. "Surely — "

"Suzanne's parents were Protestant," Mauriac interrupted smoothly. "Her convent upbringing would not be a deterrent."

"You've said nothing of her parents," Keith said pointedly, his eyes guarded.

"Rest assured, Keith," Gilbert responded with an undercurrent of anger, "Suzanne's bloodlines are as fine as your own."

"She's been raised in France," Keith stalled. "My French is not the best."

"Suzanne Duprée came from a Southern family. She's equally at home in English, French, and Spanish." Mauriac rose to his feet. Keith saw the glint of understanding in his eyes. Mr. Mauriac knew he was asking for time to reconcile himself to what must be done. "Suzanne must not know that we have discussed marriage," Mauriac exhorted. What was he trying to pull off, Keith wondered with fresh irritation. "You must court her." Mauriac smiled faintly at Keith's astonishment. "Suzanne has known few young men. She's charmingly romantic. You'll know how to win her, Keith. I trust you to do this."

"I don't know that your confidence is merited," Keith warned. Damn Mauriac for pushing him against the wall this way! And what was so special about Gilbert Mauriac's ward that she must be handled with such delicacy? He must win her, his mind taunted.

"Keith, you are the most eligible young man in the parish. I'm sure the young ladies in Washington must have been in ardent pursuit. Of course," he added indulgently, "you can be confoundedly stubborn. That's why you play such a solid game of chess. But you must give this deep consideration, Keith." Again he was serious.

"I'll think about it, Sir," Keith promised with deference as he moved towards the door with Mauriac.

His mind in rebellion, Keith stood watching from the front door as Gilbert Mauriac climbed into his carriage. Only when the carriage was rolling down the driveway did he turn away, and was startled to see his sister's tall, lean frame hovering in the doorway of the small sitting room to the right of the hall.

"What did Mauriac want?" Jane demanded.

"The bank is pushing him," Keith explained evasively.

"Come in here and talk," Jane ordered, walking back into the sitting room. She loathed having the servants overhear discussions of their private affairs.

Keith closed the door behind him. Jane had to know the truth. How long could he pretend that they could cope with the bank's demands for payment?

"It's not good," he began tersely.

"The crop was fine," she shot back defensively, but her keen blue eyes were troubled. With one hand she brushed the fair, prematurely gray-streaked hair back from a face of near-classic beauty, marred by an air of deep-seated bitterness. "In January we should have money."

"Jane, the crop will see us through until the next season, no more," Keith said tiredly. "What I had hoped to give to the bank will have to go for repairs to the equipment. And even that," he acknowledged, "would have been insufficient to meet the loan."

"Keith, the bank dealt with Papa for twenty-five years!" she burst out angrily. "Savage Oaks is one of the finest plantations in the South. They know its value."

"They want their money, Jane."

She clasped one hand nervously with the other.

"You'll have to sell some slaves. Papa would forgive us."

"Jane, we would have to sell every able-bodied slave on the plantation to meet the loan," he said bluntly, and saw her recoil with shock. He took a deep breath. "There is a way. Mr. Mauriac came out to talk to me about it. He has a ward. She's been in a convent near Paris since she was very small. She has a large inheritance."

"He expects you to marry this girl for her inheritance?" Jane stared at him with a mixture of disbelief and fury. "Gilbert Mauriac expects you to marry a girl you've never seen? Someone about whom we know nothing?"

Keith's eyes avoided hers.

"She's been tenderly reared, she's seventeen, and supposedly beautiful. She would come to live at Savage Oaks as my wife, but you'd remain its mistress, Jane." Keith's tone was soothing. "You know that."

"Keith, how could you consider it?" Jane blazed. "Who are her parents? Is she French or American?"

"Mr. Mauriac didn't discuss this," Keith said unhappily, "though I gather her parents were from the South. He says she comes from a fine family. Their name is Duprée."

"There are Duprées in New Orleans," Jane pinpointed. "Is this her family?"

"I doubt it," Keith pointed out. "If they were, it isn't likely that Mauriac would be her guardian."

"Who is she, Keith?" Jane pushed arrogantly. "Gilbert's bastard child that he's hidden away all these years?"

"The girl is his ward," Keith said with deliberate calm. "Gilbert Mauriac would never have sent away his own blood."

"If his grandmother didn't approve, he would have," Jane guessed with disdain.

"Jane, if the girl were Mauriac's, Mme. Mauriac would have raised her as her great-grandchild," he rejected sternly.

"Keith, I can't believe you're seriously considering this!"

"Do you want to see the bank take over Savage Oaks?" he flared.

"She'll be like all the other plantation wives." Jane's voice trembled. "There'll be constant parties and visiting. Keith, you'll hate that!"

"We have no choice. We'll have to adjust. The girl arrives in ten days. We'll go through a pretense of courtship. I must woo her," he said sardonically. "But quickly, in deference to the bank's demands. That's the way it must be, Jane. There's no other way to save Savage Oaks."

★★★

As he approached the sugarhouse, Keith frowned in rebellion. Let Reagan handle the crew alone for the rest of the day. He was efficient enough as long as he stayed away from the whiskey, and he was too smart to drink this time of year. Reagan would be roaring drunk for a week when the hogsheads were loaded and the sugarhouse inactive.

Keith swung away from the path to the sugarhouse, headed for the stables. In the distance, along the levee, he spied Philip's tall, slender figure poised before an easel. Now Phillip was painting during every waking hour. Six months ago he drove the household insane with his incessant practicing at the piano.

He frowned. Damn, Phillip had commandeered Raoul from the sugarhouse to pose for him! Phillip knew how shorthanded they were this time of year. When they were out of this bind, he must sit down and talk to Phillip.

At the stables he dismounted and ordered that a carriage be readied for him. He would go into New Orleans and visit with Jacques. He had seen little of Jacques since he had come home from Washington. They had not been truly close the four years they were roommates at Princeton. Actually, it had been their similar backgrounds that brought them together. Jacques Rochambeau was flamboyant, fun-loving, and prone to taking off for holidays in Philadelphia — and on some occasions in New York City. But Jacques came from a fine Creole family, and in the Creole tradition had entered into a marriage arranged by his family, only four weeks after graduation. *Yes, go talk with Jacques.*

Fifty minutes later, arriving in bustling New Orleans, Keith realized how isolated he had allowed himself to become in his frenzied efforts to bring in a crop that, at best, could only faintly ameliorate their situation. Twice during the spring, when he had come into the city on business, he had stopped by Jacques' office near the St. Louis Hotel. Jacques was set up now as an attorney, with clients supplied by his parents and in-laws. Each time Jacques and he had gone to a restaurant near the French market that was said to make the best jambalaya in New Orleans, and talked for two hours about the years at Princeton. A half dozen times Jacques had sent a man out to invite him to dinner at his home or to a family ball. He had pleaded work at Savage Oaks.

Jacques received him with delight.

"What's the matter with you, Keith?" he rebuked. "Every time I invite you for dinner or to a party, you're too busy." Jacques spilled over with Creole charm. "Come, we'll go somewhere to eat and talk. Carlos — " He turned to his somber-faced clerk, "if anybody comes to call, I have been taken away on business."

Jacques hurried Keith out into the narrow, congested street, lavishly sprinkled with cafés and casinos, to Antoine's on St. Louis Street. For a few moments they were occupied with choosing from the menu, then Jacques settled back with an expansive smile.

"So," he jibed ebulliently, "when will you get married, Keith?"

"Why are you suddenly concerned about my marital state?" Keith demanded sharply.

Jacques shrugged, but his eyes were analyzing Keith.

"When a man works as hard as you, I think he's concerned about his future."

"I'm concerned about saving Savage Oaks," Keith said somberly.

"Keith, if you need a loan," Jacques offered, serious now.

"Jacques, my father went into horrendous debt to keep Savage Oaks afloat through three bad crops. I need a miracle," he said flatly.

"I didn't realize the situation was so bad." Jacques' air of conviviality was replaced by solicitude.

"Raising sugarcane is not like raising cotton," Keith reminded. He frowned, hearing his father's voice again. "Papa used to say that operating a sugar plantation was like betting on a throw of dice. Two years in a row we lost the entire crop to early frosts. Last summer there was a crevasse that ruined the whole year's work."

"Why didn't your father ever switch to cotton?" Jacques asked curiously.

"Damn it, man, we've got a fortune tied up in machinery!" And Papa remembered the years when the molasses alone paid all the expenses and the sugar brought twenty-five percent on his investment. "Jacques, how are things with you?" he asked with startling intensity.

"*Comme ci, comme ça.*" His smile was philosophical. "It's a comfortable life. I find my pleasures."

"What about your marriage?" Keith pinpointed.

"My wife is very pretty, an elegant hostess, and under the blankets she's as cold as a Northern winter." He grimaced with distaste. "In six months she's to give me an heir, so now I'm completely denied the privileges of her bed." He shook his head with an aura of bafflement. "I still remember our wedding night. She seemed to adore me. And then we got into bed. Her Mama had told her, 'You must do whatever your husband wishes.' But she was outraged when she discovered what her husband wished." He spread his hands in Gallic eloquence.

"Gilbert Mauriac came to me this morning." Keith's eyes were darkly unhappy. "He spoke to me about his ward, who has been brought up in a convent near Paris. He's eager to arrange a marriage between us."

"She's rich?"

"Quite," Keith conceded. If he married Suzanne Duprée, everything she owned under Louisiana law would become his.

"Have you seen her?" All at once Jacques was practical. "If she's presentable, then you've found your solution."

"I'll see her in about ten days. Mauriac says

she's very pretty, beautifully educated." Jacques flinched; he detested women with brains. "Hell, I have no choice, Jacques. I'll have to marry her if she looks like a flounder."

"Believe me, Keith, it won't be the end of the world for you," Jacques soothed. "You'll survive." He grinned. "You'll survive in luxury, free of debt."

The waiter arrived with their sumptuous meal, and by tacit agreement they abandoned serious talk for reminiscences about college friends, with whom Jacques meticulously kept in touch. Yet as they talked, Keith found his mind returning to the painful encounter with Gilbert Mauriac. Mauriac was right, of course. He could not allow Savage Oaks to revert to the bank. That was unthinkable. Yet the prospect of an arranged marriage remained repugnant to him. He remembered Jane's distress, her shock. But Jane was realistic; she would come to understand they had no choice.

"Bring us a Château Margaux 1848," Jacques told the waiter with a brilliant smile as he hovered at their table. The waiter, respectful of this choice, hurried off to the wine cellar. Jacques leaned forward with an air of confidentiality. "We must drink to your marriage," he said whimsically. "Let the bridegroom be the first to know."

They lingered long at the table, warmed by the wine, sipping endless cups of chicory-laced coffee. Jacques, for all his air of conviviality, sensed Keith's depression.

"Keith, I'm not going back to the office," he decided, a gleam of triumph in his eyes. He leaned forward conspiratorially. "You and I will go this afternoon to the Mansion House."

Keith was taken aback. He had heard, of course, about Yellowbird Shaw's Mansion House, which catered to the passions of senators and judges, planters and businessmen with impeccable backgrounds.

"Jacques, at this hour of the day?" he protested.

"Yellowbird receives gentlemen of quality — and money," he added humorously, "any time after three in the afternoon. Have you ever been there?"

"No," Keith acknowledged.

"Then you are in for something special!" Jacques' eyes brightened. "No house in Louisiana can compare with it. Remember when we went to New York to Flora's on Greene Street? And the time we went to Josie's farther uptown? We only got in because I had that letter of introduction from Judge Davis. We thought that was fancy!"

"It *was* fancy," Keith said drily. "I was broke for three months after that."

"You haven't been living like a monk at Savage Oaks," Jacques said slyly.

"Like a monk." Like Papa he had an aversion to miscegenation. "Anyway, I've been too busy."

"God, man, I don't believe you!" Jacques was incredulous. "No man's ever too busy."

"I was," Keith insisted. "But not happily."

"All right, that's the answer. We go to Yellowbird's Mansion House right now," Jacques decreed. "Nobody compares with Yellowbird. Her girls are magnificent. Her house is fantastic. And even if you are not in the mood, Yellowbird has provided diversions to change this."

They left Antoine's and drove to the Mansion House, set discreetly at the edge of town. Why not? Keith asked himself defiantly. Gilbert Mauriac was plotting to tie him down for life in a loveless marriage. What would convent-bred Suzanne Duprée know about pleasing a man? She'd recoil from that side of marriage, like Jacques' wife.

From the exterior the three-storied Mansion House seemed another of the fine town houses favored by wealthy New Orleanians. Keith and Jacques descended from their carriage to approach the gate that provided admittance through the wrought-iron fence that surrounded the stuccoed, slate-roofed structure, shaded by tall live oaks and magnolias. At the door Jacques sounded the knocker sharply against the heavy door. A liveried black man, after inspecting them through a grille, opened the door and bowed obsequiously, then gestured them into the expansive, crystal chandeliered foyer, from which rose a staircase lit by a massive fixture of sculpted bronze. The baluster appeared to be made of onyx.

"Please folluh me, Suhs."

The butler led them down the hall, its walls

hung with crimson damask, to a pair of double doors. With a flourish he pushed the doors open for Keith and Jacques. Keith guessed there was a series of such parlors. He was impressed by the sumptuous furnishings, the chairs and sofas upholstered in brocade and satin, the floor carpeted in velvet. Gilt-framed mirrors and fine paintings hung on the walls. Marble statues sat on lacquered Chinese tables. One walnut paneled wall was lined with bookshelves, laden with books bound in ivory and red leather.

"Nobody in this country has a collection of erotic literature to match this," Jacques said with a flourish. He walked to the bookshelves, pulled forth a book at random, opened it. "Keith, come over here and read this — " Already Jacques was aroused.

"Rather better than what you used to hide under your mattress at Princeton," Keith conceded self-consciously as he read over Jacques' shoulder.

"She has all the works of the Marquis de Sade. All the best of the French and Italian books."

"I don't read Italian," Keith reminded, clearing his throat with an unfamiliar nervousness. He was furious with himself for reacting to this erotic literature.

"You read French," Jacques shot back. "Don't tell me this doesn't make you want to throw one of Yellowbird's girls on her back."

Of course he was aroused. He was a man with normal desires, though admittedly living like a monk. But this afternoon — this whole day — was unreal. He should be back at the mill supervising operations.

"Good afternoon, gentlemen."

He swung about with a start as a feminine voice greeted them from the doorway.

A tall woman of about forty — square-jawed yet handsome, big bosomed but with an astonishingly small waist — walked toward them with a radiant smile. She wore yellow, setting off her honey-colored hair. Keith wondered if this explained her name.

"Ah, M. Rochambeau," she greeted Jacques in the French manner that her Creole clientele preferred. "It's good to see you." She turned inquiringly to Keith.

"This is a friend of my college days," Jacques said with an unexpected delicacy, avoiding identifying Keith by name. "I've told him how marvelously you cater to the pleasures of New Orleans gentlemen."

"At more conventional hours I would have more young ladies at your disposal," she apologized, but there was an air of confidence about her that spoke of success. "But at any hour I have two who are available to entertain you. Today there is Colette," she said with a smile at Jacques, who nodded appreciatively, "and Manon. I'm sure your friend will find her delightful."

"I'm sure." Jacques was impatient to be upstairs with Colette.

As ever in such situations, Keith was uncomfortable. But the moment Manon approached him, he was drawn to her. She was a tall, ivory-skinned quadroon, delicately built and exquisite of features. She smiled with a glint of admiration in her eyes that stirred Keith into desire.

Manon led him upstairs to a gold carpeted sitting room furnished with gleaming antiques, its windows tightly drawn against the day with red velvet drapes. In an alcove stood a red velvet covered bed, made of the finest of woods encrusted with ivory. The vaulted ceiling of the alcove was ornately painted with a scene depicting a trio of nude nymphs at play. The walls parallel to the bed were mirrored from floor to ceiling.

"Please sit down," Manon coaxed in a low, melodic voice, her eyes promising much. "I must change."

Keith sat in a velvet chair, every nerve aware of Manon's presence in the adjoining bathroom. Restless, he picked up a book that lay on the table beside his chair, and felt heat rush to his face as the opening words of the erotic novel reached to greet him. His legs tightened. Jacques was right; he had been too long without a woman.

He started at the knock on the door, went to respond. A uniformed houseman bowed politely, entered to place a tray with a bottle of champagne and two stemmed glasses on the table. Quickly the man departed. His hands perspiring, Keith opened the champagne, poured the pale liquid into the glasses. For a little while he would forget about Gilbert Mauriac's ward and the marriage that was being forced upon him.

"I'm sorry to have been so long," Manon apologized demurely, and Keith swung about to face her. His throat constricted as his eyes swept over the gossamer black dressing gown that she had not bothered to close. He was aware of the heady scent she wore.

"You're here," he said with a surge of passion, walking to her with two glasses in his hands.

As they sipped the chilled champagne, Keith allowed his eyes to rest on the small, high breasts that emerged from the dressing gown, nipples unexpectedly large and taut. His mouth went dry despite the champagne as his eyes moved down the length of her.

"You're beautiful." He took the glass from her hand before she had more than sipped from it and deposited it with his own on a nearby table. "I want to take you to bed this minute, Manon." His voice was husky.

"Come." She took him by the hand and led him to the bed.

As the black dressing gown fell to the floor beside the bed, Manon's hands reached for the buttons of Keith's shirt. An enigmatic smile on her face, she stripped him of his clothes while his eyes clung to the vision of her in the mirror. She was naked and perfect.

She lifted her faintly parted mouth to his. With a muffled groan he lowered his mouth to hers, pushing past her pearl-like teeth. Her body moved against his as they swayed together.

"I'm glad you're so passionate," she whispered with satisfaction when his mouth released hers. "Love me quickly, *mon ami*."

He prodded her across the velvet coverlet, crouched above her in towering excitement. His hands rippled about her responsive body as his mouth burrowed at her breasts and his manhood grew hard between her thighs.

Manon moaned softly, reached with slender fingers to find him. A white heat shot through him as they moved together, the sounds of their pleasure filling the room.

At Manon's gentle prodding he turned over on his back, lay with eyes shut while her mouth made love to him. The girls at Flora's and at Josie's had not touched the wells of passion that Manon discovered in him. He reached to pull her above him so that they could merge again in a fresh burst of satisfaction. This was what he had needed. Damn Mauriac and his convent-bred ward.

"We will bathe together, yes?" she invited.

"Yes." He read the message in her eyes. Afterwards he would love her yet again. He was twenty-three and passionate, and Gilbert Mauriac was sentencing him to a lifetime of emptiness.

Keith followed Manon into the bathroom. The floor was marble, partially covered by a rug of white fur. The walls were mirrored. The bath, like the other fixtures, was of solid onyx, dramatically reflected in the mirrored walls. A small dressing table held a dozen crystal bottles.

Manon leaned over to turn the gilt tap, sculpted and set with colorful stones, that brought warm water into the tub. She took a crystal decanter from the dressing table and poured perfumed nuggets into the water. Almost immediately the room was heavy with an indefinable, exotic scent.

Watching Manon, Keith remembered the succession of quadroons who had lived in the small, perfect cottage secluded in the woods, which his father had built seventeen years ago, two years after his mother's death. Papa would never touch a slave at Savage Oaks. He preferred to keep a quadroon mistress.

Manon stepped into the water, her body alabaster against the onyx of the tub. Desire rising in him again, Keith lowered himself beside her into the water, pulled her to him. But in the midst of his passion Keith's mind became startlingly clear.

He would marry Suzanne Duprée to save Savage Oaks. But he would install Manon in the cottage in the woods.

Three

The first pink streaks of dawn paraded through the portholes of the lavishly appointed cabin of the steamboat, intruding upon Suzanne's light slumber. She opened her eyes with an instant awareness that the days along the Mississippi were coming to an end. In four hours they would be in New Orleans.

Despite the luxury of life aboard this queen of the Mississippi, Suzanne had been tormented by conflicting emotions. She had never envisioned the homesickness that would attack her at unwary intervals. Yet, while part of her yearned to return to the comforting familiarity of the Convent and Mère Angélique, the other grappled with the tide of impatience to arrive in New Orleans, where she could confront Uncle Gilbert with the myriad questions about Maman and Papa that clamored to be answered.

She emerged from the berth and dressed with stealthy quietness, lest she wake Mme. Vauban, who snored noisily in the other berth. Disturbing

47

uncertainties, which had not surfaced in the protective atmosphere of the Convent, assailed her now. She was going to live on a plantation. *Her* plantation, where a hundred slaves cared for the house and raised the cotton crop. *She loathed slavery.* It was a sin against God for one human to own another. But she owned a hundred slaves.

Again she asked herself why she had been recalled to New Orleans so precipitately. She had no memory whatever of that city. How could she, when Uncle Gilbert had arranged for her to be brought to the Convent when she was three? Still she clung to the poignantly shadowed memories of Maman and Papa.

She reached for a shawl as the late October mornings were quite chilly, and left the cabin to go on deck. Standing at the rail, glad for the early morning silence that surrounded her, she watched the fine mansions, swathed in fog, that appeared along the river banks at intervals, flinching at the now familiar clusters of huts that another passenger had identified as slave quarters.

In a little while she would be in New Orleans. Her heart pounded with expectancy. The years of loneliness, of silent night tears, would be swept from memory because here she would, somehow, reach out and touch the memory of her mother and father. *Finally, she would discover who she was.*

Suzanne remained at the rail, mesmerized by the passing scenery, until a sudden awareness of hunger sent her below deck to the still-empty dining room. A solitary waiter on duty, seeming to understand her impatience to be in New Orleans, came forward to serve her.

She lingered at the table until the first straggler came in for breakfast. This morning the dining room rippled with a special aura of excitement. The journey was coming to an end. But no one, Suzanne thought with young extravagance, had so much at stake as she.

She went to her cabin, where Mme. Vauban was awake and packing frenziedly.

"Suzanne, you must pack!" she exhorted. "Soon we'll be in New Orleans." She had not seen her sister for twenty-three years; she was aglow with anticipation at this reunion.

"I'm packed," Suzanne soothed her. "Everything is ready."

"Suzanne, are you as nervous as I?" Mme. Vauban asked, speaking in French as always. "To think I will see three nieces and two nephews for the first time!"

"I'm nervous," Suzanne said softly. She would see her birthplace. "I hope I recognize Uncle Gilbert." Suddenly she was uneasy.

"He will recognize you, *chérie,*" Mme. Vauban reassured her.

Together they went on deck to watch for the first sight of New Orleans. To many Americans, Suzanne remembered, New Orleans was the most fascinating city in the country. Uncle Gilbert said that one day it would be the greatest city in the world, surpassing London and Paris.

Slowly the deck filled with passengers, all eager

for their first sight of the city. They were three-deep at the railing. At last New Orleans came into view, its buildings, chimneys, church spires bathed in golden sunlight.

"The turret there," a man beside Suzanne said to his companion, pointing to the loftiest object before them, "That's the turret atop the St. Charles Hotel. From up there you can see the whole city sprawled before you. The French Quarter, the American section, even the lake in the distance."

Suzanne fought to control the trembling that overtook her. All those years in the Convent she had felt herself in exile. Now she was coming home.

With only part of her consciousness, she was aware of the colorful charm of the waterfront, the levee bustling with vessels of every description. Grand steam-packets, flatboats, keepboats, smaller craft. It was possible, Suzanne thought with momentary absorption as their ship moved into its slot, to walk for miles, perhaps, stepping from boat to boat, not once touching shore. But that was a fleeting distraction. She gazed at the city before her with an exhilarating awareness that her mother and father had lived here. She had been born here. Tears filled her eyes. Suzanne Duprée had come home.

They had barely touched ground when Suzanne spied Gilbert Mauriac striding towards them. A smile lighted her face; she had recognized him, as though she had seen him only yesterday instead of three years ago. A small, stocky woman was struggling to keep up with him as he pushed his way through the crowd. Instinctively Suzanne knew this was Mme. Vauban's sister.

In the noisy confusion about them, Gilbert Mauriac greeted her with affection, introduced Mme. Vauban's sister, was in turn introduced to Mme. Vauban. In moments Mme. Vauban made her effusive farewell to Suzanne and allowed her sister to hurry her off to a waiting carriage. Suzanne watched Mme. Vauban leave with a startled, wrenching sense of loss. It was not that they had grown so close, Suzanne analyzed; it was that Mme. Vauban was her last contact with the Convent.

"Suzanne, you must be exhausted from your traveling," Gilbert Mauriac said sympathetically, an arm at her elbow. "Come, let's go to the carriage."

"I'm not really tired at all." She tried to appear at ease, though the moment of separation from Mme. Vauban had left her shaken. "The trip was fascinating."

All at once she felt herself adrift on a strange isle. She had seen Uncle Gilbert only three times in her entire life! They had written regularly ever since she was able to put down her first words on a piece of paper — but he was a stranger.

As Mauriac helped her into the brilliantly polished black carriage that waited for them, Suzanne tried to imagine what life at Tintagel would be like for her. Mrs. Cantrell, who had been housekeeper at Tintagel for many years, remained in that position. Uncle Gilbert said there was an overseer, accountable to him, who managed the slaves and the cotton-growing. But what would she do with herself in that lovely old house alone with Mrs. Cantrell? All at once the prospect of living at Tintagel was unnerving.

"We'll go to my house in town where you can meet Grandmère and refresh yourself before we leave for Tintagel," Gilbert intruded on her introspection. "Grandmère is eager to meet you."

"Is Tintagel far from New Orleans?" she asked hesitantly.

"Little more than an hour's drive. Close enough to come in often to the theater and the Opera and, I hope, to dinners with Grandmère and me. You're fortunate that the plantation is so accessible."

"Uncle Gilbert," Suzanne said impulsively as the carriage moved slowly ahead in the dray-clogged traffic, "please tell me about Maman and Papa." Her eyes clung to him. Why did he seem so disconcerted?

"Suzanne, you know," he said patiently. "They died in an explosion aboard a steamer en route from New Orleans to Natchez. You were in the care of a nursemaid in New Orleans — to that you owe your life."

"Uncle Gilbert, I've often thought that I must have — somewhere — an aunt or an uncle or a cousin. Somebody." She stammered in her haste to broach the subject that had been the driving force in her life ever since she could remember. "I want so much to know more about Maman and Papa!"

"Suzanne, I've told you. Your parents were absolutely alone in the world. That's why your father appointed me as executor of his estate. He knew I would do everything possible to manage your money well, and to arrange for your proper upbringing." He was visibly distressed. "Is there something that displeases you, Suzanne?"

"It's that I have nothing of Maman and Papa," she whispered, fighting tears of frustration. "Not even a daguerre of them."

"My dear, there were no daguerreotypes in those days," he reproached gently. "Only in the past few years have there been studios in Louisiana."

"A painting?" Suzanne persisted. "Is there a painting somewhere of Maman and Papa? A miniature?"

He sighed, his eyes troubled. "Nothing. I'm sorry, my dear."

"But where did they live? Show me their house, Uncle Gilbert." Her gaze swung towards the window of the carriage. "Can we drive past their house?"

"When they visited New Orleans, they stayed at my house," Mauriac explained.

Suzanne's eyes shifted from the window to him.

"Visited New Orleans?" she echoed in bewilderment. "But I — I've always believed they lived here."

"Your parents came from Savannah, Georgia. They were contemplating moving to New Orleans. I was encouraging this. Your mother wished to see Natchez before they made a final decision. That was when they died."

"But I — I always understood that they lived in New Orleans!" Her eyes fastened on him with consternation. She had plotted so hopefully to search — and find — blood relatives, no matter how distant, that would make her feel less alone in the world. She would talk to relatives who remembered Maman and Papa, who would make her feel that she could reach out and touch them.

"Suzanne, I'm sorry you received this wrong impression from me." He seemed almost distraught. "I didn't intend to mislead you. Believe me, you've always been very dear to me. And to Grandmère, though she has not seen you since you were three."

"My mother's family. What was their name?" Suzanne groped for something to which she could cling.

"I'm sorry." He gestured apologetically. "I never knew. I met her after she had married your father. Her name before her marriage never happened to be mentioned."

"Their house in Savannah," Suzanne pressed. "What happened to it?"

"I arranged for its sale through an attorney. The money is part of your estate." Now he forced himself to regain his composure. "But Suzanne, you are seeing nothing of the city," he rebuked as

54

the carriage rolled over the cobblestoned streets. "In a few moments we'll be passing the St. Louis Hotel. It would do honor to Paris itself."

But Suzanne cared little about the sights Gilbert Mauriac pointed out and meticulously described as they rode to their destination. Her parents had lived in far-off Savannah, Georgia. Uncle Gilbert seemed so sure there were no relatives. If there had been, her mind reasoned, one of them would have been named as her guardian in Papa's will. But instinct drove logic from her mind. Somewhere, there must be a cousin, perhaps twice or three times removed. *Somehow, she must find that cousin.*

"Here is our house," Mauriac said as the carriage pulled to a stop. "My grandfather built it many years ago when he brought Grandmère here as his bride."

The simplicity of the ivory stucco house with its array of tall French windows was made dramatic by the contrast of two-storied galleries with delicate ironwork railings, scrolled filigreed panels. The carriage turned in through a pair of tall iron gates that had been left open for their arrival.

Suzanne stepped down from the carriage, one small hand in Gilbert Mauriac's, and was almost breathless with the realization that her mother and father had walked up those stairs before her. For a little while they had lived in this house!

Already the front door, set between half-columns under an arched fanlight, was being opened. With her guardian's hand at her elbow,

Suzanne ascended the short flight of wrought-iron railed stairs that led to the door.

"Mawnin', Mist' Gilbert, Young Missy." A buxom, white-turbaned black woman smiled warmly at them, her huge brown eyes admiring Suzanne.

"Suzanne, this is Amelia, who has been with the family for forty-three years." Both Gilbert and Amelia chuckled at Suzanne's astonishment. Amelia looked no older than forty-three. "Amelia is a free woman," Gilbert said with pride. But at Tintagel I own a hundred slaves, Suzanne remembered unhappily.

Mauriac guided Suzanne past the curving staircase in the entrance foyer to a high-ceilinged, chandeliered room golden with sunlight just off the hall. The floor was covered by an Aubusson rug. The furniture was an eclectic collection of fine French and English antiques.

"Come meet Grandmère," Gilbert said with deep affection, and only then did Suzanne see the tiny, small-featured, still beautiful old lady with dark eyes and a wide smile sitting in a blue damask armchair before the fireplace.

"You must come close," Mme. Mauriac encouraged with a low, surprisingly strong voice that bore a faint reminder of her English birthplace. "I do not see so well these days." She leaned forward as Suzanne shyly approached and focused on Suzanne's face for a moment. "You were right, Gilbert," she said with satisfaction. "She is beautiful. Sit down, Suzanne. Here, beside me." She reached for a bell, shook it into a tinkling musical message. "We will have pralines and New Orleans coffee."

"Grandmère, at this hour of the morning?" Gilbert rebuked with an air of indulgence.

"The young and the very old adore sweets," Mme. Mauriac said firmly. "And not until Suzanne has eaten pralines and tasted our coffee will she know that she is truly in New Orleans."

Suzanne longed to ask information about her mother and father from Mme. Mauriac, but she did not dare. It was as though she were back in the Convent, hearing Sister Catherine's admonitions about how a young lady was to conduct herself in the presence of her elders.

With genuine interest Mme. Mauriac questioned Suzanne about her journey to New Orleans. Her dark eyes seemed young suddenly as she reminisced about her own trip from England with the young man, Gilbert's grandfather, whom she had secretly married. There was no luxurious Collins liner in those days, and the journey was long and hazardous.

"My family were Sephardic Jews," she said with a proud lift of her head. "In Spain, before the Inquisition, they had been physicians to the Court. When I fell in love with a Frenchman, who was an agnostic and whose family was Catholic, they were outraged. His French family was outraged that he wished to marry a Sephardic Jewess. We married and came to New Orleans." All at once she seemed to age. The glow was gone from her face. "When I lost my husband twenty-two years ago, I lost half my life."

"Grandmère, you are not to be morbid," Gilbert reproached gently.

"I think perhaps there is a touch of the actress in me," Mme. Mauriac chuckled. "And when I have such a sympathetic audience, I overplay."

"Tonight you'll sleep at your plantation," Gilbert said to Suzanne with an air of satisfaction. "You'll be pleased with Tintagel."

"I'm sure I will," Suzanne said politely because this was expected of her. Mme. Mauriac was so friendly, so warm, why couldn't she bring herself to say, "Please, tell me about my mother and father. How did they look? How did they think?" They loved her. Of this she was triumphantly sure. "Mrs. Cantrell expects me?" She must walk into Tintagel and meet not only Mrs. Cantrell, the housekeeper who would also be her chaperone, but all the house slaves *whom she owned*. It was a disconcerting prospect.

A tall, erect but elderly black man, his hair as white as his teeth, appeared with a tea cart laden with a richly decorated silver coffee service, a porcelain plate piled high with what Suzanne guessed were pralines, and three delicately painted porcelain cups and saucers. The delicious aroma of strong, fresh coffee permeated the room.

"This silver service was given to me by my maternal grandmother on my sixteenth birthday, in preparation for the day I married. It was all I

58

took with me, along with the clothes I wore," Mme. Mauriac added humorously, "when I left London."

"Mme. Mauriac," Suzanne asked impetuously as Madam poured for them, "please tell me about my mother. Was she pretty?"

It seemed to Suzanne that Mme. Mauriac's hand trembled as she carefully finished pouring.

"Your mother was lovely, Suzanne," the old lady said slowly. "You are very like her. Except for your eyes," she stipulated. "You have your father's eyes."

"Suzanne, tomorrow evening Grandmère and I are going to the Opera," Gilbert broke in almost brusquely, destroying this precious moment for Suzanne. "We would like you to attend with us." Gilbert reached for the cup his grandmother extended, his eyes in a secret exchange with hers.

"Thank you." *Why didn't Uncle Gilbert want his grandmother to talk about Maman?* "I've never been to the Opera." It seemed almost a command that she go with them.

"Wear your prettiest ballgown because attending the Opera in New Orleans is a very special occasion. And tell Mrs. Cantrell you will dine with us before the Opera," Mme. Mauriac instructed warmly, "so that she'll arrange for the carriage to bring you in early."

"Mme. Mauriac, may we talk sometime about my mother and father?" Suzanne's voice was tremulous but determined.

"We'll do that, Suzanne," Mme. Mauriac promised gravely.

Before Suzanne could press further, Gilbert launched into a lively discussion about Tintagel; but all Suzanne heard was the echo of Mme. Mauriac's voice. *You are very like her. Except for your eyes. You have your father's eyes.*

Gilbert pulled forth an enameled gold watch.

"Suzanne, Mrs. Cantrell will be expecting you. We should leave."

"Of course," Suzanne forced a smile. She would have liked to remain here with Mme. Mauriac, without Uncle Gilbert's presence. If they were alone, Mme. Mauriac could be coaxed to tell her more about Maman and Papa. *Why was it so difficult for Uncle Gilbert to talk about them?*

"You'll enjoy the Opera," Mme. Mauriac said with persuasive charm. "*Au revoir,* Suzanne."

Gilbert guided Suzanne through a side door. The carriage waited for them, Sebastien talking good-humoredly to a maid at a downstairs window. He hopped down with alacrity to open the carriage door for them. The Mauriac servants were all free people, Suzanne guessed with fresh discomfort in her own situation. Could she free her slaves? Would Uncle Gilbert allow her to do that?

En route to Tintagel Gilbert talked about the magnificence of Savage Oaks, which adjoined her plantation. He spoke with warmth and admiration of the three members of the Savage family

60

in residence there. Suzanne listened, striving to quell her misgivings about this new way of life.

"Tintagel is just ahead," Gilbert said with an air of anticipation, yet Suzanne felt an inner tension in him. "It's far smaller than Savage Oaks, of course, but just as beautiful."

The carriage turned into a long, pebble-covered driveway flanked by towering oaks and pecans that formed an imposing arch as spreading boughs met high above the ground. She ought to be breathless with excitement, Suzanne thought guiltily; but her initial delight at the prospect of living in Louisiana had dissipated with the realization that Maman and Papa came not from this state but from Georgia.

Tintagel was a three-storied brick structure fronted by a Southern favored double gallery upheld by four Doric columns and surrounded by lush gardens. As the carriage drew close to the house, Suzanne saw that the windows and outside doors were faced with white marble, as were the entrance steps and portico. Mère Angélique would admire this house, Suzanne thought wistfully. Would she ever see Mère Angélique again?

As Suzanne and Gilbert Mauriac walked up the steps, a black-frocked woman appeared in the doorway. She was of average height, carrying herself ramrod stiff despite her heavy build. She wore her dark hair severely plain, and her faintly sharp features showed the strain of time. Suzanne knew instinctively that this was Mrs. Cantrell.

"Welcome to Tintagel, Miss Duprée," she said with a formality that, to Suzanne, indicated disapproval.

"Thank you." Suzanne forced herself to smile. She would not be intimidated by this forbidding woman.

Gravely Suzanne accepted the introductions made by Gilbert, then followed the housekeeper into the large hall that divided the house. Her eyes lingered admiringly on the beautifully executed murals that adorned the walls of the entrance foyer.

"There are two rooms on either side of the downstairs floor," Mrs. Cantrell said with impersonal politeness. "The music room and the library." She pointed to her left with one heavily veined hand. "The Judge's law library was one of the finest in the South. Every book is here," she said proudly, "as it was when Mr. Joseph was alive. On the other side — " she walked to a pair of double doors and swung them wide " — are the parlor and the dining room."

"What a beautiful room!" Suzanne said spontaneously, her eyes sweeping about the golden splendor of the parlor. The upholstery and hangings were of gold satin damask, the curtains caught with tiebacks of white grapes against gilt-bronze grape leaves. Gold-leaf mirrors hung about the room and over the mantel. A half-dozen paintings dominated one wall.

"The dining room is here." Mrs. Cantrell slid open a pair of doors to reveal an expansive dining room furnished with what Suzanne was certain was authentic Chippendale. "The glassware is Waterford. The silver by Tallois of Paris. The china was brought from England by Mr. Noah's grandmother." For a moment, so fleeting Suzanne warned herself that she might be mistaken, Mrs. Cantrell gazed at her with a barely controlled fury. *Mrs. Cantrell resented her intrusion in Noah Ramsay's house.* A chill darted through Suzanne. And she was to live in this house with Mrs. Cantrell? Now Mrs. Cantrell turned to Gilbert Mauriac with an impersonal smile. "You will stay for dinner, Mr. Mauriac? It is served early from habit because Mr. Noah wished it that way." Her cold green eyes challenged Suzanne to object to this.

"Thank you, but I must leave," Gilbert apologized. "Business calls me back to New Orleans. Suzanne, there is a shining black beauty of a horse in the stables. I'm sure you'll enjoy riding Othello. Please ride tomorrow morning," he said ingratiatingly. "You must see the woods at their best. Promise me you'll ride early tomorrow morning." His eyes were almost hypnotic as they held hers.

The strange air of command in his voice was disconcerting. She was away from the Convent. The mistress of Tintagel. Was she not old enough to make her own decisions? "I promise, Uncle Gilbert," she said quietly.

Four

Keith left the stables and rode towards the east, where Savage Oaks property would eventually blend into that of Tintagel. His face was taut with hostility as he remembered Gilbert's admonition when he was at Savage Oaks yesterday. *"Suzanne will be riding early in the morning. Make sure you encounter her. Talk with her for a few moments. Then send word to me about your decision."*

What decision? He had to play this as Gilbert Mauriac called it! But pride insisted that he see Suzanne Duprée before he courted her. He felt a cool sweat break out across his forehead. The young ladies at Mrs. Slidell's Washington parties had been shockingly aggressive in their pursuit of him, but what about this romantic Suzanne Duprée? What would he do if Suzanne Duprée rejected his courtship?

Birds sang in the still-green woods. The air was fresh and sweet. But where usually he enjoyed an early morning ride, which he would not allow himself during this hectic milling season, he sat tense in the saddle this morning. The future of Savage Oaks was riding on his ability to persuade Suzanne Duprée to marry him.

She rode every morning at the Convent. It was fashionable for young ladies to ride, he remembered derisively. She had promised Mauriac she would ride this morning.

Last night he had lain sleepless in his bed, plotting this campaign. She was romantic. She probably read Sir Walter Scott and dreamt of being wooed by a knight in shining armor. Approach this as a chess game. He needed a gambit, a calculated drive to an early victory.

If he had not been dragged back from Washington in January, he would have been ready now to take his examinations for admittance to the bar. It wasn't law in itself that so intrigued him. It was government. He must have a solid law background to push himself forward in government. Damn it, there was so much that was wrong in Washington! In the years ahead he could have become a force in changing this. But his destiny had been wrested from his hands, he thought bitterly. First, the need to leave Washington to take over running Savage Oaks — and now he was being thrust into an arranged marriage.

Keith surveyed the stretch of woods about him. To his left, discreetly hidden in a grove of pecans and orange trees, was the cottage where he had brought Manon last week. Just ahead was Tintagel property. He tightened his jaw with determination to see through the charade he had devised as he lay sleepless in bed last night.

He rode another eighth of a mile through the woods and dismounted. Suzanne was sure to come this way, over the path beaten by three generations of Ramsays. His eyes fell to the ground, searching. There. He bent to pick up a small pebble. It was a matter now of waiting.

He heard Suzanne before he saw her. He stiffened to attention, poised for action. She rode into view. Pretty, he acknowledged detachedly. She rode well. And then, with calculated accuracy, he threw the pebble. Suddenly the horse charged forward as though he were at the Metairie track.

"Slow, Othello!" Suzanne's voice was startled, faintly shrill. She struggled to maintain her seat, hampered by her side-saddle position. "Slow! Slow!"

Keith leapt onto his own horse, urged him forward. Every muscle was geared for the action ahead. He came up beside Suzanne. She was fighting frenziedly not to be unseated. He leaned forward, reached out with one strong arm, scooped her up by the waist, and imperiously pulled his horse to a halt. Gently he deposited Suzanne on the ground. Her color was high, her eyes a golden glow. She was not frightened, he realized with astonishment. She was furious that she could not control her horse.

"Are you all right?" he asked solicitously, dismounting to stand beside her. "You might have been killed."

"I'm fine," she gasped, gazing up at him with gratitude. "I can't imagine what happened to Othello to bolt that way." She smiled suddenly and Keith realized that she was beautiful. "Thank you."

"You're sure you're all right?" Keith probed, his eyes showing admiration along with concern. This episode might have been written by Sir Walter Scott, his mind taunted.

"Absolutely." Her voice was light, musical. She spoke the King's English, he thought with ironic amusement.

"I'm Keith Savage," he introduced himself. "From Savage Oaks. Actually, I'm poaching," he added humorously. "But the Savages and Ramsays have done that for three generations." Why must Gilbert Mauriac insist on this marriage? Suzanne Duprée would encounter no difficulty in acquiring suitors. Willing suitors. Or was her background such that it did not warrant probing? Was Jane right? Was this Mauriac's bastard child?

"I'm Suzanne Duprée," she introduced herself. "My guardian, Mr. Mauriac, bought Tintagel for me when Mr. Ramsay died. I arrived from France yesterday."

"Let me take you to the house," Keith said, and reached to lift her by the waist and into the saddle. Mauriac was right; she was a romantic. To her this was a storybook encounter. Already she looked upon him with that softness of the eyes that he had seen in smitten young ladies in

Washington. This conquest would be easy.

They rode together back to Tintagel while Keith forced himself into an animated conversation about New Orleans. Would there be sufficient money in Suzanne's estate to allow him to buy and maintain a town house in New Orleans, where he could escape from time to time? If he were to be deprived of both his Washington life and his personal freedom, let him have some pleasures, he thought with grim defiance.

He deeply missed the stimulation of that year and a half in Washington, where he had been so close to the workings of the government. While he had recoiled from much of the necessary Capitol socializing, he had relished being among those invited, by virtue of his association with Judge Campbell, to sit in on sessions of Congress and attend the parties of the Supreme Court set, where he encountered the most brilliant minds in Washington. Within this charmed circle, philosophy, history, inventions and the arts were the subjects of discussion. And now, he mocked himself with distaste, he would be subjected — as Jane had warned — to endless plantation parties where the talk would be spiked with parish gossip, fashion news, and racing results.

"Uncle Gilbert tells me that Savage Oaks is one of the showplaces of the South," Suzanne interrupted his reverie.

"I love it dearly," he said with sudden intensity. Only his love for Savage Oaks brought him here this morning.

Suzanne lifted her face to his, her eyes all at once oddly troubled. She seemed on the point of some confidence, then frowned and turned her face resolutely ahead.

"I used to visit Tintagel regularly when I was growing up." Keith was uncomfortable in this subterfuge. Couldn't Mauriac realize what he was doing to Suzanne, guiding her this way into a contrived marriage? "The Ramsays are our distant cousins. Noah taught me to play chess when I was twelve. I went over to play with him when I was home from school and college. Sometimes I watched him play with Mr. Mauriac. That was a treat. They were both chess masters." He hesitated. "Noah was something of a recluse. Did Mr. Mauriac tell you about the family?"

"No. But when I was sitting in the parlor with Mrs. Cantrell last night, she told me about the tragedies that plagued the Ramsays." Suzanne's voice was sympathetic. "How Joseph Ramsay died in an accident when his three sons were small, and how his wife became an invalid right after that. She told me how Mrs. Ramsay and two of her sons died within weeks of each other when the boys were young men."

"Robert and Adrian died at the hands of political assassins. Robert on the eve of his election to the Legislature. Adrian, who was an artist, allowed himself to be pushed into replacing his brother, and he was killed. My sister, Jane, remembers them. Adrian had taught her to paint."

"How sad." Suzanne's eyes were poignantly reflective. "My parents, too, died when I was three. In a boating accident."

They were approaching the house now. Mrs. Cantrell had always been pleasant to Keith because Noah liked him, but he had always found her forbidding. Now she kept Tintagel a shrine to Noah. Everything the way he had liked it. Fresh flowers on his grave throughout the year. She must resent Suzanne's presence at Tintagel.

"I'll have to send someone after Othello," Suzanne said anxiously. "I don't know why he bolted that way."

"Perhaps he caught a briar in his hoof. He'll be all right. Mrs. Cantrell will have someone from the stable round him up."

Mrs. Cantrell appeared in the front doorway as they walked up the steps, Keith's hand solicitously at Suzanne's elbow. She squinted nearsightedly at him. The last time he was at Tintagel was the summer before Noah's death, when he had been home from Princeton.

"Keith, how nice to see you." She seemed genuinely pleased. But her eyes were curious. She was trying to figure how he came to be here with Suzanne.

"Mrs. Cantrell. I'm afraid someone will have to go after Othello. He bolted, and Keith rescued me." Suzanne was breathlessly apologetic. "Othello went charging off through the woods."

"I must send word to Mr. Mauriac," Mrs. Cantrell said agitatedly, her eyes darkening with

70

concern. "He'll have to sell that horse. You might have been killed."

"Please don't say anything to Uncle Gilbert," Suzanne pleaded. "Othello's a magnificent animal. I'm sure he won't do it again." She lifted her head determinedly.

Stubborn little wench, Keith guessed, despite that delicate air of damsel in distress. She might just prove to be harder to handle than he had suspected.

At Mrs. Cantrell's insistence Keith joined both ladies for coffee on the gallery, a habit that Noah had instituted many years earlier. At intervals he allowed his eyes to linger admiringly on Suzanne, and each time he saw her color in pleasurable confusion. Ten minutes later he rose to his feet and excused himself.

"It's been delightful to meet you, Suzanne," he said with quiet charm. "I hope to see you again." He would. Gilbert Mauriac would arrange that. As soon as he reached Savage Oaks, Keith ordered himself, he would send Edward into New Orleans with official word of his acceptance of this marriage. Now he turned to Mrs. Cantrell with a deferential smile. "It's been good to see you again, Mrs. Cantrell. But this is the milling season. I'm spending most of my waking hours with the hands." His eyes told Suzanne he would much prefer to spend them with her. Damn Mauriac for making him play this asinine game!

In a little while the carriage would pull up in

front of Tintagel to take her into New Orleans. Suzanne sat before the mirror in her bedroom while Patrice, the elderly Haitian slave who had been appointed her maid, lovingly brushed her hair.

"*Trés beaux, les cheveux,*" Patrice crooned in her melodic voice, proud of the French she learned long ago from her mother. "Lil' Missy gonna be de pretties' thing at dat Opera tonight."

Suzanne was glad that she had packed the gown made for her by M. Worth for Cecile's wedding. Without the train it should be right for the Opera.

She remembered the day that her gown and matching cloak had been delivered by one of M. Worth's assistants. That same evening, returning from the theater, they had seen a poor Parisienne in a boat, washing clothes in the Seine to earn a few sous. How many thousands of sous had her gown cost? Most workmen in France earned no more than three or four francs a day, but Cecile said that the favored courtesans in Paris earned ten thousand francs in a single night. What a disturbing world! How little the Revolution seven years ago had done for the poor in France!

Sometimes she suspected that Mère Angélique disapproved of the lavishness of her wardrobe, though it was not so lavish as Cecile's or the two young ladies from Rome. But Uncle Gilbert had been so generous; and she adored, sinfully, to feel herself encased in beautiful materials.

Endlessly throughout the day, her thoughts

had focused on Keith Savage. Color flamed along her high cheekbones as she remembered his arms about her while he held the reins in his hands as they rode to the house. Troubling new emotions surged within her. *She must not think about Keith Savage.*

"Patrice, I must go downstairs," Suzanne said firmly after another few minutes.

"Some fine young man gonna go after you tonight," Patrice teased. "You is so pretty."

"I'm going to dinner and to the Opera with my guardian and his grandmother," Suzanne said with mock reproach.

"Ol' Patrice got the gift for seein' ahead. You is gonna meet a fine young man tonight. And you is gonna marry him," she wound up triumphantly.

Absurdly, Suzanne's heart began to pound. She had never known a young man as handsome as Keith Savage, as charming as he. But she was not one to think of marriage, she reminded herself. She had come to Louisiana with a vow, made that day in the Cathedral of Notre-Dame.

For one moment this morning, when Keith talked about his mother's family coming from Georgia, she had felt an impulse to confide that her family, too, came from Georgia. If she saw Keith again, she must ask him if he had ever heard of the Duprées of Savannah.

When she had settled in at Tintagel, she would ask Uncle Gilbert if she might visit Savannah. She was conscious of a faint rebellion that she must ask Uncle Gilbert's permission in such matters. She was seventeen years old and well educated, but because she was a woman she was therefore helpless and treated as if she were not overly bright. Those ladies who were fighting for women's rights knew that the masculine world must change its archaic ideas.

"Patrice, my yellow cloak, please," Suzanne said softly, rising to her feet. Would she ever be able to accept the attention of a maid with the poise of Cecile and her mother?

Suzanne went downstairs to wait on the gallery for the carriage. She was relieved that she would not be required to sit down to the evening meal with Mrs. Cantrell. She felt such an undercurrent of hostility in the housekeeper, directed to *her*.

The carriage pulled up before the house. Suzanne hurried eagerly down the steps, to be helped inside by Merlin, the coachman who had been what Mrs. Cantrell called "Mr. Noah's most spoiled slave."

The carriage rolled along the river road towards New Orleans. The Mississippi was faintly gold with the departing rays of the sun. South winds from the Gulf brought a pleasant scent of sea to shore. As they arrived in the city, Suzanne was aware that the hectic pace of the day had diminished.

At the Mauriac house, Suzanne was greeted with affection.

"Dinner will be served immediately so that we

may arrive at the theater before the overture," Mme. Mauriac announced convivially.

Mme. Mauriac, Gilbert, and Suzanne sat down to an elegantly laid table in the small, perfect dining room. The menu, Suzanne thought with admiration, would have been a credit to Magny's in Paris. Gilbert talked earnestly about the trouble in Kansas — the ballot stuffing by armed Missourians in the election of the territorial Legislature last March.

"This is going to lead to terrible bloodshed," Gilbert prophesied worriedly. "Force such as this is evil."

Suzanne had read in the London newspapers about the determination of the South to establish slavery in Kansas, though this must be accomplished by the action of squatters; at the same time anti-slavery forces in the North were fostering the emigration of anti-slavery people to the area.

Gilbert consulted the French ormolu clock with Sèvres china panels, which sat atop the marble mantel, as they sipped coffee from exquisite porcelain cups.

"After Annette's *bavaroise* we should sit in appreciative contemplation for twenty minutes," he said with wry apology. "But the Opera calls us."

There had been no moment, Suzanne thought with frustration, when she might ask Mme. Mauriac questions about Maman and Papa. She knew it was futile to attempt to question Uncle

Gilbert. But she *would* visit Savannah, she silently vowed.

The Mauriac carriage brought them to the Théâtre d'Orléans, on Orleans Street between Bourbon and Royal. Suzanne was intrigued by the brilliant spectacle of the arriving audience, the air of anticipation that permeated the atmosphere.

"Anyone with any pretensions to social standing must be seen at the Opera," Mme. Mauriac said with sardonic amusement.

"Maman," Gilbert clucked with indulgent reproach, "New Orleans is a town where everyone loves the Opera. John Davis loved it enough to spend eighty thousand on the Théâtre d'Orléans," he added whimsically.

Gilbert ushered his mother and Suzanne into the beautifully appointed, commodious Opera house, illuminated by a massive gas chandelier and avenues of wall sconces. He escorted them down the richly carpeted aisle to a stall in the dress circle. Behind the stalls were rows of single seats, flanked by loges.

"The curtained loges are for those in mourning or who wish privacy," Gilbert explained as they settled themselves in the Mauriac stall.

Suzanne gazed eagerly about the festive assemblage. Her eyes swept above the boxes on the first level to the tiers that rose up to the ceiling. The first tier was occupied mainly by lovely, strikingly gowned mulatto women. The tier at the top was for free blacks.

As Gilbert helped Suzanne to remove her

cloak, his eyes moved to one of the loges. He nodded with a faint smile to a woman seated there. In the stall beside them a pompous, moustached gentleman was staring at the same loge.

"Good Lord," he said with distaste, loudly enough for Suzanne to hear, "isn't that Yellowbird Shaw in that loge? How does the madam of the Mansion House dare show her face at the Opera?"

Hastily Suzanne lowered her eyes. Uncle Gilbert had never married. Cecile said it was natural for unmarried gentlemen to have secret liaisons. Curiously she shifted her gaze so that it might fall upon the woman in the loge, but the curtains already were discreetly drawn.

"Jane — Keith! How pleasant to see you!" Gilbert said with a jocularity that was foreign to him.

Suzanne turned towards the aisle with an effervescent smile, delighted at this unexpected encounter. This intimidating woman was Keith's sister? How unlike Keith she was.

"We don't have a subscription this year," Keith was explaining, "but a friend offered us his seats this evening." His eyes met Suzanne's. She felt giddy with exhilaration.

As Gilbert introduced Jane and Suzanne, the gaslights dimmed. The overture was about to begin. Keith hurried Jane to their seats.

Throughout the first act Suzanne sat at the edge of her seat, entranced by the performance, yet every moment conscious that Keith sat in a stall only a few feet away. Four times during the first act she was aware that Keith's eyes deserted the stage to search out her face in the shadows. She strained to appear absorbed in the production, but her heart pounded.

At intermission, Jane and Keith came to the Mauriacs' stall to chat. Jane was painfully uncomfortable with strangers, Suzanne realized sympathetically, remembering her own shyness as a child. Mme. Mauriac strived charmingly to put Jane at ease.

"Jane, we'd better return to our stall." Keith broke off a discussion with Gilbert about the expansion of railroad lines about the country. "The second act is about to begin."

Jane frowned, took a deep breath, and spoke hastily to Suzanne.

"Why don't you join Keith and me in our carriage for the trip home? It's a desolate ride alone. We can drive you to Tintagel." Her eyes were uncommunicative; Suzanne suspected that Keith had asked her to extend this invitation.

"I would like that," Suzanne accepted with a shy smile.

On the long drive home Suzanne sat between Jane and Keith. Jane spoke little. Keith talked earnestly about the evacuation of Sevastopol just last September after the eleven-month siege by the English, French, and Turks. Suzanne, turning toward Keith, spoke eloquently about Florence Nightingale's heroic efforts in the Crimea.

"Lord Tennyson wrote a beautiful poem about

Balaklava," Jane broke her silence. "Do you know *The Charge of the Light Brigade?*"

"Yes," Suzanne said with sudden intensity. "A beautiful collection of words, but I cannot accept its ideals."

"You disapprove of the honor of the military?" Jane bristled.

"Lord Tennyson glorified the concept that a soldier must blindly obey his orders. But the newspapers have told us plainly that more than two-thirds of the men in the Light Brigade died because they obeyed orders from high-ranking British officers who were stupid and overly ambitious."

"But you can't have soldiers making decisions. Their officers must lead them. Otherwise there would be chaos in the army!" Jane stared at her with overt disapproval.

"I can't believe that soldiers should follow a leader they know is leading them, out of his own ignorance and personal greed, to destruction!" In the shadows of the carriage Suzanne felt her face grow hot with color. The Sister at the Convent had been so upset when she expressed this conviction. She must learn not to be outspoken. And yet, she thought rebelliously, she was glad to have conquered her shyness. And why should she not speak her mind? God gave her the ability to think.

"Suzanne, tell us about Paris," Keith diplomatically intervened.

"I saw little of it," Suzanne conceded with a

slight smile, "but what I saw was fascinating."

Keith drew her out about her knowledge of Paris. Suzanne, basking in his attentions, spoke with animation of the week she had recently spent at the de Mirabeau mansion.

"It'll be lonely for you at Tintagel with only Mrs. Cantrell to keep you company," Jane said as the carriage turned into Suzanne's driveway. "Won't you come for dinner tomorrow evening? We don't have dinner at the fashionable hour of three," she said with a touch of irony. "All of us at Savage Oaks prefer to have our dinner in the evening. Particularly in the milling season, when Keith spends such long hours at work."

"Thank you." Suzanne was confident that Keith had prompted this invitation. "I'll look forward to it."

Suzanne sat at the elegantly laid dining table in the Savages' handsome family dining room, striving not to appear self-conscious as she participated in the strained table conversation. Only Phillip seemed relaxed. She had liked Phillip on sight, instinctively feeling they would be friends. His resemblance to Keith was astonishing. But why was Keith so moody, so strangely withdrawn tonight?

"I hated military school," Phillip was saying with vehemence. "I loathed everything about it. Getting up at five in the morning. The rotten food. All the ridiculous rules. And Princeton was little better. I couldn't wait to leave."

"The feeling of the Princeton faculty was similar," Jane said drily. For a second Suzanne feared an explosion from Phillip, but he tightened his mouth grimly and helped himself to more of the red snapper. Jane turned to Suzanne with an impersonal smile. "Do you play the piano, Suzanne?"

"Not well," Suzanne said candidly. "Though I love music."

"Keith plays beautifully." Jane's eyes softened as they rested on her older brother.

"Keith does everything well," Phillip shot back. Suzanne was startled by the blend of hostility and pain she saw in his eyes.

"You'll play for us after dinner, Keith," Jane said coolly.

"Jane, I'm tired," he protested with irritation. "I've been working since sunup."

"Keith, you're not being very hospitable," Jane rebuked, her eyes holding his.

"Suzanne, I'm sorry," Keith apologized with a contrite smile. "Of course, I'll play."

Later Suzanne, Jane, and Phillip sat in the library while Keith played Beethoven with a skill that delighted Suzanne. Yet as he enveloped himself in the music, Suzanne sensed a towering sadness in him.

Earlier than she would have liked, Suzanne announced that she must return to Tintagel. She knew that Keith would be up with the sun. He loved Savage Oaks, but he was unhappy at having been brought from Washington at his father's death. Unhappy and rebellious, she analyzed, subduing a disconcerting impulse to go to comfort him.

When Suzanne arrived at Tintagel, Mrs. Cantrell was waiting up for her in the parlor.

"I know there has never been a slave uprising at Tintagel. Mr. Noah took pride in hiring trustworthy overseers to keep the slaves in hand. But I never go to bed until I have personally locked every door that leads into the house. And I sleep with a pistol beneath my pillow. Mr. Noah taught me how to use it."

Within the next two weeks it seemed to Suzanne that she was constantly at Savage Oaks or Keith was at Tintagel, despite the demands on his time. He alternated between tenderness and a discreet show of affection that entranced her and a dark moodiness that disturbed yet drew her to him. Still, she was stunned, at the end of those two weeks, to sit in the parlor with Gilbert Mauriac and to hear what had brought him to Tintagel so unexpectedly.

"You must know, Suzanne, that Keith has been taken with you," he pointed out indulgently. "I admit that this request to speak to you about marriage may seem premature, but Keith is desperately lonely. Since Keith's mother died when he was four, there has been none of the entertaining at Savage Oaks that is so frequent at other plantations."

"But I've known him such a little time," Suzanne stammered.

"You've seen much of him these last two weeks. I've thought you felt something special for him." Gilbert was gazing at her seriously. "Was I wrong?"

"Uncle Gilbert, I'm not sure that I'm ready to be married. I'll think about it," Suzanne said with a strength she had not suspected she possessed. Uncle Gilbert seemed aghast. He had expected her to fall into Keith's arms. Oh, she wished she could do that! But there was the vow she had made to herself. Nothing must stand in its way.

"Suzanne, it would be a fine match for you." Gilbert was dismayed at her reaction. "I've known the Savages since before Keith was born. He's the most eligible young man in the parish. I can't imagine any other young lady hesitating a moment in your position."

"I'll think about it," she said unsteadily. How could she become Keith's wife, mistress of Savage Oaks, and devote her life to searching for her family? And yet the prospect of his marrying someone else filled her with distress. "I'll think about it, Uncle Gilbert," she reiterated.

Suzanne walked with Gilbert to the gallery, stood watching while he climbed into his carriage. Keith Savage loved her. He wished to marry her! *And she loved him.* She knew this the moment he swept her from Othello's back, though she hardly dared admit this even to herself.

The carriage was moving down the driveway. Suddenly she was darting down the steps from the gallery and down the road.

"Uncle Gilbert, wait!" she called breathlessly. "Uncle Gilbert!"

The carriage came to a stop. Gilbert leaned out. Suzanne's face was alight with exhilaration.

"Uncle Gilbert, tell Keith 'yes'! Yes, I will marry him!"

Five

Suzanne sat on the gallery with Mrs. Cantrell's Scotch collie sprawled at her feet. Her head was light, her heart still pounding. *Had it truly happened?* For the twentieth time in the hour since she had run after Uncle Gilbert to tell him, yes, yes, she would marry Keith, that brief scene replayed itself in her mind.

The collie pushed his silken head beneath her hand, his dark eyes pleading for affection.

"Of course, I love you," she murmured, leaning forward to scratch him behind the ears. "I adore you," she said extravagantly and brought her face down to his. She was living in a fairy tale. Keith Savage loved her! She was going to be his wife.

"Come, let's go for a walk, Perceval." With a joyous smile, she rose to her feet, and walked down the steps, the collie at her side. She halted at the sound of a carriage coming up the road. "Perceval, wait — "

Uncle Gilbert was coming back to the house.

All at once she was fearful. Had Keith changed his mind? Had Uncle Gilbert misunderstood him? She waited with a small, anxious smile as the carriage pulled up before the house and Uncle Gilbert came to her. He was smiling warmly.

"Suzanne, I've spoken to Keith. He's delighted that you've accepted his offer of marriage." Then it was all true, Suzanne told herself with relief. Gilbert hesitated. "Keith said he would like to hold the wedding a week from today." Suzanne stared at him in shock. "If that's all right with you," he finished uneasily.

"But Uncle Gilbert, a week from today? Such a short time?" All at once she was uncertain.

"I know that's rushing you," Gilbert sympathized. "But you must realize how lonely Keith is at Savage Oaks. He's impetuous and romantic," Gilbert said indulgently.

Cecile would say, *"Marry Keith now before somebody else whisks him away from you."* She could not bear to lose him!

"A week from today," Suzanne consented. "I'm sure everything can be arranged," she said with shaky confidence.

"It must be a quiet wedding because Keith's father has been dead less than a year," Gilbert reminded regretfully. "I know every young lady dreams of a fine wedding."

"Uncle Gilbert, I don't mind," she reassured him effervescently. She would be happy to marry Keith in the cane fields.

"Tomorrow you come into New Orleans to stay with Grandmère and me until the day before the wedding. Grandmère will bring in her favorite French seamstress and make sure your bridal gown is ready. The wedding will be held here at Tintagel." He paused, tired from his efforts of the last hour but clearly exhilarated by the results. "Jane suggested Savage Oaks, but I insisted you be married at Tintagel."

Suzanne reached to press his hand in hers. She was pleased that Uncle Gilbert had been insistent.

"Jane will arrange for a wedding dinner at Savage Oaks. Now," he said briskly, "we must go to Mrs. Cantrell and tell her the news."

Mrs. Cantrell struggled to conceal her astonishment. Her eyes said plainly that she could not understand this rush into marriage. It was not because the bride was *enceinte,* Suzanne thought humorously. Cecile talked wickedly about how so many young ladies in Paris blessed the crinoline for concealing their urgency to marry.

Gilbert took his leave again, and Suzanne called to Perceval to resume their walk. She must write Cecile tomorrow and tell her everything. She wished wistfully that Cecile could be here for the wedding, though it would not be so grand as her own. She must write Mère Angélique, too, Suzanne reminded herself conscientiously. Would Mère Angélique be disturbed at the speed with which she was going into marriage?

She was not forgetting the vow she had made that day in the Cathedral of Notre-Dame. She was as determined as ever to learn every small detail about Maman and Papa, to ferret out any living relatives. She could do this, even as Keith's wife.

Maman and Papa would wish her to marry. But how desperately she wished that they might be here with her. They would have been as charmed by Keith as she. Uncle Gilbert, who surely was one to know, had great respect for Keith, she remembered with pride.

Thanks to Cecile, she would not go into marriage blinded by romantic novels, as so many young ladies did. She knew what happened between a man and his bride. Cecile, who at fifteen had been initiated into the rites of love by a young cousin, had described the wedding night with gusto, in minute detail. After her initial shocked protestations of distaste, Suzanne acknowledged, she had come to understand that it could be beautiful to give herself to the man she loved. Even now she was aware of strange tremors of excitement as she envisioned her wedding eve. But she must not be too forward. Keith would not like that.

In one week she would stand with Keith before the Episcopal priest and hear the words that would make them man and wife. Only a few short weeks ago she had sat in the Cathedral at Notre-Dame and watched Cecile marry a young man she hardly knew. Her own marriage would be different, she told herself exultantly. She was in love with Keith and he loved her.

The following morning Suzanne left Tintagel with her portmanteau filled with sufficient attire to carry her through these next few days. Only yesterday morning her trunks had arrived from the Convent, and fleetingly she had been brushed by a devastating wave of homesickness.

In New Orleans, Mme. Mauriac welcomed her affectionately, her face bright with anticipation.

"In the afternoon the seamstress will arrive with her assistants," she reported happily. "And any moment her man will arrive from the shop to show us materials."

"My gown must not be too fancy," Suzanne reminded with a conciliatory smile. "Keith's family is still in mourning."

"Suzanne, your wedding day will be the most important day in your life. You will wear a white gown so beautiful you will treasure it," she said resolutely. "Someday your daughter will wear it." Her eyes were suddenly wistful. "My two daughters and my son died early. My three granddaughters, Gilbert's sisters, are married and living in Europe. Two in Paris, one in Lucerne. I have eleven great-grandchildren, whom I have not seen for almost six years. Crossing the Atlantic has become too much for me; and each time they plan to come to me, there is some family crisis." She gestured philosophically. "So I have adopted you as my great-granddaughter, Suzanne. I am going to be the great-grandmother of the bride."

Suzanne's eyes were tender. She understood

now the closeness between Gilbert and his grand-mother.

"Mme. Mauriac," she said impulsively, "you said that Maman was very like me — "

"Suzanne, she would have been so happy to see you married to Keith," Mme. Mauriac said sentimentally. "As your father would be." She frowned in sudden consternation, distressed that she had allowed the conversation to take this turn. "Why hasn't Amelia brought us tea?"

"Please, can we talk about Maman and Papa?" Suzanne pleaded.

Mme. Mauriac seemed incapable of speech. Her eyes betrayed her panic. *Why couldn't they talk about Maman and Papa?*

"Someone is arriving." Mme. Mauriac rose unsteadily to her feet with an air of reprieve. "Amelia!" she called. "Please go to the door."

Suzanne sat back in her chair. She must not corner Mme. Mauriac this way. She was a fragile old lady. It was too upsetting to her. *Why?* All at once her mind focused on a supposition that left her dizzy. Was it because Mme. Mauriac was, in truth, her great-grandmother?

Was the story about Maman and Papa dying in a steamboat accident a fantasy? She felt herself teetering at the edge of a breakthrough. If Uncle Gilbert was her father, then who was her mother? She must watch for a sign, something that would reveal the truth to her.

Amelia ushered the man from the shop into the drawing room. He approached slowly, lugging bolts of material in his arms. Suzanne forced herself to concentrate, along with Mme. Mauriac, on choosing materials. White tulle illusion and white satin for her gown, gossamer fabrics for nightdresses and dressing gowns, so sheer that pinkness touched Suzanne's high cheekbones as she visualized herself appearing before Keith in them.

The day swept by with astonishing speed, yet at unwary moments Suzanne grappled with the possibility that Uncle Gilbert was her father. At the dinner table Mme. Mauriac filled him in on the day's happenings.

"You must tell Jane that the ceremony is to be performed at nightfall," Mme. Mauriac told Gilbert as they ate a perfect chocolate mousse. "A candlelit ceremony is always beautiful. Then we'll go to Savage Oaks for the wedding dinner."

She was marrying Keith, Suzanne reminded herself, but she must live at Savage Oaks with Jane and Phillip as well. Though Jane had been scrupulously polite to her on all the occasions that she had been at Savage Oaks, she had felt an intimidating wall between them.

While Suzanne sat in the room, talking with Uncle Gilbert about the continuing trouble in Kansas, Mme. Mauriac excused herself. She returned in a few minutes to sit on the sofa beside Suzanne.

"When Gilbert was last in Europe, I asked him to buy a châtelaine for me to present to my first great-granddaughter on her marriage. Since they seem to be slow in arriving at this, I wish you to have it, Suzanne. My adopted great-granddaughter," she said with a dazzling smile.

"Mme. Mauriac, how thoughtful of you." Suzanne opened the small, velvet box that Mme. Mauriac placed in her hands. "Oh, it's lovely!"

A decorated enamel case, whose central motif was surrounded by twelve floral decors, highlighted by bands of tiny pearls, hung from a delicate, golden chain.

"There is a watch inside," Mme. Mauriac explained, pleased at her delight. "Lift the top of the case and you'll see. It is the creation of a Monsieur Gubelin of Lucerne, a jeweler highly favored in Europe."

"It's perfect." Suzanne leaned forward to kiss Mme. Mauriac.

"Tomorrow we'll visit the Episcopal priest. He'll be eager to meet Keith's bride," Mme. Mauriac pursued. "And Keith has asked that we go to the jeweler's so that you can choose your wedding band and have it adjusted to your finger."

Suzanne stared in dismay. Wouldn't Keith choose her ring? Was it proper for the bride to go to the jeweler's and choose it alone?

"Keith is frantically busy at Savage Oaks," Gilbert said quickly, reading her reaction. "He's spent so much time with you these past two weeks that he must concentrate on the milling these next few days."

"Isn't he coming into New Orleans before the

wedding?" Suzanne asked. She needed Keith's presence to reassure her that she was not making a terrible, impetuous decision. Mère Angélique always cautioned her against this tendency.

"He'll try, I'm sure," Gilbert soothed. "But you'll have the rest of your lives to be together. As a sugar planter's wife, you'll learn how critical this time of year can be. But next year, with the Tintagel acreage and hands added to Savage Oaks, Keith might find himself in a more comfortable position."

When she married Keith, Tintagel — everything in her estate — belonged legally to him. She knew that she loved Keith; she wished it to be that way, she reproached herself guiltily. Yet she recognized a rebellion deep within her that her estate would pass from Uncle Gilbert's care to Keith's, as though she, Suzanne Savage, was incapable of thought.

"Suzanne, you're tired," Gilbert said compassionately when she tried to cover a yawn. "Go upstairs now to your room and to bed."

Suzanne was certain that she would fall asleep the moment Patrice pulled the coverlet about her shoulders and left the room, but sleep was elusive. Disturbing suspicions that Uncle Gilbert could be her father charged through her mind. Was everything he had told her about her parents a myth? Even that they had come from Savannah?

Recurrently she remembered the ring that Papa had worn. Uncle Gilbert wore no such ring.

No, Uncle Gilbert was *not* her father. If she were his child, surely he would have acknowledged her.

She stirred restlessly, her mind too active for sleep. She hoped that Keith would come into New Orleans to see her before the wedding. It was not easy to understand him. He was a man of striking contradictions. One moment so affectionate, the next moody and withdrawn. And yet these contradictions in themselves intrigued her.

It would have been so wonderful if they could have gone away together after the wedding, but this time of year that was impossible. She wished passionately that they could spend their wedding night away from Savage Oaks.

Mme. Mauriac swept Suzanne along in a burst of activity. The seamstress and her workers were constantly in the house, caught up in the urgency of finishing Suzanne's wedding gown, the night-dresses and dressing gowns by the scheduled date. Slippers must be made and Mme. Mauriac insisted on white satin. The wedding band was too loose; the jeweler must make it small enough for Suzanne's slender finger.

As she stood with concealed impatience while the seamstress enveloped her in endless yards of white satin and tulle illusion, Suzanne remembered Cecile standing before M. Worth while he created the masterpiece she wore at her wedding at the Cathedral of Notre-Dame.

Cecile had entered philosophically into a marriage arranged by her parents. She was marrying Keith, whom she loved. Yet as each day brought her closer to the wedding, she felt increasingly insecure.

Had she made too impetuous a decision? Uncle Gilbert was practical. He saw Keith as a fine young man of good family, whom every young lady in the parish was out to marry. But this was her whole life being arranged so precipitately.

She loved Keith. But she would not be a wife who abandoned her capacity for thinking in return for marriage. She had made a vow to herself, and in some fashion she must convince Keith that this was an inseparable part of her.

Why couldn't Keith come into New Orleans just once to spend an hour or two with her? It was his absence that caused these doubts in her. First she saw him daily, now not at all.

The morning before the wedding, Suzanne and Mme. Mauriac settled themselves in the Mauriac carriage while Sebastien hoisted the portmanteaus and multitude of parcels on top. Suzanne felt herself living a role in a play. Was she truly going to marry Keith Savage tomorrow?

She was grateful for Mme. Mauriac's light chatter as they drove towards Tintagel. She was conscious of being swept up in a tidal wave over which she had no control. She had not seen Keith since before Uncle Gilbert came to her with the marriage proposal. She had expected him to come to her that evening.

Oh, she was behaving like a spoiled little girl! Uncle Gilbert had explained how urgently Keith was needed at the sugar house this time of year. He must make up for the two weeks in which he had spent so much time with her.

At Tintagel they were welcomed by Mrs. Cantrell with a stiff, small smile. Again, Suzanne sensed her hostility at the presence of strangers. Was Mrs. Cantrell anxious about what would happen to Tintagel, now that Suzanne was marrying Keith? It was a question that rose regularly in her mind.

After a brief rest, Mme. Mauriac organized a group of house slaves into helping her rearrange the drawing room for the wedding. Mrs. Cantrell watched with grim disapproval while the piano, bought thirty-one years ago so that Adrian Ramsay might learn to play, was moved into the drawing room.

"Suzanne, you will come down the aisle with Gilbert," Mme. Mauriac planned with the vivaciousness of a woman one-third her age, "to stand here. There will be masses of flowers on either side of the aisle. Lilies, roses, and camellias. The camellias have just begun to blossom," she said with satisfaction. "Pick the flowers tomorrow afternoon," she told Merlin. "So they'll be fresh for the ceremony."

At last Mme. Mauriac was satisfied with the rearrangement of the drawing room. Suzanne and she joined Mrs. Cantrell for lunch. Mme. Mauriac was disarmingly charming to the housekeeper, but Mrs. Cantrell did not relinquish her somber mood. After the meal, at Mme. Mauriac's order, they prepared to retire to their rooms for naps.

"You must rest, Suzanne. This has been such a chaotic week for you. Even if you don't sleep, stay in bed until dinner."

"I'll rest," Suzanne promised.

Late in the afternoon, Suzanne abandoned her futile attempt to nap. She was conscious of a need for physical activity. Walk along the levee, she exhorted herself.

The sun was low, painting the river with ribbons of gold. She walked compulsively, a cashmere shawl drawn closely about her shoulders because the temperature had dropped sharply. She relished the freshness of the air, not realizing the distance she had walked until suddenly daylight was gone. How strange it was in Louisiana! No twilight, no hovering between light and darkness. Now a fog was moving in about her with eerie beauty, settling low above the trees.

She must return to the house. Mme. Mauriac would grow concerned if she were not there when Patrice called her for supper. She walked swiftly, skirting the stable. She started at the sound of Phillip's voice. He was talking to someone within a lamplit room at the rear of the stable.

"Raoul, I mean it," Phillip said with conviction. "Keep writing the poems and give them to me. I promise to send them out to a newspaper up North. They'll publish them. They're beautiful!"

"Mist' Phillip, I wouldn't even know how to read if you hadn't taught me." Raoul's voice was rich with gratitude.

"Didn't you teach me how to swim when I was eight?" Phillip countered with an effort at levity. "After you pushed me in head first!"

Suzanne smiled faintly. She could understand Phillip's being sympathetic to a stable boy at Savage Oaks, who secretly wrote poetry. Again she felt a sense of pain that, in truth, she was a party to the slave system, which she found so reprehensible.

Suzanne stood motionless in the hall while the neckline of her billowing wedding gown was carefully adjusted by Mme. Mauriac. A cluster of servants, including Patrice, hovered sentimentally behind her. Some of them, like Merlin, had been here before Keith was born.

"The moment you hear the music, Suzanne, you are to enter with Gilbert. And after the ceremony you'll pose for a daguerreotype. The man is waiting on the gallery with his equipment." Tears glistening in her eyes, Mme. Mauriac leaned forward to kiss her. "Suzanne, be happy. This will be a fine marriage." But Mme. Mauriac's eyes were troubled.

A few moments later, Phillip began the wedding music by the German composer, Mr. Mendelssohn. Jane said Phillip had been practicing all week. Suzanne's hand was ice-cold as she slid it through Gilbert's arm. The drawing room was fragrant with the scent of the flowers. Trying not to appear nervous, Keith waited at the improvised altar. The Episcopalian priest smiled benignly upon Suzanne as she approached.

She was about to marry Keith. He stood beside her, his eyes so serious on this occasion. For an instant she remembered the splendor of Cecile's marriage, the awesome assemblage of relatives and friends. If only Maman and Papa could be here today. They would love Keith, as she loved him.

As the priest's sonorous voice filled the room, Suzanne's eyes clung to his face. This was the most momentous occasion of her life. And then the priest was saying the words that would make her Keith's wife. She made the necessary response in a whisper. Keith's reply was strong and clear. *They were married. Man and wife.*

Self-consciously Keith leaned down to kiss her. The others in the room came forward with congratulations.

"May I kiss the bride?" Phillip asked with a whimsical smile, and without waiting for a reply brushed his mouth gently against her cheek. "Welcome to the family, Suzanne."

"Please step away from the bride and groom," an unfamiliar voice ordered cheerfully, and Suzanne realized this was the man who had come up from New Orleans to take the daguerreotype of Keith and her. She must ask if she could have two copies to send to Mère Angélique and Cecile. "Now perfectly still, please."

The wedding party left Tintagel to ride in two carriages to Savage Oaks, where they were greeted by a cluster of servants eager to express their good wishes to the bride and groom. Phillip and Mme. Mauriac were determinedly convivial, in sharp contrast to Jane, who seemed pale and drawn today. Keith was disconcertingly formal.

The dining salon had been opened for the wedding dinner. A long table, resplendently set, dominated the impressive salon. A crystal chandelier hung from the ceiling, which was ornately designed in dark green. The walls were pale green, the windows draped in a green damask that matched the ceiling.

Pointedly Jane seated Suzanne at the foot of the table, as the new mistress of Savage Oaks, with Kevin at the head. Arthur, the majordomo, hovered uncertainly at the sideboard, bewildered about where to stand, then crossed to stand behind Jane's chair.

"Arthur, no," Jane admonished. "Behind Miss Suzanne's chair."

Suzanne felt her face grow hot. Jane was going to be a hostile sister-in-law.

Jane had ordered a sumptuous menu, prepared with the help of a French chef brought from New Orleans for the occasion. Champagne was served rather than the usual wines. Along with the coffee came a silver dish with lumps of sugar blazing with spirits to be put in the tiny Sèvres cups.

Mme. Mauriac complimented Jane on the wedding feast, striving to elicit some air of festivity from her. Jane's face remained impassive, her eyes telegraphing her disapproval of this marriage. Never mind Jane, Suzanne told herself defiantly. *She* had married Keith.

As soon as they had finished dinner and retired to the drawing room, the priest and Mrs. Cantrell excused themselves after the perfunctory good wishes. Half an hour later the Mauriacs departed for New Orleans. Suzanne was conscious of a painful tension in the room. Only Phillip and she talked. Jane and Keith sat submerged in silence.

Did Keith feel the same oppressive distress as she at the prospect of spending their wedding night here at Savage Oaks, beneath the same roof as Jane and Phillip? Why had she not discussed this with Keith, she berated herself. But when could she have talked with him?

Keith frowned sharply as they heard a knock at the door. Edward was going down the hall to answer it.

"Keith, are you expecting someone?" Jane asked irritably.

"No one." He rose to his feet as they waited to learn the identity of the caller. They heard the heavy footsteps of a man in a hall. Keith strode to the door.

"Reagan!" he said in astonishment. "What's happened?"

The short, stocky overseer came into view. His

florid face was etched with indignation.

"Mr. Keith, I think you'd better come to the sugar house," Reagan said tersely. "Some lunatic put out the fire under the boiler and then messed up some of the machinery."

"How did you let that happen?" Keith shot back furiously.

"You told me to let the hands off from five to midnight," the overseer reminded, embarrassed at being chastised before the family.

"You should know enough to leave somebody to tend the fire! It should never go out!"

"I left a hand there," Reagan said miserably. "He fell asleep. They've been working eighteen hours a day, Mr. Keith — and you gave them that whiskey — " His voice trailed off.

"What exact damage was done?" A vein throbbed in Keith's forehead. He was fighting to control his temper.

"I went in for a routine check," Reagan explained. "I saw the fire was out under the boiler, and the kettles and the pans had all been dumped over. I took a closer look and I saw somebody had dumped sand into the steam engine."

"Oh, Lord!" Keith's face was pained. "We can't afford a slowdown now. Come on, Reagan." At the door he paused, swung around to face Suzanne. "Suzanne, I'm sorry," he apologized. "I must go to the sugar house."

With a forced little smile on her face, Suzanne listened to the sounds of the two men rushing from the house.

"The sugar house should have been in operation," Jane said agitatedly. "It must go twenty-four hours a day in season. The hands work in shifts. Eighteen hours' work, six hours' rest. I don't know what got into Keith to give them those hours off."

"Let's go into the library and I'll play some poor piano for you," Phillip offered as an awkward silence engulfed them. "Of course, I'm not up to Keith's playing," he said with sarcasm.

"I'll have Edward bring us more coffee in the library." Jane rose to her feet with an air of distraction, and then she paused, her eyes focused on Suzanne, her face taut. "Or perhaps you would prefer to do that yourself, Suzanne?"

"No, please," Suzanne said uncomfortably. Jane saw her as a threat to her position as mistress of Savage Oaks. She knew nothing about managing a household. "Nothing must change because I've married Keith."

They moved into the library, the room at Savage Oaks that Suzanne most liked. Phillip settled himself at the piano while Arthur started a fire in the grate.

"Arthur will bring the coffee in a few minutes," Jane promised stiffly, ill-at-ease in Suzanne's presence.

How long would Keith remain at the sugar house? How long must she sit here with Phillip and Jane? This was her wedding night.

Phillip appeared rooted at the piano. Jane grew restless as he moved from one musical mood to another without taking a moment to talk. Suzanne heard the first rumble of thunder, and remembered the overcast sky that greeted them as they drove earlier from Tintagel to Savage Oaks.

"We're in for a storm," Jane predicted. "Phillip, go out to the kitchen house and tell Arthur to see that all the shutters are closed."

Phillip obeyed, then returned to sit in the drawing room with Jane and Suzanne. Suzanne strained to make conversation. What was happening at the sugar house? Why was Keith staying so long?

Outside, Edward was moving about the house with another servant, closing the shutters against the impending storm.

All at once, in the midst of a sonata, Phillip stopped playing and rose to his feet.

"I'm going to bed," he said with irritation. His eyes lingered speculatively on Suzanne, and she felt her face grow warm. "Goodnight, Suzanne. Goodnight, Jane."

Suzanne searched her mind for something to talk about with Jane, but her sister-in-law seemed oblivious of her presence, involved in some private anguish.

Jane flinched as a burst of lightning flashed across the sky and sent an unnatural brightness into the library.

"It's late," she said tensely. "Let's go to our rooms."

Suzanne turned to her with an air of uncertainty. Where was Keith? Ought she not wait downstairs until he returned to the house?

"Keith will be at the sugar house till dawn," Jane said with unexpected gentleness. "I'll show you to your room."

Jane left Suzanne at her door with a constrained goodnight. Assailed by conflicting emotions, Suzanne opened the door and walked into the elegant corner bedroom where her portmanteaus had been deposited earlier but which she had not seen until this moment. The bed was elaborately canopied in *toile de Jouy*, the walls covered with a delicate ivory silk. A pair of Regency side chairs and a small cane-backed settee, cushioned also in *toile de Jouy*, flanked the low-manteled fireplace. A finely crafted mahogany armoire, a Sheraton washstand, a marquetry chest-of-drawers, and a writing table were positioned between tall, narrow windows draped in ivory damask.

Patrice came forward with a broad smile.

"Ah unpack ever'thing an' iron an' hang dem away, Young Missy." She glowed with a possessive pleasure. "Mah lady be de pretties' bride Ah eveh did see!"

"Thank you, Patrice." She forced an answering smile. Jane said Keith would be at the sugar house till dawn. On his wedding night?

"Lemme he'p yo' outta dat dress, Young Missy. An' den Ah'll press de sheets so's dey won't be so cold."

"You don't have to do that, Patrice," Suzanne

said quickly. "Just unhook my dress, please."

Her eyes romantically aglow, Patrice helped Suzanne out of her wedding gown, reverently hung it away. Fighting self-consciousness, Suzanne changed into a dainty, diaphanous nightdress, pulled on a matching peignoir. She shivered slightly in the night chill, and instantly Patrice was at the fireplace, putting more wood into the grate.

"Ah could press dem sheets in jes' a few minutes, Young Missy," Patrice offered again.

"No, Patrice," Suzanne said with polite firmness. She just wished to be left alone. "Goodnight."

Suzanne stood uncertainly in the center of the room as Patrice closed the door behind her. Outside lightning crackled repeatedly. Suzanne started at the sound of a tree being struck in a grove nearby. She crossed to the window and gazed out at the stormy sky.

Perhaps Keith would not come back to the house till dawn, but she would be waiting for him.

Six

Jane walked into her room, its somber darkness faintly alleviated by the fire that smoldered in the grate. She closed the heavy oak door behind her and locked it, as she inevitably did before retiring for the night. She had survived the day without the roof falling in, but knots between her shoulder blades and a dull throb at the back of her head were evidence of the tension that had been insidiously growing in her since she awoke this morning with the knowledge that this was the day Keith must marry a girl he scarcely knew.

She crossed to the commode near her four-poster canopied bed and lit the brass-based, glass-shaded lamp. Thunder rumbled overhead, to be followed by a flash of lightning that penetrated the worn-thin drapes at her windows. The wind was ripping through the trees. Her mouth tightened in rejection. She loathed storms.

Elaine had laid out her nightdress and pressed the sheets. She crossed to the fireplace to change by the warmth offered there, flinching with each fresh clap of thunder, each new flash of lightning. This would be another of the sleepness nights that plagued her.

Phillip pretended to be amused by Keith's hasty marriage.

"Jane, don't be so depressed," he had mocked. "Keith's marrying to save Savage Oaks. And I don't think it's such a hardship. The girl's damned pretty."

But tonight Phillip had been moody, almost sullen. When he stayed at the piano that way, she knew he was disturbed.

They would not have trouble with Phillip and Suzanne, would they? She always worried about Phillip. Papa had been so shaken when Phillip had to leave Princeton that way. But nobody in the parish knew that he had been expelled for being more friendly than he should have been with a faculty member's wife.

She stood before the fireplace in her severely plain nightdress and remembered the day when Papa, who was the soul of gentleness and had never laid a hand on any of them, had flogged Phillip on his fifteenth birthday for taking a pretty slave to bed. After that, Phillip never touched a slave. He would not be too free with Suzanne, would he?

Jane reached for the poker, separated the smoldering logs to coax them into a blaze. It had been stupid of her to give Suzanne the room right next door to hers, when there were eight bedrooms on the floor and only three occupied. *The room that had been closed up for nineteen years.* But some per-verse pride had prodded her into putting Suzanne into the one upstairs room that did not betray their pinched financial condition.

She started at the cautious knock on her door. "Yes?"

"Phillip," he said quietly, and she crossed to unlock the door and pull it open.

"What is it?" she asked in exasperation.

"Temper, temper," he taunted with a sly smile.

"Phillip, I'm tired. What do you want?"

"Keith hasn't come back to the house yet." His eyes were quizzical.

"What do you expect me to do about that?" she demanded coldly.

"Send somebody to the sugar house to remind Keith that this is his wedding night," Phillip said, and Jane was astonished by the compassion she saw in his eyes.

"Phillip, don't be absurd," she said impa-tiently. "Go back to your room."

He shrugged and walked back down the hall while she watched him from the doorway. Was Phillip harboring ideas about standing in for his brother? It was lonely here for Phillip, but he re-fused to go away to school again. What were they going to do with him?

Jane closed the door, crossed to her bed. The night was cold and damp, the fire in the grate sending warmth within a range of only a few feet. She would not sleep — not on a night like this — but she could at least be more comfortable in bed.

As she settled herself beneath the comforters, the rain came down in torrents, slashing against the shutters, which Elaine had closed earlier. It was absurd to waste oil, but she was reluctant to turn down the lamp just yet.

Jane struggled to keep her mind from hurtling backwards, as too often happened in the midst of a storm. When she was a child, she had been scolded indulgently by Mama because she loved to stand on the gallery in the midst of a violent storm and watch the trees bending before the elements, seeing the mile-wide Mississippi churn darkly between the levees.

No! No, don't think about that night! Not tonight, with Keith's bride lying in the room next door. In the room that had been hers until the summer of her fourteenth year.

She had been so delighted when the tall, handsome stranger arrived to stay at Savage Oaks for a few days. Where usually there were constant guests at the plantation, the last few months there had been none because Mama had been quite ill before Phillip was born, and was slow in regaining her strength after his birth. Jane had been so lonely, feeling herself overshadowed by the arrival of another brother, though she adored Keith.

When they sat down to dinner with the stranger, who talked so eloquently that he mesmerized her, Papa and Mama were cold and silent. She was bewildered. But the stranger singled her out for attention, and she had been deliriously pleased.

Each night she sat at the dinner table, glowing because he teased her with such affection, called her pet names, complimented her on her long, fair hair and blue eyes. To her amazement, Mama was rude to him. Maybe because he always liked a glass of bourbon at his hand, she'd decided. Mama hated having whiskey served in the house, though she politely made it available to their guests.

Their guest told fantastic stories about life on the boats along the Mississippi until Mama would cut him short, despite Jane's protestations. She knew it was wrong to gamble, but the tales he told were so exciting.

Jane tensed beneath the comforters, straining not to remember that final night; but remorselessly recall overtook her. She was fourteen again. All that evening a summer storm had been threatening. The shutters had been closed in anticipation, but she had thrown them open in her room so that she could lie in bed and watch the clouds move together in the ominous sky.

She had fallen asleep despite her determination to stay awake until the rains came. She had awakened with a start, conscious that someone stood beside her bed.

"Don't be frightened, Janie," he whispered. "I've come to say goodbye." *Their guest.*

She sat up in bed with a sense of desolation.

"You're leaving now? In the middle of a storm?" Yet she felt it was oddly right that he should do this.

"Beautiful little Janie." His voice was a caress. "Will you miss me?"

"Yes," she said fervently.

"Your Mama thinks I have overstayed my welcome," he said with charming wistfulness. "But I couldn't leave without saying goodbye to you." He dropped to the edge of her bed and she was conscious of his bourbon-scented breath. "May I kiss you goodbye?"

He had kissed her on the mouth. *Nobody had ever kissed her that way before.* And suddenly she was conscious of his hand fondling her throat and she grew frightened when the hand crept inside her nightdress. When she tried to pull her mouth away from his, he refused to release her. His mouth stayed on hers while he pried between her teeth with his tongue with a terrifying frenzy.

It was a nightmare! It wasn't happening! She heard the tear as he ripped her nightdress to the waist, and with one hand, caressed her budding breasts. And then she felt the strange, ominous weight of his body above hers, and he began to move above her.

He was trying to choke her to death with his tongue, she thought frantically. And then, all at once his hands were leaving her breasts to rip the nightdress to its hem. *What was he doing to her?*

He separated her ice-cold legs with one of his, and she felt an unfamiliar hardness between them. A cry of outrage died in her throat as he thrust that hardness towards her, pushing impatiently until she was conscious of a sharp, fleeting pain.

In the lightning that flashed into the room she saw his face contorted in some unknown emotion. While he groaned in some secret pain, she screamed wildly.

"Mama! Mama! Mama!"

Jane swung to one side and buried her face in the pillow. Why could she never erase that night from her mind? It was nineteen years ago.

And in that room where her life had ended, Suzanne waited to be taken by her husband. Why did Keith have to bring his bride to Savage Oaks? Why must she lie here in her bed and know what was happening in the next room?

Seven

Keith hovered above Reagan as the overseer labored over a piece of equipment. The hands who had come in to work at midnight were subdued in the face of the destruction in the sugar house. The kettles and the vacuum pans had been set up properly again, and the rollers cleaned out. A fire burned healthily under the boiler. But unless Reagan could make this final repair, they would have to shut down until he could go into Leeds in New Orleans and buy replacement parts.

"How's it coming, Reagan?" Keith asked anxiously.

"It's not," Reagan admitted. "I've tried everything I know how." He straightened up, frowning with frustration. "I can fix almost any piece of machinery used in the South, but this here has got to be replaced." His eyes met Keith's guardedly, and Keith felt guilty about his outburst in the drawing room.

"You're a good man, Reagan," Keith said

apologetically. "I'm sorry I yelled at you that way."

Unexpectedly, Reagan grinned.

"I guess a man's got a right to be nerved up when he's dragged away from his bride on his wedding night."

Keith managed a responsive smile. Reagan had no way of knowing how he had welcomed this intrusion, even while he was disturbed about the infernal vandalism. For a few hours he had pushed from his mind the realization that he had married Gilbert Mauriac's ward. Guilt welled in him as he remembered Suzanne's startled face when he told her he must go to the sugar house. But it was urgent, he thought defensively.

"You'll have to go into New Orleans first thing in the morning," Keith said somberly. "Let's hope Leeds has the parts in stock."

"They will, Sir," Reagan said optimistically.

Keith left the sugar house, strode out into the wetness of the night. The rain had stopped at last. The ominous blackness of the sky was giving way to the first gray of morning. Damp leaves, swept to the ground before their time by the force of the storm, flattened beneath his feet as he walked towards the house. Here and there twigs cluttered the ground.

Who the devil had gone into the sugar house and caused that damage? Nothing like this had ever happened at Savage Oaks. Papa had always run a model plantation, and he was doing everything possible to follow that path.

Sure, the hands were working long hours. So

was he. But they enjoyed the grinding season; they were glad when it arrived. They were more cheerful then than at any other time of the year. Their food was better, more varied. They had their rations of whiskey. They relished the demands of the season. And they knew, when the season was over, they would have special rewards and a big party. Better to give them rewards than to drive them with a whip, Keith thought with distaste for those few plantation masters who sanctioned brutality. Thank God they were few.

Approaching the house, he spied the light in Suzanne's room. Damn, he would have to go to her. He was hoping she could capitulate to the emergency and postpone their wedding night. God, he was tired. Right now he would like nothing better than to have George bring him the tub to his room and fill it with hot water. He would like to soak there till his skin was waterlogged. Instead he must play the amorous bridegroom.

The bough of a towering pecan splintered by lightning lay across his path. He stepped absently over it, then paused to watch a cottontail dart into the woods behind him. Manon would still be awake, he thought tentatively, staring through the woods though he knew no light could be seen at this distance. Nobody in the big house knew that the small, perfect cottage existed. Except Phillip. Phillip knew everything that happened at Savage Oaks.

Manon would still be awake. She stayed up until dawn, chattering away with Lily Mae, the little thirteen-year-old he had released from the fields to be her maid, or reading those cheap romantic novels of which she was so inordinately fond. He hesitated indecisively. Manon would be delighted if he walked into the cottage now. She would take him to that silk-sheeted bed and make him forget he was tired, that his head pounded remorselessly.

He dismissed this, annoyed with himself. Not on his wedding night. He suspected that Manon was hurt that he had married so soon after setting her up in the cottage. But damn it, she knew that what happened between them had nothing to do with his life at the house.

He walked with a quickened pace, his shoes wet, droplets from the trees falling upon his head and shoulders. He had married Suzanne Duprée. Now he must show himself her husband.

On the gallery he removed his shoes, walked in stocking feet up the stairs and towards his room. He saw the spill of light that showed beneath Suzanne's bedroom door. His face tightened. He must change into a dressing gown and go to his bride.

Suzanne sat up in bed as she heard the sound of a door close down the hall. Keith was home. All at once her heart was pounding. She tossed aside the light coverlet and rose to her feet, reached for her peignoir, listening for sounds from Keith's room.

A few minutes later she started at the tentative knock on her door. She had not heard him approach. Eagerly, her mouth parted in a welcoming smile, she hurried to respond. She knew he would come to her.

Keith stood before the open door in the faint spill of light from the wall sconce that offered illumination for the night. How handsome he was in that fine, deep red, silk dressing gown!

"I'm sorry to have been kept so long at the sugar house," he said apologetically, and walked into the room and closed the door behind him. He stood there awkwardly, his smile strained.

"I understood." Suzanne's eyes were luminous with the love she felt for him. "You look exhausted," she said sympathetically. Waiting for him to touch her.

"You look beautiful," he said with peculiar intensity. "You were a beautiful bride."

"You were a handsome bridegroom," she said lightly, yet strange unease stirred within her. Why did he sound so formal? Why was he standing here before her this way without taking her into his arms? Was she a wanton to feel such impatience? But she loved Keith. He was her husband. She wanted him to hold her in his arms and teach her to love.

"Suzanne, turn down the lamp," he said tersely. His smile had ebbed away.

"Yes, Keith." Was he angry with her? She searched her mind to think what she might have done to vex him.

In the darkness she moved towards him, unsure and anxious. She realized he had discarded his dressing gown. Trembling, she pulled away her peignoir and dropped it to the foot of the bed. His hands were cold when they reached to pull her towards him. He had worn nothing under his dressing gown.

He lowered his mouth to hers and suddenly she was responding with a passion of which she had not suspected herself capable. He drew her in against the lithe hardness of his body, and she was starkly conscious of his maleness.

She was disappointed when he released her mouth, but then he swept her into his arms and carried her to the bed. She had never felt so totally alive, she thought with exhilaration as she waited for the newness of marriage to be taught to her. She was conscious of an unfamiliar pulsating low within her, a sense of waiting to receive.

He kissed her again, his hands moving about her breasts. The weight of him lay above her, sweetly heavy. She waited with ecstatic anticipation for the moment that would truly make her his wife. The gossamer folds of her nightdress rose to her hips under his guidance. A faint sound of desire welled in her throat when she felt his first thrust. Her hands tightened at his shoulders.

All at once, Keith was driving himself within her. His breathing labored. No tenderness in him, no awareness of *her*. She stiffened in rejection, cried out for one reproachful instant in pain. He waited, then drove again within her with a grim, methodical thrusting. She submitted to the invasion that she had expected to be beautiful. She lay beneath him, unresponsive, immobile, tears stinging her eyes.

Keith was taking her in anger. He had not come to her with love. *This was not the way it should be.* She was relieved when he, at last, lay limp above her. She gritted her teeth to keep back the accusations that welled in her when he perfunctorily kissed her before he lifted himself from the bed. Where was the Keith she had known before the wedding?

"Goodnight, Suzanne," he said matter-of-factly, reaching for his dressing gown that lay upon the floor.

"Goodnight, Keith." She struggled to keep her voice even, uncolored by the disappointment that filled her.

She waited until he had left the room, then crossed to the door and locked it. Tears filled her eyes, spilled over as she leaned against the door. She was furious with Keith. She felt herself used, as though she were some slave girl he had brought to his bed for a few minutes of passion. This was her wedding night. It was supposed to be the most eventful night of her life.

With a sigh of anguish she darted across the room to push aside the drapes at one of the windows that overlooked the Mississippi, gazed out at the first grayness of morning. Her instinct was to pack a portmanteau and flee to Tintagel, to wash away forever the memory of tonight.

She stood at the window, watching the first

pink streaks of dawn stain the sky. No, she must not make a hasty decision. Keith had been upset tonight. He was exhausted from the long hours he spent each day at the sugar house, and then tonight that awful business of the destruction of the equipment. She must not hold tonight against Keith. He was her husband. He would come to her again, and it would be different.

Suzanne struggled to settle into this strange new life at Savage Oaks, tried to adjust to the disappointment of her wedding night. The days passed with Keith constantly at the sugar house. When he appeared at the table for meals, he was tired and distracted, speaking little. He made no effort to come again to her bed, though each night she waited. Some nights he did not come home at all.

She spent long, lonely hours reading on the gallery, walking among the gardens. Occasionally she took Othello out for a canter, feeling guilty that she did not do this daily, though Abram assured her that Raoul exercised the horse regularly.

She visited the small family cemetery surrounded by trellises of late-blooming roses, and read each tombstone as though here she might find some insight into Keith's complex nature. He was polite and solicitous when he spoke to her, yet there was this wall between them that had not existed before their wedding.

How had she failed Keith? She had not pleased him that one night he came to her. But how could she have been warm and responsive when he came to her in anger? Why had he changed? What had she done?

She sat on the gallery this sunlit morning in November and tortured herself with recriminations. She should have responded to Keith. She should have made him understand that she loved him. There had been no fear of the wedding night in her. He was exhausted and disturbed over the trouble at the sugar house, and she had not understood this.

With a need for action she put down the *Harper's Weekly* she had been reading and left the gallery. She walked without direction, fighting the restlessness that surged through her at regular intervals. As she walked away from the house, she spied Jane's tall, spare figure emerging from a side door. Under one arm Jane carried a small square box that, Suzanne knew, contained the remedies she dispensed each Monday in the quarters. In her free hand Jane carried a copy of *Gunn's Domestic Medicine.*

Last night Phillip had told her, with that faintly cynical smile of his, that Savage Oaks retained a doctor on an annual fee of six hundred dollars. But he came to the plantation only in dire emergencies.

Jane would return to the house in time for the light midday meal, Suzanne surmised; and shortly afterwards she would disappear in the chaise, driving herself. Where did Jane go every afternoon, she wondered with recurrent curiosity.

Should she ask Jane to allow her to help in the duties of running the house? She shrank from this, though Jane worked as hard as any farmer's wife. Every morning, except on Mondays, she shut herself up with half a dozen servants in the large sewing room up on the third floor to supervise the weaving and the cutting and sewing of clothes for the plantation slaves. In the afternoon, when she returned from her daily jaunt away from the house, Jane worked on the household accounts or supervised the making of soap for the plantation and planned the meals for the family. Yet Suzanne knew intuitively that Jane would resent any offers of help.

Occasionally Phillip would join Jane and her in the drawing room after dinner; but when he did, Jane and he seemed involved in some covert hostility.

She could tolerate Jane's coldness, her slightly supercilious attitude, if there were some relationship between Keith and her: but since their wedding night they might have been strangers living beneath the same roof. She had hoped that Phillip would become her friend, but Phillip burrowed in a private world of his own. She was so alone at Savage Oaks, she thought with soaring frustration.

She walked towards the levee now, intent on sitting on one of the benches to watch the boats coming down the river. This was a view that captivated her. She stopped short at the sight of a small, fenced-in clearing to her right, that she had never before observed. A single tombstone was erected here, nearly hidden by the weeds allowed to grow unheeded.

Suzanne stooped to read the inscription: *A Stranger Who Stayed Briefly Here.* A chill passed through her. Who was the stranger? How had he died? Oh, she must control this wild imagination of hers! Someone traveling through the area fell sick, took refuge at Savage Oaks and died. He was buried here before his name could be ascertained. It was absurd to feel frightened because a stranger lay buried at Savage Oaks, beneath a tombstone that bore no name.

She rose to her feet and walked resolutely to the river. She must stop wallowing in self-pity. She was married to Keith. She loved him. She must find a way to bring back those romantic first days when he had been so warm, so charming. She would remember forever how he rescued her when Othello bolted that way.

She knew the compassion of which Keith was capable. When Mrs. Cantrell came to Savage Oaks for the wedding, he had so delicately assured her that they would not be closing up Tintagel. Once the grinding season was over, he planned on spending hours there each day, reading in Judge Joseph Ramsay's law library. Mrs. Cantrell would always have a home at Tintagel.

By the time Suzanne returned to the house, the table was being set for the midday meal. Jane sat in the library going through the mail that had been brought up from New Orleans. It was too early to expect a reply from Cecile or Mère Angélique, Suzanne reminded herself. Her letters must have just arrived in Paris.

Jane glanced up with a frown.

"Suzanne, will you please have someone go find Phillip? We're sitting down to the table in five minutes."

"Of course." Suzanne smiled and darted down the hall to find a servant to send in search of Phillip.

A few minutes later Suzanne settled herself awkwardly at the table, still feeling self-conscious in the chair that had long been occupied by Jane, with Arthur stationed behind her to see that the meal was properly served. She could hear Phillip talking with Jane, sparring as usual. Both Jane and Keith were annoyed that Phillip refused to help in the activities at the sugar house.

"I saw George coming back with the carriage. Did he go into New Orleans for the mail?" Phillip asked as Jane and he came into the family dining room.

"He always goes on Mondays," Jane reminded.

"Any earth-shattering news?" he mocked.

"There was a letter from Savannah," Jane said and Suzanne was instantly alert. Maman and Papa were from Savannah. How earnestly she wished to go there! "Belle will be married in ten days."

"And you're expected to attend," Phillip said with a taunting smile.

"Phillip, you know I have too many responsibilities to go running off to Belle's wedding." She paused reflectively. "Cousin Eleanor particularly asked for you to come, since Belle and you were so friendly as children."

"I saw Belle for three weeks on their plantation each summer until I was twelve," Phillip drawled. "After that Cousin Eleanor kept her favorite grandchild away from my predatory eyes."

"She had hoped that someday you two would marry," Jane shot back.

"We're cousins," Phillip retorted.

"Cousin Eleanor and Grandfather Savage were cousins. That's sufficiently removed for you to have married."

"But Belle didn't wait for me," Phillip pointed out with a glint of amusement. "Pity."

"Phillip, you'll have to go to the wedding," Jane said firmly. "We've avoided these obligations for years. They're at the town house. That's where Belle will be married. And take Suzanne with you," Jane said after a speculative moment. "You two will represent the family."

"Will Keith agree to this?" Suzanne asked, dizzy with anticipation. At the same time she felt a discomforting wrench at the prospect of putting such distance between Keith and her.

"Keith will agree," Jane said with conviction. "Neither he nor I can leave Savage Oaks at this time of year. The family must be represented. As Phillip said, Belle is Cousin Eleanor's favorite grandchild. She'd never forgive us for not being at Belle's wedding."

"My parents came from Savannah," Suzanne said tremulously. "Perhaps your cousins knew them."

"You never mentioned that," Jane said sharply.

"You never asked," Phillip tossed back with a sardonic smile.

"I knew that Suzanne was an orphan and grew up in a convent near Paris." Jane's face was cold. "I never questioned her parentage."

Oh yes, she had, Suzanne silently challenged. What had Uncle Gilbert told them about Maman and Papa? Whatever, Jane had resented her marrying Keith, still resented her presence at Savage Oaks.

"I'll ask Keith at dinner this evening about my going to Savannah," Suzanne said with contrived calm. It was not Jane's decision to make. But to go to the city where Maman and Papa had lived! Where she had been born! Surely she would meet somebody who remembered Maman and Papa.

All through the meal, while Jane and Phillip engaged in their customary verbal fencing, Suzanne thought about Savannah. In her mind she formulated the questions she would ask. A whole new world would open up to her.

She spent a restless afternoon, impatient for Keith's approval, waiting to know that she *was* going with Phillip to Savannah. They had barely settled themselves at the dinner table when Jane apprised Keith of the wedding and her decision that Phillip and Suzanne would attend.

Jane would find pleasure in her being absent from Savage Oaks, Suzanne told herself, even if only for a short time.

"Suzanne tells us her family is from Savannah." Jane's eyes held Keith's in secret communication.

"I grew up thinking my parents were from New Orleans because that's Uncle Gilbert's home," Suzanne explained uncomfortably. "But their home was in Savannah."

"Would you like to go to Belle's wedding?" Keith asked politely.

"Yes, if you approve." She made a show of eagerness. Neither Phillip nor Jane must guess that Keith had not come to her bedroom since their wedding night. Even if he were working eighteen hours a day at the sugar house, he could find time to come to his wife.

"You'll enjoy the trip, Suzanne," Keith assured. "Savannah's a beautiful city, though quite unlike New Orleans."

"We'll go by boat," Phillip said. "It takes four or five days." He seemed to anticipate the voyage.

"Patrice will go with you, Suzanne," Keith stipulated. He smiled faintly. "I'm sure she'll be delighted."

"Cousin Eleanor will expect an expensive gift," Phillip warned.

"That won't be a problem," Jane said crisply. "You'll go into New Orleans tomorrow and buy a silver tea service at Mallards. Have it engraved with Belle's initials. Explain this must be done immediately. I know you'll choose carefully. You have a taste for such things."

"I believe there's a boat leaving on Thursday," Keith squinted in thought. "That'll get you there in plenty of time. Phillip, make the arrangements while you're in the city."

"We're taking the next boat back after the wedding," Phillip said firmly. "I can't take more than three or four days of Cousin Eleanor."

Suzanne was silent through dinner, struggling to suppress her elation. It was truly happening. Day after day she had searched her mind for some excuse to visit Savannah. And here it was!

But her joy at the impending trip was tarnished by the suspicion that Keith, like Jane, was relieved that for two weeks she would be away from Savage Oaks.

Eight

This evening both Phillip and Keith accompanied Suzanne and Jane into the drawing room after dinner. Keith knew she was going to Savannah. Perhaps tonight he would come to her room. Let her go away knowing everything was all right between Keith and her, she silently prayed.

Keith and Phillip were talking animatedly about Keith's stay in Washington City.

"If it was so hot in Washington City in the summer, why did you stay?" Phillip needled Keith. "You could have been comfortable here."

"When you do something, Phillip, do it all the way," Keith said impatiently. "I was there to read law in Judge Campbell's office, and, by God, I wasn't going to waste a minute of it."

"Campbell didn't stay in Washington City all summer," Phillip scoffed. "Everybody leaves in July and August."

"Campbell stayed and I stayed," Keith said tersely.

"Did you like Washington City?" Suzanne asked curiously.

Keith smiled faintly.

"I was mesmerized. The pace in the city is un-believable. There's always something happening. From Embassy affairs to the annual visits of the American Indians."

Jane appeared startled.

"Indians in Washington City?"

"The chiefs arrive with interpreters and camp in a square in the barracks. Unfortunately many of the local residents consider them a traveling circus," Keith recalled with irritation. "The chiefs come to ask for agricultural tools and for grist mills so that their women won't have to grind corn between stones. They don't come begging. They feel — and can you blame them? — that they've been robbed." Something in Suzanne responded to the zealous glow in his eyes. "The very ground on which the Capitol stands belongs to them."

"Some Indians are rich men," Jane objected.

"A handful," Keith parried. A reminiscent smile softened the sternness of his face. "Last year I encountered old Chief Apothlehole in Harper and Mitchen. His face was painted and he wore a bright red blanket. He's supposed to be worth eighty thousand dollars. He has a farm in the West worked entirely by Negroes."

"That I'd like to see!" Phillip chortled with amusement.

Keith ignored the interruption.

"He's eighty years old and as erect and powerful as any man a third his age. He was buying a hundred dollar scarf for his daughter, but his eyes were sad."

"Were you ever able to visit the Senate and the House of Representatives when they were in session?" Suzanne asked. "I would dearly love to do that some day."

Keith gazed at her with astonishment. Did he think her totally mindless?

"I was often in the Senate and the House," Keith said matter-of-factly.

"What was it like?" For the first time since their wedding, Suzanne thought, Keith was looking at her as though he truly saw her.

"The Senate proceedings are quiet and dignified, but in the House there's a lot of noise and confusion. I was shocked by the indifference often shown by both Senators and Representatives towards the man on the floor. Sometimes they forget to answer to their name when a vote is taken." Keith leaned forward, seeming to talk only to her. "Members of the House obstruct the aisles. They laugh, talk, sit with their feet on the desks. Sometimes so many leave the Speaker has to send the Sergeant-at-Arms to round up a quorum." Keith's eyes glistened with distaste.

"I'm sure our Senators Slidell and Benjamin don't behave in such a fashion," Jane broke her silence with an aura of reproof.

"Our Louisiana Senators are earnest and aggressive," Keith said defensively. "I wasn't speaking ill of them." He stifled a yawn, shifted tiredly in his chair. Another few weeks, Suzanne thought hopefully, and the grinding season would be over. Then Keith would be the delightful young man who had wooed her so ardently. He was exhausted, driving himself at the sugar house day after day.

"What about all those Washington parties?" Phillip jibed. "Don't tell me you were so deep into law you didn't have time for them?" Phillip was self-conscious about not helping at the sugar house, when every hand was working so hard; and at the same time he was defiant, Suzanne thought sympathetically, because he loathed taking second place to Keith.

"When Mrs. Slidell or Judge Campbell's wife invited me, of course I attended," Keith conceded.

Had there been a special girl in Washington City that Keith liked? Had he turned to her because he was lonely, and now he longed for that girl he had known, perhaps loved, in Washington City? Suzanne's heart pounded as she considered this. For a moment she was on the point of withdrawing from the Savannah trip. No, she sternly reproached herself. She must go to Savannah.

"I understand Mrs. Slidell is famous for her matinée dances," Phillip said shyly. "And you were young and eligible."

"I went to Mrs. Slidell's matinee dances because it was a personal obligation." Suzanne saw the glint of hostility in his eyes. Senator Slidell had arranged for him to read law in Judge Campbell's office, and Phillip knew this. "But there were parties that I enjoyed." He was angry with himself for having allowed Phillip to bait him. "When Mrs. Campbell entertained, guests could be sure of meeting the wittiest and weightiest minds of the Capitol. The talk was of philosophy, history, inventions, and the arts. No fashions, no cheap gossip."

"Keith, you're a snob," Phillip laughed.

"That's not true!" Suzanne objected passionately, and flushed as she felt Keith's eyes on her. "Keith's of a serious turn of mind," she said matter-of-factly.

"I'm tired." Jane rose to her feet. "Why don't we call it a night?"

"I have to go back to the sugar house." Keith's eyes were moody. "My work day isn't over yet."

In her room, Suzanne prepared for the night. Patrice was bubbling over with delight at their imminent trip; but Suzanne, sitting in the rosewood slipper chair she particularly fancied while Patrice brushed her hair, was assaulted by conflicting emotions. The prospect of putting so many miles between Keith and herself distressed her. But Keith would be busy with the sugar until almost Christmas. She must not lose this wondrous chance to learn about Maman and Papa.

When Patrice left her, she crossed to a window and gazed out into the night. Above the grove of orange trees she could see the smoke spiraling into the sky from the towering chimneys of the sugar house. She hated this season, she thought violently.

Restless, she left the window to walk to the bed. Maybe tonight, when Keith returned to the house, he would knock at her door. He knew she was going away for two weeks. *Let him come to me. Please, let him come to me. It'll be different this time.*

She lit the ormolu Argand lamp that sat on the table beside her bed, settled herself beneath the light coverlet, and reached for the novel — *Wuthering Heights* — which Mme. Mauriac had sent to her a few days ago. Absorbed as she was in the passionate, melancholy novel, she listened for the sounds in the hall that meant Keith was home for the night. Exhausted, her eyes too tired to read, she refused to give way to sleep. Close to dawn she heard the door open and close downstairs. She thrust aside the coverlet and sat at the side of the bed. Keith must have seen the light in her room as he walked to the house. He knew she was awake.

She listened, hoping he would stop at her door. He walked so softly she had to strain to hear his footsteps. He was walking past her door. He was going into his room. Perhaps he would change into his dressing gown and come to her. She would not think of the way it had been that night. Only how it would be if Keith gave them another chance.

She waited, her heart pounding, silently praying. But at last she knew Keith was not coming to her. Determined not to cry, she burrowed her face against the pillows.

Early next morning Phillip left for New Orleans. He returned just before dinner, jubilant about having arranged for their accommodations. Again, Keith's dinner was taken to him at the sugar house; but Phillip strived to bring an air of conviviality to the dinner table, even eliciting a reluctant laugh from Jane. He was elated that they were going to Savannah, but Suzanne suspected it was the prospect of being aboard ship rather than Belle's wedding that he anticipated.

Keith appeared briefly at the dining table early Thursday morning as Suzanne and Phillip sat sipping Clarissa's strong black coffee. Her first morning at Savage Oaks Suzanne had gently discouraged Patrice's efforts to bring a breakfast tray to her room.

"Phillip, you'll see to Suzanne's comfort," Keith said self-consciously. "It's a long trip."

"Not half so long as the trip from Liverpool to New York," Suzanne said effervescently. But the next moment she was already wistful at the prospect of not seeing Keith for the next twelve days. Phillip estimated that it would be no longer than that. It was painful to be with Keith and feel this wall between them, yet not to see Keith at all would be more of a trial for her.

"Patrice will be sleeping in your stateroom," Keith reminded Suzanne. "You'll be properly chaperoned."

"Keith, I'm not at all worried," she told him earnestly. Why did he appear so disturbed? Did he feel guilty at shipping his bride away before the marriage was a month old?

"I have to go to the sugar house," he said awkwardly, hesitated, then leaned forward to kiss her lightly on the cheek. "Enjoy Savannah, Suzanne."

In a few minutes Jane strode into the dining room to tell them that Caleb was waiting with the carriage to take them into New Orleans. They hastened out to the gallery. Patrice, in a snowy white turban and her best black dress, sat proudly beside Caleb. She should have told Uncle Gilbert and Mme. Mauriac that she was going to Savannah, Suzanne thought belatedly.

"Will there be a few moments to stop by Uncle Gilbert's office?" she asked Phillip.

"Not unless we equip these horses with wings," Phillip said whimsically. "You'll see him when we get back." He was whistling as he helped Suzanne into the carriage. She had never seen him in such high spirits.

The carriage moved down the long roadway towards the public road. The day was delightfully cool and sunny with the early morning frost still glistening with pristine whiteness on the ground. Suzanne wished that the four days on the ship were already past and they were setting foot in Savannah.

Phillip leaned forward slightly, smiling at a tall, slender, golden-skinned young man who was sawing a birch brought to the ground by an earlier storm.

"We're on our way to Savannah, Raoul," Phillip called out with warmth. "Make sure you exercise Othello for Miss Suzanne."

"I'll be sure to do that, Mist' Phillip," he promised shyly.

As Phillip had prophesied, they arrived at the wharf with no time to spare, and hastily followed the other passengers aboard the immaculately white double-stacked steamboat. Suzanne went to her stateroom with Patrice, was charmed by its luxurious appointments. Mère Angélique used to rebuke her for her pleasure in earthly comforts, Suzanne remembered with a touch of homesickness.

"Missy, yo' res'," Patrice ordered with mock sternness. "We is got a long trip aheada us." Her dark eyes sparkled. Suzanne suspected that Patrice had been no farther than New Orleans in her whole life.

"Patrice, I'm going up on deck to see what's happening. We've got to be sure the Captain knows where he's going," she teased.

They were going to Savannah, where Maman and Papa had lived. Suzanne felt herself suffused with well being. In four days they would be at their destination, and she would pursue the vow she had taken in the cathedral of Notre-Dame. She felt poignantly close to Maman and Papa. She closed her eyes for an instant, grasping at the shadowy memories that had been her constant companions during the years at the Convent.

Each day blended pleasantly into the next, but Suzanne was plagued by restlessness. Despite the charm of the voyage, she was impatient to be in Savannah, to be asking questions about Maman and Papa.

As Suzanne had suspected he would be, Phillip was a charming companion onboard ship. He was attentive, amusing, seemingly enjoying every moment of the voyage. They stopped briefly at Mobile, Tampa, then sailed around the Florida peninsula and northward. On their last night aboard ship, as they stood on deck watching the lights on the distant shore, Suzanne told Phillip the special import of this journey to her.

"I'll do anything I can to help you find your family," Phillip promised. "I never knew my mother," he said with a sense of loss. "No memories at all. I was a few months old when she died." He reached to cover her hand with his; she felt that confiding in him had created a special bond between them.

On the fifth morning Suzanne arose early to find Patrice already awake and packing. Suzanne dressed quickly, eager to go on deck and watch for her first view of Savannah. With a sense of adventure, she left her stateroom. The air was fresh and salty, pleasantly cool. Fresh excitement soared in her this morning. Maman and Papa had lived in Savannah. She had been born there. She would meet these cousins of Keith's, and she would ask them about her parents. They would surely help to find the aunts, uncles, or cousins who, hopefully, lived in their city.

"We won't be arriving at Savannah for a while."

Suzanne swung about to face Phillip.

"I know." She felt so close to him, yet he had not truly revealed himself to her. It was as though they had a secret pact to talk neither about Savage Oaks nor Keith and Jane. She had talked much about the days at the Convent, about Cecile, and he had told her about the hated years at military school and his year at Princeton.

"There's a seventeen-mile trip up the river to the city," he reminded. "Stand here and watch. We'll be turning in soon."

The Savannah River was muddy, its current strong. Suzanne was conscious of a slightly fetid odor.

"We're going to pass the northern point of Tybee Island in a few minutes," Phillip said, "then we'll go up the north channel of the river."

Suzanne watched avidly as the ship moved forward. The north channel was separated from the south channel by a series of small islands. After a while the two channels merged for a short distance before dividing again. Then they were following a very narrow, tortuous route, the currents strong.

"I hate to tell you how many ships collide here or are grounded," Phillip said wryly.

"Phillip, don't say that!" she protested, and laughed.

Suzanne was disappointed at her first view of

Savannah. This was the city of whose beauty Phillip had boasted so heartily? Phillip identified the most prominent building in view as the Exchange, which since 1812 had housed the city government offices. It was a square, barn-like structure with a cumbersome watchtower. On either side of the Exchange stretched the city's drab antiquated business houses.

As the ship moved closer to its destination, Suzanne saw the wharves that stretched the full length of the city. Houses and railroad depots fronted on the river. Ships were crowded two and three deep, testifying to the prosperity that had come to Savannah in the past decade.

Not until they had docked, disembarked, and taken a carriage that transported them some forty feet up the hill to the bluff did Suzanne see the splendor of Savannah.

"Oh, Phillip, how beautiful!" she breathed, leaning forward as the carriage clattered over the planks of Bay Street.

Here was the city that Phillip had extolled as more unusual and more romantic than any described in a novel. On the Bay — the major business street, Suzanne realized — were stores on one side and rows of trees with benches interspersed along the side of the river, which the stores faced. Beyond Bay Street were shaded green squares, broad streets lined with oaks, chinaberry trees, magnolias, and a variety of shrubs. Here was an air of a delightful rural village, when Savannah was, in truth, one of the larger cities of the South.

As they rode over the sandy streets, Phillip pointed out the beautiful Greek revival United States Customs House, the County Courthouse, the handsome Presbyterian Church, the Hall of the Georgia Historical Society. Private homes were a blend of old and new, dingy wooden tenements and handsome brick mansions. Had Maman and Papa lived in one of these fine houses they were passing?

"Cousin Eleanor's house is one of the showplaces of Savannah," Phillip said with respect. "It was built thirty-five years ago and designed by William Jay, the English architect. He was in Savannah at the time to supervise the building of the Richardson house, which now belongs to the Owens family. He was only twenty-one," Phillip said with unexpected strength, "but already people had great regard for his ability."

In another few minutes the carriage pulled up before a massive wrought-iron fence, behind which sat an imposing white-brick town house. Gravely Suzanne inspected the charming bowed portico — with its gracefully curving double staircase, the parapet roof.

"You won't see many Southern homes that look like that," Phillip said humorously. "It might be a corner of Regency London."

"It's magnificent." She had never visited London, Suzanne thought wistfully, though Cecile had talked much of her trips there with her mother.

A servant darted forward to open the gates so that the carriage might pull up before the portico. Suzanne felt a tightness in her throat as Phillip helped her down from the carriage. Here lived the Savages' cousins, who must surely remember her parents. Never had she felt so close to reaching out to Maman and Papa.

She walked beside Phillip to the portico, where a maid, hearing the carriage turn in, already waited to welcome them. Masses of camellias were in bloom about the grounds, lending dramatic color to the tall, stately mansion. The sound of light laughter and the chatter of many voices drifted through the windows. Probably wedding guests had already arrived to stay at the house, Suzanne surmised. Suddenly weddings were so prominent in her life, she thought with a touch of amusement. Cecile's, her own, and now this unknown cousin's in Savannah.

They walked into a wide marble floored entrance hall with a pair of elegant Corinthian columns, which led to a chandeliered stairway. The stairway divided to form graceful double stairs to the second floor.

"The bog oak for these stairs was brought from Ireland," Phillip whispered.

On the second floor they followed the maid to the light, airy family parlor, furnished with Duncan Phyfe, Allison and Sheraton pieces. The rugs were muted orientals. A tall, spare, white-haired woman with a hearing trumpet sat reading *Punch* on a cane settee. In an armchair at right angles to the sofa dozed a bewhiskered, corpulent man of impressive stature.

The maid crossed to touch Eleanor Rankin gently on the shoulder to indicate that guests had arrived. Instantly she discarded her magazine to welcome her guests. Dutifully Phillip kissed her and introduced Suzanne.

"Lyle, wake up," Mrs. Rankin exhorted her husband loudly, and immediately turned her scrutiny on Suzanne. "So you are Keith's bride. I'm surprised that Keith married so hastily. His father not dead a year yet." Her eyes focused speculatively on Suzanne's waistline, and Suzanne's smile lost its spontaneity.

"Keith was lonely and I was alone in the world except for my guardian," she said with contrived demureness. Cousin Eleanor would be disappointed to learn that she was not *enceinte*.

"Jane wrote very little about you," Eleanor said bluntly. "Except that you are a Duprée. The New Orleans Duprées?" she probed.

"No," Suzanne said softly, startled to discover there were Duprées in New Orleans. But if they were related, Uncle Gilbert would have told her. She took a deep breath. "My parents lived in Savannah. I've been hoping that you knew them."

Cousin Eleanor frowned, her hearing aid obviously ineffective.

"Lyle, what did she say?" Mrs. Rankin demanded in irritation, and loudly he repeated Suzanne's information.

"There are no Duprées in Savannah," Eleanor Rankin said with arrogance. "If there were, we would know them."

Suzanne felt the color drain from her face. She turned pleadingly to Phillip.

"We'll ask around town." His voice was too low to carry to their elderly cousin. "Suzanne, don't look so stricken."

"What's the matter with Keith?" Eleanor picked up querulously, "sending his new bride all the way to Savannah with his brother?"

"Keith's too busy with the grinding season to come, Cousin Eleanor," Phillip explained politely, though he knew that Suzanne was indignant at Eleanor's implication. "He couldn't possibly leave Savage Oaks."

At that moment, a cluster of cousins, along with the bride, converged on the parlor; and Suzanne was caught up in a flurry of introductions.

"Don't worry," Phillip whispered, noting her consternation at the flood of names that had been thrust upon her. "Just smile prettily. Nobody expects you to remember everybody's name."

Belle was a vivacious nineteen-year-old beauty enjoying every moment of her prenuptial celebrations.

"Grandma was just scared to death I'd be an old maid," she effervesced. "Mama stays most of the time up at the plantation, and I'm always here in town, so Grandma and I are specially close." She inspected Suzanne with lively curiosity. "I don't know why Cousin Thorne never built a town house in New Orleans." Because the money went to buy new equipment for the plantation, Suzanne surmised practically. Sugar-making was an expensive undertaking. "Don't you just die living all the time at Savage Oaks?"

"I've only been married three weeks," Suzanne said awkwardly. She wished earnestly that Keith were here beside her.

"I can't bear staying on the plantation," Belle pursued. "Not for more than two or three weeks. After that it's like being in exile." Suzanne frowned unconsciously. She had spent most of her life in exile. "I read every morsel of gossip in the newspapers and I hanker for the city pavements and the gaslights and the theater and whatever is newest in the city."

"I'm so tired of all these books against slavery," somebody was declaring loudly to Suzanne's right. "Like this new one by C. P. Persons. Do you know, he researched it right here in Savannah — and it's so unjust, so grossly false in spirit!"

Suzanne was relieved when she was finally ushered upstairs to her bedroom, where Patrice was industriously pressing the clothes she had unpacked. A mahogany bed was elaborately draped in pink and white silk, which was duplicated on the cane settee and in the window drapes and reflected in the Samarkand rug. An English Chippendale mahogany washstand stood against one wall beside a mahogany chest of drawers with elaborate brass pulls, over which hung a French Directoire mirror. A Chinese lacquered writing table held a pair of antique silver candlesticks.

"This heah is a fine house, Missy," Patrice said respectfully, "but nothin' can touch Savage Oaks." Pride glowed in her eyes.

"Do you miss it?" Suzanne asked with sudden comprehension.

"Ah reckon it'll be good to get home," Patrice conceded. "Ain't no place in de world like what we's got at home."

Suzanne went to a window and gazed out into the gardens. No Duprées in Savannah, Cousin Eleanor had said. How could that be? Uncle Gilbert said definitely that Maman and Papa had lived here. *They had owned a house here.* How she wished she could remember Maman and Papa more clearly! She could close her eyes and hear Maman's laughter, Papa's teasing voice as he tucked her into bed each night. Why must her memories be faceless?

Phillip promised to show her Savannah tomorrow. She would ask everywhere about Maman and Papa. There were over twenty thousand people in Savannah, according to the last census, one of the cousins had told her. How could Cousin Eleanor know every one of them? *She would find someone who remembered Maman and Papa.*

Dinner was served in the regal formal dining

room because, in addition to the family, a dozen guests already had arrived to stay at the house until after the wedding. Here the draperies and chair seats were of red and gold silk brocade. A French Empire chandelier hung from the lofty ceiling, crystal sconces adorned the walls. An antique wine cabinet sat between two windows, a sideboard against another wall. Suzanne was fascinated by the narrow, amber horizontal windows set in a niche high above each of the two doors, and by the rounded fireplace wall, like nothing she had ever encountered.

No doubt Cousin Eleanor had confided her curiosity about their new cousin's background to her guests. Suzanne was aware of their covert glances, masked by native Southern politeness.

Talk was lively as those at the table in the gas-lit dining room ate their way through the sumptuous meal. Normally Suzanne would have relished this animated conversation, but tonight she was crushed because these new cousins had never heard of the Duprées of Savannah. Cautiously she had made inquiries among them.

"There are four cardinal sins to up-country folks," Belle was saying brightly to Phillip and Suzanne. "Card-playing, dancing, theater-going and novel-reading. How would Savannahians survive without these? Of course, there are some up-country folks who make trips into Savannah to go to the theater or the Opera, but they know better than to talk about it when they get back home."

"It's a shame how badly the lectures are

attended," an elderly maiden-lady cousin said sorrowfully. "Just nobody shows up unless it's something sensational. Like Dion Boucicault when he talked here last year on 'Woman — Her Rights and Her Wrongs.' And of course, Thackeray when he was here the year before that."

"I think it's just terrible," Eleanor was saying loudly at the foot of the long table, "how we have to put up with all this dust in the city. And all that trash and litter on the streets. Garbage dumped regularly on the outskirts of the city. Some folks are just pigs," she wound up contemptuously.

"That comes along with prosperity," Lyle shouted so as to be heard by his wife. "Savannah's growing, splitting its sides. We can't get enough houses or stores to accommodate the growing population. Why, new houses are rented before the walls are up!"

"And the rents are up," the middle-aged gentleman on his right pointed out grimly. "Have you any idea what they're charging at the hotels and boarding houses? It's outrageous."

"You don't have to worry about that," Lyle pointed out expansively. "We've always got room for family."

Suzanne was relieved when it was time to retire to her room. Patrice was awed by the bathing apartment that had been set up on the lower floor. She spilled over with all the details she had learned while she helped Suzanne out of her dress.

"Missy, the water comes in all the way from the backyard. They's got a pump that pushes it!"

"It sounds very grand, Patrice." She tried to appear interested.

Patrice shrewdly sensed her depression, began to chatter with determined cheerfulness about earlier days at Tintagel. She had come to the plantation at the age of twelve when Joseph Ramsay moved his bride into the fine new house. She had no children. The Ramsay children were her children. Now Suzanne was her "baby," and she fussed over her, striving to bring a smile to her face.

"You go to sleep, Miss Suzanne," she ordered softly. "All this travelin' wore you out."

"I am tired, Patrice," she acknowledged affectionately. But she would not sleep; she was too impatient for tomorrow to arrive so that Phillip and she could go about Savannah asking questions.

Despite her conviction that she would twist and turn in bed till dawn, Suzanne fell asleep almost immediately. She awoke to a deliciously cool and sunny morning. Patrice had started a fire in the grate so that Suzanne might dress by its warmth.

"Ah go downstairs for your breakfas', Missy," Patrice said firmly, and Suzanne realized this was the routine for the ladies in the house.

While Patrice was gone, Suzanne dressed, hoping Phillip would not sleep late this morning. Outside a servant working in the garden was whistling a Mozart melody. She laughed aloud when he switched to Beethoven. She remembered now that Cousin Lyle said they frequently held musicales in the house.

When she had finished breakfast, with Patrice cajoling her into eating every morsel of her scrambled eggs and grits, she hurried downstairs. Phillip was in the downstairs drawing room she realized with relief. She heard him in conversation with their host.

"We're having perfect weather, Phillip," Cousin Lyle was saying complacently. "Would you believe that one winter — it was in March of 1837, on the day Van Buren was inaugurated — we had a terrible snowstorm. Can you imagine? In Savannah, Georgia!"

Phillip whisked her away from the house in the fashionable buggy that Cousin Eleanor put at their disposal. They went directly to the bustling business district below the bluff, where they left the buggy and began to walk. Long rows of brick buildings four and five stories high extended along the waterfront. Along the quay were cotton presses, rice mills, sheds to protect the goods in the process of loading or unloading. Phillip kept a solicitous hand at Suzanne's elbow; the sidewalks were obstructed with endless barrels and boxes. Workmen were busily unloading merchandise from drays, carrying on good-natured, raucous conversation. Clerks darted back and forth with bills of lading and marking pots in their hands.

Phillip pointed out the new gas lighting under the bluffs, which were so welcomed by the merchants and seamen. Suzanne tried to match Phillip's optimism as they walked endlessly, going from store to store inquiring about Mr. Duprée and his wife. Two hours of inquiries brought nothing but a shake of the head and polite regrets. Somberly Suzanne considered their next approach.

"Phillip, someone at dinner last night talked about a census in Savannah in 1840 and 1850," she said contemplatively. "The census records of 1840 must have a listing of Maman and Papa!" And of other Duprées. "How can we go through those records?" she asked expectantly.

Phillip pursed his lips and thought. "They ought to be at the Exchange Building. Let's go back to the buggy," he said briskly. "We'll check the census records."

After numerous inquiries, Suzanne and Phillip were directed to the proper office. A genial clerk allowed them to search the census records for 1840. There were no Duprées. Suzanne's eyes filled with tears of frustration.

"Suzanne, I'm famished," Phillip said with false cheerfulness. His eyes betrayed his compassion for Suzanne's disappointment. "Let's go find a tavern and have something to eat. Unless," he jibed mischievously, "you're too much the fine young lady to go with me to a public tavern."

"I'll go," she shot back at the challenge.

Phillip took her to a tavern where they were served an astonishingly good seafood meal in unprepossessing surroundings. He strived to coax her into a less depressed mood, but Suzanne found it difficult to respond.

"Suzanne, in what year were you born?" he asked, suddenly serious.

"In 1838." She gazed questioningly at him.

"You said you were at the Convent since you were three. The year your parents died. Since 1841," he pinpointed. "Maybe it was late in 1840. They were not included in the census records because they had died that year. Let's go back and try the 1830 census."

"Phillip, do you suppose that's what happened?" Her face glowed with hope.

"Drink your tea and we'll go back to the Exchange Building," he said exuberantly.

Again they confronted the clerk in the office where the census records were filed. Obligingly he brought them the 1830 records. Suzanne was trembling as Phillip turned the pages. Here! They must be here! Phillip turned to the *D*'s and ran a finger down the list of names. But no Duprée was listed in the Savannah census. Not in 1840. And not in 1830.

"Phillip, why did Uncle Gilbert tell me Maman and Papa lived in Savannah?" Suzanne demanded in a tortured whisper. "Why did he lie to me?"

"Ask him," Phillip said, his eyes glinting with rage. "When we get back to New Orleans, you go to Mr. Gilbert Mauriac and you ask him!"

Nine

After her deep disappointment, Suzanne was impatient for the festivities to be over and to be on board ship for the return trip to New Orleans. The knowledge that Gilbert Mauriac had not been honest with her endlessly broke into her thoughts. Why had he lied? What was he hiding?

It was a relief when at last they saw Belle married and they sat down to the sumptuous wedding banquet. The next morning, while the other guests still slept off the effects of the festivities, Phillip and she left Savannah with Patrice, despite Cousin Eleanor's exhortations that they must remain at least another week.

The days of their return trip dragged interminably. Phillip became increasingly moody as they grew closer to Savage Oaks, though he loved it with a passion that matched Keith's and Jane's. On their last morning aboard, Suzanne left the dining room to go alone on deck. Phillip, again, had not appeared at breakfast.

A faint drizzle greeted her. The deck was deserted. But Suzanne welcomed the oddly refreshing wet chill of the morning. She stood at the railing, unconscious of the passage of time. Her eyes focused on the horizon, willing New Orleans to appear before her.

"Suzanne, what are you doing out here in the rain?"

She spun about to face Phillip. He smiled at her with mock reproach. His mood was lighter this morning.

"I'm watching for first sight of New Orleans," she confessed.

"Maybe you ought to forget about what happened in Savannah." All at once he was serious. But in Savannah he had urged her to confront Uncle Gilbert. "Mr. Mauriac will be terribly upset if you accuse him of lying. He prides himself on his integrity."

"Phillip, I'm not going in like a battering ram," she protested. "I'm going to ask him, politely, for an explanation." But already her heart pounded as she visualized this confrontation.

"Wait a few days," Phillip coaxed.

"No." She lifted her head defiantly. "I've waited too long already."

"It might be better if you dropped the whole thing," Phillip pursued. "You're married. Your name is Savage now."

"Phillip, I *must* know about Maman and Papa. It's torturing me not knowing about them." Her voice dropped to a pained whisper. "I remember so little. Not even their faces.

"My mother died when I was a few months old," Phillip remembered, his eyes rebellious with recall. "My father hardly knew I existed. Keith was the one he was always so proud of. Keith did so well in military school. Keith graduated from Princeton with honors. Keith studied law with Judge Campbell. Everything was always Keith!" A vein was distended in his forehead as he relived every imagined slight in a swift, painful mental kaleidoscope.

"Phillip, you must not believe that," Suzanne urged. "I'm sure it wasn't true."

"Are you happy with Keith?" Phillip asked unexpectedly.

"I — I see so little of him," she evaded, startled by the question. "You know how busy he is."

"You're in love with him." Phillip's voice was gentle.

"Yes," she acknowledged. Color touched her cheekbones. "He's my husband." Did Phillip and Jane guess that Keith never availed himself of his husbandly privileges?

"Talk to Keith about this business with Mauriac," Phillip persuaded.

"No," Suzanne refused stubbornly. "I have to talk to Uncle Gilbert."

"Then at least come down to the dining room for breakfast," he ordered brusquely. "It's ridiculous to stand out here in the rain."

"I've had breakfast."

"Then have more coffee with me," he said, taking her arm, and she realized he did not wish to leave her alone in this gray, dismal drizzle.

Only a few minutes behind schedule the boat docked at New Orleans, and Suzanne and Phillip pushed their way through the colorful hordes to where Lewis waited with the carriage.

"We'll go straight home," Phillip said wanly as he helped Suzanne into the carriage. "It looks as though it's going to storm."

"No," Suzanne contradicted. "The rain has stopped. Tell Lewis to take us to Uncle Gilbert's office."

Suzanne sat tensely as the carriage inched slowly ahead, caught in the morning rush of drays and carriages. Drivers shouted stridently at the tie-ups that were inevitable. When the Savage carriage arrived at Gilbert's office, Suzanne accepted Phillip's hand in alighting, then darted ahead of him into the building that housed Gilbert's office.

"I'm sorry," the elderly clerk who greeted her said apologetically. "Mr. Mauriac had to go to Algiers on business this morning."

"Thank you." Suzanne forced a smile. "I'll see him another time." But as Phillip helped her back into the carriage, she told him to instruct Lewis to take them to the Mauriac house. "And Phillip, please, let me go in alone."

Mme. Mauriac greeted her with rich affection. She knew that Suzanne had been in Savannah. Last week she had sent a man to Savage Oaks to invite Keith and her for dinner and to go with Gilbert and her to the theater.

"Did you enjoy your trip, Suzanne?" she asked with the familiar charm, yet Suzanne sensed that she was uneasy. "What a pity that the wedding came at a time when Keith could not go with you." She smiled effusively as she rang the bell to summon Amelia.

"I was disappointed," Suzanne said softly. "I thought in Savannah I would surely find people who had known Maman and Papa." She took a deep breath. "Keith's cousins have never heard of any Duprées in Savannah."

"Suzanne, the families of planters know only other planters' families. Didn't Gilbert tell you? Your father was an attorney, like Gilbert. They went to college together, at Princeton." Uncle Gilbert had never confided even that to her. "Professional people move in different social circles. And Savannah is a city," she reminded with tender reproof. "How could Keith's cousins be expected to know everybody?" She turned to Amelia, who came into the room with a welcoming smile for Suzanne. "Amelia, please bring us pralines and tea."

Suzanne recoiled inwardly from saying what she knew would distress Mme. Mauriac, yet she knew she must.

"Mme. Mauriac, I went to the Exchange Building and asked a clerk to check the census records. There were no Duprées in Savannah in 1840." Mme. Mauriac stared at her in consternation. "There were no Duprées in 1830." Suzanne waited, faintly breathless, her eyes

158

clinging to Mme. Mauriac's face. The fine lines seemed to deepen into those of the very aged. She was not saying that Uncle Gilbert lied to her, she told herself guiltily; she was asking for the truth about Maman and Papa.

"Suzanne, I don't understand this." Mme. Mauriac was fumbling, groping for words, her dark eyes troubled. "Of course they were from Savannah. There must be some mistake." Then all at once she leaned back with a relieved air of comprehension. "Oh, how stupid of Gilbert! And of me. They were not actually residents of Savannah. They lived in one of those little hamlets beyond the city itself. Gilbert always referred to their home as Savannah because they were so near." Now she leaned forward earnestly. "Suzanne, Gilbert must have told you that both your father and mother were alone in the world. Perhaps that was what drew them together."

"Perhaps." Suzanne managed a shaky smile, masking her sense of defeat. She believed not one word of what Mme. Mauriac had said. *Why all these lies about Maman and Papa?*

"Are you finding it lonely at Savage Oaks?" Mme. Mauriac asked solicitously.

"I haven't been there long enough to find out," Suzanne hedged. The brief period she had spent at Tintagel she had been constantly with Keith. Oh yes, she told herself, she had been lonely at Savage Oaks. Lonely and unhappy.

"You're extremely fortunate that the plantation is so accessible to New Orleans. Most are not, you know. That's why there's so much socializing. But Jane has always avoided the partying and the visiting. You'll change that, Suzanne," she said vigorously. "And you'll come into New Orleans often. You won't be lonely," she promised with a cajoling smile.

"I think Jane disapproves of Keith's having married me," Suzanne confided impulsively. "I suspect she meant for him to marry into an important plantation family."

"These plantation families!" Mme. Mauriac said with scorn. "They have a way of considering themselves the South. They never truly accept the fact that they are a privileged but very small part of Southern life. And Jane has little right to concern herself about family background," she pursued strongly. "She's a Savage by adoption." She paused at the sound of astonishment that escaped Suzanne.

"I didn't know!"

"No one ever talks about it," Mme. Mauriac said drily. "Jane considers herself as much a Savage as Keith or Phillip. They shared the same mother," she acknowledged conscientiously. "She's their half-sister. Jane's mother lived on the plantation below Savage Oaks. Their mother was orphaned at sixteen and entered into a disastrous marriage only a few months after her parents died. When Jane was a year old, her father discovered that he might have married into a wealthy family but the property was so tied up legally he couldn't turn any of the assets into cash. He walked out. A year later word was brought to Jane's mother of his death in a fight at a gambling table. Two years later she married Thorne Savage. He always considered Jane his own child. He was devoted to her."

Amelia arrived with the pralines and tea. Suzanne listened with a polite show of interest to Mme. Mauriac's recital about the performance she had recently attended at the St. Charles Theatre, struggling to conceal her restlessness. Phillip must be annoyed that she was keeping him waiting so long.

Phillip's eyes were seriously questioning when she rejoined him in the carriage.

"Mme. Mauriac and Uncle Gilbert won't ever tell me the truth," she said frustratedly. "Why, Phillip? *Why?*"

"Maybe it's better not to know," he suggested.

"I will know!" Suzanne flashed back at him. "Someday I'll know." She frowned, reliving the unsatisfying encounter with Mme. Mauriac. "Phillip — " She hesitated, feeling discomfort in deception. "I won't say anything to Keith or Jane about our going to the census office in Savannah. I won't mention my stopping to visit with Mme. Mauriac this morning."

"Why should you?" he shrugged. "No one will notice that we're arriving late from New Orleans. If they are aware, they'll assume the boat was late in docking. It usually is."

At Savage Oaks Suzanne went directly to her room. Jane was closeted in the sewing room, unaware of their arrival. Keith was at the sugar house, she surmised. Perhaps he might put in an appearance at dinner if he remembered Phillip and she were coming home today.

When she went down to the midday meal, Suzanne realized how eager she was to see Keith, yet pride warned her that she must not allow him to know how desperately she had missed him. From Jane's air of surprise at finding Phillip and her at the table, Suzanne realized she had not remembered they were returning today. She had not truly expected Keith to leave the sugar house at midday.

Jane questioned them perfunctorily about the activities in Savannah. Her eyes rested quizzically on Suzanne.

"Did Cousin Eleanor know your family when they lived in Savannah?"

"No," Suzanne acknowledged. "But they're a plantation family. Papa was an attorney." Jane did not believe that either, she guessed unhappily.

Suzanne returned to her room to sit before the fire that Patrice lighted against the early December chill. She knew that shortly Jane would be off on her daily afternoon drive. Phillip had stalked from the house as soon as they left the table. As deeply as he professed to love Savage Oaks, he seemed to be obsessed with restlessness when he was here.

She leaned back in her chair, closed her eyes. She had gone to Savannah with such confidence that she would find answers to the questions that tormented her. She had come home with nothing except the certainty that Uncle Gilbert was not being honest with her. Where did she go from here?

She searched her mind for a new approach. Perhaps Papa's college could put her in contact with instructors, elderly now, who might remember Papa. She would write to the college in Princeton, she decided with a surge of fresh enthusiasm. While she did not know the exact years that Papa had attended Princeton — and she would not ask Uncle Gilbert — she would explain that he attended at the same time as Uncle Gilbert.

She would write the letter now. This minute. Edward would be going into New Orleans tomorrow for the mail. She would ask him to mail the letter for her. Nobody else at Savage Oaks need know.

She was trembling when she finished writing the brief letter to the college. *Please, let somebody remember Papa.* How long would it take for the letter to reach Princeton? A week?

She started at the knock on the door. Had Keith returned and learned she was home? Discarding her earlier determination to be polite but distant to Keith. she darted to the door, pulled it wide with a welcoming smile. George stood there, an odd surprise in his eyes.

"Miss Jane say you please to come down to the drawin' room. We has company."

"Oh." Her smile was strained. No wonder George seemed surprised. Guests were rare. "Thank you. George. I'll be right down."

Swiftly Suzanne ran a brush over her hair, inspected herself anxiously in the mirror. She had met none of the Savages' friends or neighbors. Phillip had on occasion made sardonic remarks about their lack of socializing at Savage Oaks. She steeled herself for this prospective encounter.

Suzanne heard voices in the drawing room. Jane was making monosyllabic responses.

"When we heard that Keith had married, we simply had to come calling on his bride," a slightly shrill feminine voice gushed.

"Did Keith meet his wife up there in Washington City?" a younger voice inquired.

"No, Suzanne has been in a convent in France for many years." Jane sounded tense and formal. She loathed this intrusion. "She came to live at Tintagel recently." Jane did not say how recently, Suzanne thought as she walked slowly down the stairs, fighting her reluctance to meet their visitors. "That's how Keith met her."

"It must have been a whirlwind courtship," another feminine voice said coyly.

"It was," Jane said succinctly.

"I'm sorry to have taken so long," Suzanne apologized with contrived graciousness as she walked into the drawing room. Their visitors were a middle-aged woman forty pounds heavier than she should have been and two young ladies of startling plainness, all three dressed in expensive but overly ornate frocks. Had their mother hoped that Keith might marry one of her daughters?

Jane introduced her to their guests. They lived at a plantation forty minutes from Savage Oaks, Jane explained with strained politeness. The two young ladies stared, bright-eyed with curiosity, as their mother began a cross-examination.

"Jane was telling us you were living at Tintagel when you met Keith. Are you related to the Ramsays?" Mrs. Andrews asked.

"No, I'm not."

"But your family came from these parts?" Mrs. Andrews probed.

"No, my family is not from Louisiana." Suzanne fought to conceal her irritation. "We're from Savannah." Nobody in this room could prove to the contrary. "But I've lived in France since I was three."

"Clara and Rose speak beautiful French," Mrs. Andrews said with cloying pride. "And they play the piano exquisitely. Do you play, Suzanne?"

"Not well." She loathed this insipid conversation. "But Keith plays magnificently." Unexpectedly, Jane smiled.

"Do you like to read? Clara and Rose have their noses constantly in a book. I keep telling them they're going to ruin their eyes."

"I adore Sir Walter Scott," Rose said dreamily. "I could sit and read his novels all day long."

"Southern ladies all seem to adore Scott," Jane

said, faintly acerbic. "No doubt that's where they acquire their romantic views of life."

"What do you like to read, Jane?" Clara asked with deceptive sweetness.

"This year I'm reading all the Henrys." Their visitors gazed blankly at Jane. "Shakespeare's Henrys."

Edward arrived with a tea cart. Jane was compelling herself to be gracious, but Suzanne saw her furtive glances at the gilt clock on the mantel as Mrs. Andrews prattled with hollow vivacity about her husband's plans to run for alderman in the spring elections.

"Do you know," she said indignantly, "that there's talk again about consolidating the school system in the city? Mr. Andrews says this could lead to removing Bible reading from the schools!"

Earlier than Suzanne had dared hope, their visitors rose to leave. Suzanne suspected they were eager to get away from Savage Oaks so they could dissect Keith's bride. She had seen the covert, sly exchanges between mother and daughters.

"We'll be having a Christmas party," Mrs. Andrews said sweetly, though Clara was tugging at her arm. "It's informal. I won't bother sending invitations. You-all must come."

"Thank you." Suzanne murmured, hoping they had not noticed Jane's heavy sigh of impatience.

"What about Phillip?" Rose asked avidly. "We

heard he didn't go back to college this fall."

"We'll tell him about the Christmas party," Suzanne promised, ignoring the question. "Thank you for coming to call."

Jane was livid at their prying into Phillip's activities. She stood stiff and unsmiling while Suzanne walked with the other three to the gallery. When Suzanne came back into the foyer, she saw Jane already striding towards the rear of the house. She was hurrying by way of the back door to the stable, rather than waiting to summon the chaise to the front of the house.

Suzanne returned to the drawing. room. She reached for the most recent issue of *Putnam's Monthly Magazine*, intent on sitting on the side gallery where sunshine poured with cozy warmth. As she walked out onto the gallery, Clara's voice — simultaneously contemptuous and triumphant and clearly audible in the afternoon stillness — drifted to her.

"Mama, it's just like we figured. He married her for her money. Everybody knew the Savages were just one step away from foreclosure. Papa said Keith paid off his loan at the bank just two days after the wedding! It had to be a marriage settlement. Where else would he have gotten all that money?"

Ten

Suzanne stood immobile, cold as ice, trying to assimilate what she had heard. *Keith had married her to save Savage Oaks.* Now she understood his impetuous courtship, the hasty wedding. The bank was demanding payment on a loan. He knew the bank could take over Savage Oaks. Her marriage, like Cecile's, was an arranged one. To Uncle Gilbert an arranged marriage was normal; it was in the French manner.

Did everyone know this except her? Phillip? Jane? Obviously their neighbors suspected this. But on her side it was not arranged, she thought with fresh young bitterness. Foolishly, she was in love with her husband.

Could Keith ever come to love her? No, he must hate her! Only his love for Savage Oaks, his sense of responsibility towards Jane and Phillip, had pushed him into this charade. She closed her eyes, fighting back tears. Remembering the anguish of her wedding night. Now she understood Keith's sullen anger.

Who had decided that Keith must play the ardent suitor? It could hardly have been Keith's idea. Uncle Gilbert, solicitous for her sensibilities, must have ordered Keith to play this game with her. The naive, Covent-bred young lady would never suspect the practical negotiations. It was enough, Uncle Gilbert thought, that she loved Keith. Uncle Gilbert was a romantic.

She lifted her head defiantly. She was Keith's wife. She would live at Savage Oaks and nobody — except Keith and herself — would know that theirs was a play marriage. She didn't *want* Keith to come to her. Not unless he came to her with love.

Restless, driven by a need for action, she hurried upstairs to change into her riding dress. She would go to the stables and ask that Othello be saddled. She was glad Othello had been brought from Tintagel to Savage Oaks.

She rode through the beaten horse trail towards Tintagel, reliving her first encounter with Keith, remembering every instant of those ecstatic two weeks of his courtship. Angrily she rode towards Tintagel, her plantation, that now belonged to her husband under the law.

Her first instinct was to stop at the house to visit with Mrs. Cantrell, but curiosity propelled her away from the house and towards the quarters. She would see how their slaves lived here at Tintagel. Keith talked with pride about the good living conditions of the slaves at Savage Oaks, but she had never ventured down to the quarters. What did it matter how they lived when their bodies and their souls were in bondage to the Master? The whole institution of slavery was a blot on the nation.

Seeing smoke rise from a chimney, she rode curiously in that direction. Emerging from the woods, she saw a modest cottage that sat, like a gate house, about a hundred yards above two rows of small cabins. As she approached the cottage, she could see children cavorting in the wide swathe of dirt between the rows of cabins. Chickens wandered among them, and a goat nibbled at a patch of grass. These were the children of the field hands. The house servants looked down upon the field hands with good-natured contempt, Suzanne remembered, but who among them would not give up their way of life to be free?

She started at the sound of an hysterical outcry. Alarmed, she drew Othello to a halt before the cottage, dismounted, and hurried to the door. Someone within the cottage was sobbing in terror.

"You stop that, you hear?" a man's voice yelled. "You do like I say or I'm beatin' the daylights outta you! What you got is just the beginnin'!"

Furious, Suzanne pulled open the door and stormed inside the cottage. Nobody was beating a slave at Tintagel! She dashed across the drab, sparsely furnished sitting room to the open door of the bedroom. A small, slight black girl, no more than twelve or thirteen, cowered on the bed, her dark eyes terrified. The short dress she wore had been ripped to the waist. Already a welt was rising on one budding breast. She sobbed convulsively as the man hovered over her, his large, squat hands pushing the torn dress above her thighs.

"Get away from her!" Suzanne ordered strongly, and the burly sun-bronzed man spun about in astonishment. "How dare you behave like that on this plantation!"

"Who in blazes are you?" He stared belligerently at her.

"Suzanne Savage. I own Tintagel." The girl on the bed, suddenly conscious of rescue, scrambled to her feet, her eyes moving from Suzanne to the overseer.

"You don't belong here," he taunted. His eyes roamed arrogantly about Suzanne. The girl ran. "You can't tell me what to do. Go back to the big house with Mrs. Cantrell!"

"No overseer at Tintagel lifts a whip to any slave on this plantation," Suzanne insisted, surprised at her own strength, as he moved towards her, his breath soured by whiskey. "I'll report this to my husband."

"You don't come from these parts," he guessed, gazing down at her speculatively. "Not the way you talk. Spunky, too." Unexpectedly he reached and pulled her roughly to him.

"Take your hands off me!" Her eyes flashed with rage. "Let me go!"

She struggled in his embrace. His hands were rough on her, his body thrusting hard against hers.

"Go on, fight!" He chuckled drunkenly. "I like a woman with spirit!"

Suzanne kicked him in the shins with all her strength. He howled, put a hand at her breast and ripped her riding dress to the waist.

"Let me go!" she ordered with mounting alarm. "Let me go!"

"Take your hands off Mrs. Savage!" Dizzy with revulsion, Suzanne heard Mrs. Cantrell's voice, but the overseer ignored her. He lifted Suzanne from her feet, despite her desperate flailing efforts to free herself, and threw her upon the bed.

"I told you to let her go!" Mrs. Cantrell shouted.

Without releasing Suzanne, the overseer turned his face towards the housekeeper with a menacing scowl.

"Get outta here, old woman!"

A shot sounded in the room. The overseer grunted with pain, clutched at his left leg, then sank to the floor. Mrs. Cantrell stood, white but determined, with the revolver still outstretched.

"You won't die from a shot in the leg," she said caustically. "I'll send Mama Cassie to take care of it. But you be off this property before dark. Because if you're not, Mr. Keith's going to kill you for this."

Mrs. Cantrell focused solicitously on Suzanne as she rose shakily from the bed, clutching the torn bodice of her dress with one hand.

"Are you all right?"

"Yes," Suzanne reassured Mrs. Cantrell,

though her voice was unsteady and her eyes blazed with indignation.

"We'll go to the house and some tea." Mrs. Cantrell seemed embarrassed by the strength of her emotions. "I'll have someone come for Othello." She turned to the prone overseer, who was glaring at them as he grasped his wounded leg. "You remember what I said. You be off this property before dark."

Suzanne and Mrs. Cantrell left the cottage. The children in the clearing between the cabins played with noisy good humor. If they had heard the shot, Suzanne surmised, they thought the overseer had been after small game.

"He was attacking a young girl," Suzanne explained as Mrs. Cantrell and she walked towards the house. "I heard her scream and ran into the cottage." Suzanne shuddered. "He had taken a whip to her. I saw the welts."

"I never trusted that man," Mrs. Cantrell said with distaste. "But it's so hard to find a good overseer, and Mr. Mauriac was pleased with the way he was bringing in the crops."

"Thank you for coming to my rescue, Mrs. Cantrell," Suzanne said fervently. "I was terrified."

"We've never had any trouble at Tintagel, but I make a habit of having my revolver with me when I go to the quarters. My oldest sister was killed in the insurrection at Southampton County, Virginia, thirty-three years ago. You don't forget something like that." She gazed grimly into space for a moment, then turned again to Suzanne. "I'll sew your dress for you before you return to Savage Oaks. Shall I send a note to Mr. Keith about our being without an overseer, or will you tell him?"

"I'll tell him," Suzanne promised. She still trembled from the encounter.

"I'll arrange for the head count to be made tonight," Mrs. Cantrell said somberly, "but tomorrow there must be a man to take charge."

Suzanne sat on the sofa in the parlor and sipped fragrant jasmine tea while Mrs. Cantrell sewed the bodice of her riding dress with a series of minute stitches. Mrs. Cantrell no longer felt hostile to her because Keith had made it clear that they would not close up the house at Tintagel.

Rejecting the housekeeper's offer of a carriage, Suzanne left the house to mount Othello and head back to Savage Oaks. Keith must be told immediately about the lack of an overseer at Tintagel. She would face him calmly. He would not suspect how cruelly she had been hurt by Clara Andrews' revelation. She lifted her head proudly. He would never know.

She cut off along to the sugar house. She saw the plume of smoke that arose from the chimneys. Drawing near she heard the whir of the machinery that would not stop until close to Christmas. Her breath quickened. In a few moments she would see Keith.

She dismounted, tied Othello's reins about a slender tree, and approached the great door of the sugar house. She knocked, then realized this was ineffectual in the face of the noise within. She opened the door, startled by the wave of sweetened steam that greeted her, the intense heat of the sugar house. She saw the mill, three iron rollers placed at considerable height from the floor, through which the cane was being pressed. Her eyes skimmed past the mill to the five deep cast-iron kettles, arranged in solid masonry so that they were in a line, and heated by a furnace whose mouth was outside the building.

Children as well as men and women worked at a variety of tasks with an air of high spirits that she had not expected. Hogsheads of sugar and barrels of molasses sat in neat rows at the far end of the building. She was aware of the pungent aroma of coffee boiling.

"Suzanne!" Keith's astounded voice spun her about to face him. "I'm sorry," he said apologetically. "I had forgot that you were to return this morning."

"That's all right, Keith. I know how busy you are." She compelled herself to smile while Clara's voice echoed in her brain.

"Mama, it's just like we figured. He married her for her money."

"How was your trip?" he asked self-consciously.

"Lovely." She paused, faintly breathless now. "I — something has happened at Tintagel. I have to talk to you about it."

"Reagan, I'll be back in a few minutes," he

called tersely over the noise and piloted her towards the door. "We'll talk outside." When they were outside the sugar house, he inspected her worriedly. "What's the trouble?"

Haltingly she told him that the other plantation was without an overseer and explained why. She saw the rage that welled in him as she told him what had happened in the overseer's cottage.

"Keith, I had to go into the cottage when I heard her cry out that way. I told him you would not allow that at Tintagel." He was gazing at her oddly. Was he angry with her? Subconsciously one hand moved to the bodice of her dress. She saw the shock in his eyes as he became aware of the tear in her bodice, which Mrs. Cantrell had so carefully sewn.

"Suzanne, did he do that?" Keith demanded.

"Yes," she whispered, dropping her gaze.

"I ought to kill the bastard!" His voice shook with anger. "Excuse me, Suzanne," he apologized, "but I can't believe this could happen at Tintagel."

"The man was drunk. Mrs. Cantrell said she never trusted him, but he was a good overseer."

"I'll go right over," Keith promised grimly.

"No," Suzanne objected with alarm, and she saw a glow of startled comprehension in his eyes; he realized she was afraid for him. "Mrs. Cantrell said she would arrange for the head count tonight," Suzanne said unsteadily. "The driver can handle the crews today. Tomorrow morning will be soon enough."

"I'll ride back with you to the house," he said tentatively.

"I'm all right, Keith." Was Keith upset because he cared for her? Something new and infinitely precious seemed to generate between them. *Was she imagining this?* "Will you be home for dinner?"

"Of course," he promised.

Keith returned to the sugar house, shaken by Suzanne's experience at Tintagel. He felt a strange guilt that this had happened. He would never have expected a young girl with her tender upbringing to go fearlessly into that cottage in defense of a slave. Suzanne had a way of surprising him.

In the sugar house he summoned Moses to him, briefed him on the problem at Tintagel without saying why the overseer was departing so precipitately. His father had expressed his respect for Moses' capabilities. He was as competent as any white overseer. Moses would be able to handle the situation at Tintagel until Keith could go into New Orleans and hire a new man. In four or five days the grinding season would be over. Christmas, he realized with a start, was only eight days away.

"You'll go over tonight and lend Mrs. Cantrell a hand with the head count," he said briskly. Mrs. Cantrell knew Moses. From time to time he had been sent to Tintagel to repair furniture. If Moses were a white man, Keith thought uncomfortably, he would be able to make a fine living for himself as a furniture maker.

Keith tried to concentrate on activities at the sugar house, but his mind kept returning at regular intervals to his brief encounter with Suzanne. He was astonished that she had not hesitated to rush into the cottage to stop a flogging. He felt a towering rage at the vision of the overseer laying hands on her, and at the same time he was conscious of arousal.

He arrived at the dinner table just as the others were sitting down and quickly realized that Suzanne had said nothing to either Phillip or Jane about what had happened in the quarters at Tintagel. When he told them, both were visibly upset.

"Suzanne, you said not a word about it!" Jane was pale.

"It's over," Suzanne said quietly. She had not expected Jane to be distressed. "Thanks to Mrs. Cantrell."

"But suppose she had not happened to be walking in the quarters?" Jane shivered.

"Next time you want to go over to Tintagel," Phillip said firmly, "I'll go with you."

"Nothing's going to happen again," Suzanne said with determined lightness. Everybody was amazed that she had not taken to her bed in shock. "Mrs. Cantrell said she never trusted the man."

"I've sent Moses over. He can handle the situation until Christmas." Keith frowned. That damned overseer had ripped Suzanne's dress. If Mrs. Cantrell had not shot him, he would have raped Suzanne. Again he was conscious of arousal, and felt guilt that he could feel this way. "I'll have to put in the order for the Christmas presents in a day or two." He smiled at Suzanne's gaze of inquiry. "I'm going around with a notebook these days, asking what everybody wants," he explained. "Then I have the order filled in New Orleans. They're modest gifts," he conceded. "Clarissa wants a new head handkerchief. George asked for a pipe and Edward for a pair of shoes for his oldest boy."

"Raoul would like a book of poetry," Phillip volunteered with an air of defiance.

Jane squinted in annoyance.

"Phillip, it's time you grew out of this nonsense about Raoul. You're not helping by giving him pretensions of being white."

"His father was white!" Phillip shot back, and turned to Suzanne with a bitter smile. "Papa bought Raoul when he was eight because his resemblance to his father was an embarrassment to the family. The plantation ladies were talking. You might say Raoul and I have grown up together. I taught him to read and do figures. Surreptitiously, of course," he said with a mocking bow to Jane. "And he taught me what it means to be neither black nor white."

"Phillip, enough of this!" Jane's voice was strident.

"Oh, Elaine tells me she wants a mourning

veil," Keith said, firmly diverting the conversation from Raoul.

"But she's being married at Christmas." Jane stared at him with astonishment.

"I know." Keith smiled whimsically. "But Elaine's decided she never mourned properly for Elijah. That was her first husband, who died a year ago," he explained to Suzanne. "So before the wedding she wants to mourn for a few days."

"If her bridegroom were more choosy, he could marry one of Elaine's daughters," Phillip suggested amusedly. "We'll have to go to the wedding, Suzanne. We're expected to attend all the quarter weddings."

"Keith, could I do the Christmas shopping this year?" Suzanne asked. "I'd like so much to do it," she added persuasively.

"If you like," he acquiesced. "You'll probably want some money for yourself," he said self-consciously. "Mr. Mauriac has arranged for your dividend check from your stocks to come directly to you now. It arrived while you were in Savannah. I'll give it to you after dinner."

"Thank you." Her eyes sparkled. He had given her money before she left for Savannah, but this was different because it was her own, Keith sensed.

Sometimes he suspected she was not entirely happy here at Savage Oaks. She had been disappointed in their wedding night. His fault. But damn it, they were in the midst of the grinding season. He was too tired to play romantic games.

While the others lingered over dessert and coffee, Keith excused himself to return to the sugar house. Tonight Suzanne disturbed him. It was guilt, he told himself. He hated having deceived Suzanne with that spurious courtship. She had been so charming, so appealing, so believing. If it had been simply an admittedly arranged marriage, he would not feel this way. He loathed deception.

Halfway to the sugar house he suddenly changed direction and went to the stable. He would ride over to the cottage. Manon would be pleased to see him. She was sulking because he allowed days to pass without going to her. He could find time to go to Manon, an inner voice taunted, but not to go to his wife.

Smoke spiraled from the chimney of the cottage. Manon kept a fire going incessantly. The drapes were discreetly drawn in the bedroom, where the faint glow of a lamp showed through despite the heavy brocade of the drapes. Keith could hear Manon singing as he reached the door. He recognized the aria from the new opera by Verdi. *La Traviata.*

He walked into the small, darkened living room. Manon had not heard him come into the cottage. He crossed to the bedroom door, impatient to be lying between those silken sheets with Manon. Manon would insist on playing her romantic game. Tonight he wished she would dispense with this.

He knocked lightly. The quadroon's face wore

a dazzling smile as she pulled the door wide for him. The bedroom was overly warm, heavy with the scent of the perfume she favored.

"Lily Mae, go," Manon said imperiously without moving her eyes from Keith's face. Swiftly, with a wise young grin, Lily Mae darted from the room and out of the cottage. Tonight she would sleep in the quarters. "Keith, I've missed you," Manon said reproachfully. She always wore those filmy dressing gowns that set a man's teeth on edge, Keith thought.

"What were you doing?" Keith reached for her.

"I was making my hair pomade," she said airily. "Come into the bedroom and watch me finish it."

Reluctantly he released her. She was punishing him for staying away so many days.

"What the devil goes into it?" he asked curiously, settling himself at the edge of the bed while she walked to the marble-topped commode on which sat a deep bowl filled with a white substance.

"Beef marrow and castor oil. First the marrow has to be rendered, then the oil added. I beat and beat it," she said with satisfaction, reaching for a small bottle. "Now I add the essence of bergamot and I beat it again." Industriously she performed this small task while Keith sat with tense thighs.

"Enough of that," Keith said tersely, rising from the bed and going to her. "You'll worry about your hair pomade later."

"Keith," she murmured while he brought her

tall, slim body against his own, "do you know I heard about a woman who went to Paris and had her face enameled. She was warned not to smile or laugh, but one day she forgot and laughed and the enamel cracked. She went dashing back to Paris to have it repaired!"

"Oh, shut up," he said mockingly and brought his mouth to hers.

"You've been wicked," she chided after a few moments. "I haven't seen you for six days."

"I'm here now." His breathing was labored. He wanted to throw her across the bed this instant.

"Naughty." She lowered her opened mouth to nip at one shoulder while her thighs pressed his.

"Take off that thing." Lord, these quadroons knew how to arouse a man!

The filmy dressing gown and nightdress lay on the floor in a pool of lamplight. She posed before him, knowing what she was doing to him. As his hands reached for her, she dropped to her knees before him, and he closed his eyes to savor the passion that wracked him. Manon smiled with a secretive satisfaction when, at last, he drew her to her feet and prodded her across the bed.

When they had made love, Manon pushed him against the mound of silk pillows and rose from the bed, a glint of triumph in her eyes because he had been so pleased with her.

"I'll bring champagne, and then I'll make supper for you." She enjoyed preparing small, exotic suppers for him.

"No supper, Manon," he said regretfully. "I'll

have to go back to the sugar house in a few minutes. They'll be changing shifts."

Manon clucked in disappointment as she pulled her nightdress over her head.

"Champagne," she insisted and strolled from the room. Champagne was a ritual finish for their lovemaking.

Keith's thoughts focused on Suzanne. She had not been the unresponsive bride that Jacques had warned he would surely encounter. She had come to him willing to be loved. But he had been resentful, angry, performing an obligation. And she had known that.

Eleven

Suzanne lay sleepless far into the night, tossing beneath the comforter, straining to thrust from her mind the words that Clara Andrews had etched there this afternoon. *Keith had married her to save Savage Oaks.*

His pretense of ardor would be difficult to forgive, yet for a while this afternoon — when she told him what had happened in the overseer's cottage and saw his deep concern — she had fancied that he was beginning to feel something for her. Had she imagined this because she wanted so desperately for it to happen?

Not till dawn did she fall at last into deep, exhausted sleep. She slept late, waking to lie in bed in somber contemplation of her situation. She must not be impetuous; she must not act in haste.

At dinner Keith gave her the notebook in which he had been jotting down Christmas gifts she was to buy for the field hands. Earlier she had observed Keith in muted conversation with

Phillip and suspected he was asking Phillip to shop for a Christmas present for Jane and her.

"Phillip will go into New Orleans with you tomorrow," Keith said briskly. "He knows which stores will stock what you're looking for."

"We'll leave early," Phillip decided highspiritedly. "The stores will be busy this time of year. It'll take us all day to shop." He turned ingratiatingly to Jane. "I'll go into the woods tomorrow and choose a tree."

Jane seemed irritated.

"We shouldn't have a tree this year," she protested. "Out of respect for Papa's memory."

"It's almost a year." All at once Phillip was hostile. "We've had a wedding at Savage Oaks. Why, can't we have a Christmas tree?"

"All right," Jane capitulated wearily. "We'll have a tree."

"This year let's hang the servants' presents as well as the family's," Phillip pursued, seeming to be pleased by this small victory.

Before Arthur indicated that dessert was to be brought to the table, Keith rose to his feet and excused himself. In a matter of a few days the sugar house would be silent, the fires unlit, Suzanne thought with a tremor of hope. Would Keith come to her then? Only in Keith's arms would she be able to know if there was a chance for them. If Keith brought only a sense of duty to her bed, she silently vowed, she would leave Savage Oaks.

As Suzanne and Phillip prepared to leave early next morning for New Orleans, Jane came out on the gallery with the list of presents to be bought for the house servants. There was to be a gift from each member of the family. Though Phillip had been moody last evening as he sat with Jane and her in the drawing room, this morning he seemed caught up in the Christmas spirit.

This was the first Christmas within her memory that she would not be desolately lonely, Suzanne thought. Each year that Cecile had been at the Convent she had extended an invitation to go to the de Mirabeau mansion in Paris; but Suzanne had been too proud to accept when she knew she could not reciprocate.

"All we have to do with the plantation lists is to present them to the stores and they'll pack everything up for us," Phillip explained, leaning back in the carriage with an air of well-being.

"But I'd like to choose," Suzanne scolded gently.

Phillip laughed.

"Believe me, these fellows know exactly what to choose. They've been doing it for years." He paused, his eyes opaque for a moment. "Except for the book of poetry for Raoul. I know what he'd like to have."

"We'll have to stop at the bank and cash my check," she remembered. She had been impressed by the amount that was hers to spend as she liked. "You must help me choose something for Keith. And for Jane," she added conscientiously. "I thought I'd try to find a particularly beautiful paperweight."

"Jane collects them." Phillip seemed intrigued that she had decided on this.

"I saw the way she handled the paperweight in the library," Suzanne smiled. "As though she loved it."

"She has little enough to love. Jane should have married," Phillip said somberly. "It wasn't enough for her to have raised Keith and me."

"She could marry still, Phillip."

"Jane will never marry," he said with finality.

"Why do you say that, Phillip?" There was an ominous undercurrent in Phillip's voice.

He turned to her, his eyes stormy.

"There's so much you don't know about Savage Oaks," he said with an intensity that left her shaken. "I pray that you never will."

Phillip leaned back in the carriage, his gaze concentrated on the passing countryside. Not until they approached Carondelet Street, with its pleasant rural homes, did he speak again.

"We'll stop first at the bank, then we'll go to Carrere's for the pocketknives. We'll need about a dozen of those. From there we'll go to Moody's at Canal and Royal streets."

New Orleans reflected the holiday season. Suzanne was fascinated by the throngs of shoppers. At one point on Camp Street all traffic stopped before a flock of turkeys, guided by a man and boys carrying long poles. Phillip and Suzanne were convulsed with laughter.

But Suzanne flinched at the sight of the seemingly endless slave "yards." Sympathetic with her reaction to these, Phillip told her there were at least twenty-five of them on Gravier, Baronne, Magazine, and Esplanade streets. He told her, too, about the sales in the rotundas of the St. Charles and the St. Louis hotels, which Suzanne had no curiosity to visit.

"I'll tell Lewis to take us to Morgan's," Phillip decided when their transactions at Carrere's and Moody's were completed. "You'll want to stay there forever," he teased. "It's a fantastic book-store."

Because of the congested traffic they left the carriage a few blocks from Morgan's to walk the rest of the way, past tall buildings and cafes and casinos. They were within minutes of Uncle Gilbert's office, Suzanne realized; but she had no intention of stopping by for a visit, no matter how brief. How long, she wondered, before she would receive a letter from the Princeton College?

In front of the block-long aristocratic St. Louis Hotel, with its air of an Italian palace, Phillip pointed to the lockjaw pathway opposite them.

"We turn in here at Exchange Alley," he said, and they swung into a flagstoned passage. Blocking the entrance to the post office, a man sat selling buckskin purses and suspenders. Beside him a colorfully dressed black girl sold flowers and cakes. Between customers she complacently knitted. They pushed farther along the alley, past the cigar man, past law offices and legal libraries. Notaries and lawyers walked

189

briskly en route to the courthouse. Everywhere was the seductive scent of mint lemons.

"Here's Morgan's." Phillip prodded Suzanne inside the bookstore. "You can buy any kind of newspaper you want here."

Suzanne gazed in amazement at the array of newspapers. English, Irish, French, Spanish along with the New Orleans and New York dailies. There must be two dozen New Orleans papers, in four languages! Close by were the weeklies like *Punch* and *Nation* and *Sun*. A wood box was provided to receive the proper coins in payment.

"The novels are farther along," Phillip directed her after Suzanne had delightedly bought a collection of papers. "And in that railed-off corner over there are the magazines." His eyes moved speculatively about them. "Is it all right if I leave you alone for a few minutes? I want to inquire about the book of poetry."

"I could wander here forever!" Suzanne said enthusiastically. "What are those books all the way in the back?"

"Textbooks," Phillip said with a grimace of distaste and walked rapidly away.

Suzanne wandered about the store, shopping with abandon because there was so much time for reading at Savage Oaks. Moving farther back into the store she searched her mind for books to buy for Keith. After Christmas he would have time to read.

She stopped short before a group of leather-bound books, the titles eliciting excitement in her. *The Memoirs of the Life of William Wirt.* She had read his biography of Patrick Henry and admired it deeply. Wirt was a lawyer, she recalled. At one time he was the Attorney General of the United States. Surely Keith would like to own his memoirs. Happily she took the two volumes that comprised the memoirs from the shelf and gave them to the clerk who came forward with a smile.

When they left Morgan's, they deposited their books in the waiting carriage and Phillip took her to a small, unpretentious restaurant where they had magnificent gumbo, jambalaya and salad plus a bottle of Bordeaux. The proprietor beamed upon them, thinking they were a young married couple, Suzanne guessed in discomfort. She was seeing far more of her brother-in-law than of her husband. What had Phillip meant when he said, "There's so much you don't know about Savage Oaks. I pray that you never will."

After the long luncheon, Phillip took her to the jewelry store where she had chosen her wedding ring. The clerk greeted her effusively. No doubt he remembered the bride who had chosen her wedding ring alone, Suzanne taunted herself. Phillip was in deep consultation with another clerk, intent on completing his personal shopping.

To Suzanne's delight the jewelry store had a small collection of exquisite paperweights. Her eyes moved with soaring admiration from an apple paperweight — the delicate green and red apple resting on a cushion of crystal, to a Clichy garland weight with nine white and green roses, and then to a Baccarat pansy weight with wine-red petals above three smaller yellow and mauve petals centered on a whorl and stardust cluster.

"This one is particularly beautiful," the clerk said with something akin to reverence. "It's quite expensive," he conceded as Suzanne leaned raptly over the counter, knowing this was Jane's gift. This four-colored crown weight consisting of blue and yellow, red and green alternating with white latticinio.

While the clerk wrapped the paperweight, Suzanne chose a handsome cravat pin for Phillip. She wished that she had shopped early for gifts for Mère Angélique and Cecile. She must buy something for Mme. Mauriac and Uncle Gilbert, she remembered belatedly, and chose for romantic Mme. Mauriac an exquisite porcelain figurine of a musician, colorfully painted in enamel, and for Uncle Gilbert a silhouette of an attorney at the bar, by the celebrated August Édouart. On the point of leaving the shop, she stopped to buy a double pendant garnet brooch for Mrs. Cantrell, who would be going to her sister in Natchez for the Christmas to New Year's week.

When they left the jewelry store, Phillip decided they must go for a walk along the levee. They paused at a tiny shop to buy "ices" and walked with flavorsome cups in hand along the levee between Toulouse and Julia streets, where the steamboats were arriving with such frequency that the harbor master was requesting steamboat pilots to anchor out in the stream until space was available.

This was another pleasant but unreal interlude. Reality was Savage Oaks, Suzanne thought while Phillip talked compulsively. She reached into her reticule to give money to an aged beggar. There were so many beggars in this wealthy city!

"Everybody complains about the high crime rate in New Orleans. The swindlers, the counterfeiters. One group passed out almost $70,000 in bogus ten dollars recently, and a ring of Irish girls was making fifty-cent pieces." Phillip was taking refuge in impersonal conversation, regretting — Suzanne suspected — his outburst in the carriage. "The *Mirror* ran a piece lately about ten- and twelve-year-old children roaming the streets with cigars in their mouths and knives in their pockets."

"Keith told me New Orleans has at least three hundred policemen," Suzanne recalled.

"Who are controlled by the politicians," Phillip said bitterly, quoting Keith. "And who are overworked and underpaid. They get forty-five dollars a month for long hours every day, when even unskilled dock workers earn two dollars a day and skilled workers can earn four dollars a day. Can you wonder that we have such heavy crime in the streets?"

Keith was drawn to politics. After the Christmas holidays, he said, he was going to read every day in Judge Ramsay's library at Tintagel.

Would he take his bar examinations when he felt he was ready? She knew so little about Keith, she thought wistfully, when she so desperately wished to know everything.

The days before Christmas seemed to speed past, partly because the servants were so involved in the Christmas spirit. Suzanne spent hours each day wrapping the gifts for the house servants and the hands. Elaine had been given her mourning veil early so she might replace it with her wedding veil on Christmas Day.

Jane had come down from the attic one morning with a white satin ball gown that had belonged to her mother. She presented it to Elaine for her wedding gown. Suzanne offered to undertake the laborious task of letting it out to accommodate Elaine's more ample dimensions.

The night before Christmas Eve, the sugar house was at last silent. No smoke emerged from the chimney, no night showers of sparks. The last hogshead of sugar, the last barrel of molasses had been moved. Keith arrived at dinner exhausted but pleased. The crop had been impressive.

"I'm going to bed tonight and sleep till George calls me for dinner tomorrow night," he said, suppressing a series of yawns. "Every hand will be doing the same," he chuckled.

"Thank God the season's over," Jane said sympathetically.

"Now come the festivities," Phillip jeered amusedly. "The hands will be drunk until they're

194

back at work on the day after New Year's."

"Phillip, why do you make such sweeping statements?" Jane asked exasperatedly. "There's little whiskey given out on this plantation."

"Tomorrow night we hang the presents and we light the tree." Phillip coolly ignored Jane's reproach. "And later in the evening we take down our presents."

"We exchange our presents on Christmas Eve instead of on Christmas morning," Jane shot back, "because as a little boy Phillip would sneak down from his room to sleep by the tree. We solved that situation by taking down the presents before going to bed." But despite the sarcasm in her voice, her eyes were unfamiliarly tender as they rested on Phillip. She was remembering him as a small boy, Suzanne thought. Phillip and Keith were Jane's children more than they were brothers to her.

Immediately after dinner, Keith retired to his room. The others followed shortly after. The tree Phillip chose had been cut down and set up in the drawing room. Arthur had brought masses of holly into the house, creating a festive air that was a new experience for Suzanne.

The grinding season was over. Keith would not be spending eighteen hours a day in work. She trembled as she considered Keith's becoming, once again, the ardent young man she had known in their two weeks of courtship. *Would* that happen? These last few days, since the ugly encounter in the overseer's cottage, she had sensed a new awareness of her in Keith. If he came to her again, she would be warm and responsive. *She could forget that he married her to save Savage Oaks if she knew that he loved her now.*

She awoke next morning with an instant realization that Christmas Eve was only hours away. She was eager to learn if Keith liked the books on Wirt that she had bought for him. After breakfast she would hang the presents for the house servants on the tree, along with her presents for the other members of the family. In the afternoon she would bring Elaine into the sewing room for the final fitting on her wedding gown. Though let out to its fullest extent, it would not accommodate Elaine's proportions without an inset.

As Suzanne had expected, the hours dragged with interminable slowness. Keith slept all day. Not until late afternoon did she see George, a grin on his face, go up to Keith's room with a pot of coffee. The knowledge that Keith was awake and rested exhilarated her.

She left the house to walk towards the levee. This afternoon she found herself drawn to the solitary grave with its enigmatic tombstone in the small clearing. On impulse she stooped before a mass of lilies of the valley and with bare hands dug up a clump of earth in which grew a profusion of the delicately fragrant, small white blossoms. Carefully she replanted the clump of earth before the tombstone, happy that she had made this effort.

As Suzanne continued her walk to the levee,

her thoughts turned wistfully to Maman and Papa. Always on holidays Maman and Papa seemed sweetly close to her. Soon she ought to be hearing from Mère Angélique and Cecile. And from the college in Princeton.

Scarcely twenty yards from the levee she spied Phillip and Raoul sitting on one of the benches. Phillip was reading aloud to Raoul, slowly because he was translating from the French. Suzanne realized it was the book of poems about which he had talked to her. A collection by seventeen mulatto poets who had all lived at one time or another in New Orleans. Some of the poets, Phillip said, were friends of Victor Hugo. One had several plays presented in Paris. The two on the bench were too engrossed to be aware of Suzanne's nearness. Hastily she turned away and on silent feet sped towards the house.

Clarissa had prepared a sumptuous Christmas Eve dinner. Oyster soup, turkey and capons fattened on pecan nuts, wild duck, mutton, platters of yams and red beans and rice. Arthur brought bottles of sauterne, burgandy, sherry and Madeira to the table, then went to the rosewood wine cabinet to bring forth the stemmed Waterford glasses used on special occasions. Along with coffee, Edward brought in plum pudding and mince pie. Despite the festive spirit at the table, both Jane and Keith spoke little. Phillip and Suzanne talked animatedly about Paris, which Phillip had never seen, but which he longed to visit.

Immediately after dinner they went into the

drawing room and Phillip lit the candles on the Christmas tree. As he lit the last candle, melodic voices welled in song right outside a window. With an incandescent glow on her face, Suzanne darted to open the window. A cluster of slaves of varying ages, including three gangling ten-year-olds, wrapped against the night chill, had come to sing Christmas carols for their "white folks."

They sang until they were breathless, and then Jane called to them to go to the kitchen house. Arthur would serve them hot chocolate. As Jane closed the window, Suzanne was astonished to see that her eyes glistened with tears. Jane, so rigidly disciplined against revealing emotions.

A holiday air pervaded the room as Phillip took upon himself the task of handing out the family presents. No doubt it was Phillip who shopped for Keith and Jane, Suzanne guessed humorously.

Suzanne started at a series of small explosions somewhere in the distance.

"It's that stupid habit of the children to fire crackers on Christmas Eve," Jane said with distaste, but her eyes were tender. "I don't know where they get them."

"I do," Phillip said with sly amusement, his eyes defying Jane to deny any part in this.

Smiling radiantly, Suzanne settled down to open her packages, but covertly she watched Keith. He was opening her present first. He was pleased! She watched as he fondled the fine leather bindings of the two volumes, then opened one to skim the first pages.

"Suzanne, thank you." His voice deepened with warmth. "I've wanted to own these since they were first published."

"I thought you would like them." The Savages were land and slave rich, she realized. Money was something the family spent personally with care. Only now was she beginning to see the genteel shabbiness that threatened Savage Oaks. When her next check came in, she resolved impulsively, she would buy new draperies for the drawing room and the dining room.

Only now did Suzanne open Keith's present.

"Thank you for the cameo, Keith," she said with a surge of pleasure. "It's exquisite." Phillip had shopped for the dainty cameo of stone set in a frame of pearls. He might have bought it while they were separately involved in purchases at the jewelry shop.

From Jane she received a fanciful music box from Switzerland, and from Phillip a slender volume of poetry by a new writer named Walt Whitman. Phillip expressed lively admiration for the cravat pin she had chosen for him, and Jane seemed profoundly touched by the paperweight.

The servants were brought to admire the tree and to receive their gifts with jubilant smiles and a solemn "Thankee," for each member of the family. Jane had chosen with an intuitive knowledge for each servant's likes, Suzanne thought with respect. But Jane had not yet truly accepted her as Keith's wife. Neither had Keith, she reminded herself unhappily; and she asked herself if a rival in Washington City stood between them.

They went up to their rooms early because Jane pointed out that the field hands would be eagerly awaiting their gifts in the morning. Suzanne hoped wistfully that Keith would come to her room. Tonight she had sensed a warmth in him that was a poignant reminder of their brief but beautiful courtship. Not until the first pink streaks of dawn showed in the sky did she acknowledge that Keith would not come to her.

Patrice woke her the next morning, bearing a pot of fragrant hot coffee. Her eyes were light with the spirit of Christmas Day as she shyly offered Suzanne a gift.

"Oh, Patrice," Suzanne murmured with gratitude that might have been elicited by the most expensive of gifts. "You made this for me yourself."

"Yes'm," Patrice said complacently, while Suzanne gazed admiringly at the colorfully woven bookmark. She was aware that Suzanne spent much time reading. She had seen that Suzanne's bookmark, from long use at the Convent, was ragged at the edges, fading. "Ah figgered you could use that. Miss Suzanne."

"Oh, I will, Patrice," Suzanne promised seriously.

"Ah expect you best get downstairs now," Patrice urged. "Them field hands be comin' any minute."

Suzanne dressed swiftly and hurried downstairs. Christmas Day. How different from waking on Christmas Day at the Convent! She heard voices on the back porch. The field hands must be gathered there. She walked swiftly down the hall to the rear of the house.

Keith was talking good-humoredly to the hands while Jane and Phillip distributed the gifts. She was welcomed with a chorus of "Merry Christmas!"

When all the gifts had been handed out, Arthur and Edward came to the back porch with a jug of whiskey and a mass of tin cups. The family drank along with the hands. It was a tradition on most plantations, Keith whispered to Suzanne, smiling at her absorption in the festivities. She was seeing a side of the master-slave relationship that was new to her. There was an affection here on both sides.

Dinner was served early so that the family might attend the "quarter wedding" and the Christmas ball to follow. Suzanne, with Patrice proudly leading her, set off immediately after dinner for the quarters to help dress the bride. It was the first time since her arrival at Savage Oaks that she had seen the quarters.

The neat, whitewashed cabins were elevated above the ground, each containing two rooms, a chimney in between, and a porch in front.

"There's de church," Patrice said with a proprietary pride, pointing to a modest structure a few hundred feet beyond the cabins.

Suzanne and Patrice joined the giggling girls

who were struggling to fasten Elaine's let-out wedding gown. Suzanne stepped in to show them how the wide gap at the waist must be covered by the inset of discarded ribbons that she had designed for this purpose. Then a tiny crown of white lace veil and white lilies of the valley was placed on Elaine's head, and the bride was ready.

In the church, bedecked with blossoms, Elaine and her much younger husband stood solemnly before the plantation preacher in his cast-off swallowtail coat that twenty years earlier had belonged to Thorne Savage. Tears welled in Suzanne's eyes as she listened to the marriage ceremony. Twice her gaze moved to Keith, to find his eyes on her. She remembered the night of the Opera, when she had felt his gaze on her at intervals during the performance. That had been part of a contrived courtship, her mind derided. But he had no such motive now. Hope brought a becoming touch of color to her face as she smiled hesitantly at him.

After the ceremony, in the tradition of his father and grandfather, Keith spoke to the wedding couple.

"You must both remember this is a solemn tie," Keith said seriously. "You must behave and be faithful to each other. There must be no shirking of your duties as husband and wife."

After the ceremony, everyone moved to the big quarters' nursery, adorned with much greenery and a vast collection of cut-paper flycatchers. A long table was laid with roast mutton and pig and hot biscuits, brought from the kitchen. The young girls had made sweet potato pies and molasses gingerbread in the oven in the quarter cook house. Everyone ate with noisy relish. But Jane, Suzanne suddenly realized, had withdrawn from the festivities.

"The dancing will begin as soon as they've moved away from the table," Keith told Suzanne. "They wait all year for this ball."

Now the slaves from Tintagel began to arrive, eager to share in the celebration. The young girls wore colorful head kerchiefs, some of the women resplendent in turbans with marabou feathers. The noise became so loud it was all but impossible to hear what Keith and Phillip said to her.

The fiddler sounded his A, corrected the pitch, then began to play. The others waited expectantly until he rapped with his bow.

"Git yo' pardners for the kwatillion! Come on now, stomp yo' feet an' lift 'em high!"

Impulsively Suzanne moved towards the dancers. Phillip jumped forward to join her.

"S'lute yo' pardners," the fiddler called out exuberantly. "An' don' go bumpin' into ever'body!"

The dancers moved spiritedly, grinning in pleasure while the fiddler exhorted them to do their best. As Suzanne swung about the floor, caught up in the revelry, she spied Raoul standing away from the dancers, his face somber and unhappy, his eyes clinging to Phillip's every movement.

They danced tirelessly for hours. At intervals

the fiddler stopped for a quick swig from a convenient jug, then began to play again. Keith did not join the dancers but stood on the sidelines, obviously approving the activities.

It was late in the evening, when Suzanne saw a very young girl come into the nursery and go to Keith. She rose on tiptoe to whisper into his ear. He frowned, seemed to hesitate, then nodded in agreement to whatever she was saying. As Keith straightened up, she darted from the room with a happy smile.

Keith was trying to catch Phillip's eyes.

"Phillip, I think Keith wants to speak to you," she said as they moved together in the dance.

Startled, Phillip glanced in Keith's direction. Keith beckoned to him. Phillip disengaged himself and crossed to Keith. Suzanne continued to dance, but her eyes concentrated on Keith. He was whispering to Phillip, then he strode from the nursery.

Where was Keith going? Who had called him away in the midst of the Christmas ball? She smiled determinedly when Phillip rejoined the dancers, but questions plagued at her.

Why had Keith left the ball?

Twelve

With an impassive smile, Phillip rejoined the dancers. He ignored the questions in Suzanne's eyes. He must be the dutiful younger brother, he told himself with sardonic amusement. When they left the ball, he would see his beautiful sister-in-law to the big house.

"Hol' up yo' faces! Yo' ain't supposed to be lookin' at yo' feet!" the fiddler exhorted boisterously.

When the dancers were at last panting for breath, the fiddler held up his hand, waved somebody from the throng of dancers to join him. A squat, perspiring field hand came forward with a drum held high above his head, to the accompaniment of rousing cheers from the others.

"That's a *bamboula*," Phillip whispered in Suzanne's ear. "Watch this."

His glistening face uplifted, his mouth parted in a wide grin, the man with the drum began to beat on the hide, singing loudly. Another hand leapt forward, bringing with him a tall, lithe slender girl, and the two began to dance. For an hour, it seemed, the man kept spinning the girl around while she waved a bright red kerchief above her head and everybody sang in a peculiar sort of French.

Finally another couple began to dance. An oddly exciting dance. The woman was dancing almost without moving her feet while the man kneeled, turned, gyrated about her. Now the drummer pounded with a mesmerizing violence. The woman's face became contorted with arousal as the others began to chant in the French that was unfamiliar to Phillip. The excitement of the chanters matched that of the dancers, who seemed oblivious of their audience.

"Let's go," Phillip said abruptly. "This will go on until dawn. The hands don't work for the next week. I'll take you back to the house."

"Where's Keith?" Suzanne asked when they moved out into the night.

"He was called out," Phillip explained uncomfortably. How could he tell Suzanne that Keith's quadroon mistress had summoned him? Keith was unaware that Phillip knew about the girl in the cottage.

Suzanne walked silently beside him. Did she suspect that Keith had a mistress? Was Keith sleeping with Suzanne? God, he was forever at the sugar house these past weeks. Still, Keith found time to go to the cottage. Did he find time to go to his wife?

"Merry Christmas, Phillip," Suzanne said re-

206

servedly when they walked into the house. "I enjoyed the evening."

He waited until Suzanne was upstairs in her room before leaving the house again. Knowing every inch of Savage Oaks, he walked purposefully through the dark woods. Compulsively he strode towards the cottage, intent on discovering if Keith had gone to the girl. *Couldn't Keith recognize what he had at home?*

He saw the faint glow of lamplight behind the heavy drapes in the small sitting room where his father had been entertained through the years by a series of mulatto and quadroon mistresses, even though he flogged his younger son for taking a pretty slave. What was the difference between Papa and him? But after that flogging, he thought with bitter humor, he had never touched another of the young bitches.

"Manon, stop it!" Keith exhorted desperately. "Stop crying that way."

"You neglect me! You leave me alone!" she shrieked. "It is Christmas and you don't even come to me! Don't you know how lonely it is for me, with only Lily Mae to talk to? I can't read all day and night. I'm a prisoner here in this awful house!"

"Manon, I'm sorry," Keith soothed. "I've been terribly busy."

"With her!" Manon wailed. "I don't please you anymore."

"Manon, you're magnificent," Keith said with sudden passion. "There's no one like you.

Tomorrow I'll send a carriage over for you," he promised cajolingly. "Go buy yourself something pretty, spend the day in New Orleans."

"Keith, I adore you." All at once Manon was spilling over with sweetness. "Come, *mon ami*, let me show you how much I love you."

Phillip turned away from the window, hurried through the grove of trees. Keith's woman, he thought with distaste. Anybody could buy her favors. As he moved toward the house, he could hear the noisy carryings-on in the quarters. They would stay there till dawn, listening to the end of Mama Marie's gruesome tales of conjurers and ghosts and devils.

The morning after Christmas was sunny, crisp and invigorating. Phillip strode to the stables, ostensibly intent on a morning ride.

"Yo' gonna ride dis mawnin', Mist' Phillip?" Abram, the elderly slave long in charge of the stables, asked respectfully.

"I don't think so," Phillip shrugged. "I'll go for a walk with the dogs." He reached down to fondle the head of one of the stable pups eager for play. He glanced about for a twig, found one, tossed it. The pup charged off in pursuit.

"Yassuh." With an affectionate gleam in his eyes, Abram lumbered over to the brougham to rub a cloth over its compact closed carnage.

So Keith was sending the discreet brougham to take Manon into New Orleans. What did Abram think about that? Phillip wondered.

Nothing happened at Savage Oaks that Abram did not know. How many times had he induced Abram to talk, with the aid of a bottle filched from the wine cabinet? His eyes were suddenly moody, bitter with recall. Perhaps it would have been better if he had never flushed out Savage Oaks' secrets.

Phillip made a pretense of romping with the dogs as he covertly watched Abram, talking aloud to himself about the "lazy stable boys," hitch up the brougham to a horse and then go off in search of a coachman. Quickly Phillip crossed to the carriage, pulled open the door, climbed inside and dropped to the floor. Cautiously he drew the carriage blanket over his crouched figure.

He waited for the coachman to come. Abram and Lewis stood beside the brougham talking for an interminable period. At last Lewis climbed up and ordered the horse forward.

Phillip flung aside the carriage robe, but remained on the floor, anticipating Manon's astonishment when she discovered she had a guest to accompany her into New Orleans. The carriage came to a stop. He could hear Manon talking vivaciously to someone. The girl who had come to the ball last night to fetch Keith to her, he surmised.

"Take me into New Orleans," Manon ordered imperiously. "When we arrive in town, I'll tell you where to stop."

Lewis was not jumping down from the driver's perch to open the door as Manon apparently expected. Phillip suppressed a chuckle. Lewis was not jumping down for any quadroon. The door pulled open, Manon drew herself up into the carriage, her eyes dark with fury at the slight just encountered. Hastily Phillip lifted a finger to his mouth to indicate she was to remain quiet.

Her initial shock was almost immediately replaced by curiosity. Eyebrows lifted provocatively, Manon settled herself on the seat. Phillip lithely rose from the floor to sit beside her. The carriage moved ahead at a fast gait.

"Who are you?" Manon demanded arrogantly, yet Phillip knew she was intrigued by this unorthodox situation.

"I'm Keith's brother." Phillip's eyes moved over Manon with overt admiration. "I'm Phillip."

"Did he tell you I was in the cottage?" she demanded warily.

"He told nobody. But I know everything that goes on at Savage Oaks. I make it my business to know." He leaned forward, sniffing appreciatively. "I like your scent."

"It's made especially for me," Manon boasted.

"Keith never notices," Phillip challenged. "He's always too busy with the scent of molasses in the sugar house."

"He notices," Manon contradicted airily. She tilted her head to one side and inspected him. "Does Keith's bride know he has a woman in the cottage?"

"If she knew," Phillip guessed, "she wouldn't be at Savage Oaks."

210

Manon leaned back and laughed.

"What does a girl like that know about love?" she scoffed. "Tell me, Phillip — " She leaned slightly towards him. "Was she relieved when her bridegroom never came to her on their wedding night?"

"How do you know he didn't go to her?" Phillip demanded.

"Phillip, he was at the sugar house looking after the equipment that had been messed up," she reminded. "He must have been there most of the night."

"*You* went into the sugar house and wrecked that equipment!" Phillip accused and broke into laughter.

"I was furious with him. I had just arrived at the cottage, and he comes to me and tells me he's marrying this girl from a convent." She made a low sound of disrespect. "A man as passionate as Keith with a wife who was brought up by nuns!"

"Does he suspect that you were responsible?"

"Phillip, darling, Keith suspect me?" she rebuked extravagantly. "Never. He's far too much of a gentleman."

"I'm not a gentleman," Phillip drawled, moving forward to drop an arm about her shoulders.

"Are you going to tell this little girl from the convent about me?" Manon challenged.

"No." He leaned closer to her, nipped one dainty earlobe. "I'm going to make love to Keith's woman."

"Phillip, you're out of your mind!" But her

211

eyes glowed. "Here in the brougham?"

"We don't have to drive." He leaned past her to close the curtains on her side, then closed the pair on his side of the carriage.

His mouth reached for hers. His hand fondled her breast. Where had Keith found this beautiful bitch? Keith didn't deserve her. He would not know what to do with a woman like this. All at once Phillip was aware of Manon's arousal. Without drawing his mouth from hers, he maneuvered her into a semiprone position, pushed a hand under her skirt. This one traveled for action. She wore nothing beneath her skirt.

"Phillip, this is crazy!" she remonstrated when he released her mouth, but her voice was deep with passion. Could Keith excite her the way he would? "In a carriage?"

"Why not?" he countered. "We're a long way from New Orleans."

She moved with him while the carriage rolled along the bumpy road. He gloried in this feeling of total command. He knew how to love a woman like Manon.

When he entered her, his passion matched her own. Triumph surged through him as they clung together in mutual satisfaction. He was taking Keith's woman, he thought exultantly.

Phillip listened good-humoredly to Manon's seemingly endless tale of Keith's neglect, surmising she was inwardly uneasy that she had admitted to the vandalism in the sugar house. What a temper in this one! He would be wary of crossing her.

He had not broken his vow to his father, he told himself complacently. He had not laid a hand on any of the wenches at Savage Oaks. Only Keith's woman.

"Where are we going today?" he interrupted, reaching for Manon's hand, his eyes calculatedly amorous. He could have Manon any time he wished.

"I'm going to see my mother," she said self-consciously, "and then to shop for jewelry. Keith gave me money," she said with an ebullient smile. "And already I'm hungry," she added with a pout. "Will you eat with me on Baronne Street?" Her eyes challenged him to invade this largely Negro area. "Between Perdido and Poydras."

"Since Keith has been generous with you and I have almost no money, you can take me to lunch," he countered. "But not on Baronne Street. In a restaurant on St. Louis Street," he stipulated.

Manon's eyes widened in disbelief. A touch of color showed becomingly on her ivory cheeks.

"Phillip, I can't go to a restaurant on St. Louis Street," she protested.

"You'll go with me," Phillip insisted with an audacious smile. "You know you can pass," he said indulgently.

"Phillip, I'm afraid," she whispered, and he saw the angry humiliation in her eyes that she should be in this position. Even in these more en-lightened days a "woman of color" might be whipped until her back was raw for flaunting herself before the whites of New Orleans.

"You'll go with me," Phillip repeated, enjoying this prospective adventure. "My lady," he emphasized with a flourish. "You're a guest at Savage Oaks. Nobody will dare to question me."

Manon smiled dazzlingly.

"We'll go to the restaurant on St. Louis Street," she capitulated. "After we stop to see my bitch of a mother." Phillip laughed. "You don't know my mother," she said with disgust. "She works in a coffee house, and the way the men talk to her!" She spit eloquently out the window. "But she looks down on me because I went to live at the Mansion House. That's where Keith found me. I was one of Yellowbird Shaw's girls."

"The most beautiful girls in New Orleans," Phillip acknowledged.

"My father left my mother when I was barely a year old. What else could she expect? She let herself grow fat. He gave her money to open a little shop. She lost it at the gambling tables."

"Do you know who he was?" Phillip asked curiously.

Manon shrugged.

"He was a rich planter. But the devil with him, Phillip! I'm going to see my mother to show her I have found a rich protector. And I'll keep him," she said triumphantly. "I won't grow fat like her."

They drove along Baronne Street, slowing down at Perdido while Lewis searched for the address Manon had called out the window earlier. There was a colored church, an ice-cream saloon, a restaurant, a coffee house, and a barber shop. Lewis stopped before the barber shop. Maliciously missing the coffee house, Phillip suspected.

He opened the door, grinning at Lewis' astonishment at his presence in the carriage. He waved at Lewis to remain on the driver's perch, and helped Manon down. Together they went briefly into the squalid coffee house where Manon's mulattress mother worked, then hurried back to the carriage to be taken to the French restaurant on St. Louis Street, where the Savages had been known for many years.

"M. Phillip!" the owner welcomed him effusively. "It is so long since we have seen you. Months!"

"René, we won't bother to order," Phillip was pleased at this reception. Manon was attracting admiring glances from the few diners who had arrived early like themselves. No one, he decided triumphantly, suspected Manon was a quadroon. "We entrust ourselves to you, René."

René personally served them a gourmet meal, which both Phillip and Manon ate with gusto. René was astonished that they did not linger in the restaurant, as was the custom. Phillip went with Manon to the jewelry shop, where she dickered with the shopkeeper over the price of the pendant she proposed to buy.

"Where now?" he asked as they emerged from the shop.

"To the Mansion House," she said saucily. "I'll take you to meet Yellowbird and the girls. The House won't open for another hour yet. We can visit for a while," she said nonchalantly. Again, she wanted to boast of her success, Phillip thought with amusement.

The brougham took them to the edge of town, to deposit them before an elegant town house. So this was the Mansion House. Phillip inspected it appreciatively. He had never been affluent enough to present himself as a prospective client.

Manon and he were admitted by a liveried black man who, after his initial astonishment at Manon's presence here, greeted them with warmth and led them to a small parlor.

"Lloyd, tell Yellowbird I've just come to visit for a little while with her and the girls," Manon said effervescently. "Tell her I'm here with my 'protector's' brother."

Phillip gazed about with lively interest at the lushly furnished parlor. So this was where Keith had met Manon.

"You've missed us, Manon?" a teasing feminine voice inquired, and Phillip swung around to face Manon's former employer.

"It's lonely out there on the plantation," Manon conceded with charming wistfulness. "So I've come into New Orleans for the day."

Yellowbird's eyes narrowed speculatively.

"There are few plantations close enough to New Orleans to permit that. You're lucky."

"I was sorry that I had to leave you with so

216

little warning," Manon apologized prettily. "But my 'protector' was insistent that I move instantly into the cottage he had prepared for me."

"Manon, you have not introduced me to your escort," Yellowbird scolded, smiling charmingly at Phillip.

"My 'protector's' younger brother," Manon murmured. "It would be indiscreet of me to say more." She was obviously enjoying her new position. "He's been anxious to meet you."

Yellowbird chuckled.

"Not me, Manon," she corrected. "My girls."

How long could Keith keep Manon at Savage Oaks without Suzanne's finding out? Suzanne was not a demure little Creole bride who would cry nightly about such an arrangement, but who would accept it.

Phillip listened politely to an exchange of gossip, then Manon inquired about her friend Colette.

"Is Colette awake yet?" she asked.

"Go on up to her room," Yellowbird told her. Her eyes met Manon's in a secret exchange. "Take your young friend up with you."

"Phillip," Manon whispered to him as they moved up the lushly carpeted staircase, "Colette and I will show you how some of New Orleans' most famous gentlemen take their pleasure. You'll be most appreciative," she promised, allowing one hand to ripple up his back.

"My talents are greater than your famous gentlemen's," Phillip boasted.

"I know," Manon pointed out with a seductive smile. "Why else am I taking you upstairs to Colette's room?"

Keith could never have achieved this dubious honor, Phillip thought ebulliently. Being entertained by two of Yellowbird's girls as a guest of the Mansion House! His brilliant brother was paying for Manon's favors, which he could enjoy at his will.

If he tried, Phillip thought with soaring confidence, he could take Suzanne away from Keith.

Thirteen

The sugar house was shut for the season. Spiders spun nets about the dust-gathering kettles, hung fanciful veils from the tall rafters. Mice roamed about the floors, cavorted in the walls. The hands were working in the fields.

Immediately after New Year's Day, when Savage Oaks took no part in the ceremonial entertaining that was traditional in the South, Suzanne had decided to ride each morning. Her inactivity made her restless. She was disturbed that Keith made no effort to resume their marital relationship.

While she waited at the stable for Othello to be saddled for her, her mind shot back to last night's dinner conversation. Only at dinner was there any semblance of a family life at Savage Oaks. She strived so desperately to make Keith aware of her as a person, and last night she had reveled in a fleeting success. She asked him about William Wirt's involvement in the Indian problem, and he launched into an eloquent diatribe against President Jackson's treatment of the Indians.

"We may have renamed the Place d'Armes as Jackson Square, and we're building that $30,000 statue that should be unveiled next month; but I can't forget that Jackson accepted the frontiersman's estimate that the only good Indian is a dead Indian. It was outrageous the way he robbed the Indians of their lands by treaties that were imposed by force or chicanery."

"Keith, you belong in politics," Phillip jeered.

"If you took some interest in running Savage Oaks, Keith might have time for that," Jane said sarcastically. It was the first time she had spoken since they sat down to dinner.

"This country is painfully in need of reform." Keith leaned forward earnestly. "Take our Electoral College system of choosing a President. It's wrong. Every American should have the right to vote *directly* for the President."

"Every American," Suzanne declared passionately, "should include every American woman."

"Hear, hear!" Phillip chortled.

"That time will come, Phillip," Suzanne promised. "I hope in our lifetime."

"Suzanne, did you know that under the Electoral College system we can elect a President who hasn't received a majority of the popular vote?" Keith said. It was almost as though they were alone at the table, Suzanne thought with exhilaration. "It happened with John Adams, with Polk and with Taylor. And there's more wrong than just the electoral system. Look at our position right at this moment. If something happens to Pierce — if he should die — the Secretary of State, an unelected official — would take over."

"But what about the Vice President?" Suzanne was puzzled.

"Our Vice President, Mr. King, died a few weeks after the Inauguration," he explained wryly.

But after dinner Keith had settled in a chair with the first volume of the Wirt memoirs. Away from the table, she thought unhappily, the magical closeness between them disappeared. He remained in the drawing room after Jane and she retired to their rooms. He had not gone up to his room until almost midnight. Nor had he stopped at her door, as she had prayed he might. With the grinding season over and the holiday week of leisure behind him, Keith could not hide behind an alibi of exhaustion.

This morning on impulse Suzanne deviated from her normal route and guided Othello to the edge of the south fields. Here Reagan supervised the ploughing of the fine, dark, sandy loam of fallow land while Keith hovered absorbedly before the mule-drawn cart, which had brought stalks to be used for seeding. Hands waited beside him to carry armfuls from the cart to be laid by the side of the furrows. A second team of hands would plant the cane, and a third would cover it. Suzanne realized that Keith was inspecting the stalks to make sure the cuttings were such that vigorous plants would be produced.

At dinner last night, Keith had explained to her that the cane grew for several years from the roots of the old plants. However, to insure a healthy crop, it was the practice in Louisiana, Keith said, to plant every three years.

Suzanne dismounted, her gaze steadily focused on Keith. If he was aware of her presence, he gave no recognition of this. Reluctantly she prodded Othello away from the fields. She would not see Keith again until dinner. Every afternoon these past three weeks since New Year's he had been riding over to Tintagel to read in Judge Ramsay's law library.

She dreaded the oppressive evenings when Keith, Jane, Phillip and she sat together in the drawing room after dinner, each supposedly engrossed in a newspaper or magazine or book. Each of them imprisoned in private torment. Occasionally she glanced up from whatever she was reading to discover Keith gazing at her with such intensity that she found it difficult to breathe.

Suzanne left Othello at the stable and walked to the house. Edward had just returned from New Orleans with the mail. She followed him into the library, where Jane worked on the plantation records. She struggled to hide her impatience while Jane stopped totaling figures to sort the letters.

"A letter for you." Jane looked up curiously as she handed the envelope to Suzanne.

"Thank you." Suzanne's hands trembled as she turned the envelope over to see who was the sender. The letter was from Princeton.

She ran from the library and up the stairs to her room, praying that Patrice would be downstairs. She wanted to be alone when she read the letter.

She opened the door and walked into her bedroom. Patrice was not there. She ripped open the envelope, pulled out the letter. Her eyes raced over the small, precise handwriting. Slowly, disbelievingly, she reread the brief, polite note.

"We have searched our records for a period of fifteen years, but regret to inform you that Mr. Charles Duprée was never a student at Princeton."

She dropped into a chair, sick with frustration. Again Uncle Gilbert had lied to her. Why? She would go to him with this letter. Make him tell her the truth about Maman and Papa. She would not be put off any longer!

She crossed to the armoire, brought out her cape and a reticule. Downstairs she sought out Arthur and asked him to have a carriage brought to the house. She waited impatiently on the gallery for the carriage to arrive.

The carriage pulled up before the house. Raoul jumped down to help her into the carriage. She was momentarily disconcerted to discover that Raoul was driving her into the city. How unhappy he seemed this morning. A man with the sensitivity to write poetry must be doubly sensitive to the indignities of slavery.

As they drove along the rough road, Suzanne gazed at the passing scenery. This morning at a turn in the road she noticed a cluster of children, scantily clad in the mid-January chill, who played before a run-down shack. Behind the shack a pair of women washed clothes in a black tub, paused in their scrubbing to check who was passing. Suzanne waved. They weakly returned the greeting. These would be one of the "poor white" families that clung so tenaciously to their small patches of land. Phillip had talked about them one night.

There were several such houses along this stretch of road, built of wood or clay in the old French peasant style. The residents, Phillip said, grew a little corn and cotton, raised a hog when they could steal one. Keith had reproached him for this callous attitude.

Those children ought to be in school, Suzanne thought worriedly. The nearest schools must be in New Orleans, a trip not likely to be undertaken daily. The slave children on the plantations should also be in school, but the laws of the state made this illegal.

Suzanne tapped restlessly with one foot as the carriage rolled along the road to the city. She opened the enamel case of the dainty watch that hung from a chain about her neck. The Gubelin watch, that Mme. Mauriac had given her with such a display of affection. They must arrive before Uncle Gilbert left his office to go home for the midday meal.

By the time the carriage arrived at the outskirts of the city, Suzanne was sitting on the edge of her seat. Today she was irritated by the noisy, colorful traffic that glutted the New Orleans streets. When Raoul pulled to a halt at her destination, she pushed open the carriage door and leapt down to the cobblestoned street before Raoul could assist her.

"I won't be long, Raoul," she called over her shoulder as she darted towards Gilbert's office.

The elderly clerk Suzanne remembered from her earlier visit was just emerging from the office.

"Is Mr. Mauriac here?" Suzanne asked breathlessly.

"He's with a client," the clerk said uncertainly, holding the door for her.

"I'll wait for him," Suzanne said charmingly. "Please don't let me keep you here. I'll sit in a chair and wait until he comes out," she insisted because the clerk seemed ambivalent about leaving her alone.

"Yes, ma'am," he acquiesced with a quick bow.

Suzanne sat self-consciously in the pleasingly furnished reception room, trying to form the sentences in her mind with which to face Gilbert. She stiffened as the door to the office was flung open, and Gilbert Mauriac walked out in the company of a lady dressed elegantly in yellow. Gilbert appeared dismayed to find Suzanne waiting for him, but he quickly recovered.

"Suzanne, how pleasant to see you!"

"I must go, Gilbert," the lady with him said

quickly. "Thank you." She smiled at Suzanne as she swept past her en route to the door.

Uncle Gilbert had made no effort to introduce them, Suzanne thought curiously. How unlike him! And then all at once she understood. This was the lady in the loge grillé at the Opera, the night she had attended with Uncle Gilbert and Mme. Mauriac. The lady whose identity had been established by an outraged Opera-goer as the madam of the Mansion House.

"Suzanne, I'm going home for luncheon. You'll come with me," he said warmly. "Grandmère will be delighted to see you."

"Uncle Gilbert, I must talk to you," she said urgently.

"At the house," he hedged. "You are in New Orleans. I will not deprive Grandmère of the privilege of seeing you."

In the carriage from Savage Oaks, Suzanne and Gilbert went to the Mauriac house. Raoul was dispatched to the kitchen at Gilbert's insistence, where Amelia would serve him a meal. Suzanne, after an affectionate welcome from Mme. Mauriac, was ushered into the dining room amidst animated conversation. When would Uncle Gilbert allow her to tell him what had brought her to his office?

Sebastien served them delicious claret-soaked chicken baked with mushrooms, a salad of lettuce, dressing and shrimp. French bread, hot from the oven, accompanied this. For dessert Amelia prepared sugar-coated crepes. Sebastien brought them to the table, poured a pony of brandy over them, and ignited them with a flourish.

When Sebastien had served their coffee and withdrawn from the dining room, Suzanne took a deep breath and turned to Gilbert.

"I had a letter this morning, Uncle Gilbert," she said gravely. "From the college at Princeton. They wrote me that there has never been a Charles Duprée registered at their school."

Gilbert's face was drained of color. Mme. Mauriac's hand was unsteady as she lifted her cup to her mouth.

"Suzanne, I'm sorry," Gilbert said unhappily.

"Uncle Gilbert, why?" Suzanne asked earnestly. "Why can't I know about Maman and Papa? What are you hiding from me?"

"Suzanne, your mother and father were two admirable people. I had the deepest affection for them." Gilbert was struggling to retain his composure. "Their deaths were a terrible shock to me."

"Who were they?" Suzanne persisted. Why wouldn't Uncle Gilbert look at her?

"Gilbert, it's time Suzanne knew the truth," Mme. Mauriac said with gentle insistence. "Your father, Suzanne, was a talented but poor sculptor who lived in New Orleans. I adored him. Your mother was a lovely young Irish girl whose parents refused to allow their only child to marry a man they felt was incapable of steady support. I met her only once, when Charles brought her here to meet me. Not long after that they ran off together to Paris."

"But where did all the money come from?" Suzanne was bewildered.

"Charles acquired a very rich patroness. She settled much money on him. He arranged for Gilbert to invest most of it. When your parents died on a ship crossing the English Channel, Gilbert was notified by a Paris attorney. He went to Paris to arrange for your upbringing at the Convent."

"My grandparents," Suzanne pinpointed, her heart pounding. "They lived in New Orleans?"

"Yes. They've since died. I'm sorry, Suzanne," Gilbert said somberly. "I thought I was doing the best thing to tell you that Charles and I had attended college together. I don't know why I said they had lived in Savannah," he apologized.

"Thank you for telling me," Suzanne said quietly.

But she did not believe one word of what Mme. Mauriac and Uncle Gilbert had just told her.

Suzanne fought to conceal her depression at this latest failure to fulfill the vow she had made in the Cathedral of Notre-Dame. And she had failed as a wife on her wedding night, she taunted herself. Perhaps she should have remained at the Convent as Mère Angélique had wished.

A rainy afternoon three days later she confided to Phillip the contents of the letter from Princeton, along with what the Mauriacs had told her later that day.

"I suspect the Mauriacs are trying to be discreet," Phillip said seriously. "They told you your father and mother ran away to Paris together when her parents objected to a marriage. They may be concerned that a marriage never took place."

Suzanne stared at him in shock. She had never considered this. No! She would not believe that! But did Keith suspect this? Jane? No, he would not have married her.

"No, Phillip," she said shakily. "I can't believe that."

"No matter," Phillip dismissed it. "You're a member of the Savage family now."

"Phillip, I have to know about my mother and father," she insisted urgently. "You've had your father most of your life. You know so much about your mother. You told me you have a painting of her in your room. You can feel close to her."

"My mother should not have died." Phillip's eyes smoldered. "It should not have happened that way. Excuse me," he said abruptly. "I'm going for a walk."

"In the rain, Phillip?" Suzanne objected, but he was already striding from the room.

Suzanne was at the piano playing Chopin, daring to do this because she was alone in the house except for the servants, when Arthur knocked lightly and walked into the room.

"Miss Suzanne, the boy from the Andrews' place is here with invitations," he said politely, and instantly Suzanne remembered Clara's words as she walked with her mother and sister down the steps from the gallery the afternoon of their visit here. "He wants you to pick out one for the family, please ma'am." Arthur approached to extend a silver basket laden with envelopes.

"Thank you, Arthur." Belatedly she realized that neither the Andrews' servant nor Arthur could read.

She searched among the envelopes, found one addressed to "Mr. and Mrs. Keith Savage, Miss Jane Savage, Mr. Phillip Savage."

"I have it here, Arthur," she said with a smile. "Thank you."

The Andrews were entertaining at a ball ten days hence. Her heart hammered at the prospect of arriving at their home in Keith's company. Did the whole parish share their belief about Keith's marriage to her?

Suzanne tried to suppress a yawn. She was tired from the parade of nights when she lay sleepless until dawn, and the dreary weather was oppressive. With the invitation in hand she went upstairs to her room. She slept until Patrice woke her to go downstairs to dinner.

Not until after dinner, when the family had taken their usual places in the drawing room did Suzanne remember the invitation to the ball at the Andrews' plantation.

"We've been invited to a ball at the Andrews' house," she announced with self-conscious vivacity. Jane immediately lowered her book. Neither Keith nor Phillip appeared to have heard her.

"I'll send them our regrets." Jane frowned slightly, as though even the invitation was an imposition.

"It might be interesting to go," Suzanne demurred, her eyes charmingly guileless though she was inwardly determined not to be governed by Jane's decision.

"I'll send my regrets," Jane corrected herself, her eyes suddenly appraising Suzanne.

"Keith, would you like to go the Andrews' ball?" Suzanne pursued. "Keith — "

"Oh, I'm sorry," he apologized. "What were you saying?"

With an air of anticipation she reported the invitation.

"Mr. Andrews is running for alderman in the spring, isn't he? Wouldn't you enjoy hearing him express his views?"

"I don't always agree with Mr. Andrews' views," Keith said drily, "but I would like to hear where he stands. I imagine the ball is part of his campaign strategy."

"They'll expect us to invite them here," Jane reminded agitatedly.

"Perhaps it's time we started entertaining," Keith said thoughtfully. "I can think of a few people I'd enjoy seeing at Savage Oaks. Like Senator Slidell and his wife, and Senator Benjamin."

Suzanne lowered her eyes. Jane was furious with her.

"I'll go to the Andrews' ball with you," Phillip

said casually, putting down his newspaper. "Why not?" He shrugged cynically. "These are not exactly scintillating evenings at Savage Oaks."

"You could go hack to school," Jane shot back.

"We can't afford it," Phillip rejected. "Papa was breaking his back to keep me there. That's why Keith didn't go to Yale for his law studies."

"We can afford it," Jane insisted, her eyes holding his.

A coldness crept over Suzanne. They could afford to send Phillip back to college because of the marriage settlement.

"Aren't you forgetting, Jane?" he asked sarcastically, switching tactics. "They threw me out of Princeton."

"Other schools will accept you," Jane pushed.

"Sorry." Phillip's voice was truculent. "I don't want to go back to college."

Jane opened her mouth to retort, then abandoned this. She was at a loss to handle Phillip. Suzanne sympathized. He seemed so lost sometimes, so troubled. He blamed his mother for dying when he was a baby, she recalled. In some ways he was still a small, hurt boy.

Tonight Suzanne was the first to leave the drawing room. The invitation to the Andrews' ball had brought again into glaring focus the reason behind Keith's ardent courtship. In her room she prepared for bed, knowing she faced another sleepless night

In nightdress and peignoir designed to please her bridegroom, Suzanne stood at a window gazing down at the wide, turbulent Mississippi. She spied Phillip's slender figure striding purposefully towards the levee, and quickly averted her eyes. A few moments later she heard Jane come upstairs and go into her room.

How much longer could she play in this charade? There were beautiful moments when Keith looked at her and she could almost believe that he loved her. But they were such fleeting moments.

She left the window, pulled the slipper chair close to the fireplace, and sat down. She looked into the fireplace without seeing the log smoldering in the grate. A door closed down the hall. Suzanne stiffened. Keith had gone to his room.

She would not stay here at Savage Oaks! She would live at Tintagel. She must go to Keith now and tell him, she commanded herself defiantly. She went to the armoire, pulled out the demure dressing gown from her Convent wardrobe. With trembling hands she discarded her bridal peignoir for the schoolgirl dressing gown, and left her room.

She walked down the night-shadowed hall to Keith's door. She lifted a fist to knock, hesitated an instant, then rapped sharply.

"Yes?" Keith sounded distracted.

"Suzanne — " Why was she trembling this way?

Keith pulled the door open.

"Come in, Suzanne." He tried to conceal his astonishment at her presence.

"Keith, I'll only be a moment, but there's

something I have to say." She must keep her voice even. She must not let Keith know how deeply he had hurt her.

"What's happened?"

"Keith, I know why you married me." Her anguished eyes dared him to deny this. "You married me to save Savage Oaks."

"Who told you this?" he demanded furiously. "I'll horsewhip him!"

"It doesn't matter who told me. Keith, why did you play games with me?"

"I've felt guilty every moment," he acknowledged miserably. "But let me make it up to you, Suzanne. Everything is different now."

"Yes, everything is different." Suzanne lifted her head with pride. "I'm leaving Savage Oaks. I'll remain your wife in name. I'll go with you to the Andrews' ball. But I'm going to live at Tintagel."

"Suzanne, no!" Keith protested. "I don't want you to leave!"

"Why?" she challenged. "Because your friends may discover I'm living at Tintagel and talk about it? Will that disgrace the Savages?"

"Suzanne, Savage Oaks has been different since you've come here. I don't want you to leave. I'm discovering you're a very special person, Suzanne." He reached to draw her to him.

"I don't believe you," Suzanne disputed. How could she think clearly when Keith held her this way? "You're trying to save face before your friends."

"Suzanne, I wanted to kill that overseer for touching you. I couldn't forget him for days. I've never felt this way about anyone. Suzanne, I love you. I've tried to deny it, but why should I?"

His mouth reached for hers. His arms folded her against him. There was no pretense tonight, she thought, while tears stung her eyes. Oh, Keith, Keith!

With exquisite tenderness he lifted her off her feet and carried her to the bed. In the golden glow of the lamplight he swept aside her peignoir, allowed one hand to touch her breasts.

"You're beautiful," he murmured. "And bright and sweet and utterly desirable."

"Keith, I love you," she whispered.

She smiled expectantly while he pulled away her nightdress, not caring that he had not turned down the lamp. Rejoicing in his passion. How handsome he was, she thought with pride as he stood beside the bed and thrust aside his clothes.

And then he lay with her, warm and gentle and knowing. She whimpered softly as he brought himself to her. Her arms tightened at his shoulders. Tonight, she told herself exultantly, was her wedding night.

Fourteen

Early morning sun filtered in through the drapes to lie in ribbons of gold across the bed. Keith frowned against the intrusion, slowly opened his eyes. Instantly he was conscious of Suzanne's warmth beside him. He lifted himself on one elbow to look at the loveliness of her face in sleep. He was conscious of a stirring of passion in him, was tempted to wake her so that they might make love again.

No, he exhorted himself with a surge of unfamiliar tenderness. Let her sleep. He reached with one hand to brush the tawny fan of silken hair that spread about the pillow. Suzanne was a revelation to him. He had never known any girl like her.

How many girls had he known, he mocked himself? All the years he was growing up, strangers rarely came to Savage Oaks. Jane had rejected all efforts to include the Savages in the parish socializing. At military school and later at Princeton he had lived in a totally male word, except for those occasions when Jacques had bullied him into going to Philadelphia or to New York, where they had defiantly visited the brothels.

In Washington City he had been at first in awe of the hordes of pretty, stylishly turned out young ladies who had flocked to the dinners, dances, receptions and balls that were endless. And then he had discovered that most of them viewed him as favorable husband fodder, and he had cautiously retreated. At Supreme Court parties he occasionally met a young lady whose conversation was intelligent and challenging, but unfortunately her appearance was such that she was probably doomed to be forever a maiden aunt.

His last few months in Washington City there had been the very pretty, very willing maid at the Willard Hotel. Of her own volition she came regularly to his tiny apartment. It was tacitly agreed that there was to be no social exchange between them. Their regular relationship in his hotel bed had been mutually, overwhelmingly satisfying. By now she was, no doubt, married to the waiter at Gautier's, with whom she demurely attended the concerts of the Marine Band on the White House grounds once each week.

Keith smiled faintly when he saw the basin of still-warm water on his washstand. George had come in and diplomatically left. Keith washed and dressed quickly, pleasantly conscious of Suzanne's presence in his bed.

When he came down to breakfast he found Jane already in the dining room. She appeared tired, strained. Suzanne's presence in the house upset her. She would learn to accept Suzanne, he promised himself optimistically as he sat at the table.

"Reagan sent a man to the house," Jane said briskly. "He's having trouble with one of the plows. I told him you would be in the fields directly after breakfast." Keith pushed back his chair in irritation. This was not the time of year for the plows to break down. "Keith, eat your breakfast first," she insisted.

"All right," he capitulated with an unexpected smile. Jane enjoyed this quiet time with him each morning. He remembered his mother, but more clearly he remembered Jane at his bedside through childhood illnesses. Why had Papa allowed her to sacrifice herself for them? She had been a beautiful girl. She should have married.

Leaving the house, he forced himself to face the situation with Manon. He would have to send her away. It had been a mistake to bring her here. It had been a rebellious decision because Mauriac had forced him into the marriage. How could he have known then what Suzanne would come to mean to him?

He dreaded the confrontation with Manon. She was sure to cry and to reproach him dramatically. He would give her money to live on until she was settled. That was the usual arrangement. She would have little difficulty in finding a replacement. At worst she could go back to the Mansion House. Yellowbird Shaw was sure to

238

welcome back one of her best girls.

In the fields he found Reagan working over an idle plow. Reagan gazed up exasperated as Keith approached.

"I'm sorry, Mr. Keith. This one's had its day. No way we'll use it again."

"We knew it was coming, Reagan," Keith said with a calmness he would not have felt six months ago. "I'll have to go in town and shop around. And fast," he conceded. "We don't want to hold up the planting." By the time the cane was in, they should put in vegetables for the hands. A lot of idle acres at Tintagel could be utilized for this.

"Mr. Keith, I heard about some plows being up for sale at the Maire plantation. You know the place. It's about two hours up-river." Keith squinted in thought, then nodded in recall. "You might pick up one at a good price."

"I'll go up today," Keith promised. "But first I want to see how the cuttings are coming in."

An hour later Keith returned to the house. He would go to the cottage and talk to Manon when he got back from the Maire plantation. She ought not be too upset, he thought guiltily. She knew these arrangements were transient. Dozens of men had shared her favors.

Heading for the library to take money from the safe, Keith heard Suzanne and Phillip talking over breakfast in the family dining room. With a sudden compulsion to see Suzanne, he detoured into the room.

Suzanne, radiant in a dark brown riding dress, gazed up at him with an effervescent smile. Her eyes glowed with a recall that made him involuntarily tense his thighs. If Phillip were not here, he would take Suzanne by the hand and up to his room again. How right Gilbert Mauriac had been when he said Suzanne would be the perfect wife. Not only beautiful, intelligent, and understanding, but passionate as well. Manon was a beautiful body for an occasional hour. Suzanne was a wife to share every moment of his life.

"Have you had breakfast, Keith?" Suzanne's voice had a special lilt this morning.

"Over an hour ago. But I'll join you with more coffee."

He sat at the head of the table, resenting the separation between Suzanne and himself. He watched while she poured coffee for him, passed it to him via Phillip.

"You look beautiful this morning." His eyes held hers in a private exchange.

"I feel wonderful." Her voice was a caress.

"I have to make a trip up-river. A plow broke down this morning. Reagan knows of one for sale at the Maire plantation."

"You'll be back for dinner?" she asked expectantly.

"I'll make sure I am." Phillip was watching them oddly. Suzanne and he were close. She had never talked to Phillip about the inactivity of their marriage, had she? No, he dismissed this guiltily. Not Suzanne. And that was past. No bridegroom could be more avid than he to claim his bride.

"Tell Clarissa I'll be expecting a masterpiece of a dinner tonight." Again his eyes were in secret communication with hers. Phillip, aware of something new between Suzanne and Keith, was annoyed.

"I'll check on the menu myself," she promised. Jane gave Clarissa instructions each morning about what was to be served for dinner, but Suzanne had acquired the confidence to go out to the kitchen house and countermand this.

"I'd better go if I expect to be back for dinner." He pushed back his chair and rose to his feet. Hesitating a moment he walked to the end of the table to kiss Suzanne lightly on the mouth.

"I've been drinking enough coffee this morning to launch a battleship," Suzanne laughed as she poured herself yet another cup. Phillip was astonished by Keith's show of affection this morning. Phillip was discerning; he knew that Keith had made love to her last night. Did he guess that it was the first time since their wedding night, all those weeks ago? No matter, she thought with exhilaration. A miracle had come to Savage Oaks. Keith loved her.

"Are you going riding this morning?" Phillip asked.

"I go riding every morning. I have since I was thirteen." Why didn't she hear from Cecile and Mère Angélique, she wondered with fresh impatience? Twice a week Edward went into New Orleans to the post office to pick up their mail, and each time she hoped there would be letters for her from France.

"I'll go with you this morning," he offered impulsively. "If you don't mind company."

"I'd love it," she said warmly.

"I'll change and be back downstairs in ten minutes." All at once he radiated charm again. "Wait for me."

Suzanne went out to the kitchen house to confer with Clarissa about dinner.

"Miss Jane tol' me what I was to fix," Clarissa said uneasily.

"Mr. Keith would like something special tonight," Suzanne said coaxingly. "Ask Miss Jane if there's any venison," she added diplomatically, "and make one of your wonderful sweet potato pies. He particularly likes that."

"Yes'um," Clarissa agreed reluctantly. She would check first with Jane.

Suzanne walked out to the gallery to wait for Phillip. This morning she saw Savage Oaks with new vision as she stood in the sunlight, enjoying the spill of warmth about her. This afternoon, she decided with a surge of high spirits, she would ride over and talk with those children she had seen when she was going into New Orleans several days ago. It disturbed her that they were not in school.

Walking with Phillip to the stable she confided in him the plan that had been forming in her mind.

"I'd love to teach those children, Phillip. I'm sure I could," she pursued enthusiastically.

"Those white trash families?" Phillip asked with astonishment. "Their parents don't care about their children getting an education."

"*I* care," Suzanne shot back, her eyes flashing. "I'd like to open a classroom at Tintagel and teach them for two or three hours every morning."

"Jane and Mrs. Cantrell would love that," Phillip said derisively.

"Phillip, it doesn't concern either Jane or Mrs. Cantrell," she said spiritedly. "I'll discuss it tonight with Keith; and if he agrees, then I'll do it." She would not be defiant with Jane, but neither would she be cowed.

"First talk to the parents," Phillip cautioned. "What makes you think they'll send their children to you?"

"I'll talk to them," Suzanne said confidently. The prospect of this school activity was exciting.

Abram brought out their horses and they mounted them. Suzanne spoke affectionately to Othello for a few moments, then turned to Phillip.

"Let's ride down to the shack at the turn in the road," she said persuasively. "I'll feel better talking to them if you're with me."

"I wanted to show you something special in the woods." His eyes were strangely bright. "Later we'll go and talk to them."

"Now, Phillip," Suzanne insisted. "Of course, it's just an idea. They'll have to understand I must talk to Keith about it if they agree."

"All right," Phillip accepted reluctantly. "But you must see this place." His face was flushed. Was he coming down with a fever, Suzanne wondered uneasily. "Promise?"

"I promise," she said seriously. Sometimes he seemed so young. Younger than she.

The rode in silence, each engrossed in private thoughts, until they approached the turn in the road. The children played with a litter of very young kittens this morning. They looked up with wary smiles when Suzanne and Phillip dismounted and tied their horses to nearby trees.

"Phillip, don't look so annoyed," Suzanne exhorted under her breath as they approached the children.

At first the children hung their heads and were reluctant to talk. Phillip, surprising Suzanne, produced a handful of hard candies; and all at once they were communicative. No, they never went to school, they said solemnly, astonished that Suzanne might think they had.

A shabbily dressed sun-bronzed man and a small, gaunt woman who looked old beyond her years deserted the fields behind the house and suspiciously approached Suzanne and Phillip. Swiftly, exuding friendliness, Suzanne explained that she might possibly be able to open a classroom at Tintagel to teach their children and those of their neighbors.

"I'll have to talk to my husband about it first," she said ingratiatingly, "but I would dearly love to have a classroom. It would give me something to do. The children tell me they don't go to school."

"Why should they?" the man demanded truculently. "What's book-larnin' gonna do for 'em?"

"It'll give them a chance to better their lives," Suzanne said calmly. "You want that for them, don't you?" The woman glanced swiftly at her husband.

"We couldn't send 'em to school down in New Orleans," he said defensively. "It's too fur. Besides, we don't want no charity."

"The public school system in New Orleans is not a charity organization," Suzanne said firmly.

"Most places 'tis," the children's mother said defiantly. "Most anywhere in the South you gotta stand up and say you're too poor to pay. We got too much pride for that."

"Not in Louisiana," Suzanne insisted. "But I know the schools are too far away," she continued with a conciliatory smile. "And I would so enjoy teaching the children if you'll let me. Provided my husband will agree." The children were standing about them, wide-eyed and solemn.

Their father frowned, then looked at his wife. Suzanne was touched by the hope she saw in the woman's eyes. She knew the future that awaited her children. Each generation led a life of drudgery. They raised corn and sweet potatoes and a little cotton. They depended on patent medicines rather than doctors. Here was a faint hope that their children's lives might be better.

"Well, I reckon we'll let 'em," their father consented. "Since you say you'll like to do it. But it ain't charity."

"It's not charity," Suzanne confirmed. "I'll come back here tomorrow and talk to you about it." Joy welled in her. Surely Keith would not object to her running her classroom at Tintagel.

Suzanne and Phillip rode back to Savage Oaks, cutting into the woods through a break in the whitewashed fences. Phillip seemed in a brighter mood. He told Suzanne about the efforts on the part of Southern educators to expurgate the school books, most of which were written by Northerners.

"The bias is unbelievable, Suzanne. Educated in France the way you were, you couldn't know this. But take the geography books," he said contemptuously. "They devote two full pages to Connecticut onions and broomcorn and no more than ten lines to Louisiana and sugar. And antislavery sentiments are written right through some of the histories. I remember reading Wayland's *Moral Science* in college — you never saw anything so biased."

"Phillip, where are we going?" she asked curiously when he guided her through a pecan grove so thick with trees they could do no more than walk the horses.

"I'm going to show you one of Savage Oaks' secrets," he said with an ironic smile.

"Whatever is it?" Suzanne pressed. She remembered the stranger's grave down near the levee just beyond the house, and questions hovered on her lips.

"You'll see in a few minutes," Phillip soothed. "It's far from the bridle path. Nobody ever goes there." There was a peculiar excitement in his voice. "A cottage Papa built a year after my mother died. He swore he would never marry again. He brought his quadroon mistresses to live there."

"How sad that he never married again," Suzanne said compassionately.

"I would have hated him if he had!" Phillip said intensely. "I don't mind that he took himself mistresses. He filled the cottage with fine antiques and priceless wall hangings and exquisite porcelain. He needed that refuge, the way he fought year after year to keep Savage Oaks afloat. To the small farmers and the poor whites, we're rich planters," he said derisively. "We have over four hundred slaves. But they forget how many are too young or too old or too sick or too lazy to work. We have to support them all."

Suzanne forced herself to remain silent. Would those same slaves that Phillip concerned himself about their supporting not prefer to be free and maintain themselves? Keith was uncomfortable with the slavery system. Unwarily he had revealed this when he talked with such dislike about Robay's slave pen and auction block so close to the Capitol grounds in Washington City.

She remembered the chills that had darted through her when, as a small girl in France, she had read the Declaration of Independence. *We hold these truths to be self-evident, that all men are created equal.* But those who interpreted the Declaration chose to close their eyes to black men and to all women.

For all the uproar the Abolitionists created, they ignored the prejudices against the blacks in the North, Suzanne recalled reading. In the Northern states black children were forced to go to black schools. Black people were not allowed into places of public amusement. Some states even prevented the immigration of free blacks into their territory.

"We turn off here," Phillip directed, indicating a narrow, beaten path. His hands, holding the reins, were trembling. "Nobody in the big house was supposed to know about the cottage. But I followed Papa there once when I was nine. After that I used to come often. I would stand close by and listen to the laughter inside and wish I could be part of it. Once, when there was no woman in the cottage for a few weeks, I went inside and stayed there all day. Jane thought I was fishing with Abram."

Suzanne inspected him anxiously. He was so distraught. The cottage brought back bad memories, she surmised; but he was taking her there to prove to her that they were friends.

Then, through the trees Suzanne could see a clearing. The horses took them closer. A low, white stuccoed cottage with a wrought-iron railed gallery came into view. What a charming cottage, Suzanne thought. Thorne Savage's retreat from the hard realities of running a sugar plantation.

All at once the cottage door flew open. A tall, beautiful, ivory-skinned girl walked onto the gallery.

"Lily Mae, bring me the *marrons glacés*," she called imperiously and instantly a very young black girl came into sight.

Frozen in the saddle, Suzanne felt dizzy with shock as her mind absorbed what she saw. The younger girl was the one who had come to the Christmas ball in the quarters and whispered to Keith. He had left the ball to come here Christmas night. He was following in his father's footsteps. *The beautiful ivory-skinned girl was Keith's quadroon mistress.*

Suzanne swerved Othello about and galloped off at a hazardous pace, Phillip in silent pursuit. At the stable she dismounted without a word to Abram and walked rapidly towards the house. Phillip dismounted and caught up with her.

"Suzanne, I didn't know," Phillip stammered agonizedly.

"I don't want to talk about it," Suzanne said, her voice held with perilous control. "You never took me to the cottage."

They walked to the house in strained silence, Suzanne fighting determinedly against tears. Keith would never touch her again. She would not share her husband with a quadroon mistress.

Fifteen

"Miss Suzanne, you ain't changed from your ridin' clothes and Elaine's already puttin' food on the table," Patrice scolded gently.

Suzanne turned over on her bed to face Patrice.

"I have a headache, Patrice," she fabricated. "Will you please tell Arthur that I won't be down for luncheon." She could not go downstairs and face Jane and Phillip. Keith, she remembered, had gone up to the Maire plantation to look at a plow. She never wanted to see him again, she thought with painful intensity. No, that was a lie. She loved Keith as she had never thought it possible to love any man.

"I'll bring you a tray." Patrice searched her face anxiously.

Suzanne managed a faint smile. "That'll be nice, Patrice."

While Patrice went downstairs Suzanne listlessly changed from her riding dress into a demure blue flannel dressing gown brought from the Convent. Why was she staying here? She ought to pack immediately and leave Savage Oaks forever. But not to see Keith every day, not to hear his voice, was inconceivable. What were the chains that held her here? Where was her will? Where was her pride?

In Europe, and probably here in the United States, many wives turned their backs when their husbands took mistresses. Cecile had talked quite calmly at regular intervals about the series of actresses of whom her father was enamored. Her mother accepted this. But she could not accept Keith's having a quadroon mistress.

How could she bring herself to leave, feeling the way she did about Keith? She would die away from here. She would stay. But her door would be locked to him. He would not touch her again until she knew that girl was gone. And that another would not replace her.

In a few minutes Patrice arrived with a tempting tray. Because of the maid's solicitude, Suzanne forced herself to eat a little and drink the strong coffee.

"Now you sleep, you hear?" Patrice said affectionately when she took the tray. "I'll come up and wake you when it's gettin' close to dinner time."

Suzanne spent the afternoon trying to read, haunted intermittently by visions of the girl on the gallery of the white stuccoed cottage. She listened subconsciously for the sounds that would tell her Keith had returned from his trip. She remembered the way he had kissed her goodbye this morning, and fresh agony welled in her. She was entrapped by her love for Keith.

Not until she was dressing for dinner, with Patrice pleased that she had chosen a particularly pretty frock, did she hear the sounds that told her Keith had returned. Her heart pounded as she anticipated, with mixed dread and elation, facing him at dinner. He must not know she had seen the secret cottage. She must pretend that nothing had happened in those hours he was away.

The others were already seated at the table when Suzanne arrived in the dining room. Keith's face lighted at the sight of her. Ignoring the thumping in her chest she smiled impersonally and seated herself at the table. Phillip seemed so miserable. He sat with shoulders hunched, his eyes on his plate.

"We're having a hammock of venison," Keith said in a convivial mood. Arthur was at the wine closet bringing out the Madeira.

"I know." She refused to meet his gaze. Jane's mouth was compressed with annoyance at her interfering in the dinner menu.

"When will the plow be here, Keith?" Jane asked. "You won't lose too much time in the fields?"

"We'll have it tomorrow," Keith told her. "Reagan will make up for the day we've lost."

"I was talking with that family that lives at the turn of the road." Suzanne's voice was tense.

"What on earth were you doing down there?"

Jane asked in astonishment.

"I saw the children playing there the day I went into New Orleans." *Don't let anybody know she was falling apart inside.* "I rode down there this morning." She compelled herself to look at Keith. "Keith, do you know those children have never been to school?"

"What would they do with education?" Jane asked contemptuously. "They're lazy, dirty, and ignorant. They've been living on that tiny piece of land for three generations, doing nothing about improving it."

"Teaching their children to read and write might help them to do it," Suzanne said heatedly. "Keith, I'd like to set up a room at Tintagel to teach them each morning. I'm sure I could." She was breathless with the effort to declare her plans.

"Suzanne, how can you consider such a thing?" Jane was outraged. "How could you bring those dirty children into Tintagel?"

"They'll come to school clean," Suzanne said firmly. "I'll teach them that."

"It's out of the question," Jane snapped.

Suzanne stared at her. Jane could not order her around this way! But before she could retort, Keith intervened.

"Jane, one room at Tintagel could be set aside for a classroom." His eyes pleaded for indulgence. "Suzanne might enjoy teaching and it would give her something to occupy her time."

"I want the classroom very much." She could

just move to Tintagel and set up the school herself. Yet she knew she wished for Keith's approval. Not Jane's. Keith's.

"How can I help, Suzanne?" Keith was uncomfortable before Jane's displeasure.

"I can handle everything," Suzanne said crisply. "I'll go into New Orleans to Morgan's to buy some textbooks. I'll ask Mrs. Cantrell to have a room cleared for me. We'll need only a large table and some chairs." She turned to Jane with a conciliatory smile. "Nothing will be damaged." Tintagel was hers, she railed inwardly. Why must she be apologetic?

"I'll go into New Orleans with you tomorrow," Keith offered.

"You're too busy with the planting," Suzanne demurred. "I can go alone." Keith was approving the schoolroom because it would keep her busy, she tortured herself. She would be less likely to discover the cottage at the edge of the property.

"I'll take you into New Orleans, Suzanne." All at once Phillip was in a congenial mood. "We'll go in the morning."

After dinner Phillip went directly upstairs to his room. Jane and Suzanne retired to the drawing room, Keith excusing himself to go to the library.

"Reagan asked me to check on some equipment I have on order," he apologized.

Was Keith going to use this as an excuse to disappear from the house in a little while? Suzanne sat stiffly in her chair, pretending to be engrossed

254

in her book, listening for sounds from the library. All at once there was a burst of music. Keith was at the piano.

Suzanne went to her room while Keith continued to play. She prepared for the night, dismissed Patrice. For the second time since her arrival at Savage Oaks, she locked her bedroom door. She pulled up the slipper chair before the fire Patrice had started earlier and sat down to read.

The piano music stopped. Suzanne laid aside her book and she waited for sounds in the hall. Keith and Jane were coming up the stairs, discussing repairs Jane thought were necessary in the quarters. Now there was money for that, Suzanne tormented herself.

Jane and Keith went to their respective rooms. Suzanne left her chair to stand before the fire. She was sure Keith would come to her. She waited, assaulted by memories of last night. From heaven she had been thrust into hell. She closed her eyes, willing herself not to think of Keith with that girl.

She clenched her teeth at the light knock, the turning of her doorknob. Keith thought she would be expecting him.

"Suzanne," he called softly and knocked again.

She stood unmoving, fighting tears. She would not cry. *She would not.* Then she heard Keith's retreating footsteps, heard the door to his room open and shut. He would not be welcomed in her bed, she reiterated her vow. Not until she knew the cottage in the woods was unoccupied and that Keith planned no replacement.

When she came downstairs the next morning she found Phillip waiting at the breakfast table for her. He greeted her cheerfully, apparently anticipating their trip into New Orleans; but at unguarded moments she sensed his preoccupation with what happened yesterday. He was chastising himself for having taken her to the cottage. But how could he have known what they would find?

"You'll be able to buy everything at Morgan's," he promised. "They're sure to have those *Peter Parley* readers that are adapted for the Southern trade. And you'll want the Webster's Spellers and arithmetic books." He hesitated. "Did Keith give you money for them?"

"I have my own," she explained with satisfaction. Not much but it would be sufficient. "From the dividend check I cashed just before Christmas."

After breakfast they went out to the gallery to wait for the carriage. Within minutes, Lewis pulled up before the house. Phillip helped her gently into the carriage. He knew she was still distraught. Still, it was difficult for her to feel at ease with him.

When they reached the small shack at the turn in the road, Suzanne impulsively ordered Lewis to stop for a few moments. She greeted the children affectionately and told them their school would begin in a few days. When the carriage moved on again, she felt less desolate.

Phillip began to talk lengthily about the schools Keith and he had attended.

"I don't know how Keith liked Princeton so much." His eyes were moody as he reminisced. "The damnable cold up there!" He shivered expressively. "And we went there with not enough mathematics behind us. I had to be tutored. God, no school puts so much importance on mathematics! Not even West Point. And the damnable rules! A student in my dormitory was given two demerits for returning from vacation with a beard."

Suzanne listened with a polite show of interest, but she was remembering Keith's light knock on her door last night, his voice calling her. She had lain awake for hours, torturing herself in the belief that she was sending him to the cottage. But he had not gone there.

She went with Phillip to Morgan's, pretending to enjoy this excursion; but at intervals she looked up to see Phillip's eyes focused unhappily on her. As she waited for a clerk to find a sufficient number of the blue-backed Webster Spellers to suit her purpose, she overheard a pair of gentlemen talking about a lecture series to be offered at Odd Fellows' Hall next month. William Makepeace Thackeray was coming here to New Orleans. How she would adore to go to the lecture with Keith if only the memory of yesterday morning were not burnt into her brain.

"Are you taking me out to luncheon?" Phillip

asked ingratiatingly when they emerged from Exchange Alley. "I would take you," he apologized, "but I have no funds."

"I'll take you," Suzanne laughed. She was grateful for Phillip's friendship. And she knew that Jane kept him in a straitened financial situation, hoping he would capitulate and return to college.

Phillip escorted her to a restaurant where the Savages were well known. Grandly Phillip introduced her as his new sister-in-law, and the proprietor was effusive in his attentions. As they ate the superb luncheon served to them, Phillip talked about the fine parties held at Savage Oaks before he was born, the important Louisianans who had attended them.

"We can have parties again," Suzanne said in a burst of enthusiasm, and suddenly she flinched. She recoiled from the image of herself in the mold of Cecile's mother, the Comtesse, who gave fantastic parties while her husband was entertained by one of his charming actresses. No, that was not for her.

"You haven't changed your mind about going to the Andrews' ball?" Phillip asked seriously.

"No, why should I?" She struggled to retain her convivial air. "I'll probably need a ball gown." She was painfully unhappy that Phillip knew about the girl in the cottage. Who else knew?

"You don't have much time," Phillip laughed.

"Mme. Mauriac's seamstress has a shop on

Chartres Street." She frowned. "I don't know the address."

"We'll find it," Phillip said ebulliently. "And I'll help you choose the material. Even Jane admits I'm good at that," he said ironically.

They left the restaurant and sought out the shop on Chartres Street. Phillip persuaded the seamstress to delay her other clients in favor of Suzanne. He insisted Suzanne choose an expensive beige brocade imported from Lyons with a design woven into the fabric that had been copied from a rare Chinese shawl.

"Keith can afford to buy you a fine ball gown," he said coolly.

With arrangements about the fitting scheduled, Suzanne and Phillip returned to the carriage. Phillip talked divertingly all the way back to Savage Oaks. She was relieved that little was required of her.

At dinner she dutifully reported her day's activities to Keith. He sat across the table from her, seemingly intrigued by her every word. If Phillip had not taken her to the cottage, she would be rapturous at his attentions.

Keith must have convinced himself that she was asleep when he came to her room last night. But soon enough he would realize the door was locked to him. How long would it be before he realized she was too proud to share him?

"When will you start the school?" Keith asked with lively interest.

"I'm going over to talk to Mrs. Cantrell tomorrow. I hope to have the children come the following day."

"It's unfortunate that we don't have public schools to teach these country children," Keith said seriously. "There are public schools in New Orleans, of course."

"Louisiana has an excellent public school system on paper," Phillip emphasized with the faint air of superiority he sometimes adopted, Suzanne suspected, to conceal his true emotions. "But the laws are not being carried out."

"More schools just mean more taxes," Jane said fretfully. "We pay enough now."

"Jefferson introduced a bill in the Virginia Legislature way back in 1779 that would provide public education for all children for three years. Then the brighter children would be chosen to go on to another school, and from these," Keith pursued, "the best would be chosen to study at the College of William and Mary at public expense. He hoped to bring forward the best minds of the country from all classes to be educated to lead the nation. The bill didn't pass," he said wryly.

"Terribly idealistic," Phillip shrugged. "But so impractical." His eyes were stormy. "Almost like trying to teach the slaves to read."

"Was the new plow delivered, Keith?" Jane redirected the conversation.

Suzanne made a pretense of eating. She would allow no one to be aware of her distraught state. She had earned a small victory with the classroom. This would help her to survive at Savage Oaks.

Keith was taken aback when she went up to her room immediately after dinner. But tonight she could not endure to sit in the drawing room, knowing what she knew.

She prepared for bed early and dismissed Patrice. She turned down the lamp, knowing no ribbon of light would show beneath her door if Keith should come to her room.

He came. He knocked lightly. And then he went back to his own room.

Commanding herself not to think about Keith's thwarted efforts to come to her last night, Suzanne rode over to Tintagel to talk with Mrs. Cantrell about setting up a room for her class. Mrs. Cantrell was aghast.

"A classroom in this house for those children?" She stared at Suzanne in disbelief.

"Any room will do, Mrs. Cantrell," she said cajolingly. "You can have it cleared of all furnishings. Just have someone bring in a large study table and some chairs. The children won't break anything," she promised.

Unpredictably Mrs. Cantrell's face softened.

"Mr. Noah would rather have liked that, I suspect. Every Christmas, right up to the time he died, he always had Merlin shop presents for those children and take them down to them on Christmas morning. And Mr. Adrian was forever keeping candies in his pockets to give to the little ones." Her eyes misted in recall.

The following morning Suzanne launched her classroom. The children arrived, at first abashed; but they warmed quickly before her friendliness. Perceval slumped on the floor of the classroom, happy for their presence. Midmorning Mrs. Cantrell came into the room with a tray of cookies and a pitcher of milk. A warmth suffused Suzanne. She was helping the children, but they were helping her.

She returned from Tintagel to find the seamstress had arrived early from New Orleans for the fitting on her gown. Delivery was promised for the morning of the Andrews' ball. If there were any adjustments needed, she would make them immediately.

The days moved past. Keith made only one more effort to come to her. Sick with the knowledge of this breach between them, she ignored the puzzled glances he bestowed on her at regular intervals. He was not a stupid man. Let him figure out for himself why her door was locked to him.

Dressing for the Andrews' ball, she wished she had not committed herself to attend. Keith's bride would be the prize exhibit. She recoiled from the necessity to be cordial to Clara and Rose Andrews and their mother.

In the carriage, Phillip coaxed Suzanne to talk about her activities in the classroom. Keith seemed preoccupied. Only when they approached the Andrews' plantation did he join the conversation to tell her that the Andrews' home had been in the family almost a hundred years.

The entire lower floor of the stately Georgian mansion was brightly lighted. The sound of music and laughter greeted them as they left their carriage to walk up the steps to the gallery. Too vividly Suzanne recalled Clara Andrews' triumphant declaration, which she had not been meant to hear. *"Mama, it's just like we figured. He married her for her money."*

As a liveried servant opened the door, Suzanne managed a dazzling smile. Everyone at the Andrews' ball must be convinced that Keith and she were most happily married.

Their host, a portly man with appraising hazel eyes, welcomed them in the huge, ornately furnished foyer. He paid extravagant homage to Suzanne's loveliness, then with her on his arm walked into the multichandeliered ballroom. With the air of an ambassador at court he introduced Suzanne to an endless array of ladies, all of whom were beautifully polite because good manners demanded this of them; but Suzanne suspected that Clara and Rose and their mother had gossiped about her with every lady present. She was relieved when Keith appeared at her side again.

As Keith predicted, the conversation at supper became largely political. Suzanne suspected that Mr. Andrews was a shrewd and ruthless politician. Tonight national politics gave way to the imminent local elections.

"We can't have the violence and bloodshed at the polls that we had last fall," Andrews said righteously. "Despite the new voter registration laws, I'm concerned about what's going to happen."

"It's difficult to elect a mayor as colorless as Mr. Elmore," Keith said bluntly.

Suzanne listened earnestly, as the conversation grew more heated, although the ladies were completely ignoring the political talk to gossip among themselves. She was irritated when, after supper, the ladies pointedly withdrew to leave the men to talk politics in male solitude. What a dull world among the ladies! If there would be parties at Savage Oaks, she vowed she would circumvent this separation of the sexes.

Driving back to Savage Oaks, Keith seemed exhilarated by the evening's socializing, though his respect for Andrews was low.

"William Wirt said he hated politics, that he could never be a party man," Keith said thoughtfully. "He had a good conscience and he doubted the practicality of a politician possessing such an attribute."

"But he did become a politician," Suzanne reminded. "And a statesman." Keith was looking at her in that disconcerting way of his again. "Wasn't he our Attorney General at one time?"

"Yes, he was," Keith said quietly. "For both Monroe and J. Q. Adams. And a fine one."

Now Keith seemed to withdraw into himself. Phillip, who had been openly pursued by several young ladies, broke the silence that fell between them to report amusingly on some of his conquests, none of which he took seriously. At last they turned into the driveway at Savage Oaks and rode up towards the house, darkened except for the night sconces burning on the stairs.

Suzanne said goodnight to Keith and Phillip and went up to her room, where Patrice waited to help her out of her gown. Tonight she kept Patrice with her far longer than usual. If Keith knocked on the door tonight, she doubted that she had the will to refuse him. But tonight Keith did not come to her door.

At the conclusion of her third week of teaching, Suzanne returned to Savage Oaks to discover that two letters and two packages had arrived for her from France. One was from Cecile, who seemed to have settled into marriage with none of the rebellion Suzanne had expected. Already she was *enceinte* and both her husband and she were hoping this first child would be a son.

Cecile was intrigued by the swiftness with which Suzanne had entered into marriage and clamored for details. Her wedding gift was an exquisite Louis XV ormolu clock that combined the work of the great Paris clock-master Étienne LeNoir with delicate Chantilly porcelain.

Mère Angélique, no doubt aware that this was a marriage arranged by Uncle Gilbert, expressed her best wishes. She sent Suzanne and Keith a

Queen Anne taper stick that Suzanne remembered from Mère Angélique's apartment. The taper stick had been in her family for generations. Tears filled Suzanne's eyes as she fondled the octangle silver form. It was as if Mère Angélique had sent her part of herself.

After dinner, in the presence of Jane and Phillip, because she made a point of never being alone with Keith, she told him about the gifts they had received. She was polite, sweet, but impersonal. He seemed bewildered by her attitude. *When was he going to understand?*

Suzanne and Jane went up to their rooms. Phillip left the house with some vague remark about needing fresh air. Keith discarded the book by Benjamin Disraeli, which Senator Benjamin had sent to him because he knew Keith's admiration for the British statesman. He had read hardly a word in the last hour.

What had happened to Suzanne? Yes, he had married her to save Savage Oaks; but surely she knew after that night in his room how deeply he loved her! Yet each time he went to her, she ignored his presence at the door.

Was it because she was fearful of their having a child so early in marriage? She didn't *have* to have a child. Any girl at the Mansion House could tell her that, he thought with bitter humor. Stubbornly she gave him no chance to talk to her.

He rose restlessly to his feet. He had delayed in

266

sending Manon away because he cowardly shied from an ugly scene. Perhaps it was just as well that he had not sent her away. His wife refused him entrance to her bedroom. Manon would receive him with pleasure.

Suzanne knew that the tall, ivory-skinned quadroon continued to live in the cottage. With guilty stealth she had twice approached the clearing, each time with a wistful hope that Keith had sent the girl away. She saw that he had not.

In the mornings she rode Othello to Tintagel for her class, grateful that she had the children to occupy these hours. She spent most afternoons — when Keith was at Tintagel reading in Judge Ramsay's law library — in Phillip's company. He talked amusingly to her while she sewed, or they took long walks about the plantation.

On an afternoon that was prematurely laden with the breath of spring, Suzanne impulsively asked Phillip to take her on a tour of the quarters.

He stared at her in odd discomfort.

"Suzanne, you were in the quarters," he reminded. "On Christmas Day."

"All I saw was the nursery and the cabin where we helped Elaine dress. And that was at night." All at once she was eager to see the quarters. At dinner last night Keith had mentioned that he would have to schedule the whitewashing of the cabins. The cabins and the miles of fencing were whitewashed every spring.

"What could you possibly enjoy seeing at the quarters?"

"I'd like to see how the hands live," she said seriously. It was absurd to be afraid to go alone to the quarters at Savage Oaks, but her experience with the overseer at Tintagel lingered in her memory. "I've lived here for months now, and I know so little about the plantation." Color suddenly flooded her cheeks. She knew too much, her mind taunted. Phillip was looking at her with concern. Was he remembering the morning he took her to the cottage, never suspecting what they would find? "Phillip, it's such a beautiful day. We'll walk to the quarters and you'll show me everything."

"All right," he agreed, almost sullenly. "I'll send Edward for a carriage."

"Phillip, no," Suzanne rejected. "Let's walk." She was conscious of a need for physical activity.

They left the house and walked along the levee towards the quarters. The oranges were still green on the trees and buds were swelling on the jessamine vines. The camellia-japonicas were in full bloom. Sparrows chirped as they flitted from tree to tree, and close by a mockingbird whistled noisily.

Sun shone brilliantly overhead and was reflected on the river. They stopped to watch a Mississippi queen moving majestically towards New Orleans. Uncle Gilbert had told her that Maman and Papa had died in an explosion of a steamer between New Orleans and Natchez.

Then he had told her they had died on a boat crossing the Channel. Would she ever discover the truth about her parents?

"I don't know what you expect to see," Phillip complained as they approached the quarters. "All the cabins are locked. The hands hang the keys around their necks by a cord while they work."

"Phillip, I don't want to go snooping in the cabins," she rebuked. "I want to see the nursery and the infirmary and the quarters kitchen — and whatever else there is."

"You've been in the nursery," he reminded shortly, "and why do you want to see a bunch of sick slaves? Most of them are malingerers," he said arrogantly.

"I saw the nursery at night when it was cleared for the party," she said stubbornly. "And I'd like to see where Jane goes every Monday morning with her medicine kit. Phillip, I'm interested in how we care for the slaves."

Phillip pointed out Reagan's cottage, which stood at the head of the cabin-lined "street" of the quarters. Children played high-spiritedly, grinning curiously at Phillip and Suzanne as they walked towards the infirmary at the far end of the "street" without ceasing their good-humored play.

The infirmary was a large two-story building to the left of the cabins, surrounded by orange trees. Smoke spiraled from the chimney. The windows were glazed and sparkling with cleanliness. Grimly Phillip escorted Suzanne inside where she was welcomed delightedly by a pair of elderly women who served as nurses.

The two women took her from bed to bed, in each of the four neat rooms, where she was introduced as "Mist' Keith's lady" and fussed over, she thought, as though she were Queen Victoria. She saw the three new babies and pronounced them beautiful. She talked with respect to the few aged slaves doomed to spend the rest of their lives on the beds on which they lay and who were excited at this visit. The midwife urged her to stop briefly by the bedside of two field hands, both expected to deliver within the hour, and she wished them easy deliveries and healthy babies.

She rejoined Phillip, who waited for her in the first room, where those injured on the plantation were received for treatment.

"Satisfied?" he mocked.

"I'm glad I came."

Tense and silent he led her to the nursery. On the gallery and steps a cluster of eight- or nine-year-old girls tended the babies, calling out exhortations to the toddlers on the steps. The crawlers were in a pen. A handful who seemed to be about four or five danced about a small fire that had been made for them, singing happily. When they were twelve, Suzanne recalled with discomfort, they would be sent to the fields.

A small, wiry, elderly woman, her hair snow white, was soothing a crying infant as they walked into a large square room lined with cribs. At the huge fireplace a collection of pots and pans hung in readiness for feeding time. Her mouth parted in a wide, toothless smile.

"Mist' Phillip," she greeted him joyfully. "Now ain't you a fine sight!"

Self-consciously Phillip introduced Suzanne to Mammy Charlotte, who was in charge of the nursery. Mammy Charlotte, who had been at Savage Oaks for over fifty years, reminisced with Phillip about the days when she had been a servant in the big house.

"I was with his Mama when he was born," Mammy Charlotte told Suzanne. "She was the finest lady that ever walked on this earth."

"Suzanne, let's go," Phillip said with an abruptness that startled her. Mammy Charlotte had upset him.

"All right, Phillip," she placated.

They walked away from the nursery towards the "street." A pair of children playing alone on the gallery of one of the cabins captured her attention. A boy and girl about five and four, Suzanne estimated, who were so fair they could have passed for white.

"Phillip, wait," she said, and crossed to talk to the pair, who smiled shyly at her. What lovely children. She stooped to draw them to her with spontaneous affection, talked with them about the game they were playing. "Phillip, aren't they sweet?" She lifted her eyes to his. Phillip's face was etched with torment.

"Suzanne, I told you not to come here — " He turned away from her.

271

"Phillip?" she said bewilderedly. And then she returned her gaze to the children, inspecting their appealing upturned faces with fresh awareness. Her heart pounded as she recognized the Savage family features. *They were Savage sired.*

Suzanne rose shakily to her feet. This was why Phillip tried to dissuade her from coming to the quarters. lHe did not want her to see Keith's children.

Sixteen

The river was golden with the departing rays of the sun, a spectacle of beauty to which Phillip was oblivious as he strode along the levee. He fought to erase from his mind the vision of Suzanne's anguished face as she looked at Peter and Elizabeth and knew that the Savage blood flowed in their veins. How could he have allowed her to believe Peter and Elizabeth were Keith's children?

He paused to gaze unseeingly at a ship that moved upriver. He had tried to keep her from the quarters to hide his own shame. Not until she looked at him that way had he realized she believed Keith was their father.

All at once he was cold. Suzanne would not leave Savage Oaks, would she? The house would be desolate without her. How could he sit down at the table with her tonight? How was he going to spend the evening in the drawing room with her, knowing how distressed she was and that he was responsible?

Don't stay here. Go into New Orleans. He needed only a small stake to play at one of the casinos on Carondelet Street. Maybe tonight he would be lucky.

He strode away from the levee towards the house. Arriving at the gallery he could hear Jane talking with Arthur. His hands perspiring with nervousness, he went into the hall. Jane turned to him. Her eyes wore the glow of concern he saw perennially there when she looked at him.

"Arthur, tell Edward to be sure he cleans the silver tomorrow," Jane reminded.

"He be sure to do it, Miss Jane," Arthur assured her.

"Jane, I'm going into New Orleans," Phillip said offhandedly. "I thought I'd play a little poker."

"Phillip, that's such a waste of money," Jane protested. She knew he had no funds.

"Let me have a small stake, Jane," he coaxed with the charm that had won him his way into beds since he was fourteen. "When that's gone, I'll just watch. It's an inexpensive diversion. I can't get into trouble," he reminded wryly, "with only a few dollars to splurge."

"I'll give you the money after dinner," she capitulated. She knew how damnably boring it was for him here.

"I'd like to go now," he said persuasively. "I'll eat at the casino. They serve a buffet supper."

"All right, Phillip." Jane sighed, but she started towards the library where cash was kept in the safe.

Twenty minutes later Phillip pulled himself up into the carriage that Lewis had hooked up and brought from the stables.

"Lewis," he leaned out of the carriage with a belated thought as Lewis prodded the horses forward. "Stop by the cottage at the edge of the plantation first. You know where."

"Yessir," Lewis acknowledged guardedly.

Every hand at the stable knew that Keith had brought Manon to the cottage. The way they had known about Papa's women. They gossiped among themselves like a herd of old women. Lewis knew Phillip had gone into New Orleans with Manon, but he would never say a word to any of the family.

Manon received him with affection, but she was uneasy at his presence. Was she expecting Keith?

"I'm going into New Orleans," he said casually. "Why don't you come along?"

"I can't, Phillip." She smiled wistfully. "I wish I could."

"I thought I'd go to Carondelet Street and play a little poker. Until I run out of cash," he said disarmingly. "I don't suppose you have some spare cash around?"

"Wait." She surprised him with her acquiescence. "Keith will give me more when I ask him."

Manon returned from her bedroom to give him a sheaf of bills that widened his eyes.

"And if you go to the Mansion House," she said wisely, "tell Colette I miss her."

Fortified by Manon's bankroll Phillip chose a casino he would have been reluctant to enter with lesser funds. He had heard that here the croupiers and dealers were required to wear evening dress, and that the free buffet suppers were as sumptuous as any supper at Delmonico's in New York.

For a little while, winning heavily to his elation, he forgot the agony that afflicted him since Suzanne had come upon Peter and Elizabeth in the quarters. And then he saw a girl arrive at the casino who had the same tawny hair as Suzanne's, the same small, slender figure, and the agony returned.

He cashed in his winnings and went to the Mansion House. Yellowbird Shaw seemed surprised that he had come to the Mansion House on his own. Why not, he thought defiantly? He was a man. He had the cash in his pocket to buy what he wanted.

"Is Colette available tonight?" Phillip asked, discreetly displaying his bankroll.

"Yes, she is," Yellowbird said with professional charm. She was trying to figure out who was Manon's protector, he decided with amusement. She would not learn that from him.

Colette came into the small parlor where Lloyd had deposited him on his arrival. Tonight, Phillip reminded himself, he was a paying client. Colette's green eyes lighted at the sight of him.

"I'm so glad you came," she said with a brilliant smile.

Colette led him up to the bedroom where Manon and she had entertained him on his first visit. She inquired solicitously about Manon, whose arrangements she envied.

"*Chéri*, I will make you so happy," she whispered confidently, closing the door behind them. "This time just you and I."

He kicked off his boots and stretched on the bed while Colette disappeared into the bathroom. Moments later, Lloyd arrived to place a bottle of champagne on the table. Phillip nodded appreciatively.

His throat tightened when Colette appeared before him in a filmy black nightdress that displayed every inch of her golden skin. To the devil with what happened in the quarters this afternoon!

"Take off that thing," he ordered and crossed to uncork the bottle of champagne.

Colette posed naked before him, her smile provocative as he handed her a glass of champagne and brought his own to his mouth. She wanted him to make love to her, he thought with savage satisfaction. She was tired of Yellowbird's fat, aging clients who sweated their backsides off trying to make themselves passionate.

"You're beautiful," Colette murmured as he shucked away his clothes. "With you, I will do anything."

He pulled her roughly to him, kissed her. Why did he keep thinking about Suzanne?

"*Chéri,*" Colette scolded when he released her. "You're angry with me?"

"Lie down," he ordered brusquely, and with a look of reproach in her eyes Colette lowered herself into a seductive pose on the silken counterpane. "Not that way!" He shoved her onto her stomach.

"So," she shrugged philosophically. "We have the whole evening to make love."

"Come on, Colette," he jeered, his voice uneven. "Show me how good you are!" Make him forget everything but this feeling that was taking him over. Make him forget this morning in the quarters.

While he lay momentarily drained and relaxed, Colette went to the table to pour more champagne for him. His eyes followed her fluid nakedness. He was not one of her old men. He was nineteen and passionate.

How could Keith go to Manon when he could have Suzanne in his bed? How often did Keith love his wife? He would lay odds she was passionate. Absurdly he was aroused again. He would like to make love to his sister-in-law, he taunted himself; but in her absence, Colette would have to do.

"Take the glasses away and come back to bed," he commanded, amused at the alacrity with which she complied. Colette had no idea how many times he could do this in one night.

The carriage turned into the long roadway that led to the house. Everybody would be asleep, Phillip surmised. Was Suzanne lying in Keith's arms, or had he gone to Manon? No, Keith would not be sleeping with his bride tonight, Phillip told himself with guilty satisfaction. Suzanne was too hurt, too distraught by what he had allowed her to believe.

He had tried to stop her from going to the quarters, he reminded himself again. At the Christmas party it was different; he knew she would not see Peter and Elizabeth. Why had he allowed himself to fall in love with Suzanne? As always, Keith got what *he* wanted.

All the way home from New Orleans he had been wrestling with his conscience. He could not live with the guilt that fermented in him. Tomorrow he must go to Suzanne and tell her the truth. That Peter and Elizabeth were his children. How could he ever hope to take Suzanne from Keith? Once he had hoped that he could.

He lay awake until dawn, the tortuous years of his young life unfolding before him. Nothing had ever been right for him! He could never compete with Keith, and more than anything in the world he wanted Papa to look upon him with pride and joy.

He awoke early with an instant recall of his resolution to be honest with Suzanne. He flinched at the prospect of the confrontation, his mind moving back through the years to the morning encounter with Papa when he first returned from Princeton.

Papa had charged into his room without bothering to knock, expecting to surprise him with that pretty bitch who had been brought into the kitchen from the laundry house. He was alone. Sure, he had mentally stripped away her dress while she served dinner the night before, but he had not touched her.

"Phillip, I saw the way you looked at that girl last night!" Papa was florid with anger. "I couldn't sleep all night thinking about it. I hate miscegenation. It makes me physically sick to think that Savage blood could run in the veins of a slave, that an overseer might flog a grandchild of mine in our fields."

"Papa," he said irreverently, "you don't allow flogging."

"It happens," his father shot back. "Phillip, I want you to go with me to the quarters. I'm going to show you something. Maybe then you'll stop looking at the wenches."

"I can look, Papa," he defied. "I don't touch."

But he had accompanied Papa to the quarters. He had stood with Papa before the nursery and looked at Peter and Elizabeth playing on the porch.

"All last night I wrestled with the question of whether or not to tell you. Your children, Phillip," Papa said. "Our blood in the veins of slaves."

Phillip thrust aside the covers and crossed to the window. He gazed out for a few moments without seeing, until George opened the door cautiously, and came into the room with Phillip's coffee. In a little while he must go downstairs to the dining room to face Suzanne over breakfast.

He waited until he heard Suzanne leave her room. Jane had gone to the laundry house a few minutes earlier. Her voice had filtered upward to his open window as she walked below with Elaine. Suzanne and he would be alone at breakfast. His hands clenched into fists as he fought the urge to bolt. Go downstairs. Be honest with Suzanne.

He felt sick with remorse as he forced himself to leave his room and go down to the breakfast table. Suzanne was sitting there alone. How pale she was this morning.

"Suzanne, I have to talk to you," he said desperately.

"About what, Phillip?" All at once she was tense.

"Not here. After breakfast. We'll walk along the levee."

"All right." She avoided meeting his eyes.

While the servants moved in and out of the room bringing in plates of food, Phillip and Suzanne limited themselves to impersonal conversation. They did not linger over their coffee this morning. As they left the house and went down to the levee, Suzanne made no effort to rush him, yet Phillip sensed her anxiety.

"Suzanne, when we were in the quarters yesterday, I should have told you the truth about Peter and Elizabeth." He stared somberly ahead of him. "They're not Keith's children." He heard her sharp intake of breath. "They're mine. Born of my fourteenth and fifteenth summers at Savage Oaks."

"Oh, Phillip — " her breath rushed out.

"I knew nothing about Peter and Elizabeth until I came home from Princeton. Only then did Papa tell me." He shook his head in disbelief. "I never once thought about there being children."

"Phillip, you were so young."

"I had done the one thing Papa could never forgive. He had seen this on so many plantations, and now it was here at Savage Oaks." Fresh self-recriminations smote him.

"Is there some way to help Peter and Elizabeth?" Suzanne asked gently.

"Papa agonized about that. He thought about sending them North or to Paris to be raised, but how could he take the children away from their mothers? That was the kind of separation he condemned in other planters. But I wanted you to know the truth," he said, his voice uneven.

"Thank you, Phillip." Her eyes glowed with sympathy. "Thank you for telling me."

For the rest of the day Phillip wandered along the levee, not bothering to go to the house for the midday meal. *He was in love with his brother's wife.* How was he going to survive at Savage Oaks, feeling the way he did about Suzanne?

At the approach of the dinner hour he returned to the house. The mail had been brought up from New Orleans. He was surprised to find a letter addressed to him among those on the marble-topped Louis XV table in the foyer. The letter was from a New York City newspaper.

With rising excitement Phillip opened the envelope, read the brief letter. The newspaper in New York was going to publish Raoul's poem under the pseudonym Phillip had stipulated. No doubt they suspected the pseudonym was his. The check enclosed was minuscule, but its significance would lift Raoul to the heights of ecstasy.

Phillip left the house and hurried through the early evening darkness to the stable. Raoul was exhorting one of the hands about the hazards of the camphene lamp the man was suspending from the rafters.

"Sure, you get a better light from that than from whale oil," Raoul said worriedly, "but look how many fires start from it, too."

"Raoul, I'd like to talk to you." Phillip masked his elation. "Come outside with me, please."

"You want me to do something, Mist' Phillip?" Raoul asked as they stood alone outside the stable in a spill of silver moonlight.

"That newspaper up in New York, Raoul — they're going to publish your poem," he said softly. No moment in Raoul's life could ever match this one. "They'd like to see more. Here's the letter and the check."

Raoul's hand trembled as he reached for the sheaf of paper and the check. His mind was struggling to assimilate the news that Phillip had brought him.

"I'll give you money for the check," Phillip explained gently, knowing, however, that it meant little to Raoul in this moment of triumph. Yet an inner rage tore at Phillip. This was all there could ever be for Raoul. Writing his poems behind a pseudonym. He was a slave, a possession. Poor Raoul. So talented, so bright, and so doomed.

"Mist' Phillip, I did it!" Raoul's voice was a mixture of disbelief and joy. "I'm a poet. *I'm a poet.*"

Phillip returned to the house. Suzanne and Jane were already at the dinner table.

Jane explained Keith's absence at dinner saying that he had gone to a political meeting being held at the Andrews' plantation.

"With the spring election coming up, people are concerned that we'll have the same intimidation, violence, and bloodshed we had at the polls in the fall." She grimaced in distaste. "It's barbaric."

"It's barbaric to keep women from the polls," Suzanne said with fervor.

"Hear, hear!" Phillip applauded, but his eyes betrayed his unhappiness.

"Jane, don't you believe we should have the right to vote?" Suzanne prodded her zealously.

"To tell you the truth, Suzanne, I doubt that I would bother if I could," Jane said with candor. "I have enough to concern me here at Savage Oaks." Her prison, Phillip thought tenderly.

All through dinner he was conscious of Suzanne's covert solicitude for him. She talked vivaciously about the invitation brought to Savage Oaks from the Mauriacs. Keith and she were invited to attend one of the Thackeray lectures with them. She strived to persuade Jane

284

and Phillip to send someone in to New Orleans for tickets to another of the lectures.

"There'll be five, Jane," she said coaxingly. "Four on the Georges and a fifth on Charity and Humor. Keith and I will hear the lecture on George III. If Phillip and you hear one of the others, then we can compare them." She was so relieved, Phillip tortured himself, that Keith had not fathered Peter and Elizabeth. But even with this he sensed that all was not well between them.

Elaine was putting the sweet potato pie on the table when Edward burst into the dining room.

"There's a fire in the stable! You can see the flames from the kitchen house!"

"Ring the bell, Edward," Jane ordered. "Quickly!"

Instantly Jane was on her feet and running from the room, with Arthur in her wake. They could hear her rapping out orders as the two of them rushed to assemble a fire crew among the house servants.

"The horses!" Suzanne's voice was shot through with alarm. "They may be trapped in the stable, Phillip!"

Suzanne and Phillip raced from the house and down the path to the stable. They could see the flames shooting into the night sky. Nearing the stable they heard Raoul's voice soothing the horses as he led them from the raging flames.

"Come on, now, you're gonna be all right. Just keep movin'."

The plantation bell was summoning the field hands from their Saturday night party. The house servants were running towards the stable with buckets of water.

"Raoul's got the horses out," Phillip reassured Suzanne as they were halted by the heat of the fire. "He's herding them towards the levee." They were whinnying with fear but they were safe, Phillip thought gratefully. Raoul had seen to that.

"How did it happen?" Suzanne asked anxiously.

"The way stable fires usually happen. One of the hands must have been careless with a lamp. Raoul warned them camphene was dangerous."

"Phillip, where's Raoul going?" Suzanne demanded in astonishment.

Phillip's eyes swung in the direction Suzanne pointed. Raoul was riding with desperate swiftness away from the horses. Instantly Phillip understood. The horses were safe. The opportunity for escape had been too powerful for Raoul to ignore on this special night.

"Suzanne, let him go," Phillip pleaded. Her eyes turned to meet his, softened with comprehension and compassion. "Let him be free, Suzanne."

Together they watched Raoul disappear into the night. Several hands were hurrying forward to round up the frightened horses. Jane was too involved in directing the bucket brigade to have noticed Raoul's flight. When his disappearance was discovered it would be too late. Keith would recoil from advertising for a runaway slave.

In a little while, with the field hands rushing up to help, the fire would be put out. And Raoul would be on his way to freedom. When would he acquire the courage to run from Savage Oaks? How much longer could he bear to remain, feeling this way about Suzanne?

Seventeen

Suzanne lay in bed, staring into the darkness of the room. She had come to Louisiana with such hopes. She had married Keith with such romantic anticipation. But she lived at Savage Oaks on the edge of a dark abyss. One push would thrust her towards eternal torment.

Keith no longer made any effort to come to her. But she must take the blame for that. She blatantly rejected him. So often in the drawing room in the evening she raised her eyes to discover him gazing at her with a blend of bewilderment and reproach. Each time he sought to speak with her privately she managed an escape.

She would not trust herself alone with Keith. Accusations would burst from her, and then she would have to leave Savage Oaks. Yet she lived in a nightmare under this roof, knowing about the girl in the cottage. It was shameful of her to ride in that direction, praying to find the cottage deserted. Each time chatter greeted her, and she fled with fresh heartbreak.

Tomorrow night Keith and she were to go into New Orleans for dinner with Mme. Mauriac and Uncle Gilbert and then to the lecture by Mr. Thackeray. Why did Mme. Mauriac and Uncle Gilbert refuse to be honest with her about Maman and Papa? Was Phillip correct in his suspicions? *Were* they trying to protect her from the knowledge that her birth was such to be a disgrace to the Savage family? No, she would not believe that.

Keith and she would leave in midafternoon; she recalled their plans, and stopped short with dismay. She would be alone with Keith for the long ride into New Orleans.

For weeks she had avoided such a situation. Her mind frenziedly sought at ways to avoid it. She would plead a last-minute headache, she plotted with panic. She could send word that they could not come in. But no, she had been looking forward to the evening in New Orleans — to hearing Mr. Thackeray. And they were to have dinner with Mme. Mauriac and Uncle Gilbert. She never abandoned hope that one of them would inadvertently let some clue slip that she could grasp and follow. She must keep the vow she made in the Cathedral of Notre-Dame.

Phillip. She clutched hopefully at this possible escape. She would persuade Phillip to go into New Orleans with them. Mme. Mauriac would not be upset if Keith and she brought Phillip along with them for dinner. Surely Uncle Gilbert, with all his connections, could arrange for Phillip to attend the lecture.

An evening away from Savage Oaks would be good for Phillip, she consoled herself. He was morose with guilt over Peter and Elizabeth. Those sweet, darling children, she thought unhappily, who would never go to school.

Suzanne awoke in the morning convinced that she must persuade Phillip to go with Keith and her into New Orleans. She was momentarily disconcerted to find Jane in the dining room when she went downstairs. Normally Jane had an early breakfast with Keith, then went about her morning activities. Jane was talking agitatedly with Phillip.

"Phillip, can't you understand how urgent it is for you to have a college education? I've managed to persuade the College of Louisiana at Jackson to accept you when the new year commences in August. They're willing to overlook your indiscretion at Princeton."

"Jane, I'm not going," Phillip rejected furiously. "Why do I have to kill myself studying trigonometry and calculus? I loathe Greek and Latin, and physiology bores me to death. I'm not going back to school," he said flatly.

"Phillip, what are you going to do with your life?" Jane demanded desperately.

"Live at Savage Oaks," he said coolly.

"Phillip, why don't you go into New Orleans with Keith and me tonight?" Suzanne suggested with a contrived air of spontaneity. "Surely there'll be one more ticket available for the lecture."

"That would be an imposition," Jane reproved. "Mme. Mauriac is expecting only Keith and you."

"I'm sure she won't mind." Suzanne turned earnestly to Phillip. "Do come with us, Phillip." Don't let her be forced to make the trip into New Orleans alone with Keith. Her eyes implored him while he silently deliberated.

"I'll go," he decided and relief flooded Suzanne. She suspected Phillip was going with them more in defiance of Jane than a desire to attend the lecture.

"I'm so looking forward to hearing Mr. Thackeray." Suzanne turned to Jane. "I was reading about his tour in the States three years ago. He made that tour despite ill-health, to be sure to have dowries for his daughters." Subconsciously she frowned. Unknowingly she had come to Keith with a dowry. "Mr. Thackeray had to raise his daughters. His wife went insane sixteen years ago."

"How do you know his wife went insane?" Jane demanded furiously. "Is that how the students gossiped in the Convent?"

"It was talked about quite openly in England," Suzanne stammered. "A classmate's father told us."

"I have no time for such nonsense." Jane rose from her chair. "I have work to oversee."

While Patrice hovered about delightedly because "her baby" was going to an important affair in New Orleans, Suzanne chose an emerald green velvet evening gown of becoming simplicity, its skirt devoid of the excessive trimmings so favored at the time. The hue was one that highlighted her tawny hair and amber eyes. She smiled with approval at her reflection in the mirror as Patrice fastened the back of her dress. Oh, she must wear the beautiful Gubelin chatelaine.

"It's gonna be cold tonight, Miss Suzanne," Patrice reminded. "You best take a cloak with you."

"I will, Patrice." Her smile glowed. This would be an exciting evening. "The white cashmere with the hood, please."

"Miss Suzanne, you is so beautiful I feel like cryin'," Patrice said solemnly. "You has a good time tonight."

"I'm sure I will Patrice."

Suzanne leaned forward to pull Patrice to her for an affectionate moment, then hurried downstairs and out to the gallery to wait for Keith and Phillip. She sat in a Boston rocker, cloak across her lap and talked with the gardener who was lovingly loosening the earth about the masses of azaleas in riotous bloom, their colors ranging from white to palest pink to crimson. Her face brightened as she spied Keith walking towards the house. She was going to allow nothing to spoil this evening in New Orleans.

"You look beautiful, Suzanne," he said softly.

"Thank you."

Keith looked at the gardener. Panic brushed her. Was Keith going to send him away? No questions from Keith now, please.

"The flowers are doing well, Amos," Keith complimented the beaming gardener, and Suzanne relaxed.

"We could use some rain, Mist' Keith. They needs a lotta water."

"I suspect they're going to get it," Keith said ruefully. "Look at those clouds."

"I doubt that rain will keep anybody away from the lecture." Why did she tremble this way at each encounter with Keith?

"It rained for the first lecture last week, and the attendance was not what was expected, but the *Picayune* said that the lecture three days ago was very well attended." His eyes lingered questioningly on Suzanne. She dropped her own. "I'd better go up and dress," Keith said, suddenly terse.

On the ride into New Orleans Phillip put himself out to be charming. Keith was taciturn, staring somberly out the window. He was annoyed that Phillip was with them. He had anticipated having this time alone with Suzanne. Why, she asked herself defiantly? What could he say that would change things between them?

They were no more than ten minutes en route when the dark clouds that had hovered ominously for the past two hours unleashed a heavy downpour.

"Lewis's going to be drenched by the time we arrive in New Orleans," Suzanne said worriedly.

"His macintosh will keep him dry," Phillip

consoled. He looked curiously at Keith. He, too, was conscious of Keith's annoyance.

"I'm so looking forward to the lecture." Suzanne forced herself to sound enthusiastic. She had been, before they had begun the long ride into the city. "Of course, most people are coming just to see the author of *The Newcomes*."

"Someone at the Andrews' ball talked about hearing Thackeray lecture in New York last November." Unexpectedly Keith joined their conversation. "They had to turn people away. But I gather some of the ladies were upset by his colorful discussion of George I and his strumpets." Keith smiled at Suzanne's laughter.

Despite the rain, they arrived in New Orleans only ten minutes later than planned. Ingratiatingly Suzanne apologized for bringing Phillip along with no prior notice; but Mme. Mauriac, regal as a dowager Empress in an antique gold moire evening dress, brushed this away with the assurance that Amelia had only to set another place at the table. Sebastien would go immediately with a note from Gilbert to see if a seat could be obtained for Phillip at Odd Fellows' Hall.

"Suzanne, you're pale," Mme. Mauriac scolded solicitously as they went into the dining room. "Are you riding every morning? Exercise is so important to the health."

"Every morning," Suzanne assured her affectionately. When she was with Mme. Mauriac and Uncle Gilbert, she forgot to be angry, yet always in her mind there lingered the knowledge that they refused to be honest with her about Maman and Papa.

"After the lecture," Uncle Gilbert confided with an air of satisfaction, "we're invited to Mr. Grimshaw's house to meet Mr. Thackeray personally. Keith, Senators Benjamin and Slidell will be there tonight, too."

"I'll enjoy seeing them again." Keith's face brightened.

"You must have heard Keith talk about our Senators, Suzanne." Mme. Mauriac sparkled in anticipation as they settled themselves at the table. "Both such brilliant, charming men. Senator Benjamin is a Sephardic Jew," she pointed out with pride. "The President wanted to appoint him to the United States Supreme Court, but he preferred to remain actively in practice."

"Grandmère, you're boasting again," Gilbert twitted. "Though you have said not one word tonight about Mr. Disraeli."

"I'm reading a book of his," Suzanne confided. "*Tancred*. The third volume." All at once she was self-conscious because she had taken the book from the library only after Keith spoke about it with such respect. He was gazing at her in that disconcerting fashion again. "Mr. Disraeli has such a great imagination, such a marvelous command of words." It would disturb Mère Angélique to know that she was reading Mr. Disraeli's reproach of the Church and the emptiness of English politics.

"I adored *Vivian Grey*," Mme. Mauriac said reminiscently. "Such a daring book. So witty, so lively. Everybody in England knew he based his characters on the important figures of London society."

"Keith, how do you feel about the Democratic Convention?" Gilbert asked. "Whom do you expect to get the nomination?"

"I'm not in close touch with Washington City," Keith reminded, "but from what I've read and what I know of the party, I expect Buchanan to be nominated. He's a safe man," Keith said with a cynical smile. "He was at the Court of St. James and took no stand on the Kansas–Nebraska Act."

"They'll try to choose a man to appeal to both the North and the South," Gilbert said judiciously, "but I have no faith in Buchanan. He's already old. He's unaggressive. I suspect he's more interested in a partisan attitude than principles." He shook his head unhappily. "I expect this to be the most bitter campaign we've ever seen."

"The Republicans are appealing to the Northern working men," Keith said somberly. "And they're using the ugly business in Kansas as propaganda. Thank God, though, that Pierce had sense enough not to try for another term."

Mme. Mauriac shuddered delicately.

"It would have been horrendous to reject an incumbent president."

How knowledgeably Mme. Mauriac spoke

about politics, Suzanne thought admiringly. Not all Southern ladies were like those she met at the Andrews' ball.

"Are you going to be active in the campaign, Keith?" Gilbert asked.

"I would like to be," he conceded slowly.

"Then do it!" Gilbert said bluntly. "We need young men at every level."

"Keith, the grinding season is over," Suzanne reminded zealously. "You have the time."

"I'll ask the Senator how I can best help," Keith said thoughtfully. Suzanne knew he meant Slidell. "King John" Slidell, the newspapers sometimes called him.

"What about Benjamin?" Gilbert pursued. "Do you think he'll switch from the Whigs to the Democrats before the election?"

"It's expected in private circles. He'll probably make the announcement at the Democratic Convention," Keith surmised. "There's hardly a Whig party left, sir."

"There's talk in Louisiana that Fremont might end up being the Republican choice," Mme. Mauriac contributed. "Mainly because these people feel Fremont and his beautiful wife are the ideal couple to live in the White House." Her voice was rich with sarcasm.

"There are a lot of Democrats already busy collecting Wall Street money to see that a Democrat gets into the White House again," Keith pointed out.

Phillip spoke little but he was not bored,

Suzanne decided. She was pleased that he was being so charming to Mme. Mauriac.

"Oh, I have started a school at Tintagel," Suzanne announced effervescently. She saw the glint of pride in Keith's eyes as she talked. "I'm teaching eleven children of the farmers in the little hamlet just below Savage Oaks."

"How like your father!" Mme. Mauriac said delightedly, then paused in confusion, her eyes stricken.

"Was my father a teacher?" Suzanne asked gently, her mouth suddenly dry.

"I meant he was eager to help those less fortunate than he." Mme. Mauriac seemed serene again, but she was furious with herself for this slip. "So generous, so giving of himself."

"In what way?" Suzanne pushed. The atmosphere was suddenly tense.

"Grandmère knows how Charles would go out of his way to help anyone in trouble," Gilbert said feelingly. Keith was listening with an absorbed air. "I've told you, Suzanne. Your father was a fine man." He turned briskly to Keith. "Keith, I understand you attended the meeting at Andrews' house. Was he any less ambiguous than usual?"

Suzanne sat back in her chair, the fork she held idle in her hand. Uncle Gilbert had so deliberately diverted the conversation. Phillip's eyes were on her, warm with sympathy. *Who was she? Was even her name a fabrication of Uncle Gilbert's imagination?*

Sebastien returned to the house and came into the dining room to whisper to Mme. Mauriac.

"You see, Gilbert has arranged for a ticket for tonight for Phillip," she announced triumphantly.

Mme. Mauriac urged them on their way the moment dinner was over. It would be unspeakable to arrive late at Odd Fellows' Hall. Under a protective umbrella they were escorted one by one to the waiting carriage. By the time they arrived at the large, three-story meeting hall, the room where Mr. Thackeray was to speak was already almost filled to capacity. The Hall was electric with anticipation as the patrons took their seats, preparatory to Thackeray's appearance.

Suzanne leaned forward avidly in her seat as a gigantic man — surely he must be six feet four inches tall — silver-haired, bespectacled, unostentatiously dressed, walked before the assemblage with a free swinging stride. His shoulders were broad and erect, his face almost clean-shaven.

"He doesn't look at all as I had expected," a woman in front of Suzanne murmured. "I thought there would be something dashing and 'fast' about his appearance."

When Thackeray spoke, his voice was clear and penetrating. His enunciation was so perfect he could be heard in the remotest corners of the room, yet Suzanne marveled that he seemed to be speaking in a colloquial tone.

The audience hung on every word that Thackeray uttered, though he spoke quietly and with few gestures. He might have been speaking to a group of friends at his own fireside. There were moments that were humorous and others that were thrilling. Suzanne was utterly absorbed as he talked with such compassion about George III, the young king who led such an exemplary life in a court as dissolute as England ever knew, until he ceased to rule in November, 1810. Suzanne felt as though she walked in the magnificent time of George III among the fascinating characters of his court.

Tears filled Suzanne's eyes when Thackeray talked about the pathetic figure of the old man, blind, deaf, and deprived of reason, wandering through the rooms of the palace issuing orders to courtiers who did not exist, reviewing troops, addressing imaginary Parliaments. He could be so compassionate towards George III because of his own experiences with his poor, insane wife, Suzanne thought.

She felt herself still woven into the tapestry of the years of George III's reign when the audience at last had ceased to applaud, and they were leaving the Odd Fellows' Hall to go to Mr. Grimshaw's house. Arriving at the elegant mansion on Bourbon Street, they were relieved of their cloaks and ushered into a resplendent drawing room furnished in the style favored by the French aristocracy and illuminated by an ornate chandelier.

"Mrs. Grimshaw is the granddaughter of the Marquis St. Pierre, who was the *dame d'jonneur* to Marie Antoinette," Mme. Mauriac whispered as their hostess. gowned in a Paris import, came forward to welcome them.

Already two dozen people congregated in small groups, each involved in lively conversation. Suzanne heard French and Spanish being spoken as well as English, and remembered that New Orleans was as cosmopolitan as Washington City. At one side of the room Mr. Thackeray was talking with a small, dark man with bright dark eyes.

"I go to Paris to visit my wife and my daughter when I can," the smaller man was saying philosophically. What a beautiful voice, Suzanne thought. "But Washington City makes much demands of me."

"That's Judah Benjamin," Keith said as Mrs. Grimshaw excused herself to welcome newly arriving guests. "And across the room is Senator Slidell."

A sharp-eyed mother with a shy young daughter in tow usurped Phillip, who seemed willing enough, Suzanne noted. Mme. Mauriac took Suzanne by the hand and firmly prodded her towards the small cluster that was gathering about Mr. Thackeray and Mr. Benjamin while Keith and Gilbert moved towards an imposing man with outstretched hand.

"Judah, we've missed you," Mme. Mauriac said charmingly. "I thought when you sold

Bellechasse we'd be seeing more of you." She introduced Suzanne, who found it almost impossible to keep her eyes from Mr. Thackeray, who towered at least a foot above her.

"I can't compete with our guest of honor tonight," Benjamin chuckled, and introduced Mme. Mauriac and Suzanne to William Thackeray.

"We were talking about my notices here in New Orleans," Thackeray said whimsically. "Only one paper whips me severely. An Irish paper, naturally." His gray eyes twinkled.

"There won't be a copy of *The Newcomes* left in any bookstore in New Orleans tomorrow," Suzanne prophesied with a dazzling smile. How easy it was to talk to these gentlemen.

"I'll tell you a secret," Thackeray confided humorously. "In every town where I lecture, I go into bookstores and poke around and ask questions. And everywhere it's the same," he said with mock remorse. "The booksellers sell five copies of any one of Dickens' works to one of mine."

"But you'll live forever, Mr. Thackeray," Mme. Mauriac promised. "For endless generations you'll be read."

A pair of servants circulated with trays and they helped themselves to glasses of champagne. At one side of the room another pair of servants were setting up a sumptuous buffet on several tables. On one was a fish larger than Suzanne had ever seen — the size of a small child, from which large rosy slices were being cut. A silver urn beside the fish provided a green sauce. At an adjacent table, succulent fillet steaks braised with tomatoes and stuffed mushrooms were arranged on silver platters. This was a repast that would honor the finest of French restaurants, Suzanne thought with respect.

"Come now, Mr. Benjamin," Thackeray was joshing, "do you truly believe that slavery is an efficient means of operation? A staff of three in an English home can do what fifteen slaves do in the South."

"We have only free men and women of color in our house," Mme. Mauriac said with pride. "And yes, Mr. Thackeray, I agree with you. A staff that enjoys liberty is more effective and less expensive."

A few minutes later, Suzanne was whisked away by Gilbert, after he was introduced to the guest of honor, so that she might meet Senator Slidell and his wife. En route, Gilbert paused to introduce her to an impressive-looking Frenchman named Pierre Soulé and to his flamboyantly gowned wife.

"That hot-tempered gentleman is a glorious orator, but probably the most undiplomatic of all American diplomats," Gilbert said in a low voice when they left the Soulés to proceed towards the Slidells. "He almost threw us into war with Spain."

Mrs. Slidell was delighted to discover that Suzanne was as fluent in French as in English.

"We always speak French at home," she confided.

Later in the evening, Suzanne found herself between Uncle Gilbert and Keith in conversation again with Mr. Thackeray and Mr. Benjamin.

"I tell you," Thackeray said with an air of pleasure, "I was served bouillabaisse on the way to Lake Pontchartrain that was as good as you can find at the reserve in Marseilles. If you haven't sampled it, waste no time. I autographed their guest book with high praise for the fish stew. New Orleans in the springtime seems to me the city of the world where you can eat and drink the most and suffer the least."

"Aside from the superb cuisine, what do you think of New Orleans?" Benjamin asked Thackeray with proprietary pride.

"I like New Orleans perhaps better than any other town in the Union," Thackeray said reminiscently. "The quaint old houses, the pictures on the quays, the sweet kind of French I hear spoken in the shops and the street. And do you know, the streets remind me much of the port of Havre."

The conversation moved adroitly into politics, which Keith relished. Mr. Thackeray was interested, Suzanne noticed with pride, in Keith's blunt denouncement of the franking privilege as indulged by the members and delegates in Congress.

"It's misused shockingly," Keith protested. "I know Congressmen who use the franking privilege to send sewing machines home to their wives."

"We had a franking scandal in England that came to a head back in 1837," Thackeray recalled.

"All kinds of stiff regulations went into effect."

"It won't happen here," Gilbert drily warned. "Our Congressmen protect their privileges."

After a while the conversation turned to Mr. Disraeli, whom both Keith and Mme. Mauriac deeply admired. Suzanne listened raptly to all that was said of the British statesman. Then the conversation took a somber turn. Several guests gathered around the two senators to discuss abolition.

"I think abolition is inevitable," Keith said seriously, after much heated debate, "but it must be carried out over a period of years, with compensation to the slave owners."

"The way it was done in the British colonies," Gilbert pointed out.

Uncle Gilbert was pleased about her marriage to Keith, Suzanne thought unhappily, because he had no knowledge of the wall between them. Did he expect her to look the other way while Keith carried on his liaison? *She would not,* she reiterated silently for the thousandth time.

It was well past midnight when they rode through the silent streets of the city en route to Savage Oaks. Keith was in high spirits. He had truly enjoyed this evening.

They ought to be entertaining at Savage Oaks. This was important to Keith's future. How exciting it would be to open up the grand salon at Savage Oaks, which had been closed for nineteen years, and give parties for the fascinating people that populated New Orleans. Mme. Mauriac, so knowledgeable about entertaining in the grand manner, would adore to help her.

Impulsively Suzanne turned to Keith, who was staring moodily out the window. A little while ago, in the Grimshaw's drawing room, he had radiated such interest in everything that was said. She had never seen him with such an air of vitality about him.

Surely somewhere in Louisiana he could find a competent man to take over much of his responsibilities at Savage Oaks. He must not be sacrificed to the demands of running the plantation. He must go on to take his bar examinations, become part of the political world. Some men were born to fight for reforms. Keith was one of them.

She had noticed that Keith and Senator Slidell had disappeared from the drawing room for half an hour of private talk. Instinctively she knew they had discussed Keith's participation in the Democratic campaign.

A wife could be helpful to a man in public service. Keith talked about the matinée dances for which Mrs. Slidell was famous, and about the endless dinners and balls given by Washington hostesses, all involved in the international scene. Suzanne spoke three languages; she could be useful as a politician's wife.

But she was not, in truth, Keith's wife, she admonished herself with sudden brutality. Not so long as his quadroon mistress remained in the cottage.

Eighteen

As Keith rode past the cane fields, he was pleased that the planting was finished. He waved a greeting to Reagan, who was moving among the hands, supervising the tillage. This morning he had sent Moses over to Tintagel to take a crew out to put in a few acres of vegetables. Next week they would start whitewashing the cabins and fences. The trees would be whitewashed as high up as the poles could reach.

The extensive repairs on the stable were finished. It disturbed Keith that Raoul had deliberately set fire to the stable before he ran away. But how could they know what anger festered in the souls of the hands? Reagan was astonished that he had not placed an ad for Raoul's apprehension. Better to take the loss than to have Raoul on his conscience. He wished the man well.

Financially Savage Oaks was in good shape, thanks to the best sugar crop in years and to his marriage settlement. But what was he going to do about Suzanne? How much longer could they go on living this way? What the devil had gone wrong? He had thought that after that night in his room everything was going to be fine for them. He had congratulated himself on stumbling into a perfect marriage.

All at once restlessness besieged him. He would take a few hours off and go into New Orleans. Have lunch with Jacques. The baby must be five or six weeks old. He should have been down to the city to congratulate Jacques before this. Reagan could carry on without him today.

With a sense of anticipation, he rode back to the stable and ordered a carriage to be brought. Suzanne had been so charming when they went to the Thackeray lecture and afterwards to the Grimshaws' party that he had hoped, when they returned to Savage Oaks, she would welcome him into her room. Yet the finality with which she had said goodnight to him forestalled any move on his part.

As the carriage rolled along past the hamlet where Suzanne's students lived, he smiled involuntarily. How many plantation young ladies would undertake such a task? What other young plantation wife would have bought her husband two volumes of William Wirt for Christmas?

Suzanne was as stubborn as she was bright, he thought with frustration. God knows, she was responsive that night in his room when he persuaded her not to leave Savage Oaks. But damn, he never knew what she was thinking! Would she never forgive him for that spurious courtship?

This morning the trip into New Orleans seemed interminably long. He was impatient to talk with Jacques. They should invite Jacques and his wife to Savage Oaks, he thought guiltily. Suzanne would enjoy the diversion. Jane must adjust to this change in their lives. They could not remain forever in a vacuum.

Jacques was delighted to see him. In ebullient spirits, he took Keith off to luncheon at Antoine's on St. Louis Street. Keith remembered coming here with Jacques to confide about his impending marriage. He had not even met Suzanne then.

They spent only a few moments on ordering from the extensive menu, then leaned back in their comfortable chairs, each appraising the other.

"Jacques, I haven't asked you about your son," Keith apologized. "He must be five — no, six weeks old."

"Seven." Jacques beamed. "The image of his father."

"And Louise?" Keith inquired politely.

Jacques shrugged.

"Louise is fine. She spends most of her time extolling the baby's virtues to his grandparents. Next month we go to the house on Lake Pontchartrain for the summer months. And you, my friend?" Jacques' eyes narrowed speculatively. "How are you taking to married life?"

"I'm having problems with Suzanne." He forced a smile. "The wedding night was a disaster," he conceded. Jacques nodded knowingly. "My fault. I was angry at being pushed into marriage. Then a few weeks later Suzanne discovered that the marriage had been arranged. We had visitors that day, I remembered later — I suspect they made a point of mentioning my financial difficulties. Suzanne came to my room. She told me she was leaving me. Lord, she was beautiful in her fury!" Visualizing that confrontation he was stirred to passion. "I insisted she remain. We made love. Jacques, it was the best ever. I couldn't believe my luck."

"So you have a passionate bride." Jacques smiled with respect.

"She's lovely, Jacques, and so intelligent." He laughed as Jacques winced. "We went to the Grimshaws' house several nights ago, after the Thackeray lecture, and you should have seen the way she handled herself with men like Slidell and Benjamin and Thackeray himself. Everybody was charmed by her."

"A wife like that could be useful to an ambitious man. Are you ambitious, Keith?" Jacques' smile was quizzical.

"I don't plan to spend my life running Savage Oaks. I want to find a man — young and shrewd, whom I can train to take over much of my responsibilities. Reagan's a good overseer, but he needs to be guided. I want to practice law, Jacques. Eventually I want to move into politics."

"What are you doing about it?" Jacques asked practically.

"I'm reading every day in Judge Ramsay's

library. I've wanted to do this ever since I came home, but it was the property of an absentee owner."

"Now you're the owner," Jacques said with rare seriousness.

"I'm going to take the bar examinations before the end of the year. If I find my man, I'll open up an office in New Orleans."

"Then you'll move into the city," Jacques pounced triumphantly. "About time."

"No. I can live at Savage Oaks and practice law in the city. That's not difficult. But what the devil am I going to do about Suzanne?" he asked intensely. "Ever since that night when she threatened to leave, she's kept her door locked. I knock and she pretends to be asleep. I try to talk to her and she adroitly avoids me."

They were silent while the waiter appeared with the bottle of Château Margaux 1848 that Jacques had ordered. His wine glass filled and in hand, Jacques leaned forward.

"Console yourself with Manon," he said indulgently and chuckled at Keith's start of astonishment. "Manon is no longer at the Mansion House. Colette told me she had acquired a 'protector.' With some persuasion she admitted it was you. Tell me, is she still as good as she used to be?"

"Manon knows how to satisfy a man," Keith conceded, "but with Suzanne there's much more. I'm in love with her, Jacques. That's the last thing I expected to happen," he acknowledged. "I can't sleep nights, knowing she's in the house and I'm not lying with her."

"Then knock down her door. She's your wife. How can she refuse her husband if he insists?"

"I don't want her that way," Keith rejected. "What about you?" he countered. "Have you ever broken down Louise's door?"

"No," Jacques conceded. "It would not be the gentlemanly thing to do." He gestured in defeat. "The baby is seven weeks old and still she says to me, 'Jacques, not yet.' So I go to the Mansion House. Expensive, but necessary."

"Maybe Suzanne doesn't want to have a child so early in marriage. I try to talk to her, but she avoids being alone with me. I could explain, delicately, that we can sleep together without her having a child. Or maybe," he said morosely, "she's still angry at me for that pretense of courtship. Maybe that one night we had together was an accident she regrets."

"For a Princeton graduate who came out high in his class, you're remarkably dense, Keith," Jacques chided. "If you want to talk to Suzanne, make the occasion."

"Maybe I'm afraid to push her into a corner," Keith said desperately. "I don't want to drive her away from Savage Oaks."

"My friend, this is becoming en obsession with you. Isolated out there on the plantation, you're building fantasies about your passion for your wife. The grinding season is over, you have too much idle time on your hands. Pass the bar examinations and take a small house for yourself and Manon in the city. You'll console yourself," he promised exuberantly.

The waiter appeared with their luncheon, and they abandoned intimate conversation to discuss the coming elections. Keith, decrying the party machine that had been created, was deeply involved in city problems. Jacques was mildly interested.

Keith left Jacques at his office and ordered Lewis to take him home. He had solved nothing by talking with Jacques, he thought morbidly. As the carriage rumbled over the cobblestoned streets in the business day traffic, he spied a familiar vehicle ahead.

The driver wore the uniform coat of an officer of artillery. Caleb, he recognized. After the War in Mexico much military clothing had been auctioned in New Orleans. Like other planters Papa had bought an ample supply. The hands were enthralled with the uniforms. Who had Caleb brought into New Orleans?

He leaned out the window.

"Lewis, Caleb is just ahead. See if you can catch up with him."

Traffic moved slowly along the narrow street. Lewis maneuvered to position himself directly behind the other carriage, though there was no room yet to pull up beside it. Keith heard Suzanne's musical laughter, and then Phillip's voice, though his words were unintelligible in the clatter of the drays.

The other carriage moved ahead. A dray precariously charged forward, putting itself between the two carriages from Savage Oaks. Keith swore under his breath.

"Lewis, try to catch up with them," he leaned forward to repeat urgently.

"Yassir." Lewis was eying the dray ahead with caution.

Keith suspected that they had come in to buy more books at Morgan's. Suzanne said at dinner last night that another little boy had joined her classroom. Phillip was always at Suzanne's heels, Keith thought with vague irritation. Was his brother becoming more important to his wife than he? Phillip would enjoy humiliating him.

When the other carriage turned into another street, Lewis followed; but it appeared impossible to catch up. Now traffic was lightening and the other carriage charged ahead. Keith frowned. Where the devil was Caleb taking Suzanne and Phillip?

The other carriage made another turn, and Keith saw them move ahead onto the road that would take them to the Metairie Race Track.

What the devil was the matter with Phillip? He knew they had not renewed their Metairie membership this year. Nor had Suzanne received the formal invitation required for admission to the ladies' stand. How dare he expose her to the public stand!

"Lewis, let's go home," he ordered tersely.

At the stable he mounted the horse that daily

took him to Tintagel. He was furious that Phillip dared to treat Suzanne as though she were some girl he had met in a dance house on Gallatin Street. How could Suzanne know that the only woman in the public stands were women of questionable background or unknowing visitors to the city?

He rode towards Tintagel, only faintly aware of the pleasantness of the spring day. His mind closed in on the growing friendship between Phillip and Suzanne. Since Suzanne first arrived at Savage Oak, Phillip had been frequently in her company; and he had been grateful for this diversion. Now their closeness was disturbing. Not that he did not completely trust Suzanne, he told himself guiltily. But Phillip, despite his being not yet twenty, considered himself a prize stud.

He had always thought about Phillip as a naughty small boy; but Papa, the most gentle of men, had not flogged him for some small boy transgression. He had been bedding down with the prettiest of the young wenches. And when Jane had pressed, the college had been explicit about their reason for expelling him.

They had all spoiled Phillip from babyhood, Keith thought tiredly. He could be so utterly charming. The children of most planters were spoiled. Most of them were passionately fond of dancing and hunting, but beyond that they exerted themselves not at all. Always dependent upon servants for everything. That was one of the reasons Phillip hated Princeton.

European visitors were always shocked at the planters' indulgence of their children. Why had Papa and Jane not restrained Phillip from his capricious ways? But he knew why; Phillip had that terrible fixation about Mama's death, as though she had deliberately died to deprive him of a mother. But Papa and Jane, who could be so strong and inflexible, allowed Phillip to manipulate them fearfully.

That evening Keith was the first to arrive at the dinner table. He bristled as Suzanne and Phillip walked in together.

"You were in New Orleans this afternoon," he said curtly, without preliminaries.

"How do you know?" Phillip asked warily.

"I went down on business," Keith fabricated. "Lewis tried to catch up with you, but it was impossible."

"Did you go into New Orleans today?" Jane asked with surprise, taking her place at the table.

"The three of us were in New Orleans today," Suzanne said with a guarded smile. "After I shopped at Morgan's, Phillip took me to the Metairie Race Track. I never suspected a race track could be such a showplace! And there must have been ten thousand people present."

"Are you out of your mind, Phillip?" Keith demanded. "Taking Suzanne there!" Suzanne gazed bewilderedly at him.

"Melody took the lead in every heat and held it throughout," Phillip said enthusiastically. "She's a saucy-looking filly."

"Phillip, you know well-bred young ladles do not attend the race track in New Orleans without a formal invitation," Jane said with tight-lipped anger. "That was unforgivable."

"But why was it wrong?" Suzanne gazed from Jane to Keith. "It was an exciting afternoon. The horses were magnificent. The finest in the country, a gentleman beside us told me." She glowed with recall.

"Phillip knows exactly the kind of women who sit in the public stands," Keith said grimly. "He had no right to expose you to that element."

"Keith, don't be so narrow," Phillip said arrogantly. "Some of the finest people from all over the South were there. Suzanne and I talked with a large group of young ladies from some Kentucky plantations who had come down to cheer their horses in the race." He grinned. "You should have heard the hollering."

"How much did you lose, Phillip?" Jane asked drily.

"Nothing," he said triumphantly. "I didn't bet. I had no money," he conceded with ironic humor.

"Next time you take Suzanne somewhere, consider if it's suitable." Keith churned with rage. Was it because Phillip had taken Suzanne to the race track, he asked himself with a tightening of his throat, or because he was all at once aware of how large a part Phillip appeared to be playing in Suzanne's life?

"Keith, we're running low on medical supplies," Jane said crisply, "I'll give you the list in the morning. The next time Reagan goes in for supplies, please ask him to stop at the apothecary."

Keith was taciturn until they rose from the dinner table.

"It's stuffy in the house with fires in all the grates," he said abruptly. "I'm going for a walk. I need some fresh air."

He walked quickly from the dining room and down the hall to the front door. Why had Suzanne looked so stricken when he said he was going for a walk?

He opened the door and went out into the pleasing coolness of the evening, fragrant with the scent of oranges and mint. He walked away from the house, down towards the levee, discomforted by the look on Suzanne's face when he had left the house.

Could she know about Manon? He stopped dead, unsettled by this possibility. No, that was absurd. How could Suzanne possibly know? She had no idea the cottage even existed. She never rode in that direction. Nobody went there.

He had meant to send Manon away right after Suzanne came to his room that night. He frowned. Why did he keep her there in the cottage? His face tightened. Manon remained in the cottage because Suzanne turned him away. He was a man with strong desires. As Jacques would say, why send Manon away while his wife would not let him into her bed?

Nineteen

Spring splashed Louisiana with brilliant color as a myriad of flowers rushed into bloom and filled the air with tantalizing scents. Riding this morning towards Tintagel, Suzanne was awed by the beauty on every side, yet part of her refused to relinquish a deep unhappiness.

Living under the same roof with Keith, knowing about his quadroon mistress, was torturous. Too often she hovered on the brink of confronting him, reproaching him; but each time she restrained herself because such a confrontation would only drive her away from Savage Oaks. How could she continue to love Keith, to dream of lying in his arms again, knowing about his secret life away from the big house?

It was futile, she recognized with frustration, to rebuke herself, to call on pride to oust him from her every waking thought. Pride was a hapless trait in the face of the emotions that Keith evoked in her.

And what of the vow she had made on the day

of Cecile's wedding? She was no closer to knowing about Maman and Papa than she had been in the Convent. And yet she felt that if she reached out a hand in the right direction, turned the right corner, she would walk into long-sought revelations. She could feel Maman and Papa almost reaching out to her. It was a strange, almost terrifying experience.

As she rode along the levee, the sky clouded overhead. She urged Othello to greater speed, a challenge he accepted with alacrity, and arrived at Tintagel only moments before a spring rainstorm burst from the heavens. The children were already in the classroom. Farmers, she thought whimsically, can smell a rain before the heavens reveal a sign.

As always, she enjoyed her time with the children. They gave her a satisfying sense of achievement. How sweet they were, she thought with a surge of affection. She never discussed her activities at Tintagel with Keith or Jane. Only with Phillip. She wished that it were possible to start a school for the black children at Tintagel and Savage Oaks; but this, of course, was forbidden by law in Louisiana. She wished that there was some way that Phillip's children — beguiling Peter and Elizabeth — could be removed from the quarters.

When the studying was over for the day, Suzanne marshaled the children onto the gallery. A father waited politely with a covered wagon to take the children home. Rain was falling again.

"Come on now, move fast so you all don't get

soaked!" he exhorted after bowing to Suzanne and Mrs. Cantrell.

"You'll stay for lunch with me, Miss Suzanne," Mrs. Cantrell said firmly when the carriage had rolled away from the house. "You can't go riding home in this rain."

"I'd love to stay, Mrs. Cantrell," Suzanne accepted with a smile. She could have gone home in a carriage, but she disliked exposing the driver to the rain. She knew, too, that Mrs. Cantrell welcomed her company.

They ate on the side gallery at a small table where Mrs. Cantrell liked to take her meals when the weather was warm enough for comfort. The rain, Suzanne thought, seemed to bring fresh fragrance from the flowers.

"Mr. Noah liked to have his midday meals with a view of the river," Mrs. Cantrell said with nostalgia. "We would sit out here and eat even when it was necessary to wear a cloak. He wished so desperately that he could put the beauty around us on canvas, but he didn't have that talent. Mr. Adrian was the artist in the family." Unexpectedly her eyes filled with tears and she focused on the plate before her.

Mrs. Cantrell had been in love with Mr. Noah, Suzanne realized. This house was a shrine to his memory. To Mrs. Cantrell, she had seemed a callous intruder.

After they had eaten, Mrs. Cantrell insisted Suzanne go upstairs to take the conventional plantation nap.

"This rain won't let up for at least an hour or two," Mrs. Cantrell prophesied, inspecting the cloudy sky. "Go up to your room and take a nap, until it lets up." The room Suzanne had occupied those brief weeks before her marriage remained her room in Mrs. Cantrell's eyes.

"All right," Suzanne acquiesced and laughed. "I ate so much, I'm sleepy already."

But in her room Suzanne found it impossible to sleep. She remembered too vividly the last few hours she had spent here. In this room she had dressed, with such joy in her heart, for her marriage to Keith.

Too restless to remain in bed and haunted by the memories this room evoked, Suzanne rose and walked out into the hall. She hesitated there in the absolute stillness of the house. Mrs. Cantrell was napping. The servants were out in the kitchen house.

In a couple of hours Keith would be arriving to read in the library. All at once her heart was pounding. But she would not be here when Keith arrived. She would leave before then. She stood indecisively in the hall, debating on her destination. Her eyes moved curiously up the staircase that circled to the third floor and to the attic.

Suddenly decisive, Suzanne started up the stairs. Cecile used to talk so romantically about rainy days when she spent hours rummaging about the attic at the family's château at Suresnes. Tintagel was hers; this was her privilege, she told herself defensively.

What would she find in the attic? Family portraits of the Ramsays? The family Bible, perhaps, with births and deaths neatly recorded. Mementos of the generations of Ramsays who had lived and died at Tintagel.

She opened the huge oak door and walked into a musty, dark, wide-beamed room of generous dimensions, where cobwebs hung in fanciful designs from the rafters. The rain beat upon the roof with a mesmerizing regularity. Furniture draped in cloths was scattered about the area. A slipper chair, on which dust lay with velvet thickness, sat before an equally dusty window, as though placed there for a browser caught up in reminiscences of times past. On one rough wall hung an avenue of paintings. At another wall portmanteaus were piled along with a collection of boxes of varying sizes.

Suzanne spied an astral lamp and crossed to where it sat atop a cloth-covered table. She inspected it to see if it contained oil. Soft light suffused a circle of space about her.

Suzanne moved forward to look at the paintings. One depicting a young woman with a baby in her arms was particularly appealing. Mrs. Cantrell said that Adrian was the family artist. These paintings must be his work.

A large square box that bore no kind of fastening captured her attention. She lifted the lid and drew forth a batch of sketches. All of them were of a little girl of about two.

Oddly disturbed by the image of the little girl who stared back at her, Suzanne took the sketches closer to the lamp. No, her imagination was playing tricks! Her eyes darted about the room, seeking confirmation of the absurd suspicions that had taken root within her.

Her gaze settled on a tea caddy veneered in ivory and engraved with English houses. With a sense of imminent discovery, she gingerly lifted the lid. On a lining of white velvet lay a topaz and silver mounted pendant, garnet brooches, a long strand of pearls, an enamel and gem-studded watch, a golden chain from which hung an exquisite cameo.

A feminine member of the Ramsay family had worn these jewels. Beside the tea caddy was a tiny red Chinese lacquer box on which had been affixed a sliver of paper bearing the name "Adrian."

Suzanne lifted the lid. The box contained a pair of jeweled cuff studs and an intricately designed ring. Her eyes clung to the ring. Her throat went dry. *Papa's ring.* Those sketches of the little girl were sketches of her. *Adrian Ramsay was her father.*

With trembling fingers she lifted the ring from its crimson velvet bed and slipped it on her finger. Papa had worn this ring. Papa had been Adrian Ramsay.

With shaking hands, she lifted the lamp to carry it to the paintings that hung on the wall, gazed raptly at the portrait of the young woman holding a baby. Maman and she.

She returned to the tea caddy, which held the

jewelry of one of the Ramsay ladies, and opened it reverently. Perhaps this was her grandmother's jewelry. *Her* family. She had found her family. Joyous tears welled in her eyes. Now she understood why Uncle Gilbert had bought Tintagel. He wanted to bring her home.

Why had he never told her the truth? She would go to him! Today. The instant the rain stopped. She lifted a golden chain with a cameo from the tea caddy and slid the ring — far too large for her slender fingers — beside the cameo on the chain. With a tremulous smile, she brought the chain about her throat, locked the clasp.

Feeling poignantly close to Maman and Papa, she left the attic to return to her room for her cloak. When would the rain stop? She must go to Uncle Gilbert and confront him with her discovery. How could he deny that Adrian Ramsay was her father?

She stood at a window, gazing out at the faint drizzle. Oh, she could not wait another minute! She reached for her cloak and hurried from the room, down the hall to the stairs. She heard one of the servants singing in the library. It was Guinevere. Breathlessly Suzanne sought her out.

"Guinevere, when Mrs. Cantrell awakes, will you please tell her I have taken one of the carriages and gone into New Orleans."

"Yes'm," Guinevere said warmly. "I'll be sure to tell her."

By the time Suzanne reached the stable, the

drizzle had stopped and the sun had burst radiantly through the clouds. She asked that a carriage be brought out to take her into New Orleans immediately.

All the way into New Orleans she sat on the edge of her seat, staring out the window without seeing. Intermittently one hand moved involuntarily to the ring that nestled unseen within the bodice of her dress. It was Papa's ring. No one could convince her differently.

She found Gilbert in his office, closeted with a client. She waited impatiently for him to be free. As always he greeted her affectionately.

"Come in and sit down, Suzanne," he invited with a smile. "Grandmère is still carrying on about the way you charmed everybody at Mr. Grimshaw's party."

"Uncle Gilbert," she brushed aside preliminaries, "I went up to the attic at Tintagel this afternoon. I discovered a painting of a young woman and a little girl. I found a dozen sketches of that same little girl. Uncle Gilbert, I was the little girl in the painting and the sketches." She pulled the chain from the bodice of her dress to display the ring. "I found this. Papa's ring. All these years I've clung to the memory of it. Uncle Gilbert, I can't be wrong. Adrian Ramsay was my father."

Gilbert's face was grave and he gently placed his hand over hers.

"Yes, Suzanne. Adrian was your father," he acknowledged. "You're the last of the Ramsays. Your mother — Moira — was a beautiful young

326

Irish girl from a working class family. Adrian's plantation-bred mother was horrified at his wish to marry Moira. She would hear nothing of it. Adrian and Moira ran away to Paris to make a new life for themselves there." Uncle Gilbert said nothing of their being married, Suzanne realized painfully. This was why she could not inherit Tintagel. "When you were three, Noah wrote Adrian that their mother was dying and pleaded with him to come home. Adrian came back to Tintagel to be with his mother in her final days. He told me he would bring Moira and you to live at Tintagel as soon as he could convince the family that this was the only way he would re-main. But in the chaotic few weeks after his ar-rival, his mother died and three days later Robert was murdered. Two weeks after that your father, too, was murdered." Gilbert hesitated, his eyes somber. "There was never a moment when Adrian could tell the family about your mother and you. Noah had a breakdown. For three months he remained in his room. He spoke to no one. Mrs. Cantrell cared for him, ran the house. When he recovered, I went to tell him about your mother and you, but Noah absolutely refused to believe you were Adrian's child."

"My mother," Suzanne asked tremulously. "She's still alive?" In Paris? Close to the Convent all these years of her growing up? *Why* had Maman put her into the Convent?

"I don't know what happened to her, Suzanne," Gilbert said unhappily. "I went to Paris to tell her

327

about Adrian's death and to advise about the funds that would be available to her from his estate. She was distraught. She gave you over to my care and disappeared. I never heard from her again. I placed you with Mère Angélique because this seemed best. Noah, the only remaining brother of the three Ramsays, refused to recognize you as Adrian's child. Suzanne, your father and mother were married," Gilbert said urgently, "but I had no way of proving that in a court of law. Your mother had disappeared. That's why Tintagel went to distant cousins at Noah's death. I'm glad I was able to buy it back for you."

"Uncle Gilbert, I must find Maman." Suzanne's eyes clung to his. "How can I do this?"

"Suzanne, there is no way," he said gently. "For fourteen years there has been no word of her. And please, Suzanne," he urged, "say nothing of this to anyone. You know. Let that be enough. Nothing is to be gained by telling anyone that you are Adrian Ramsay's daughter. It isn't likely that you'll be believed," he reminded ruefully. "Noah would never accept it."

"I'll say nothing," she promised.

Riding back to Tintagel, Suzanne searched her mind for some way to trace her mother. Maman was alive. In Paris? She could go back to Paris, search. Cecile's father was an important man in Paris. He would surely help. But where would they begin, she asked herself in frustration?

She left the carriage at Tintagel and rode Othello back to Savage Oaks. Hurrying up the stairs, she could hear Phillip at the piano. He only played when he was depressed. He hated himself for not playing as well as Keith.

She was relieved not to have to face Phillip at this moment, she thought as she closed the door to her room behind her. Then, with a start, she realized Patrice was in the room, sitting in a chair by the window, fixing the hem of a dress Suzanne particularly liked.

Patrice had known Papa. All at once she felt so close to him. Patrice had come to live at Tintagel as a small girl, years before Papa was born.

"Patrice — " She fought to keep her voice lightly curious. "You knew Mr. Adrian Ramsay, didn't you?" Again, involuntarily, her hand moved to the bodice of her dress to reassure herself that Papa's ring hung by the slender chain about her throat.

Patrice's face lighted.

"Miss Suzanne, I was his nurse. When he was born, his Mama don't have enough milk to feed him. My baby — my only black baby," she emphasized, "he was born dead just a few days befo'. I took that hungry little fella to my breast and suckled him. His Mama say nobody but Patrice take care of her baby. I raised him, Missy — him de sweetes' man that ever lived." Tears filled her eyes. "I loved him like he was my own."

"Patrice, what was he like?" She trembled with excitement. "Tell me about him."

She pulled a chair close beside Patrice and listened while Patrice reminisced about Adrian

Ramsay. As Patrice talked, she could visualize him as a small boy, then as he grew older and battled with his mother about his intention to become an artist. She could visualize the high-spirited, intense man he became. Papa, who tucked her into her small bed each night. And in memory she heard Maman's light laughter. But after Papa was murdered, Maman had given her over to Uncle Gilbert and run away in her grief. Where had she run? Where was she now? "Patrice, did Mr. Adrian ever tell you about his wife?" Suzanne asked unsteadily.

"He never married, Miss Suzanne," she said sadly. "Nuthin' I wanted more than to care for his children."

"There was never a young lady he cared for especially?" Suzanne prodded.

Patrice hesitated.

"I ain't supposed to know," she said, troubled. "But before he went away, he had some pow'ful fights with his Mama about some young lady he knew in New Orleans. His Mama, she wanted him to marry one of the pretty plantation young ladies what was after him. But he went off to Paris, and he didn't come home again till she was dyin'." Patrice was quietly weeping. "Them was terrible times here, the Missis dying that way, then Mist' Robert right after, and then Mist' Adrian."

"He was the youngest?" Suzanne asked softly.

"Yes'm. Mist' Adrian, he was the baby of the family. After they all died, Mist' Noah was strange. He never went outta the house. It made him sad that there was no more Ramsays to live at Tintagel when he'd die."

But there was another Ramsay, Suzanne told herself with pride. She was Adrian Ramsay's daughter and Tintagel was hers. But she would not rest, she vowed, until she found Maman.

Twenty

Suzanne moved about Savage Oaks in an aura of rapturous unreality. She was a Ramsay. Maman and Papa had been married; Uncle Gilbert said this and she believed him. Why had Mr. Noah — Uncle Noah — refused to recognize this?

Because he couldn't accept a sister-in-law who was not a fine plantation lady, Suzanne's mind derided. The Ramsays felt disgraced that Papa had married an Irish girl from a working-class family. And after Noah's breakdown, Mrs. Cantrell indicated, he had become eccentric.

Tintagel should have gone to her at Noah's death, not to the distant cousins who lived out in Texas. But it was hers now. Her ancestral home.

She looked forward with fresh intensity to going to Tintagel each morning. Patrice told her Papa had been born in that big front bedroom that overlooked the grove of orange trees. He had studied with his tutor, whom he shared with her Uncle Robert, in the music room. He had intended to bring Maman and their baby back to the plantation.

So many times she had to bite back the words that threatened to spill from her when she was with Mrs. Cantrell. Mrs. Cantrell had known Papa. But she had promised Uncle Gilbert that she would tell no one that she was Adrian Ramsay's daughter.

How could she begin to search for Maman? Mère Angélique knew nothing. Uncle Gilbert had brought her to the Convent. Could she write Cecile and ask her to beseech her father to help? But what could she tell the Comte de Mirabeau, she asked herself? *Where was Maman?*

As she lay in bed this morning, she realized this was Election Day. Her eyes sought the clock. Keith would be leaving shortly for New Orleans. These past three weeks Keith had been going into the city three days a week to help the Democratic forces.

When Patrice arrived with her coffee, she drank appreciatively while Patrice chattered happily about the twins born in the quarters during the night. She dressed with unusual haste, to be down at the breakfast table before Keith left for the polls. She was uneasy; she remembered the violence that accompanied the local elections. Jane would be at the table, she reassured herself; she would not be alone with Keith.

"I'm not optimistic about our putting in our man," Keith was saying to Jane and Phillip, who was downstairs unusually early this morning, as

Suzanne entered the room and went to her place at the table.

"Keith, I worry about you going into New Orleans today," Jane said anxiously. "I dread every Election Day."

"I'll be all right," Keith said briskly. "I'm not going to roam about New Orleans alone." As he leaned forward to take another biscuit, Suzanne was shocked to discover he wore a pistol at his waist.

"I thought New Orleans had a lot of policemen." The realization that Keith was armed unnerved her. "Won't they be guarding the polls?"

"The police," Keith said bitterly, "will look the other way when brutality is involved. Unless it's their side that's losing."

"You don't expect us to have a Democratic Mayor," Phillip reminded, earning Keith's irritation. "What's happening to New Orleans?"

"You know damn well what's happening," Keith shot back. "You read the newspapers." The *Picayune,* the *Crescent,* and the *Delta* lay on the sideboard. "The American Party is going to try every violent means to keep Democrats from the polls." He sighed heavily. "New Orleans hasn't had a municipal administration within memory that wasn't corrupt. Bad government is normal government."

"Including the Democratic administrations," Phillip needled. "All Louisiana knows how the Democrats have run in triple voters, taking names from tombstones. Nobody's hands are clean."

"And it must stop!" Keith said tightly. "We have to bring in honest reform."

"Robert Ramsay was murdered for trying that," Jane reminded bitterly. "And Adrian after him."

A chill swept over Suzanne. Papa had been murdered for his part in politics. Now Keith was becoming involved. And she encouraged this.

"Keith, please be careful," she pleaded involuntarily, and felt color rush to her face as Keith's eyes settled on her. "Don't take chances," she stammered in confusion.

Moments after Keith left the house, she went to the stable. Riding Othello to Tintagel she tried vainly to thrust aside her anxiety for Keith. She wished the day were past and he was safely home.

For a while Suzanne was able to submerge her alarm in her activities with the children, but returning to Savage Oaks, she was again beset by fears. Papa had been murdered, and her Uncle Robert, because, like Keith, they hoped to bring clean government to New Orleans. Dear God, let Keith be safe.

After the midday meal, Jane left the house as usual. Phillip went up to his room. Suzanne settled herself on the gallery with the latest newspapers to arrive at Savage Oaks. What was happening in New Orleans? Was Keith all right? She was assaulted by visions of him lying in a cobblestoned street, bloodied and unconscious.

Too restless to read, beset by anxieties for Keith's safety, she left the gallery to stroll down to the levee. But she could not erase Keith from her mind. He no longer made any effort to come to her room, she taunted herself. Why should he? There was the girl in the cottage. But I love him, she thought desperately. Can Keith find with that girl what we shared? Why doesn't Keith send his mistress away? That's all I ask of him.

"Suzanne — " She started at the sound of Phillip's voice. "I saw you from my window," he said gently. "You looked so alone walking beside the river."

"I couldn't read this afternoon." She knew Phillip would understand.

"You're worried because Keith's down in New Orleans in the midst of what's sure to be violence." His eyes were sympathetic.

"I know Keith can take care of himself." She tried to feel confident, but she could not forget the pistol at his waist.

"Come back to the house with me. We'll play some backgammon," he offered.

"Phillip, I've found out about Papa," she said impetuously, and paused in consternation.

"What did you learn?" Phillip demanded.

"I promised Uncle Gilbert I'd tell no one," she stammered.

"Suzanne, tell me," he coaxed earnestly. "You have to share it with someone."

"Just you," Suzanne stipulated. "But you must

say nothing to Keith or Jane. To no one." Her eyes searched his.

"Our secret," he promised seriously.

Haltingly, Suzanne told him what she had discovered, of her confrontation with Uncle Gilbert and his confirmation. Phillip listened with mounting astonishment.

"You should have inherited Tintagel," he said indignantly.

"Uncle Gilbert knew no way to prove that Maman and Papa were married, and that I should legally inherit," she pointed out. "No one would believe that Adrian Ramsay was my father. His brother Noah would never believe it. But at least I know, Phillip." She smiled joyously. "And Papa meant to bring us here." She was no disgrace to the Savage name; Papa and Maman were married.

"I don't remember Adrian," Phillip said candidly. "But Jane adored him. He taught her to paint when she was a child. The talent must run in the family," he said with ironic humor. "Didn't I tell you the Ramsays and Savages are distant cousins? But more distant than the ones who inherited," he conceded wryly.

"I remember," Suzanne said tenderly.

"And your mother?" Phillip asked. "Mr. Mauriac has never heard from her through the years?"

"Not once," she said wistfully. Why had Maman not come back to the Convent for her when she recovered from her grief? "Phillip, I

337

must find her — but I don't know how to begin to search. She could be anywhere in Europe."

"Suzanne, maybe she's in Paris." Phillip's eyes were bright. "She could be. Suzanne — " He reached for her shoulders to pull her close. "Why don't you and I go off to Paris to search for your mother? I've always wanted to see Paris. We could be happy there, Suzanne. Just the two of us. Keith doesn't deserve you!"

"Phillip, don't talk that way," she whispered, pale with shock. "You're my brother-in-law and my dear friend."

Phillip's hands were unsteady as he released her.

"Forget this ever happened. It was a crazy dream."

He stalked away from her. Suzanne watched as he disappeared into the woods. As though to remove herself from their encounter, she walked in the opposite direction, upbraiding herself for confiding in Phillip when she had promised Uncle Gilbert she would say nothing.

She emerged from a stretch of woods to view a vast sweep of fallow fields. The land had been plowed and left unseeded until next season. She had never wandered south of the big house before today.

She felt as though she were walking across a vast open plain. No human, no animal in sight. It was an unexpectedly relaxing experience, and unconsciously she quickened her pace, covering a far greater distance than she realized.

A rumble of thunder brought her gaze to the darkening skies. Another spring shower seemed imminent. All at once she was concerned about shelter. Her eyes skimmed the stretch of woods to her left. Was there a barn, a shack somewhere there in the woods?

A narrow footpath claimed her attention. With the first huge droplets falling from the sky she hurried to the path, half-running in her desire to find cover.

All at once through the thick foliage of the towering trees she spied the outlines of a house. She had roamed beyond Savage Oaks property, but the owners of the house would surely give her shelter.

A tall, white house, far from being as grand as Savage Oaks, but nonetheless of a highly pleasing appearance, stood in a clearing where flowers grew in riotous abandon. The house and grounds showed little of the constant attention that was lavished on Savage Oaks.

Self-consciously she approached the gallery. What a strange silence here! All the upstairs windows, she noted curiously, were tightly draped. There were no slaves about the grounds. Was the house deserted?

As she stood at the foot of the steps in indecision, the clouds unleashed a downpour. She started up the stairs and to the door. The rain was falling on a slant, drenching the gallery, which was devoid of chairs except for two worn rockers. Suzanne lifted the knocker, moving close to the door to avoid the rain. She waited. No one replied to her knock.

The house must be deserted. Curious about the charming old house, she opened the door and walked into a starkly bare hall. A door to the right displayed an impressively large but sparsely furnished drawing room, its walls adorned with a parade of paintings. Suzanne walked into the room with a feeling of adventure. This was used as a studio, she realized as her eyes fell on an easel by the window.

She absorbedly studied first one painting, then another.

They were oddly disturbing, obviously by an artist of immense talent.

"What are you doing here?" A furious — familiar — voice spun her around in guilt.

Jane stood in the doorway, white and shaken. At her side was a girl with fair hair that fell to her waist and delicately chiseled face with an other-world serenity. But at the realization of Suzanne's presence she seemed suddenly a frightened little girl. A short, heavy, elderly servant hovered fearfully behind them.

"I'm sorry," Suzanne stammered. "I was looking for shelter from the storm. Nobody answered. I thought the house was deserted."

"Callie, take Katie upstairs." Jane was fighting for control. She waited until the other two started up the elaborately carved staircase that led to the upper floors before she returned her accusing gaze to Suzanne. "Katie is a young cousin for whom I care," she said stiffly. "Katie has a great fear of people. She's been raised apart from everyone. You must have noticed," Jane pointed out painfully, "that Katie has the mind of a small child. This house was my mother's home before her marriage. Now it belongs to Savage Oaks."

"Jane, I'm sorry — " Suzanne began to apologize but Jane seemed not to have heard her.

"Not even Keith or Phillip know that Katie lives here. They know only that I use the old house as a studio. No one is allowed here," she wound up with formidable sternness.

"I didn't mean to frighten Katie," Suzanne said gently.

"Suzanne, I — I must ask a favor of you." With great effort she forced herself to go on. "Please, say nothing to Keith or Phillip about Katie."

"I'll say nothing, Jane," Suzanne promised.

"Joseph will take you back to Savage Oaks in the carriage. Wait here, please."

Jane stood on the gallery and watched the carriage roll away from the house, en route to Savage Oaks. For over eighteen years she had lived in fear that Keith or Phillip would come here and discover Katie. When they were young, it had been easy to restrict their activities away from this extension of Savage Oaks. When they grew older, she had sternly warned that she would allow no callers at the house that served as her studio. Keith and Phillip respected this.

341

Could she trust Suzanne? Desperately she searched her mind. Something in Suzanne's eyes had been reassuring. She could be trusted, Jane decided instinctively. She had looked at Katie with compassion.

Jane walked back into the house and into the room where she painted. Usually when she was disturbed, she found relief in painting. Not today. Her mind was hurtling back through the years to that night when she lay in her bed, terrified and shamed . . .

"What are you doing in Jane's room?" Mama screamed hysterically, pulling the drunken intruder from her. "What have you done to that child?"

"I taught her what I taught you," he roared, and laughed as Mama cried out in anguish.

"You monster!" Mama's voice soared. "I'll kill you! I'll kill you!"

She crouched against the pillows, pulling the coverlet over her torn nightdress while Mama pummeled him with her fists. He stumbled backwards. The shutters of the window behind him were open. She saw him plunge through the window, to the ground below. Even now she could hear his startled screams.

"My baby, my baby!" Sobbing hysterically, Mama swept her into her arms. "I couldn't believe he could do such a thing! My poor baby!"

Papa burst into the room, followed by three of the servants. She was conscious of Papa's shock as he saw the broken window. He crossed the room, stared down at the body lying below.

"Arthur, go down there and see if he's alive," Papa ordered as he struggled to pull Mama away from her. "Janie, are you all right?" His face was a mixture of solicitude and fury.

"He hurt me!" she sobbed and buried her face in her pillow in shame.

"Thorne, he violated my baby! His own child! Thorne, how could he take his own daughter?" *What was Mama saying?*

"Jane's going to be all right," Papa soothed, cradling Mama in his arms. But he was not her father, she realized in the midst of her agony. That monster was her father. That was what Mama just said!

"Annie Mae, bring her dressing gown," Papa ordered. But again in her tortured mind she remembered that Papa was not her father. He was Keith's father and Phillip's father, but not hers. "Callie, you go downstairs and send Abram for the doctor! Right away, Callie!"

Papa sat at the edge of the bed, holding Mama and rocking with her in mutual anguish, while she herself lay cold as ice, her face buried in the pillow, hiding her torn nightdress. She could never look anybody in the eye after tonight. *Not after what happened in this room.*

Arthur returned. When he spoke, his voice was rich with grief.

"He dead, Mister Thorne."

"We'll have to bury him, Arthur," Papa said sternly. "No one must ever know he was here."

"No, Sir."

Annie Mae came back into the room with Mama's dressing gown.

"I take care of her, Mist' Thorne," she said gently, as Papa rose to his feet as he released Mama. "Callie, she comin' up the stairs. She stay with Lil' Missy."

Annie Mae, crooning encouragement, helped Mama into her dressing gown. Mama was dazed, unseeing, sobbing under her breath as Annie Mae coaxed her to her feet.

"I take you back to you room, Missy," Annie Mae soothed. "Callie heah now. She stay with Lil' Missy."

Annie Mae took Mama back to her room. Callie, tears streaming down her face, brought a fresh nightdress, put it on her as though she were a tiny girl.

"Lil' Missy, you just sit heah while I change them sheets."

She allowed Callie to help her to the chair, shuddering when she saw the blood on the sheets. And then all at once the silence was shattered by an agonizing scream from Annie Mae.

"Missy, no! No!" But as Annie Mae screamed, a shot rang out.

"Mama, Mama!" She ran from the room to the one next door. Down the hall the baby was crying. "Mama!"

Mama was lying on the floor, blood gushing from her breast. Annie Mae rocked back and forth in grief. The gun lay on the floor.

"Oh, baby, baby," Annie Mae moaned, tugging

at her as she hovered on the floor above Mama. "She dead, my poor sweet baby. She dead."

Weeks later, when Papa could bring himself to talk about that night, he told her about the man who was her father. He had deliberately arranged for word to be sent to her mother that he was dead. Two years later she remarried. Then, all these years later, he showed up at Savage Oaks, intent on blackmail. To save the family from disgrace, Papa was trying to raise a massive loan on Savage Oaks. Their guest lied when he said he was leaving that night. He was waiting for the loan to come through.

Papa never talked again about that night. In his mind, and in hers, he was her father. Not till three months after she was violated did she know she was carrying a baby. It was Callie who noticed her swelling belly and went to Papa. Callie who moved with her into Mama's old house when it was no longer possible to hide the baby she carried.

Tiredly Jane sat in a chair by the window, the past refusing to relinquish its grip on her. She was remembering how Papa told the neighbors she had gone to cousins in Atlanta to get over her grief at Mama's death. Nobody knew how Mama died. Nobody knew about the man buried in a clearing near the levee.

Every day Papa came to the house and sat with her, comforting her. She prayed the baby would be born dead. Covertly Callie brought voodoo medicine to make her lose the baby. She brought

Mammy Eunice to the house to give her an evil-smelling concoction that only made her vomit. The baby within her grew bigger and bigger, making it so awkward that Callie set up a bedroom downstairs for her.

When Jane's pains started, Callie sent Joseph for Mammy Eunice. But he returned alone. Mammy Eunice had fallen that morning and broken her hip. He had not dared bring anybody else from the quarters. They could trust Mammy Eunice not to gossip, but any of the others who helped with the births were sure to talk. It would spread from one plantation to another that Jane Savage was not in Atlanta, that she had just been delivered of a baby. Father unknown.

Grim-faced Callie pressed Joseph into service.

"You go set the water to boilin'. Pains sure comin' fast for a first baby!"

"Callie, where's Mammy Eunice?" she asked, terrified by the pains that regularly assaulted her. "Callie!" she screamed suddenly, "Oh, Callie, make it stop! Make it stop!"

"Get outta heah, Joseph," Callie ordered. "This baby's sure in a hurry."

Despite the coolness of the day, with the fire sending little warmth to the bed where she lay, she was drenched with perspiration as the pains racked her, only moments apart. She screamed, again and again, as the mass within her thrust toward freedom.

"Callie it hurts," she moaned. "You never said it would hurt so awful!"

"Lil' Missy, you gotta help," Callie add sternly. "Come on now, you push. Push hard!"

"I am, Callie," she whimpered.

"Honey, push some more," Callie coaxed anxiously, hovering over her. "This is one big baby."

"I hope it's dead!" she cried out while she ripped at the heavy cloth Callie had placed in her hands. "I hope it's dead!"

"It's comin' the right way!" Callie said triumphantly. "I can see the head!"

With a determination to rid her body of this monster within her, she pushed with superhuman effort, feeling the tear as the baby emerged from her.

"It's a lil' girl," Callie said gently. "Joseph," she yelled through the closed door, "you come heah and take care this baby whilst I looks after Miss Jane."

Much later, when Jane lay exhausted against the pillows, Callie brought Katie to her. Not until she held Katie in her arms had she known that this child would be her whole life.

Not for many months did they understand that Katie's mind was not right, though Callie admitted later that she had been troubled that Katie lay so placidly in her cradle, hands never flailing as with normal infants. Her poor cursed baby, born of her incestuous relationship with the monster who was her father.

Twenty-one

Keith left New Orleans as the cathedral bells were chiming to vespers. The Mississippi was bright with the fading rays of the sun. Normally the busy hum of daily life would be hushing at this hour, but not on Election Day. Drunks caroused in the streets. Injury or even murder stalked the unwary. He was relieved when the carriage was beyond the city and another day of political violence was behind him.

When the ballots were counted, Waterman and his slate would be in control for the next two years. Waterman was a figurehead, he thought with contempt; the party manipulators of the sanctimonious Reform American Party, which had dropped Reform from their name, would have their way in New Orleans.

With the terrorism that surrounded the polls, too many Democrats made no effort to vote. Damn the police for standing by and doing nothing! Fear or collusion, he asked himself?

Phillip's blunt talk about the Democratic Party

had unsettled him. A man from Tammany Hall in New York came down years ago, Papa had said, to show the Democrats how to become winners. The methods they learned over the years brought no honor to the party. And now the Democratic Party cared little about local elections; only the State and National elections claimed their attention. The Senator had cannily enlisted his help because these precincts were personally important to him. When were they going to clean up local politics?

Night descended as the carriage turned into the private roadway to Savage Oaks, with the suddenness that was part of living at the thirty degrees north latitude. The lower floor of the house was brightly lighted, seeming to glow with welcome as the carriage approached. The air was fragrant, the night silence restful after the cacophony of the city.

He was exhausted from the tensions of moving about in a city where knives, pistols, and brass knuckles were considered part of the necessary dress for the day. Suzanne had worried about Keith's going into New Orleans today, he recalled with tenderness. She had not meant to let him realize that she was concerned for his safety, but at recurrent intervals today he remembered her saying, "Keith, be careful."

Lewis pulled up in front of the house, and Keith leapt down from the carriage. The front door swung wide. Suzanne stood in the spill of light from the foyer chandelier. How relieved she seemed as he hurried up the steps to the gallery.

"Jane held dinner," she said self-consciously, moving back into the foyer as he approached.

Jane appeared at the dining room door. She, too, was relieved that Keith was safely back from New Orleans.

"I'll tell Arthur to serve dinner immediately," Jane said. She was pale tonight. "We're having pompano."

"This is the month for pompano." Jane knew this was his favorite among fish. She, too, was relieved that he was back from New Orleans.

Over dinner they somberly discussed the distressing situation of the New Orleans elections.

"You know the American Party's hostility towards naturalized Americans," Keith said heatedly. "It's a miracle when an immigrant is allowed to vote. What respect can they have for the citizenship they've won?" he asked bitterly. He was silent about the roving gangs intent on beating up the Irish, the Italians, and the Germans who might dare to approach the polls.

Earlier than usual, drained by the efforts of the day, Keith excused himself to go up to his room. His eyes lingered hopefully on Suzanne. She was challenging Phillip to a game of backgammon.

As Keith had feared, the American Party swept into power. The Democratic vote had declined by over two thousand from the previous November. They carried only three of the city's twenty-five precincts. More than ever Keith wished to become involved in the fight for clean government.

The whitewashing of the cabins and the fencing had been completed. The shutters at the big house had been freshly painted. The balmy early summer air was laden with the scents of honeysuckle, cape jessamine, and Lady bank roses. The crêpe myrtle trees were rich with pink blossoms. In the freshly plowed fields, tiny spears of cane were shooting through the earth, and in sparkling water of the drains and ditches young crawfish swam.

In the midst of early summer splendor, punctured by spells of heat such as Suzanne had never experienced, word came from the quarters that two of the children were stricken with scarlet fever. When Keith quietly ordered the family to stay away from the quarters because of the fever, Suzanne's eyes moved involuntarily to Phillip. He was alarmed.

"Does it look bad?" Phillip asked.

"Scarlet fever is never good," Keith reminded grimly. "Jane, dispense with your Monday mornings at the quarters. Mammy Eunice has plenty of supplies. She knows what to do. I'll ask Dr. Kenneth to drop by the infirmary as soon as he can."

"Dr. Kenneth never comes unless somebody's dying," Phillip said contemptuously. "All he cares about is collecting his six hundred a year as Savage Oaks' physician."

"Nobody knows more than Mammy Eunice about caring for scarlet fever," Jane reproved.

"She'll keep the sick ones apart from the others so it doesn't spread."

Phillip sat tense and troubled, refusing to be cajoled into a game of backgammon. He was fearful that Peter and Elizabeth were ill with scarlet fever. How could Keith, who was so perceptive, not realize that these were Phillip's children? Or did he simply believe the children were fathered by some itinerant peddler who took his pleasure with young slaves from the quarters?

She was uneasy when Phillip abruptly left the drawing room and she heard him leave the house. Jane, too, was disturbed. She must know about Peter and Elizabeth, though she would remain silent about such knowledge.

Phillip had not returned to the house when Jane suggested to Keith and Suzanne that they retire to their rooms. The evening was uncomfortably humid. No breeze stirred through the trees to relieve the heat.

"I'll tell Arthur to bring up the baires," Jane said fretfully. "Suzanne, you must sleep under the netting to keep the mosquitos away. I've seen a few buzzing about the house today."

"Thank you, Jane." Suzanne felt a new softness in Jane towards her, and for this she was grateful. Even at dinner she had sensed this.

"Suzanne, stay out of New Orleans from now until the hot weather is over," Keith cautioned as they left the drawing room and walked to the stairs along with Jane. "The city is supposed to be taking all kinds of precautions against another outbreak of yellow fever, but I still think it's dangerous during the summer." His eyes rested on her with such intensity that she immediately lowered her own.

How much longer could she go on living this way? Under the same roof with Keith, yet lying alone each night, her door locked against him. *When would he send that girl away?*

In her room she prepared for bed and obediently allowed Patrice to settle the baire about the posts of her bed, protecting her against the mosquitos that buzzed persistently in the night stillness. Not until she was sure Patrice was downstairs and on her way to the cabin behind the house where the servants slept did she lift the baire, leave her bed and cross to the window to watch for Phillip's return.

At last she spied him emerging from the grove of orange trees.

She opened her door a few inches, drawing her dressing gown snugly about her, and waited while Phillip mounted the stairs.

"Peter and Elizabeth are all right," he whispered.

Three days later, when she rode up to Tintagel, she saw the wagon in front of the house. There were no laughing, good-naturedly squabbling children this morning. A pair of parents waited for her to pull up beside them.

"Miss Suzanne, we didn't bring the chillun this mornin' because we hear tell there's scarlet fever runnin' around in the parish. With the weather gettin' hot, it ain't good for 'em to be away from home," the mother of three of her students said apologetically.

"You understand, Miss Suzanne," their father said earnestly. "It ain't that we don't appreciate that they're learnin', but we're sure scared of the fever."

"I understand," Suzanne soothed, but she was wistful at this sudden cessation of her class. She had known, though, that this was imminent.

"Will you teach 'em again when the weather gets cool?" the farmer's wife asked hopefully.

"As soon as the weather permits," Suzanne promised. "Tell them for me, please."

She visited briefly with Mrs. Cantrell, then headed back to Savage Oaks. Leaving Othello at the stable, she encountered Phillip walking purposefully towards the quarters.

"Phillip — " He had not seen her, so engrossed was he in his thoughts. "Phillip, where are you going?" she called in alarm.

He stopped dead, startled at the sound of her voice, and waited for her to catch up with him.

"Eight children are sick in the quarters this morning," he said tersely. "Mammy Eunice sent someone to the house. She needs more supplies. I have to see if Peter and Elizabeth are all right."

"Phillip, you mustn't expose yourself to the fever," Suzanne put a restraining hand on his arm.

"Why not?" he challenged. "They're my children. Anyhow, I've had scarlet fever. I'm immune."

She stood uncertainly while Phillip strode away from her toward the grove of pecans that

354

was a shortcut to the quarters. She watched until he disappeared from view. Then suddenly she darted after him, arriving at the edge of the quarters only a dozen feet behind him.

"Phillip! Wait for me!"

He swung about in astonishment.

"Suzanne, you shouldn't be here."

"I want to help," she insisted breathlessly.

His eyes searched hers. He smiled faintly and reached for her hand.

"They're not in the infirmary," he said quietly. "Mammy Eunice has set up beds in that small outbuilding that usually stores equipment." He pointed to what was now the contagious ward.

Together they walked inside. Mammy Eunice was talking softly to herself as she hovered over a querulous child.

"Mammy Eunice, we've come to help," Suzanne said calmly while Phillip's eyes moved from bed to bed.

"Peter and Elizabeth." His face was drained of color. "They're here." He walked quickly to a pair of beds set up in one corner of the room.

"They's bad," Mammy Eunice said unhappily. "'Bout the worst of the chillun."

"Phillip, I had some training as a nurse at the Convent," she said urgently. "Trust me to help with Peter and Elizabeth."

"Keith will be furious if you stay," Phillip warned. "He'll be afraid you'll catch the fever."

"Phillip, I can be useful here." Mammy Eunice had piled blankets atop each small form. This was not what the Sisters had taught.

"Missy, it ain't right fo' you to stay," Mammy Eunice said worriedly.

"You can't handle all the children alone," Suzanne insisted. All the able-bodied women were in the fields. She went to Elizabeth, touched one flushed cheek. Poor baby, how hot she was. In her fretful sleep, Elizabeth scratched at the ugly eruptions on her face. Gently Suzanne pulled the hand away. "Mammy Eunice, take away the blankets. We must bring down their temperature."

"Yes'm." Mammy Eunice was shocked at her unorthodox order. "I was tryin' to make 'em sweat to break the fever."

"We'll try a better way," Suzanne said gently.

"Suzanne, Peter's talking strangely!" Phillip was upset. Peter's eyes were open, but he gazed unseeingly at the ceiling, muttering incoherent phrases.

"It's the fever, Mist' Phillip," Mammy Eunice explained.

"What did the doctor tell you to do for the children, Mammy Eunice?" Suzanne inquired.

"He don' come to the quarter for fever," she said with a look of surprise. "I got a bottle of brandy. I wash 'em down three or four times every day with burnt brandy and cloves. An' if they'll take it, I gives 'em tea."

"We've got to get that fever down. Phillip, go up to the house and bring back clean sheets. A lot of them. Right away. Mammy Eunice, we'll need buckets of cold water."

Without a waste of motion, Mammy Eunice moved to a window and called out.

"Sarah, Josie, you go git two buckets of cold water from the well an' bring 'em here. Move your tails!"

"Mammy Eunice, do we have enough brandy?" Phillip asked.

"Could sure use some more," she conceded.

"I'll bring a gallon," he promised.

Hour after hour, Suzanne, Phillip, and Mammy Eunice moved about the room wrapping the children in freshly soaked sheets, touching small foreheads.

"The fever's dropping in all of them," Suzanne said at last with relief, and Mammy Eunice nodded in agreement. She frowned in thought, frustrated at her lack of medical knowledge. "Phillip, does Dr. Kenneth live in New Orleans?"

"No, on a plantation about forty minutes from us," Phillip was watching her in fresh alarm. "He has an office cottage there."

"If Dr. Kenneth is too busy to come to the quarters, Phillip," Suzanne said stubbornly, "then you go to him and ask what we should do for our patients. He can exert himself that much."

"You're sure the fever's dropping?" he asked, wanting reassurance.

"Absolutely." Suzanne managed a smile.

"I'll go right over to Dr. Kenneth's office. If he's not there, I'll wait."

Suzanne and Mammy Eunice sponged each

child in burnt brandy, talking soothingly as they moved from one bed to another. Suzanne started at the sharp knock on the door. As she turned to respond, the door opened and Keith stalked into the room.

"What the devil are you doing here, Suzanne?" he demanded agitatedly.

"I'm helping Mammy Eunice care for the children." She was trembling all at once. How upset Keith was! "You mustn't stay here. You know how contagious the fever is."

"I've had it," he said bluntly. "Have you?"

"No," she acknowledged, "but I have tremendous resistance. I'm never sick." Her eyes met his defiantly.

"You should not expose yourself to it," he tried again.

"I'll stay here till the children are mending," she insisted spiritedly. "I've had some training at the Convent in the care of the sick."

Keith sighed.

"I knew you'd be stubborn about this. But I'll worry every minute you're here." If Mammy Eunice were not with them, Suzanne thought, he would pull her into his arms. "I'll have a basket of food sent from the house." He turned to Mammy Eunice. "You make sure she eats."

"Yes sir." Mammy Eunice smiled tenderly.

Keith's eyes moved compassionately about the roomful of small patients.

"If you need anything, send word to the house." He reached for Suzanne's hand, brought it to his mouth. "I'll worry every minute you're here."

"Keith, you must stay away." Suzanne struggled to keep her voice even. "You don't want to carry the fever up to the house."

An hour later Phillip returned from his consultation with Dr. Kenneth. Suzanne and Mammy Eunice waited anxiously for the words of advice he brought.

"Dr. Kenneth said to sponge them in whiskey," Phillip reported. "I told him you were using burnt brandy and cloves, and he said that was just as good." Mammy Eunice beamed. "How are they?" Phillip's eyes turned to the adjoining beds where Elizabeth and Peter lay.

"Restless but the fever's lower. All of the children have sore throats and their rashes itch. If we can keep the fever down, they've a good chance," Suzanne comforted him.

Phillip stayed in the improvised contagion ward, working with Suzanne and Mammy Eunice day and night. When Peter's ears began to run, Suzanne dispatched Phillip to Dr. Kenneth to ask for medication and a syringe with which to wash the affected ears. Phillip held Peter in his arms while Suzanne syringed first one ear, then the other. Peter seemed to understand, despite his physical distress, that they were trying to help him.

They fought a constant battle to bring the fever down, fearful in the nights when the fever of one child or another soared again. Phillip watched with a gratitude that brought tears to

Suzanne's eyes while she cared for Peter's infected ears.

During the fourth night two of the children, a five-year-old boy and a little girl scarcely two, developed difficulty in breathing. Their throats were ulcerated, swallowing almost impossible. They seemed to be threatened with suffocation. Frantically Suzanne and Mammy Eunice sought for a way to relieve them. Nothing seemed to help. In the early morning, within five minutes of each other, the two suffering little ones gave up their efforts to breathe.

Early that evening Suzanne heard the grief of the slaves as they prepared the two children for burial. From a window she watched the torchlight procession that carried the two tiny boxes to the church for the services before the burial in the slave cemetery, while the wails of their close ones echoed in the night silence. Phillip held her in his arms while she cried for the two small patients they had lost.

But now the others seemed to improve with amazing speed. They were coaxed to drink boiled milk, then encouraged to eat hominy and butter. Suzanne sent up to the big house for floating island to tempt appetites that were unenthusiastic. No fresh cases were brought to the infirmary. The disease had been checked, Suzanne decided with relief.

"Missy, you go back up to the big house," Mammy Eunice finally insisted. "You is so tired. I can take care of them children now. Mist'

Phillip," she appealed to him because Suzanne was balking. "You make Missy go home and rest."

"She'll go," he promised. "I'll stay."

Keith sat at the breakfast table with Jane. He was relieved that Suzanne was no longer nursing the children in the quarters. He had been plagued by visions of Suzanne ill with the fever, fighting against death. He listened hopefully now for sounds in the hall that would indicate she was coming down to breakfast this morning. No, not this early, he thought sympathetically. She was still catching up on her sleep.

"Keith, can you spare a few of the women from the fields today?" Jane intruded into his private reverie. "We're running behind in the weaving."

"I'll tell Reagan to send whomever he can spare to the house," Keith promised absently. He must do something about Manon. He was uncomfortable with her in the cottage. It was time to finish off that relationship, as he had decided months ago.

"Must you go to Cincinnati tomorrow?" Jane probed. "It's such a long trip."

"The Senator asked me to go out to the Convention with his contingent," Keith reminded. "I owe him that."

They had discussed this at length several nights ago. Sitting in the drawing room talking with Jane and Phillip about the approaching Convention, he had been so conscious that

Suzanne was in the quarters' infirmary caring for those poor, sick children. How he had come to appreciate her keen mind, her spirit, her candor!

"It's not as though you're working in Washington," Jane said fretfully. "You have obligations here."

"Reagan can manage with me away for a few days, Jane." He tried to sound matter-of-fact. "As soon as I can locate a man capable of taking over much of the responsibilities of running the plantation, I'm hiring him." His eyes held hers. "You know how much law means to me."

"You'll move away from Savage Oaks," she accused. It was the first time in his life that he saw panic in his self-sufficient sister. "You'll leave me here alone with Phillip."

"I'll never leave Savage Oaks. Jane, you know that." Yet he remembered with nostalgia the stimulation of living in Washington City. He loved Savage Oaks, but their isolated way of living was oppressive. If they began to entertain, he would feel differently. If Suzanne would not keep this restraining wall between them, he would not feel restless. Jacques was right; Suzanne and he ought to go into New Orleans often. There was such richness in the city.

Jane rose from the table.

"Don't forget about the women, Keith. I don't like being behind in the weaving."

Keith poured himself another cup of coffee. He sought to gear himself mentally for the confrontation with Manon. She had been silently reproachful the last few times he went to her. She felt herself neglected. She was still beautiful, still desirable; but Suzanne was a shadow between them.

He was a passionate man, like Papa. If Suzanne continued to keep him out of her bed, he would seek solace elsewhere at intervals. But he would feel less guilt at seeking relief for his desires in a few hours at the Mansion House than in this arrangement he had set up in a moment of retaliation.

Reluctantly he forced himself to leave the house and go to the stable for a horse. He would have Abram go to Reagan with the message about the women who were to go to the house. Go straight to the cottage; don't delay.

Manon would cry dramatically. She would scream reproaches. She would try to coax him to bed. But he had not taken a virginal young girl. Manon had been one of Yellowbird Shaw's choice whores, he told himself brutally. She had known many men before him. She would know many more.

Approaching the cottage, he could hear Manon screeching at Lily Mae. Though she had been going into New Orleans at intervals she was bored with the inactivity at the cottage. He would give her money, he consoled himself. She would go back to the Mansion House. It was hardly likely that Yellowbird would reject her.

He tied the horse to a tree and approached the cottage. Manon was screaming invectives that he had never suspected she knew. Her vocabulary was a combination of the most obscene of that of the Irish workmen on the docks and the most profane of the Creoles.

He knocked lightly on the door. Instantly Manon was silent.

"Manon," he called cautiously.

"Get out of here, Lily Mae," he heard her order softly. "I don't want to see your ugly face until night. Get out."

Lily Mae, both scared and relieved, darted past him and into the woods. He walked into the heavily scented sitting room.

"Keith," Manon murmured seductively, coming towards him with outstretched arms. She wore one of the filmy black nightdresses she adored, which displayed every inch of the ivory whiteness of her body. "I have been dying of loneliness for you. How can you leave me this way when you know how desperately I love you?"

"I have to leave for Cincinnati tomorrow," he began warily while she brought her lissome length against him.

"Keith, take me with you," she coaxed. "I can pass," she said with pride. "You can tell everybody I am your cousin." Her eyes were bright with silent promises.

"No, Manon," he said firmly, steeling himself for what he had come to tell her. "I'm going to a political convention."

"Keith," she pouted, "do you know we have not been together for two weeks? I feel as though I have become a nun."

"I told you there was scarlet fever in the quarters," he hedged.

"You come to the door, you tell me, and you run away. I'm not afraid of scarlet fever," she dismissed this impatiently. "I want you in my bed, *chéri.*" She smiled provocatively. "Have you forgotten how it can be with us? Keith, don't I make you happy?"

"Manon, it's over with us," he said with involuntary brusqueness, and she flinched as though he had slapped her across the face. "I'll give you money," he continued stolidly. "A carriage will come here this afternoon to take you into New Orleans."

"Keith!" Suddenly she was sobbing hysterically. Damn it, he should not have been so abrupt.

"Manon, please," he said desperately, feeling helpless. "Manon, you'll be all right. You can go back to the Mansion House. You knew this would have to happen sometime," he stammered in distress.

"Keith, don't do this to me!" Her arms closed about his neck. "Nobody can make you as happy as me!" Her mouth was at his ear. She nipped the lobe. One knee prodded between his. He would have to be a eunuch not to be aroused.

"Manon, you're as beautiful as ever," he insisted, pulling her arms away from his neck. "You're one of the most desirable women I've ever encountered." She knew what she was doing to him. His body responded of its own volition.

"But no more for us here at the cottage." Let her believe he would come to her at the Mansion House. "It's causing trouble with my wife." He grasped at an alibi she would understand.

"Did you tell her I'm here?" Manon accused.

"No," he admitted.

"Then how can she know?" Manon demanded triumphantly.

"Manon, it's over." Forcefully he thrust her away from him. She collapsed to the floor. He had not pushed her that hard, he told himself guiltily. "The carriage will be here at four." He was fumbling in his pocket for the money he had brought for her.

"Keith, don't send me back now," she sobbed. "You don't understand. I can't go back to New Orleans in the summer. Let me stay at the cottage until the hot weather is past. Don't you remember New Orleans three summers ago? That could happen again!"

"It won't," Keith insisted. Who in Louisiana — in the nation — would ever forget the summer of '53, when over eight thousand people died of yellow fever in New Orleans? "We have a Board of Health now. They quarantine those who are stricken."

"Keith, even last summer it was bad! If I go back, I'll die, Keith, please! Let me stay till the summer is past. I saw my mother die of yellow fever. It was awful. I won't bother you. I won't ask for anything." Her tear-filled eyes pleaded with him.

"You could go somewhere else," he said awkwardly.

"Where can I go except the Mansion House?" she asked with unexpected bitterness. "Yellowbird will take me back though I left with no word. But not until the summer is past. Please, Keith. I don't want to die like my mother did."

"All right," Keith capitulated unhappily. "But I won't come to you, Manon. That part is over."

"I'll miss you, *chéri*," she said wistfully. "There was never anyone like you."

Keith rode back to the stable, dismounted, and gave the horse over to Abram. He walked down to the levee, angry with himself. He had not managed the situation with Manon properly. He should have sent her packing this afternoon. But how could he, when she felt the way she did about the fever?

She would stay until the hot weather was past, but he would not go to her. It would be as though she had gone back to the city. And, of course, she was right. How could Suzanne know she was in the cottage?

His eyes settled on the rising river. There was no real reason to be alarmed. Their levees always held. The water was not so high that he would have to worry while he was at the Convention.

He would miss Suzanne while he was away. All at once he wished it were not necessary for him to attend the Convention. But it was a responsibility; he must go.

Twenty-two

Suzanne stood on the gallery with Jane and watched Keith climb into the carriage that was to take him into New Orleans. There he would board a steamer along with the clique of local Democrats who were attending the Convention in Cincinnati. As Lewis prodded the horses forward, Keith leaned from the window to wave in farewell. Smiling radiantly she waved back to him. For one precious moment it seemed to her that Keith and she were alone in the world. For this one moment she was sure he loved her.

"Keith will have his fill of politics in Cincinnati," Jane said with a conciliatory smile while they watched the carriage roll down the tree-lined road and disappear from view. "He'll be more relaxed when he comes home." Her face was tense. She was waging some secret inner battle, Suzanne thought. "Perhaps later in the summer Keith would like to bring some people out to visit." Jane broke the silence that had fallen between them. "You might like to have the Mauriacs come out."

"That would be lovely." She knew how difficult it was for Jane to receive strangers at Savage Oaks.

Without knowing why, Jane suspected Suzanne's marriage to Keith was in jeopardy, Suzanne thought, and she was disturbed. At last Jane was her friend.

"When I was a little girl, we always entertained. Mama loved company," Jane said nostalgically. "Never a summer went past, except for the summers she was carrying Keith and Phillip, that the house wasn't full of guests for weeks on end." All at once she frowned. "I must go out to the laundry house. Hear them carrying on out there? I'll bet they're lolling around, not doing a speck of work."

Suzanne remained alone on the gallery. Already Savage Oaks seemed desolate without Keith. Suddenly she could not bear the inactivity. She would change into a riding dress and take Othello out for a canter. He must have been waiting for her to come to the stable this morning, but she had not left the house with Keith scheduled to go into New Orleans immediately after breakfast.

He would be away almost two weeks. How would she endure not seeing him? When she had been caring for the children, he would show up and talk to her briefly through a window until she ordered him away. Now he was going hundreds of miles away.

At the stable she talked with Abram while Lewis saddled Othello. Abram enjoyed reminiscing about the old days at Savage Oaks.

"Neither them boys give a hoot for huntin'." He shook his head in disbelief. "Every white boy I ever knowed couldn't wait to get his hands on a gun, but not them two." All at once his eyes went opaque. His mouth tightened. "Mist' Thorne keep the guns in the house locked up de last years. He never hunt no more after the Missis died."

She rode the trail along the levee, pausing at one point to dismount and inspect the river. How high the water had risen in these past weeks! But Keith said their levees always held. A steamboat moved majestically up the river and her heart began to pound. Was that Keith's ship?

No, Keith was still en route to New Orleans, she scolded herself. Now she wished she had gone into New Orleans to see him off. But that would have meant she would have been alone with him. She was not prepared for that.

Was that girl still at the cottage? Had Keith sent her away? If he had, then she could forget the past. With a surge of excitement, she mounted Othello again and guided him towards the woods, carefully watching for the narrow turn, so easily missed, that would bring her within view of the cottage. *Maybe Keith had sent the girl away.*

She rode with fresh urgency, watching for the sight of the small white cottage, knowing she must not approach too closely. Then, through the thick summer foliage, she spied the gleam of white and pulled Othello to a halt. She dismounted, tied the reins about a slender birch tree and moved slowly forward. No one sat on the gallery this morning. The drapes were drawn tight. The only sound was that of a mockingbird flitting from tree to tree.

Keith had sent the girl away, she thought joyously. The nightmare was over! But suddenly the sweet silence was splintered by laughter.

"Oh, Phillip, you are crazy!" a girl's voice chided with levity. "Always you must think of something different!"

Her face hot, Suzanne whirled around and returned to Othello. The girl was in the cottage. A plaything for both Keith and Phillip. She would not stay at Savage Oaks, she vowed. When Keith returned from Cincinnati, she would tell him. And this time she would not change her mind.

Summer descended upon Louisiana with a devastating heat wave, slightly ameliorated in the evening by breezes from the river. The Andrews, Reagan reported, were leaving for Saratoga Springs. The Maires, from whom Keith had bought a plow, had already left for Newport.

Suzanne moved wraith-like about Savage Oaks, haunted by loneliness for Keith, yet determined to leave Savage Oaks on his return. Nor would she stay at Tintagel. She would go back to Paris. She would arrange for Uncle Gilbert to have her dividend checks sent to her. If she lived very modestly, she could manage on that, and begin to search for Maman.

The days dragged. Phillip played backgammon with her in the humid heat of the drawing room each evening while Jane read. She rode to Tintagel late each morning to visit with Mrs. Cantrell. In the house where Papa had been born and raised she felt poignantly close to Maman and him.

Mrs. Cantrell was delighted that she chose to spend part of each day at Tintagel. They ate the midday meal together, and then Mrs. Cantrell would insist that she take an afternoon nap, as was the habit during the hot months on every plantation. Jane made no comment about these new absences, suspecting that she was restless in Keith's absence, Suzanne guessed.

Riding to Tintagel today she speculated on the date when Keith would return to Savage Oaks. Another four days at the most, Jane figured. And then she must tell Keith that she was going back to Paris. She lifted her head defiantly. Let him tell his friends what he wished. Let him say that, like Senator Benjamin's wife, she preferred to live in Paris.

"Merlin brought the newspapers up from New Orleans," Mrs. Cantrell greeted her avidly. "Buchanan has been nominated. This is good for the South, isn't it?"

"The Southern Senators and Congressmen believe this," Suzanne said politely. Keith, like Uncle Gilbert, was not too happy; but he had been resigned to Buchanan.

"And Senator Benjamin is at the Convention.

He's joined the Democratic Party," Mrs. Cantrell announced with an air of triumph.

"Oh, I'm glad," Suzanne said spontaneously. She had so liked Senator Benjamin. And Keith would be pleased.

What is the matter with me? Why do I keep thinking of Keith? Soon he'll have no place in my life.

Dutifully Suzanne went to her room when they had eaten, intent on resting for an hour before riding back to Savage Oaks. But despite the heat she found it impossible to remain idle this way.

If she were going to Paris, then she must take with her Papa's painting of Maman and her. She must take the sketches. Impetuously she left her room and headed for the attic, today with a warming sense of proprietorship. This was her house. Adrian Ramsay was her father.

In the attic, she carefully lifted the painting from the wall, opened the dust-laden box where she knew the sketches lay. With the painting and the sketches lovingly clutched in her arms, she left the attic. Halfway down the stairs she stopped dead. *Could Papa have left letters behind?* Some hint about Maman's identity? Why had she never searched the house?

She deposited the painting and the sketches in her room and hurried downstairs to the lower floor. Earnestly she searched through every drawer in the drawing room, the dining room, discovering nothing. Where else? *The library.* Her heart hammered with anticipation.

She pulled forth one drawer after another of

the mahogany and satinwood desk, untouched, she suspected, since Noah's death. All at once, Mrs. Cantrell's voice, filled with fury, brought her to a halt.

"What are you doing in Mr. Noah's desk?" Mrs. Cantrell was white with rage. "You may have bought Tintagel, but you have not bought the family!"

"I'm a Ramsay!" Suzanne shot back proudly. "Noah Ramsay was my uncle. Adrian Ramsay was my father!"

"What are you saying?" Mrs. Cantrell stared in shock.

"Mrs. Cantrell, Adrian Ramsay was my father." Suzanne sought to keep her voice from trembling. "I know this." She pulled the ring from the neckline of her dress. "I remember Papa wearing this ring. I found it in the attic."

Mrs. Cantrell's eyes clung to the ring.

"He wore that ring when he came back from Paris," Mrs. Cantrell whispered. "I remember because it was so unusual. But that doesn't mean that you are his child," she challenged.

"I remember him putting me to bed when I was a very little girl." Suzanne's face glowed with recall. "He wore this ring. And I remember something else— " For a long time she had forgotten. "He had a scar above his wrist. A long one. Perhaps three inches long."

"A scar from a fencing accident," Mrs. Cantrell acknowledged shakily. "Robert and he were taking fencing lessons from a Frenchman who came to the house each week."

"Mrs. Cantrell, what do you know about my mother? I know she's alive. I must find her."

"I know only that Adrian was in love with a girl from New Orleans. Her father was an Irish laborer there. Mrs. Ramsay had been tenderly reared; she was upset that Adrian could think of marrying someone outside their own social circle. She forbade the marriage. Adrian went off to Paris. The family never knew if he took the girl with him."

"He married her in Paris," Suzanne said. "Mr. Mauriac told me this. And when his brother sent for him when my grandmother was dying, he meant to send for Maman and me. But you know what happened." Suzanne's voice dropped to a whisper. "Maman was so grief-stricken she gave me over to Uncle Gilbert and disappeared. But I must find her!"

"Suzanne, I know nothing else," Mrs. Cantrell said with distress. "I remember that Mr. Mauriac talked about a child, but Mr. Noah refused to believe this was Adrian's."

"Mrs. Cantrell, you said my grandfather lived in New Orleans. Perhaps Maman is with them!" Suddenly her mouth was dry with excitement. "What was their name?"

"Suzanne, there are over a hundred twenty-five thousand people living in New Orleans, thousands of them Irish." But she froze in thought and Suzanne leaned forward breathlessly. "Moira, that was her name."

"Moira what?" Suzanne asked urgently. "Think!"

Mrs. Cantrell spread her hands in a gesture of futility.

"Suzanne, I'm sorry. I don't know."

"I found Papa," Suzanne said tautly. "And I will find Maman."

Suzanne did not go to Tintagel the following morning. After a sleepless night she decided to go into New Orleans. She must talk to Mme. Mauriac. If she had left for the lake house, there would have been word.

Suzanne waited until Jane had left the house in the chaise to spend her afternoon with Katie. Abram was uneasy when she ordered a carriage to take her into New Orleans.

"Missy, it's the fever time," he said worriedly. "Mist' Keith, he wouldn't like you to be goin' there this time of year."

"I'll be all right, Abram," she soothed. "A lot of families stay in town until July." Jane had told her this, referring to the wealthy and the near-wealthy. The workmen and their families remained all summer.

The heat in the carriage as it rolled along the dusty road to New Orleans was hardly bearable. Suzanne touched her forehead regularly with an inadequate, damp handkerchief she clutched in her hand. Her dress clung wetly between her shoulder blades. The heat seemed to grow even more intense as they moved into the city.

Mme. Mauriac was astonished but delighted to see her.

"Sebastien, tell Amelia to bring us a pitcher of

iced coffee," she ordered, embracing Suzanne affectionately. "In the summer everyone in New Orleans abandons coffee for lemonade and iced claret, but I tell Amelia to pour the coffee over much ice, it is delicious." Her eyes inspected Suzanne keenly. She knew this was not solely a social call. "In another week I leave for the house by the lake. It isn't wise to come into New Orleans in the summer. Even Gilbert spends only two days a week at the office in these months."

Suzanne restrained herself from questions until they were sipping Amelia's delightfully refreshing iced coffee and Mme. Mauriac had paused in her rapturous description of the house overlooking Lake Pontchartrain.

"Mme. Mauriac," she said softly. "Mr. Mauriac has told me Maman's name is Moira. What was her surname before she married Papa?"

"I — we never knew this, Suzanne," she said regretfully. "To us she was simply Moira, the girl Adrian loved. Did you know your father painted my portrait before he went to Paris? It hangs in the château of my oldest granddaughter in the Loire valley."

"There must be some way to find Maman's parents," Suzanne said desperately.

"Gilbert feels towards you as though you were his own," Mme. Mauriac said gently. "He would do anything to make you happy. But there's no way to find Moira's parents." Her eyes were dark with compassion. "Adrian was like another grandson to me. He and Gilbert shared a room at military school. They were very close. Gilbert went on to Princeton and from there to study law at Yale. Adrian remained at Tintagel, preferring to devote himself to painting. But every time Gilbert came home from school, Adrian was here with us. He brought Moira to me," she said with pride. "She was sweet and beautiful, with that independence I feel in you."

"Mme. Mauriac, I *will* find her," Suzanne said determinedly.

"Suzanne, I'm an old lady, and I take advantage of that sometimes," she said with impish humor, but her eyes were serious. "Sometimes I feel that things are not going well between Keith and you — "

"I love Keith," Suzanne said intensely. "I miss him so much while he's away. But when he returns from the Convention, I'm leaving him. I'm returning to Paris."

"Suzanne, why?" Mme. Mauriac's voice trembled.

"I know it's fashionable for young men in Louisiana to keep a mistress even after they're married." Color stained Suzanne's cheekbones but she forced herself to continue. "I know this happens often. But I refuse to share Keith with someone else."

"Keith has a mistress? You're sure of this?" Mme. Mauriac asked sternly.

"I saw her. A beautiful quadroon girl who lives in a cottage at the edge of the plantation. She's still there," Suzanne said with anguish. "I prayed he would send her away, but he hasn't. So," she lifted her head defiantly, "my door is locked to him."

"Have you talked to Keith about this?" Mme. Mauriac asked seriously.

Suzanne lowered her eyes.

"No."

"Then you must go to Keith and tell him to send her packing," Mme. Mauriac said vigorously.

"I can't," Suzanne rejected. "I can't bring myself to talk to him about her."

"Suzanne, you must not leave Keith. Not yet," she added diplomatically. "I'm going to the lake house in a few days. Come up and stay with me. Let's talk about this."

"I want Uncle Gilbert to arrange funds for me to leave," Suzanne said stubbornly. "Perhaps I can borrow against the next check that is due. I want to return to Paris and search for Maman."

"Gilbert is in Newport on business," Mme. Mauriac said slowly. "As soon as he returns, I'll send word to you. But promise me you'll say nothing to Keith about leaving until you've spoken with Gilbert. Promise me, Suzanne," she ordered with astonishing strength.

"I promise," Suzanne agreed reluctantly. "But I won't stay at Savage Oaks after I've talked with Uncle Gilbert," she insisted. "I'm returning to Paris."

Twenty-three

Suzanne awoke each morning with the expectation that Sebastien would come to Savage Oaks with word that Uncle Gilbert was back in New Orleans and she could ask him to help her with the financial arrangements for her return to Paris. She slept badly these nights while she waited for Keith's return from Cincinnati.

This morning she awoke, tired from the enervating heat of the previous day and the lack of sufficient sleep. At dinner last night, when Jane said Keith should be arriving in New Orleans early this morning, she had forced herself to suppress the words that threatened to spill impulsively from her. She would not go into New Orleans to meet Keith. She was leaving him.

Last night she had rehearsed what she would say to Keith. *"I'm sorry Keith. Our marriage was a mistake. I've asked Uncle Gilbert to arrange for me to return to Paris."*

Keith would believe she was still furious at being deluded into an arranged marriage. Or he would think she was homesick for France. Let him think whatever he wished. She would not put herself through the torture of living under the same roof with him any longer.

She started at the light knock on her door. Patrice, grinning broadly came in with her morning coffee.

"Mist' Keith, he downstairs," she reported exuberantly. "He say the ship come in right on time."

"Thank you, Patrice." Her initial reaction was pleasure, but almost immediately she realized the import of his return. As soon as she talked with Uncle Gilbert, she would tell Keith she was leaving him. Uncle Gilbert would surely be back from Newport today or tomorrow.

She drank her coffee at Patrice's stern insistence, then quickly dressed. Her throat tightened as she walked down the stairs. She could hear Keith talking to Jane about the Convention.

"A lot of what happened on the Convention floor was worked out in hotel rooms the night before," he was saying soberly. "And the results were what we expected."

As Suzanne walked into the room, Keith rose to his feet with such a glow of ardor in his eyes that she felt herself almost suffocating.

"I missed you, Suzanne," he said tenderly, crossing to kiss her on the cheek. She trembled at the touch of his hands at her shoulders.

"Did you have a good trip?" she asked politely. How dare he look at her in that fashion when he kept a mistress hidden in the woods!

"I slept most of the time," Keith confessed humorously. "We had little sleep in Cincinnati."

Suzanne was relieved when Keith said he must go to consult with Reagan about the planting immediately after breakfast. Being with Keith after almost two weeks' absence was a bittersweet experience. Oh, why didn't Uncle Gilbert return from Newport? When Keith looked at her as he did now, she feared for her resolve to return to Paris. But pride would not let her remain at Savage Oaks.

Keith left to go to Reagan's cottage. *Was* he going to Reagan's cottage, Suzanne asked herself unhappily, or had he said that to mask another visit to his mistress? Jane called for Edward to accompany her upstairs where he was to take down curtains to be laundered. Suzanne, determined to be away from the house when Keith returned, walked to the stable. She was grateful for the breeze from the river that alleviated the heat of the past few days.

"That sun's pow'ful hot for ridin', Missy," Abram greeted her.

"I'm not going to ride this morning, Abram," she soothed. "Hook up Othello to the chaise and I'll take that out. He needs the run." She saw Abram's consternation and understood. "I won't be gone more than an hour," she promised. Jane would not be using the chaise until early afternoon.

"Yasma'am. I'll go fetch the chaise."

She left the stable to ride along the levee, reminding herself that she must avoid approaching the house where Katie lived with Callie and Joseph in attendance. How intimidating the river seemed this morning, she thought with a faint shiver as she viewed the churning water.

She drove along the levee until the trail veered sharply inland. For eighteen years Jane had traveled this path daily. Poor, sweet Katie, she thought compassionately.

All at once, Othello was whinnying in dismay. Suzanne tightened her hold on the reins. A wide swath of water was surging towards them, already covering Othello's hooves. A break in the levee down below! She hesitated only a moment, then prodded Othello forward. The house where Katie lived must be surrounded by water.

"It's all right, Othello," she soothed with strained calm, urging him ahead. "It's all right." But the water was rising in its forward surge.

By the time she and Othello arrived at the house, it was surrounded by water that covered the lower steps to the gallery. Othello was nervous despite Suzanne's efforts to allay his fears. At an upstairs window she spied Joseph, apprehensively leaning out a window, striving to see where the break had occurred.

"Joseph!" she called urgently. "Bring Katie and Callie downstairs. I'll take you to Savage Oaks."

"Miss Jane, she be distressed," he said uneasily.

"Miss Jane wants you safe," Suzanne insisted.

"Hurry! But don't frighten Katie!"

She brought the chaise as close to the stairs as Othello would allow, watched anxiously for the three to join her in the chaise. She must return to Savage Oaks to warn Keith about the crevasse before the fields were flooded. If the water moved into the north fields, they would lose the whole crop.

Joseph came out onto the gallery. Callie followed, holding Katie's hand in hers, talking quietly to her.

"Missy, I stay heah," Joseph said stolidly to Suzanne while he lifted Katie in his arms. Katie was bewildered but docile. "It's all right, Katie," he encouraged. "Callie's goin' with you."

"Joseph, we can all fit into the chaise," Suzanne told him firmly. "You, too." If the break spread, the foundation of the house could be undermined.

They crowded together in the chaise, Katie on Callie's ample lap. Suzanne concentrated on guiding Othello back towards Savage Oaks, urging him forward to unprecedented speed, which he seemed to relish. At last they outdistanced the raging water, slowed by the sharp elevation of the acreage surrounding Savage Oaks.

At the house, Suzanne leapt down from the chaise and darted up to the gallery.

"Arthur!" She charged breathlessly into the foyer. "Arthur!" she called. "Where's Mr. Keith?"

All at once Keith emerged from the library.

"Suzanne, what's happened?" He sensed the urgency in her summons.

"There's a break in the levee below. The water's coming fast!"

"Arthur!" Keith bellowed just as he appeared. "Hurry to the stable and fetch a horse. Ride to the fields for Mr. Reagan. Tell him we have a break in the levee!"

"Yassir!" Arthur's eyes were bright with concern as he ran to the door.

"Tell him to bring wagons of dirt and bags, and get every man on the plantation to the south fields as fast as they can move!" Keith yelled after him.

"Keith, what's wrong?" Jane asked solicitously at the head of the stairs.

"Mama!" Katie cried out in relief as she hovered behind Suzanne, flanked by Callie and Joseph. "Mama!"

Jane clutched at the banister for a moment, pale with shock. Then she was rushing down the stairs. "It's all right, darling. You don't have to be afraid." She pulled Katie to her while Keith stared dazedly at them. "Keith, what's happened?"

"A break in the levee — " He seemed immobilized.

"Then you have a rough job ahead," she said tersely. "Don't stand here!"

Without a word Keith rushed from the foyer and out of the house. They could hear him shouting as he raced towards the stable.

"Caleb, saddle up a horse for me! Fast!"

"I took the chaise out to give Othello a run," Suzanne explained. "I saw the water. I went to the house to bring them back here — "

"Callie, take Katie up to my room," Jane said quietly. "Joseph, go out to the stable. See how you can help."

Callie took Katie by the hand and headed up the stairs with her. Phillip stood at the landing above, his eyes serious as he watched them ascend.

"You're looking pretty, Katie," he said softly, and she smiled shyly back at him while Jane watched in disbelief.

"Suzanne, thank you," she said tensely, her eyes focused on Phillip. "Callie and Joseph would have been afraid to bring her here." Phillip was walking down the stairs towards them. "How long have you known about Katie?"

"Since I was thirteen. I saw her sitting on the gallery of the old house. Callie was dozing. I brought her a few violets. She wasn't frightened. After that I'd go over now and then when I was sure nobody would know. She never told you because it was our secret."

"I thought she was pretending when she talked about the friend who came to see her sometimes," Jane said huskily. "But how did you know that — "

"That she was my niece?" Phillip asked gently. "I plied Abram with Papa's best bourbon and he talked."

"Jane, will the north fields be flooded?" Suzanne asked worriedly. "The land up here is much higher," she reminded hopefully.

"It'll come," Jane predicted, "if we don't mend the levee. Just pray the break doesn't widen."

"A crevasse can widen from twenty feet in one hour to a hundred in the next," Phillip reminded. "It can be half a mile wide tomorrow. And fifteen feet high! Not even this house can take that."

"Phillip, fetch yourself a horse and see what you can do to help!" Jane ordered.

"If Keith can't slow down the water by nightfall, go to Tintagel," Phillip cautioned as he strode to the door. "That's high enough to avoid any water except in its lower fields."

Suzanne gazed anxiously at Jane, not concerned for their physical safety but fearing Jane's outrage that she had brought Katie here. She should have taken the three to Tintagel, she reproached herself belatedly; but she had been afraid to waste a moment in getting word to Keith.

"Jane, I brought Katie here because I was afraid of what would happen to the house," she said apologetically.

"Bless you for that, Suzanne," Jane said gratefully. "There's no way of knowing how bad it'll become." She hesitated. "Let's have lunch together. Then I'll go up to Katie." Jane wished her to know that she was accepting her fully as a member of the family, Suzanne thought, and was touched.

When they had eaten and Jane had gone up to Katie, Suzanne went out on the gallery. Standing at the south end she could see the water encroaching towards Savage Oaks, but so slowly as to create no alarm as yet. Because of the elevation of the land, the water was spreading into a wider swath.

A wagon piled high with dirt moved with reckless speed directly in front of the house because this was a shortcut to the levee. Another wagon followed directly behind. A few minutes later she heard the horses whinnying in initial alarm at charging through the water.

She would not go into New Orleans until this crisis was over, even if word came that Uncle Gilbert was in his office. She shivered faintly, aware of an unseasonable chill. The sun had moved behind clumps of pale gray clouds. A sharp wind blew in from the river.

She went upstairs for a shawl, then decided to change into a riding dress. She would take Othello and ride as close to the break as she could without endangering Othello and herself. The decision made, she changed swiftly into riding attire and hurried from her room. As she walked to the stairs, she heard Jane talking to Katie with rich affection.

Abram was alone at the stable. Every man on the plantation had been sent to the levee to work on the crevasse.

"Missy, where you goin' ridin'?" Abram scolded when she asked for Othello. "Till they get that break fixed, it ain't safe."

"Don't worry, Abram." She smiled reassuringly. "I'll be all right." But he watched her anxiously as she left the stable astride Othello.

She prodded Othello towards the south fields, staying close to the woods. No more than five hundred feet from the big house she saw the water churning in its effort to rise above the incline. Instead, it was spreading more widely across the fields.

She rode along the edge of the approaching water, determined to arrive within sight of the men working on the break. She rode with urgency, encircling the broadening tide that was flooding the south fields. The water was moving slower now, but it would rise insidiously until the whole plantation was flooded unless the crew could mend the break satisfactorily.

All at once the sounds of voices reached her. Cautiously she urged Othello into the low water at the edge of the onward thrust. He whinnied in protest as the water rose higher about his legs, but Suzanne coaxed him forward. There they were!

She spied Keith on horseback in water at least four feet in depth. Reagan, also on horseback, rode a hundred feet beyond Keith. Perhaps forty hands, in water above their waists, were laboring to fill the break with bags of dirt, ribaldly demanding more bags from other hands who struggled to fill them from the wagon of dirt that sat nearby, wheels submerged in water. Phillip worked with another dozen of the hands, all of them with ropes about their waists as they moved into the deepest water.

As Suzanne watched, another wagon pushed forward through the water, the horses skittish in their distrust.

"Reagan, have somebody go beyond on dry land and build a fire!" Keith yelled above the noise. "It's damn cold. Start changing shifts. One hour in the water, one hour out!" He was too involved to notice her presence, Suzanne realized.

In sudden decision, Suzanne ordered Othello away from the scene. With the speed he relished she rode back to the stable. Abram came forward anxiously.

"Abram is there a carriage available? And horses to pull it?"

"No horse not workin' 'cept for Othello," he said apologetically.

"All right. Bring out the chaise," she ordered briskly. "Hook up Othello to that. I'll be back in a few minutes."

"Missy, where you goin'?"

"To the quarters kitchen," Suzanne told him. "Have the chaise ready. I'm taking coffee and food to the men on the levee."

"In the chaise?" Abram looked startled, and then he grinned. "Mist' Keith, he sure got hisself a smart young lady!"

In the quarters kitchen Suzanne rustled up a crew of women, instructed them to make pots of coffee, hesitated about food.

"We's got corn bread and molasses," one of the women said avidly. "An' we can be makin' more whilst you take that to 'em."

"Do that," Suzanne approved. "And one of you come to the kitchen house with me. I'll have Clarissa give you bacon to fry."

"Workin' in all that water, they could use some whiskey," a white-haired, toothless woman with a gamine grin suggested.

"I'll get it," Suzanne promised.

In half an hour Suzanne was en route to the crevasse area in the chaise with pots of strong hot coffee, a gallon of molasses, and a sack full of corn bread settled on the floor. On the seat beside her sat the bottles of whiskey she had taken from the wine cabinet and a bag of tin cups. This time she held Othello in check, lest the coffee spill over. In the chill that swept in from the river the hands — and Keith — would appreciate a hot drink.

A bonfire was burning on dry ground beyond the reach of the water. A cluster of hands huddled about its warmth. Other hands were fighting to close the break with bags of earth, driving piles against the river current. Despite their efforts the river pushed through the break, though with a diminished force.

"Reagan, we'll need ground logs!" Keith called loudly. "And whatever boards are left from rebuilding the barn. Send some hands back for them. This isn't holding!"

"Keith!" Suzanne held tightly to the reins. "Keith!"

"Suzanne!" He was shocked at her presence. "What are you doing here?" He rode towards her in haste.

"I've brought coffee and food and whiskey," she said practically. "Will you have some men come take it from the chaise?" She was breathless before the admiration she read in his eyes.

"George, get somebody to help you bring over coffee!" Keith leaned forward to inspect the cargo in the chaise.

"I took the whiskey from the house," she said tentatively, reaching for the bottles. "What else can I bring?" She compelled herself to speak calmly while the hands, with hoots of delight, came forward to empty the chaise.

"More whiskey, more coffee, more food," Keith said with a smile. "We've got seventy men working here. And ask Jane to give you some bandages, a bottle of iodoform and chloroform liniment."

"Keith, drink some coffee while it's hot," Suzanne coaxed. He was probably soaked to the skin. She felt color rush to her face beneath the intensity of his gaze. "I'll be back as soon as more coffee and corn bread are ready." Her voice was uneven. This was how she had felt on the eve of her wedding, waiting for Keith to come to her. *No! She was leaving him when this was over.*

She headed for the house before returning to the quarters, mentally searching her mind for what else might be needed in the line of medical supplies in addition to what Keith had told her to bring. As she approached the gallery, Arthur appeared in the door.

"Miss Suzanne, you been down to the crevasse?" he reproached, hurrying down the steps to take the reins from her.

"Yes, and I'm going back again," she said briskly. "Keep the chaise here, please."

"Yes'm," he agreed, his eyes worried.

"Where's Miss Jane?" Suzanne asked as she hurried up the steps.

"She just come downstairs. She's in the library."

Jane glanced up with a start as Suzanne appeared in the library doorway. She was cutting lengths of cloth into bandages.

"I'm sending Arthur down to the crevasse with bandages and medication." She was pale and drawn, her hands trembling as she worked.

"Let me," Suzanne said quickly. "I went down with food and coffee and I'm going again. I have Othello and the chaise."

"Suzanne, it's dangerous," she objected.

"I'm careful. And Othello isn't afraid of the water as long as I talk to him."

Jane hesitated.

"Suzanne, the old house — has the water level reached into the lower floor?"

"Not yet." She guessed that Jane was concerned about her paintings. "And I'm sure the water's under control." Jane smiled faintly. She knew Suzanne was pointedly ignoring the probability of more breaks in the fifty-year-old levees.

"I'll have Arthur put a case of whiskey into the chaise."

Suzanne went again to the quarters kitchen. As soon as the corn bread was ready, Suzanne began to stock the chaise. Without asking, the women were already preparing another batch of corn bread, frying bacon. Suzanne knew there would be long days and nights ahead of them.

At the levee a crew had been hurriedly dispatched to an area above the present break, which was a distinct threat to Savage Oaks property. Oblivious of her presence as he consulted with Reagan, Keith swore about their neglect of the levees over the years, soothed into complacency by the lack of flooding through three generations.

Suzanne made countless trips back and forth from the quarters to the levee until night fell and Keith insisted she return to the house. But at dawn, tired but determined, she was back at the quarters kitchen. The women had already arrived to begin a new day's labor.

For four days Suzanne lived in the chaise, exhausted yet pleased by the knowledge that she was useful. She cared for the minor injuries that occurred, feeling closer to Keith than at any time since their marriage. She had not gone to the Crimea, but here she was helping. A strange camaraderie had developed between the hands and her, which she knew would be replaced by their usual deference when this crisis was past.

Late in the afternoon of the fourth day, Keith and Reagan agreed that their task was completed, though Keith vowed that in a few days he would assign a crew to work regularly on the levee until every inch that protected their property had been sturdily reinforced.

"All right, all hands back to the quarters, except for you ten working there," Keith ordered. "Go to sleep. You all need it."

With a shout the hands climbed into the dirt-empty wagons, Phillip with them.

"Suzanne, go home and go to sleep!" Phillip called exuberantly to her.

"In a few minutes," she promised.

All at once she was overwhelmingly depressed. The crisis was over. Life at Savage Oaks would go on as before the crevasse. But she would not be here.

Twenty-four

The windows of Phillip's bedroom were draped against the late afternoon sun. The house was encased in silence. But Phillip could not will himself to sleep, though he had slept little more than four hours a night since Suzanne discovered the crevasse. He had insisted on working side by side with the hands, he reminded himself with savage pride. Suzanne saw that he worked as hard as Keith.

He knew when he stood beside Suzanne in the infirmary in those awful days and nights when she cared for Elizabeth and Peter that he would never love another woman. He had reproached himself endlessly for his crassness, his total preoccupation with himself.

Ever since he could remember, he had been angry with Mama for killing herself, leaving him without a mother. Now he could understand. He had never connected Katie with Mama's suicide and the solitary grave about which Papa and Jane were so tight-mouthed. But his anger had reached out to touch Suzanne. How could he have hurt her by revealing Manon's presence here?

Seeing Suzanne in action these past four days, constantly in the carriage or on horseback, bringing food, coffee, whiskey to the crew, only intensified his conviction that he would never love another woman. Watching her he had wanted only to sweep her into his arms and take her to some secret place to make love to her. But she was Keith's wife and in love with him.

Damn, why had he bothered to try to sleep? He was too stirred up for sleep; he needed some diversion. He would take a carriage and go into New Orleans. Go over to the cottage and invite Manon to go with him. The way he had been working these last few days he deserved some amusement.

Phillip left the house and walked to the stable. Abram looked upset when he asked for a carriage.

"I'm just going visiting around here," he placated Abram without giving any destination. The canny old bastard probably didn't believe him. "I'll want Caleb to drive me." Caleb was tight-mouthed about where he went. He always slipped Caleb a few coins; that made Caleb his man.

Lily Mae was washing laundry in the tub beside the cottage as he approached. She smiled broadly and scrambled through the back door calling ebulliently.

"Missy, company comin'. He almost here!"

Manon appeared at the door.

"Phillip, are we going to be flooded?" she demanded nervously. "Lily Mae said all the hands are down at the levee trying to mend a crevasse."

"The danger's over," he brushed this aside. "Keith's down there with a few hands taking some extra precautions." His eyes swept over her provocative décolletage. Fleetingly, desire welled in him, but the inclination to put Savage Oaks behind him was a damper. "Put on some clothes. We'll go into New Orleans."

Manon's eyes widened.

"In this heat?" she objected, but he knew she was intrigued by the prospect.

"By the time we arrive in the city the worst heat of the day will be over. The breeze from the Gulf makes it pleasant enough at night. And don't worry about Keith's coming here," he chuckled. "He hasn't the strength. Tonight will be his first chance to get some sleep since the crevasse."

"All right," Manon capitulated fliply. "What will we do?"

"Play some roulette," he suggested offhandedly. Manon adored the roulette table. "If you have some cash," he stipulated. "I have enough for one spin." He gestured apologetically.

"I have no money," she said flatly, "but we can go visit at the Mansion House." Her eyes were suddenly provocative. "If Colette is not engaged, we'll both entertain you again. Yellowbird won't mind."

"Dress." Manon's invitation was a potent aphrodisiac. "I want to get away from here."

In the carriage, Manon questioned him in morbid detail about the crevasse.

"I remember when I was a little girl." Manon shivered dramatically. "A levee broke all the way up at the Sauvé's plantation, seventeen miles above New Orleans; but the water rushed all the way down to the city. It was three feet deep at Baronne Street, where we lived. Ugly muddy water," she said with distaste. "I was so frightened."

"This break has been mended, Manon," Phillip reminded with exasperation.

"Poor Keith," Manon mocked. "Working so hard." Laughter lit her eyes. "It's so easy to fool that brother of yours! Sometimes he's like a little boy, the way he believes everything I say."

"What do you mean?" He knew Manon was convinced that Keith and he were mortal enemies.

"All at once Keith is tired of me," Manon pouted, covertly watching Phillip for a reaction. Expecting disbelief.

"What makes you think that?" Phillip hedged.

"He came to me and said he is sending me away!" Her face was etched with outrage. "Why, I ask him. Have I not pleased you in every way? I know of no man I can't please," she boasted.

"You look at me like that," Phillip warned, his eyes focused on her daring cleavage, "and I'll take you in broad daylight." But behind his air of levity his mind was alert. "I did it before," he reminded, grinning.

"Later, *mon chéri*," Manon promised. "But that brother of yours," she pursued vindictively. "He wanted to send me packing, and I cried." Her eyes brightened with amusement. "How I cried! I begged him to let me stay here for the hot weather because I was terrified of the fever. I told him my mother died of the fever in '53!"

"Your mother works in that grubby coffee house in Baronne Street," Phillip recalled. *Keith meant to send Manon away*. He must tell Suzanne. He owed her that.

"Keith believed me," Manon said triumphantly. "I'll spend the summer here and in October I'll go back to the Mansion House. I'll tell Yellowbird today that I'll be back. She'll be glad," Manon prophesied with an arrogant smile. "Many New Orleans gentlemen ask particularly for me."

Phillip leaned back in the carriage, his thoughts on Suzanne while Manon chattered animately about a variety of past clients at the Mansion House.

"Then there's Mr. Simone. You know Mr. Simone," Manon said with wicked laughter. "Seventy-two years old and he still comes to the Mansion House twice a week. Between times he recuperates. But, Phillip, he insists on three girls to entertain him, would you believe that? It costs him a fortune, but he's very rich."

"It probably takes three to get him going,"

Phillip said contemptuously. "Like me," he goaded.

"Phillip, you are the most passionate, the most capable man I have ever met," she said complacently.

"Better than Keith?" he demanded.

She considered this with a seriousness he had not expected.

"As good as Keith," she conceded. "Your brother, too, is passionate," she said with an air of fairness. "But you don't let me tell you about Mr. Simone," she pouted.

"Tell me," he commanded. It pleased him that Manon rated him at least as high as Keith.

"Mr. Simone brings each of us a gift, which Yellowbird doesn't know about," she confided. "You must never tell her. Then he sends us into the bathroom to bathe. We must even wash our hair for him. He calls us his three naked nymphs. And then, oh la la!" She shrugged her shoulders dramatically. "We must climb onto the bed with him and kiss him everywhere." She leaned towards Phillip, her eyes daring him not to visualize the scene she described. "Then he kisses us everywhere. We pretend to be terribly excited." She watched him, pleased that she was arousing him. But damn it, this was not the brougham. He would not take her in broad daylight in an open carriage. He wouldn't even notice if another carriage was approaching! "And then," Manon said flamboyantly, "he is ready. For one of us," she stipulated. "But we pretend to be passionate so he takes one and fondles two. Finally, after such grunting and groaning, he's satisfied. For fourteen years, Yellowbird says, he has been coming to the Mansion House."

"That's better than the banker who insists on the whips," Phillip teased.

"I refuse that," she said with a toss of her head. "Yellowbird knows who is willing to go to the special room with him. Shall I tell you more?" she challenged.

"Tell me more," he encouraged, but his attention was moving away.

Phillip leaned back in the carriage, his thoughts on Suzanne. He must make her understand that Keith was no longer involved with Manon. What chance did he ever have with Suzanne? She was in love with Keith. For once in his life, let him do something for someone else. Let him make things right between Suzanne and Keith.

As they arrived in the city, Manon decided she must stop by to see her mother. It mattered little that her mother had only contempt for her position as one of Yellowbird's girls. Manon considered this far above her mother's station of life.

"Manon, who was your father?" Phillip asked curiously. He had asked that before, and she had always spun some romantic tale about her father being a rich planter.

"He was a no-good riverboat gambler," Manon said petulantly. She was in a mood for candor today. "But Mama could have held him if she had not allowed herself to grow fat and ugly.

That will never happen to me."

Obligingly Phillip allowed himself to be dragged into the coffee house for a brief exchange of conversation with Manon's mother, and then they returned to the carriage and ordered Caleb to take them directly to the Mansion House. Though few carriages traveled through the streets at this hour, most business people having retired to their homes for the day, every vehicle — including their own — created clouds of dust.

At the Mansion House Lloyd admitted them into the ornate foyer.

"I'll tell Miss Yellowbird you all is here," he said politely and led them past several discreetly closed parlor doors to another at the end of the hall.

"Bring us some champagne, Lloyd," Manon ordered audaciously. "We drove for over an hour in all this heat." Actually, as Phillip had predicted, a cool breeze from the Gulf made the city quite comfortable.

Manon seated herself at one end of the dark red velvet sofa and beckoned Phillip to sit beside her. Why did he keep thinking of Suzanne, he chastised himself? He was here at the Mansion House. If Colette were free, Manon and she would make him forget everything for a while. Together they could excite a wooden Indian.

Their champagne arrived. Phillip poured for Manon and himself. Yellowbird provided the best for her guests, he conceded with admiration. He drank with an abandon that brought a laughing protest from Manon.

"Drink like that, Phillip, and you'll be useless to Colette and me!"

"I never get too drunk," he boasted and poured himself another.

"This will be a busy evening despite the summer," Manon predicted. "The families may run from the city, but many of the gentlemen remain here. But never mind, Phillip. If Colette is busy, there's the long ride back to Savage Oaks."

The door opened. Yellowbird, lavishly gowned in yellow as always, walked into the room. Tonight she seemed gaunt. She had lost much weight. Dark half-moons beneath her eyes could not be disguised despite her artful use of powder.

"Manon, you're looking well," Yellowbird said casually, but her eyes were appraising.

"Phillip and I were bored," Manon shrugged. "We decided to come into the city. You remember Phillip Savage," she said, startling him. Why the devil did she mention his name? Because she was furious with Keith?

"Yes, of course." Yellowbird smiled slightly.

"I'll be free in October," Manon said airily, but Phillip suspected she was nervous. "Would you like me to come back?"

"You're always welcome, Manon," Yellowbird readily assented. "You can return immediately."

"October will be perfect," Manon said delightedly. She was relieved not to have to plead for reinstatement. "Is Colette busy? I thought perhaps — "

"Colette is entertaining a gentleman, but I

think she'll soon be able to join you." Yellowbird was elated that Manon had been deposed, Phillip decided. "I'll send Colette in to you when her gentleman leaves."

"Will it be all right if we go up with her to her room?" Manon probed delicately. Phillip intercepted the secretive exchange between the two women.

"Why not?" Yellowbird smiled and withdrew from the parlor.

"Yellowbird looks dreadful," Manon said condescendingly. "She must be afraid of becoming fat, but losing weight does not look well on her."

Phillip rose abruptly to his feet.

"More champagne?"

"I haven't finished this." She held up her glass.

"How long will Colette be?" Why the devil had Manon identified him by name? That wasn't necessary.

"Phillip, how can I know?" Manon shrugged.

Phillip poured himself another glass of champagne, drank it thirstily.

"It's hot in here," he complained and crossed to open a window.

"Phillip, no!" Manon shrieked. "In fever season you must keep the windows shut."

"If Colette is much longer," Phillip warned, "I'll finish this whole bottle." Already he felt lightheaded. He should have slept this afternoon. He should have eaten.

"*Chéri,* you are so impetuous." Manon walked towards him with calculated provocativeness.

Phillip, oblivious of this, was already pouring himself another glass of champagne. "Phillip," she scolded. "I don't please you anymore."

Phillip turned to her, his eyes focusing on the daring décolletage of her gown. He cleared his throat, leaned forward to slide one hand inside the low-cut bodice.

"Manon, let's not wait for Colette," he coaxed amorously. "Let's go upstairs right now."

"Phillip, that's impossible," Manon reminded impatiently. "Drink your champagne. Colette will come to us soon."

"I've had too much champagne already," he said with a frown, pulling his hand away from her. Unsteadily he moved to the sofa.

He knew he was becoming drunk. His vision was fuzzy; his head was reeling.

"Phillip!" Manon wailed. "Phillip, you're drunk."

"Let me sleep a few minutes. I'll be all right." Why did she have to talk so loud?

"Phillip, no!" Manon screeched indignantly.

He was conscious of Yellowbird's arrival in the parlor. He heard her talking with Manon; it was as though he were a disinterested bystander.

"It's all right, Manon," Yellowbird was saying soothingly. "I'll send Lloyd to help you take him up to my rooms. Let him sleep for a while, then Lloyd will bring a pot of coffee to you."

Phillip was conscious of being dragged to his feet, of being encouraged to walk from the parlor and up a broad flight of stairs to the second floor.

He mumbled a complaint as he realized he must manage still another flight to Yellowbird's private quarters.

Without opening his eyes, he allowed himself to be propelled across one room and into another. He was conscious of being prodded onto a bed. Someone was removing his boots. He groaned softly and fell into a heavy sleep.

He returned to consciousness slowly, reluctantly. Through slitted eyes he spied Manon across the room. She stood before a marquetry chest of drawers inspecting the contents of an intricately ornamented ivory box. He watched while she rummaged through the box, pulled forth a daguerreotype, inspected it closely, then replaced it.

Phillip tried to raise his head, groaned as a wave of sickness rose in him. Guiltily Manon put the daguerre back into the ivory box, returned the box to the drawer, and came towards him with a vivacious smile.

"I thought you would never awaken," Manon rebuked him prettily. "I was just about to call you." When she had finished snooping among Yellowbird's possessions. "How do you feel?"

"Like the Russian Army is marching through my stomach. What time is it?"

"Almost ten. We must leave for Savage Oaks. Colette will be busy all evening with a special client," she said delicately. Meaning, a gentleman with the most erotic of demands. "I'll tell Lloyd to send up a pot of coffee."

"God, no!" Phillip objected, but she was already darting from the room.

His eyes swept about Yellowbird's sumptuous bedroom. The damask draperies, the carpet, the satin coverlet on which he lay were of an effervescent yellow. The elegant furniture, he guessed, had been imported from France. He had not expected the madam of the Mansion House to have such excellent taste.

Manon came back into the room with a tray containing a coffee pot and an exquisitely hand-painted cup and saucer. His stomach rebelled as the scent of the coffee assailed his nostrils. He clenched his teeth, vowing he would not be sick.

"Drink slowly," Manon coaxed, coming towards him with the cup of coffee.

"Let it be cool a bit," he stalled. Cautiously he sat up, moved his legs to the floor. "Let me wash my face."

"In there." Manon set down the coffee and helped him towards the door.

The bathroom was beautiful without the ostentation of the bathrooms on the floor below, where Yellowbird's girls received their gentlemen. Phillip splashed water on his face with one hand, supporting himself on the marble basin with the other.

"Phillip?" Manon called uneasily.

"I'm all right," he insisted, but his head was pounding. "I'll be right out."

At Manon's insistence he drank two cups of coffee and felt slightly better. He was humiliated that he had drunk too much champagne. Manon sent Lloyd to summon Caleb with the carriage, and they headed back for Savage Oaks.

With his queasy stomach the ride was a trial. When they were a few minutes beyond the outlying areas of the city and passing a wooded grove, Phillip leaned out of the carriage window with an air of desperation.

"Caleb, stop the carriage," he called hoarsely.

"Phillip, what is it?" Manon demanded. She had been sulking since they left the Mansion House.

"Wait here," he ordered tersely.

He stalked into the darkness of the woods. The upheaval in his stomach was unbearable. Sweat broke out on his forehead as he clung to a nearby tree and was violently sick.

At last, trembling from the bout of nausea, he stood erect. He reached for a handkerchief to wipe the sweat that had collected across his forehead, dabbed at his mouth. The awful feeling was gone. Miraculously he felt himself again. He was whistling as he returned to the carriage.

Manon stared coldly at him as he climbed into the carriage.

"Can we go home now?"

"Caleb, don't drive fast," he ordered, and turned to Manon with his normal air of assurance. "What the devil were you snooping into in Yellowbird's bedroom?" he demanded curiously.

Manon laughed.

"Wouldn't you adore to know?" she mocked.

"I've discovered a scandal in a very important family!"

"Yellowbird could blackmail half the important men in Louisiana," Phillip shot back, but he waited for Manon to elaborate.

This is a family you know very well," she tantalized him. "You would not believe what I found out!"

"Tell me," Phillip ordered amusedly, leaning forward to pull her to him.

"I might," she taunted, "after we make love."

Twenty-five

Suzanne sat alone on the gallery, drawn outdoors by the onerous humidity inside the house. Tonight the scent of the flowers was cloyingly sweet. The mosquitos buzzed about her in strident concert. She sat listening for sounds of Keith's return to the house. It was almost eleven, but he remained with a few hands at the levee.

Immediately after dinner, Jane had gone upstairs to visit with Katie. Later she would come down to sit on the gallery. If Keith returned before Jane joined her on the gallery, then she must tell him instantly that she was returning to Paris. When she promised Mme. Mauriac that she would talk first to Uncle Gilbert, it was with the understanding that he would be in touch with her in two or three days.

She must tell Keith before he tried to persuade her differently. If she weakened and remained, she would grow into a bitter, vindictive woman. Her pride would be destroyed. She must not allow that to happen.

She started at the sound of the front door opening, so intensely had she been involved in her private thoughts.

"Katie's sleeping." Jane's face wore a madonnalike tenderness.

"Jane, let her come down to the table to have her meals with us," Suzanne persuaded impulsively. "We'll all be so gentle. Katie won't be afraid."

"I don't know," Jane hesitated. "She frightens so easily."

"Try bringing her to dinner tomorrow night," Suzanne coaxed and suddenly realized she might not be at Savage Oaks for dinner tomorrow night. *How was she going to bear being away from Keith forever?*

"All right," Jane capitulated after a moment of inner debate, yet she was fearful of this experience. "If Katie shows any indication of becoming frightened, I'll take her directly upstairs." But her eyes were hopeful.

"Did Phillip go back to the levee?" Suzanne asked. He had not appeared for dinner.

"No. I was worried so I sent George out to ask Abram if he had not seen him. He said Phillip had taken a carriage with some story about going visiting. I suspect he's gone into the city." She shook her head in annoyance. "Phillip knows how ineffectual the Board of Health is. The city officials are trying to keep it quiet, but there've been a number of deaths already this summer from yellow fever."

412

"Phillip will be all right," Suzanne comforted her.

"And where's Keith?" Jane's voice was edged with exasperation. "He sent most of the hands back to the quarters. Why must he stay down at the levee this way?"

"I'm sure Keith will be home soon." She would remain here on the gallery until he did return. If Jane remained, then she must postpone telling him of her decision until tomorrow. *But in the morning she would tell him.*

"Here's Keith now." Jane's face brightened.

Keith and Reagan were approaching on horseback. Keith dismounted and gave the reins of his horse to Reagan, who would return the horse to the stable, en route to his cottage.

"Keith, you must be exhausted." Jane rose solicitously to her feet as he mounted the stairs. "I'll have Clarissa prepare some supper for you."

"No," Keith brushed this aside. "I just want a bath. I haven't been out of these clothes for three days." His eyes rested warmly on Suzanne. "You were wonderful. Jane, you should have seen her! Driving back and forth from dawn to sunset. Caring for the hands when they were hurt. Raising all our spirits."

"I know." Jane smiled gently.

"I'm going upstairs to a bath, clean clothes and to sleep around the clock." Keith covered a yawn with an unfamiliarly dirty hand. "Thank God we weathered the crevasse so well."

He walked into the house. Suzanne and Jane

heard him calling loudly from the foyer.

"George! Bring the tub upstairs. I want a bath as hot as you can make it."

"I'll sit out here and wait for Phillip," Jane said after a moment.

"I'll wait with you for a while," Suzanne decided.

With a sense of relief, Keith stripped away his mud-caked clothes and stepped into the tub of hot water George had prepared for him.

"It's all right, George. Go on to bed now." He just wanted to sit here alone and feel the hot water seep into his skin.

"I put a pitcher of lemonade on the wash-stand," George said sympathetically. "You gonna be powerful hot from that water."

"Bring it over here," Keith instructed, "and pour me a glass, please."

He leaned back against the tub and sipped the ice cold lemonade, reliving in his mind the hectic, harried days just past. Each time his eyes had fallen on Suzanne he had stirred with passion. He had promised himself that when the break was repaired he would return to this house and claim his wife again. There would never be another woman for him except Suzanne.

As he soaked in the water, his tiredness seemed to evaporate. Later he would collapse into a twelve-hour sleep; but right now he was all at once fully awake, his emotions honed to new sensitivity. Why did Suzanne keep him from her bed?

With sudden resolution he rose to his feet, stepped from the tub. He reached for the towel, which George had laid handily across a chair, and dried himself. He brought down a blue silk dressing gown, pulled it on, and stepped out into the night-quiet hall. Jane and Suzanne were still sitting on the gallery. Their voices filtered up to him as he noiselessly moved down the hall to Suzanne's room, opened the door, and walked inside.

Patrice looked up, startled by his unexpected appearance.

"I jest turnin' down the bed for Miss Suzanne," she said with a glint of approval in her eyes.

"Go on to bed, Patrice," he said self-consciously. "Miss Suzanne won't be needing you anymore tonight."

"Yassir," she agreed with alacrity and darted smilingly from the room.

He walked to a window, opened but protected from the pesky insects to some extent by the closed shutters. At last a breeze from the river was alleviating the humid heat that had stalked the house earlier. He stood at the window, enjoying the pleasant air that floated in through the shutters.

He remained at the window, impatience growing in him as he listened for some indication that Suzanne was coming up to her room. Normally, even on hot nights, she was in her room by this hour.

All at once he stiffened into alertness. No sound of voices came from the gallery now. Suzanne must be on her way upstairs. But as he took a step away from the window, Keith heard Phillip down below.

"Where's Suzanne," Phillip asked agitatedly.

"She's gone to her room," Jane said.

"I have to talk to her — "

"Tomorrow," Jane insisted. "She's worn out from these last days. Phillip, where have you been all these hours?"

With heightened excitement Keith crossed to the door, positioning himself beside it in the fashion that would conceal him as Suzanne came into the room. He must convince her that he loved her, force an acknowledgment from her that she loved him. They would make love and it would be as it was that night she came to his room.

The door was opening. He tensed in anticipation.

"Suzanne," he said softly and she spun about in shock. "Suzanne, why do you avoid me?" he rebuked.

"Keith, I'm very tired. Please go." She was trembling.

"These last days, seeing you on the levee that way, I knew I couldn't go on living with your door looked to me!" He reached to draw her close. She lowered her eyes. "I was terrified for your safety when you were nursing the children in the quarters. Why can't you forget that Gilbert

416

Mauriac arranged our marriage? Suzanne, I love you. I'll never love another woman."

"I don't believe you!" She raised her eyes to his. They glowed darkly with reproach.

"Suzanne — " His voice choked with emotion as he brought her face to his. Let her know how deeply he loved her.

His mouth clung to hers. He felt the hammering of her heart against his body as his arms brought her closer to him. How stiffly she held herself! But all at once the stiffness receded. Her arms tightened about his shoulders.

"Suzanne," he whispered after a few moments. "Do you believe me now?"

"Yes." Her voice was inaudible but the movement of her lips gave him her answer. "Oh, Keith — "

He lifted her fragile slimness in his arms and carried her to the bed. Never had he been aware of such a surge of passion. A need in him to satisfy not only his own desires but to please his wife.

"Every day I've grown to love you more," he said softly as he caressed her. "Every night I've been sleepless because I couldn't be with you."

Her arms closed in about him when he brought himself to her. She was welcoming him with a passion that matched his own. And soon in the dark stillness of the night the ecstatic satisfaction they found simultaneously was a muted symphony.

Suzanne stirred into wakefulness, the memory of last night lighting her face. She felt refreshed; the tiredness that she had stubbornly denied when the others questioned her had disappeared. Tenderly she turned to Keith, sleeping heavily beside her. He would surely sleep until noon. With one finger she traced the dark crescents beneath his eyes, knowing she would not disturb him. How exhausted he was from the grueling days on the levee, yet he had concealed himself in her room last night to convince her of his love.

The girl in the cottage must be an obsession. Cecile had talked about such happenings. Keith was so sensitive to the feelings of others; perhaps he could not find a way to dismiss the girl.

She would send away the girl in the cottage, Suzanne resolved. Keith was her husband, whom she loved. She would fight for him. Quickly she dressed, pleased that Patrice had laundered her favorite green Saxony cloth riding dress. She needed the assurance that she looked her best when she confronted her rival for Keith's affections.

She inspected her reflection in the mirror, rigorously pushing aside the reservations that threatened to overtake her. She would go to the cottage. She was strong enough to fight for Keith.

Carefully, though she knew how soundly Keith slept, she opened the door and walked out into the hall. She heard Jane's voice in the guest room assigned to Katie. Callie was coming upstairs with a breakfast tray for the two of them. Jane enjoyed having Katie so accessible, she thought compassionately. And tonight, Suzanne remembered, Katie would join them for dinner.

"Mawnin', Miss Suzanne," Arthur greeted her with a smile at the door of the dining room. Both the field hands and the house servants felt a new affection for her, she realized. The knowledge buoyed her decision to follow through on the confrontation with the girl in the cottage.

She sat down to breakfast, relieved that Phillip, too, was sleeping late this morning. She ate without tasting, gearing herself for what must be done. It was early to call on anyone, she thought hesitantly while Arthur poured a second cup of coffee for her, as he automatically did each morning. But she did not trust herself to delay this confrontation.

Suzanne drained her second cup of coffee and left the house. Abram would not think it strange that she was taking Othello out this morning. Last night's heat wave had broken. As she walked towards the stable, she gazed up at the sky, cloudless and beautiful. Yet there was a strangeness in the atmosphere, as though a storm hovered indecisively in the shadows.

Astride Othello, she took the circuitous path to the edge of the clearing where the cottage sat wrapped in silence. Momentarily immobile, she reined in Othello. Her heart was pounding. She could hear Phillip's voice telling her about the cottage, before they had discovered it was no longer unoccupied.

"Papa built the cottage a year after my mother died. He swore he would never marry again. He brought his quadroon mistresses to live there. He filled that cottage with fine antiques and priceless wall hangings and exquisite porcelain. He needed that refuge."

But Keith had no need of such refuge, she told herself with a surge of confidence. They had each other. After last night she knew.

Striving to retain her composure, she dismounted, tied the reins to a nearby sapling. Her teeth clenched, she walked with small, quick steps to the gallery, knocked, and waited.

"Lily Mae!" a voice inside called querulously. "Bring me my dressing gown. Be quick about it, you lazy little slut!"

Her head lifted proudly, a strained smile on her face, Suzanne waited. The door swung open. The beautiful quadroon stood there with a dazzling smile on her face. She had expected Keith, or Phillip. Instantly the smile disappeared. Her eyes were wary.

"I'm Suzanne Savage," she said calmly. "I've come to talk to you."

"I'm Manon." The girl shrugged with an air of carelessness, but her eyes were defiant. "You can come in if you like."

"There'll be no need. I'm here to tell you to pack up your things and leave Savage Oaks. I'll have a carriage sent over to take you in to New Orleans."

"Keith didn't send you here." Manon's eyes flashed arrogantly.

"No," Suzanne acknowledged. "I'm telling you to leave gracefully. I'd prefer not to have to ask Keith to dismiss you."

"Oh, listen to this fine lady!" Manon jeered. "You don't fool me! You're no better than I!"

"I'm Keith's wife." Color flooded Suzanne's cheeks. "How dare you talk to me like that!"

"I know who you are," Manon said with deceptive sweetness. "I know about your mother. Does Keith?"

All at once Suzanne was pale with excitement.

"What do you know about my mother?" Her eyes clung to Manon.

"Go to the Mansion House," Manon said vindictively. "Ask Yellowbird Shaw to tell you who your mother is! She knows!"

Suzanne trembled so badly it was necessary to reach out a hand to a nearby chair to steady herself. She remembered the night at the Opera when a gentleman seated in a nearby stall had spoken so incautiously about Yellowbird Shaw and the Mansion House. Maman had been one of Yellowbird Shaw's girls? Adrian Ramsay had married a girl who catered to the whims of the gentlemen of New Orleans? No! No, she could not believe that! But Manon stared at her with such callous assurance.

She could hear Manon's laughter as she ran from the cottage, almost falling over a bough, to where Othello waited. She rode recklessly back

to the stable, her mind in turmoil. She remembered Uncle Gilbert's endless fabrications about
Maman and Papa. Was he trying to protect her
from the truth?

"Abram, I want a carriage immediately," she
said with a peremptoriness that elicited astonishment from him. "Hurry, please." Papa's family
had refused to recognize her, she thought with
anguish, because they doubted that she was
Adrian's child. They could not believe he had
married a girl from the Mansion House.

Caleb brought out the brougham for her, let
down the steps, and she climbed inside. As the
horses moved forward at Caleb's orders, she
heard Phillip's voice close by.

"Suzanne! Suzanne, wait!"

She could not talk to Phillip now. She leaned
out the window, pantomimed for Caleb to go on
because he seemed on the point of pulling the
horses to a halt. She was going to the Mansion
House.

She leaned back in the carriage, reliving the
precious memories she had hoarded through the
years. Papa putting her to bed each night.
Maman always laughing, making her laugh. But
now Manon's voice intruded with her ugly accusations.

Phillip rode along the levee, plagued by frustration. Damn, why had he not ordered Edward
to call him early? He had counted on seeing
Suzanne at breakfast. He had vowed last night to

tell her that Keith was not having a liaison with Manon. Except for him, she would never have known about Manon's presence at Savage Oaks, he tortured himself.

He must warn Keith to send Manon away before she decided to tell Suzanne what she knew about Suzanne's mother. He broke out in a sweat, remembering. Be honest with Keith; tell him how Manon tricked him into allowing her to stay.

Where was Suzanne going in the brougham at this hour of the morning? She had said nothing to Abram about her destination. If she had been headed for Tintagel, she would not have taken the brougham. Had she gone in to New Orleans to visit with Mme. Mauriac? No, Mme. Mauriac must have left for their lake house by now.

Was there some way *he* could persuade Manon to go back to the Mansion House now instead of waiting till the fall? Phillip searched his mind. Yellowbird was generous with her girls. Wouldn't Manon be happier there? Go to her, Phillip prodded himself. Try to convince Manon to take up the old life immediately. Why remain here till October when she was so bored? Did she expect Keith to change his mind and resume the old relationship? He would not.

With Manon out of the cottage, Phillip suddenly decided, he would move in with Peter and Elizabeth. How could he go on allowing them to live in the quarters? When they were older, he would move with them to New York or San

Francisco. They would be his reason for living.

Phillip rode briskly to the cottage. As he dismounted, he heard Manon screeching obscenities at Lily Mae. Lily Mae darted from the back door, disappearing into the woods. Phillip heard the sound of a crash inside.

"Manon!" he called brusquely, pounding on the door. She must have broken one of Papa's priceless porcelains. They should have been brought into the house at Papa's death, but Keith must have worried about how to explain them to Jane. Surely Jane knew about Papa's women.

The door swung wide. Manon stood before him. Her eyes were blazing. As he feared, the shattered fragments of a priceless Ming plate lay at her feet.

"*Chéri.*" Instantly her eyes softened charmingly. She reached to draw him into the cottage. "That slut Lily Mae — she's so stupid." She was inspecting him appraisingly. "Phillip, you know what I was thinking?" she said amorously. "How wonderful it would be if you took a small house in New Orleans. For just the two of us."

"I have no funds," he reminded bluntly. "I'm the younger, useless son."

"Keith is unfair to you," Manon flared. And then she was smiling secretly. "I had a visitor this morning." Phillip tensed. "Keith's fancy lady came calling on me. She got more than she expected." She lifted her head triumphantly. "I told her where she can find out about her mother. I'm sure Yellowbird will oblige her."

"You sent Suzanne to the Mansion House?" Involuntarily Phillip's hand swung out to deliver a stinging blow to one cheek. "You bitch!"

Manon threw herself at him, clawing at his face.

"She's no better than me! I told her! I told her!"

Phillip grabbed her flailing hands and flung her to the floor.

"Pack your things and get out! I'm telling Keith what you've done!" Phillip was white with fury.

"Do you think Keith will be happy to learn the truth?" she taunted. "Tell him! I dare you to tell him about his fancy wife!"

Twenty-six

An unseasonable chill hung in the air as the carriage approached New Orleans. Masses of dark clouds converged in the sky. Huddled in one corner of the carriage, Suzanne shivered. Caleb had been disturbed when she gave him her destination, but he had not dared to dispute her order.

They were at the outskirts of the city now. Caleb had told her the Mansion House was situated in this area. She leaned forward, wondering which of the fine town houses that lay ahead of them was her destination.

She clung fervently to her composure. How could she believe that Maman had been one of Yellowbird Shaw's girls? Yet Manon had spoken with such conviction.

In her mind she relived the moments in the Cathedral of Notre-Dame, where she had vowed to dedicate her life to learning about Maman and Papa. She was convinced that Maman was alive, so frustrated because she could find no clue to Maman's whereabouts. Would Yellowbird Shaw be able to tell her where Maman lived? Was Maman here in New Orleans?

The carriage pulled up before a three-storied mansion. His face betraying his distress, Caleb helped her down.

"Missy, you don' wanna go in there," he said plaintively. "Let me take you home."

"Wait for me, Caleb." It was as though she had not heard him.

She hurried to the wrought-iron fence, opened it, and walked to the heavy door of the stuccoed, slate-roofed structure. With one small trembling hand she sounded the knocker.

Suzanne saw a grille in the door opened. Eyes inspected her. She held her head high, mouth slightly parted. She would not be denied admission.

The door opened. A liveried black man stared at her in astonishment.

"Please tell Miss Shaw that Suzanne Savage wishes to speak with her," Suzanne said imperiously, fighting not to reveal the terrifying uncertainties that raged within her.

"Miss Shaw be sleepin' this early," he reproached gently, obviously bewildered by her appearance here. But he stood stalwartly at the door, denying her entrance.

"I'll wait," Suzanne insisted. "I must speak with her."

"Lloyd, who's at the door?" a feminine voice called from somewhere inside the house.

"Miss Yellowbird, you know what the doctor

say," he reminded worriedly. "You is supposed to rest all day."

"Lloyd, who is it?" Yellowbird's voice was weak but the tone was impatient.

"A young lady," he said reluctantly. "Miss Savage."

Her heart pounding, Suzanne waited for a reply from the woman within the house. Each second seemed agonizingly long.

"Show her into the front parlor," Yellowbird said quietly. "I'll be downstairs in a few minutes."

Lloyd showed her into a small but magnificently furnished parlor. The walls were hung in cerise silk, matched by the silk upholstery of a pair of small Empire sofas. The rug beneath her feet was surely an Aubusson, Suzanne thought with subconscious respect for its beauty. A small crystal chandelier was suspended from the ceiling.

Too distraught to sit, Suzanne went to one of the tall, narrow windows that looked out on a side garden lush with crepe myrtle that would be dazzling with clusters of bright pink blossoms in another week. The house was engulfed in silence. Suzanne strived to blot out of her mind the sordid diversions provided in the Mansion House by night. Mentally she formed the questions she must ask.

How had Manon been so sure that Yellowbird Shaw knew Maman? A coldness crept over her. Did Maman live here at the Mansion House?

"You wished to see me?" a voice asked quietly

and Suzanne spun about from the window to confront the gaunt but beautiful woman who was walking into the parlor. Her face was tired, drawn, the well-cut features seeming fragilely chiseled today, in startling contrast to the face of the robustly attractive woman she had encountered in Uncle Gilbert's office.

"You're Miss Shaw?" Suzanne asked uncertainly.

"Yes." She smiled inquiringly.

All at once Suzanne was terrified to test Manon's declaration that this woman who stood before her knew Maman.

"I was told," she stammered. . . . "Someone I met said that — that — " All at once her eyes fastened on Yellowbird's hands, which alone betrayed her nervousness. *The ring she wore. The twin to the ring Papa had worn.* Her eyes rose to Yellowbird Shaw's face. Today she saw the features of the young woman in Adrian Ramsay's painting. The same tilt of the eyebrows, the same eyes. "Manon told me to come to the Mansion House to find my mother — and I have," she whispered.

"Suzanne, I didn't want you to know." The color was drained from Yellowbird's face. "You were never to know."

"How could you have turned away your own child?" Suzanne lashed at her in rage. "Do you know how many years I cried myself to sleep each night? I vowed to seek out anybody I could find who had known Papa and you, so you would become alive to me again. And I find you here!" Suzanne's eyes smoldered with contempt.

"Suzanne, my baby — "Yellowbird closed her eyes. She was ashen.

"After being loved by Adrian Ramsay, how could you live in such a fashion? All my life I've prayed to find my mother! I wish God had never answered my prayers!" Tears flooding her eyes Suzanne swept past Yellowbird and out of the parlor.

"Suzanne! Suzanne!" Yellowbird's anguished voice followed her as she flung herself across the foyer and out of the house.

Trembling, her face tear-streaked, Suzanne allowed herself to be helped solicitously by Caleb into the carriage. How could she go back to Savage Oaks, knowing her mother was the madam of the Mansion House? How could she bring this disgrace to Keith?

"Caleb," she called distraughtly as he was about to take his position on the perch, "take me to Mme. Mauriac's lake cottage." He stared doubtfully at her. "It's on Lake Pontchartrain. We'll ask for the directions for it when we arrive at the lake."

"Missy, it's gonna storm," Caleb said uneasily.

"I must go there, Caleb," Suzanne insisted. "Drive as quickly as you can."

She sat in the carriage, impatient that Caleb drove the horses so prudently. It was at least four miles to Lake Pontchartrain, and Mme. Mauriac's cottage was far out on the lake.

"Caleb!" They were well beyond the city traffic. Why were they moving so slowly? "Go faster, please."

She felt a compulsion to put distance between the Mansion House and herself. She was haunted by the gaunt, pale face that had gazed at her with such pain. The face that Papa had painted when she was a baby. How could Maman have deserted her to go into that kind of life?

It seemed an eternity before they approached the lake. Now they were passing the resort hotels, the magnificent villas of the wealthy. Caleb pulled to a stop at the Elkin and hopped down. Why was he stopping?

"Missy, I go ask about the Mauriac place," he explained, at the same time unhappily inspecting the darkening sky. "It jes' take a minute."

"Of course, Caleb." She forced a strained smile. She had forgot that Caleb had no idea where the cottage was located.

She could never face Keith again, knowing about her mother. Manon knew. How many other people in New Orleans knew? She felt sick with shame. A Savage married to the daughter of the madam of the Mansion House. She had brought disgrace to Keith, whom she loved more than life itself.

Caleb was returning to the carriage at a trot.

"It's jes' a piece ahead," he soothed. "We be there directly."

The houses became farther apart. At last

Caleb slowed the horses down before a charming one-story house on the least inhabited part of the lake. The sprawling pine wood house had a broad gallery with chinaberry trees and oaks in front. An alabaster Diana rose from lush green shrubbery. The gallery looked out on the lake, today a churning, turbulent sickly green.

Alighting from the carriage, Suzanne was faintly conscious of the weird wind that swept across the lake. She hurried up the bricked path to the steps that led to the gallery. Enormous droplets of rain were beginning to fall.

"Caleb, take the carriage into the barn," Suzanne called as she mounted the steps.

Amelia must have heard the carriage approach because now she pulled open the front door in welcome.

"Amelia, who is it?" Mme. Mauriac inquired from within the house.

"Miss Suzanne!" Amelia was simultaneously startled and delighted at this unexpected visit. "Come in," she invited. "Looks like you just missin' the storm."

"Is Uncle Gilbert here?" Suzanne allowed Mme. Mauriac to draw her into the parlor.

"He had to go into the city today," Mme. Mauriac explained.

"May I stay here for a few days?" Suzanne asked tremulously. "I can't go back to Savage Oaks — "

"Of course you may stay, Suzanne." Mme. Mauriac was upset. "Tell me, what has happened?" She pulled Suzanne down to the green velvet sofa that flanked the fireplace, where Sebastien was laying a fire because of the sudden drop in temperature. Outside the wind was blowing fiercely. Rain pounded on the roof. "Sebastien, go out to the kitchen, please, and ask Amelia to make coffee for us." Suzanne knew this was a diplomatic move to give them privacy.

"Yes ma'am. Then I best close all the shutters."

Suzanne waited until Sebastien was beyond earshot before she spoke. Her throat was tight with the effort to retain her composure.

"Mme. Mauriac, I — I know about Maman." She saw the pain in Mme. Mauriac's eyes as comprehension came to her.

"Suzanne, tell me what you know," she ordered slowly.

"I went to the cottage to send that girl packing," Suzanne said haltingly, tears running down her cheeks. "She said I was no better than she. She told me to go to the Mansion House and ask Yellowbird Shaw about my mother. I went there. As soon as I saw her, I knew." Suzanne's voice sank to a whisper. "She wore a ring exactly like Papa's. I looked at her and I saw the young woman in Papa's painting."

"I remember the ring." Mme. Mauriac's face was touched with sadness. "There are only two rings like that in the world. Adrian designed them himself and had them made up in Paris. One for Moira, one for himself."

"I asked her how she could have deserted me.

How could she live as she does after being loved by Papa! And then I ran." She closed her eyes, wishing she could erase those moments from her memory.

"Suzanne, you listen to me," Mme. Mauriac commanded, jarring her out of recall. "I knew your parents. They were fine and intelligent. They were married, Suzanne," Mme. Mauriac said emphatically. "Adrian had every intention of bringing Moira and you to live at Tintagel — "

"She didn't have to live as she does!" Suzanne defied.

"Wait, Suzanne, before you sit in judgment," Mme. Mauriac ordered. "Hear me out." Her eyes demanded acquiescence. "Gilbert couldn't bear to write Moira the terrible news of your father's death. He went to Paris to tell her and to bring the two of you to New Orleans. You remember nothing of that, Suzanne?"

"No," she whispered.

"On board Moira was robbed of a small box of jewelry that also contained her marriage papers and your baptismal record. Both Gilbert and Moira tried to convince Noah that Adrian had left a widow and daughter, but he was stubborn. Without the papers he refused to believe this. Gilbert made every effort to contact the small French village where Moira and Adrian had been married. A fire had reduced the village to rubble. The villagers had scattered."

"But why did she abandon me? How could she allow herself to sink so low?"

"Moira was completely without funds. The story Gilbert told you about the rich patroness — " Mme. Mauriac spread her hand apologetically. "There was no patroness. When Noah refused to receive her, she went to her parents with you." Mme. Mauniac's face was taut with recall. "They cursed her and slammed the door in her face. She came to us. The two of you remained with Gilbert and me for almost a year, but Moira was proud. She refused to take any more of what she considered charity. She had a marriage behind her that nobody in Louisiana would recognize, and a child by that marriage. That she was beautiful and charming and intelligent meant nothing in the business world. She made connections in New Orleans. She acquired financing to establish herself in the only business where she could expect to earn enough to raise you as Adrian's daughter should be raised."

"I would have been happier with her," Suzanne rejected. "I didn't have to grow up in luxury."

"Your mother knew you would grow up with a stigma unless she planned your life carefully, Suzanne. You think she didn't agonize before she went into her life-long occupation?" Mme. Mauriac asked grimly. "Moira and I discussed it." Suzanne stared at her in shock. Mme. Mauriac smiled faintly. "Suzanne, a woman can be far more practical than any man. Moira opened a business. She provided a service. If she had not, somebody else would have. She did it for you." Mme. Mauriac leaned forward, her eyes commanding Suzanne to understand. "She took her baby, whom she adored, to the Convent in France and she went about earning the money necessary to bring you up to be an educated young lady worthy of your father. Every cent Moira earned was invested by Gilbert so that you would have a fortune and be able to marry well. She called herself Yellowbird because that was Adrian's pet name for her. She bought Tintagel so that she could give you your ancestral home that is rightfully yours."

The tears that filled Suzanne's eyes spilled over without her being aware.

"I didn't know — "

"A year ago, Yellowbird discovered she was desperately ill. She has only months to live. She longed to see you before she died. It was imperative for her to know that you had married well and were cared for properly."

"So that's why Uncle Gilbert sent for me so suddenly," Suzanne said, a brightness in her eyes.

"Suzanne, you must never think harshly of your mother." Mme. Mauriac's voice deepened with conviction. "Everything she did was for you."

"I said such awful things to her — " Suzanne tried to cope with all that Mme. Mauriac had revealed. "I didn't know — "

"Your maternal grandparents died six years ago, within months of each other. It didn't matter to Yellowbird that they had treated her shamefully. She supported them lavishly in their old age, buried them with honor in the St. Louis Cemetery. She's Moira Ramsay, no matter what she tells herself today. She's every inch Adrian Ramsay's widow."

"I'm going back to the Mansion House," Suzanne said shakily. "Right away. I want to apologize to my mother."

Mme. Mauriac reached for Suzanne's hand.

"When this storm is over," she stipulated gently. Lightning flashed across the sky, brightening the parlor. Thunder sounded like a dozen cannon being shot simultaneously. "Gilbert always worries about the summer storms out here, but I love this house. We've always been fortunate." Mme. Mauriac smiled with equanimity. "Four years ago, three houses below us were demolished. All we lost was a chimney." She reached for the bell that would summon Sebastien. "Why is Amelia taking so long with our coffee?"

Sebastien hurried down the hall and into the parlor.

"Amelia be ready with the coffee in a couple minutes," he said apologetically. He hesitated, obviously upset. "We's got some trouble in the kitchen house. Water's comin' up from de floor. We never has that before."

Suzanne darted to a window, opened a shutter a few inches.

"The rain's coming down too heavily to see what's happening with the lake."

"Sebastien, take some blankets and cover the

437

floor," Mme. Mauriac said briskly. "Then you and Amelia come into the main house."

"Yes, ma'am." Sebastien hurried from the room.

"The kitchen is built low," Mme. Mauriac explained to Suzanne. "That must be why the water seeped through the floor."

"The lake might be spilling over the banks," Suzanne said uneasily, returning to sit beside Mme. Mauriac.

"There has not been that much rain," Mme. Mauriac said calmly. "It's the wind that's bringing the water into the kitchen."

Suzanne and Mme. Mauriac started at the sharp knock at the front door.

"Someone is seeking shelter from the storm," Mme. Mauriac guessed.

"I'll go to the door." Suzanne walked swiftly from the parlor and across the foyer to the door, pulled it open slowly, mindful of the heavy winds. "Keith!" She gazed at him in astonishment.

"The storm's approaching hurricane force," Keith said tersely, forestalling any questions. Phillip was standing just behind him. "Where's Mme. Mauriac?"

"Mme. Mauriac is here." She appeared at the entrance to the parlor. "Sebastien tells us water is coming up from the floor in the kitchen house."

"Do you have an ice-house?" Keith asked.

"Of course." She smiled slightly but she was attentive. "It's just past the barn."

"Stone? Built into the ground?" Keith questioned. Mme. Mauriac nodded. "We'll take refuge there."

Only now did Suzanne comprehend the force of the storm.

"We'll want some light." She reached for a small lamp that sat on a nearby table.

"Is we gonna drown?" Amelia hovered in the doorway with the coffee tray.

"No, Amelia," Mme. Mauriac said indomitably. "Put down that tray and tell Sebastien not to bother with blankets for the kitchen floor. Bring them here. We're all going to the icehouse."

"Keith, let's push the armoire against that window," Phillip said. Only then did Suzanne realize the shutters had been ripped away from one of the windows. "The wind's coming from that direction."

Keith and Phillip moved the armoire protectively against the unshuttered window. Sebastien and Amelia hurried into the parlor with blankets. With each of them blanket-draped against the relentless rain, the men with supportive arms about the women, they moved out into the strangely dark outdoors. It might have been night rather than noon.

A dog was barking frantically somewhere close by. Keith stiffened, his eyes turning towards the lake.

"Somebody's on the lake!" Keith exclaimed as lightning brightened the water. "He's only a few feet out, but he's in trouble!"

"Keith, you can't go out there!" Suzanne reached out instinctively to detain him.

"Go on to the ice-house. I'll be right behind you. Phillip, hold on to Suzanne," Keith added because the wind was making their progress perilous.

Reluctantly Suzanne allowed Phillip, an arm about her waist, to prod her forward. Amelia and Sebastien were flanking Mme. Mauriac. In the distance they could hear a man's voice yelling frantically.

"Pull me in! For God's sake, pull me in!"

"Caleb and Lewis must be in the barn," Phillip said uneasily as they approached. Inside the horses whinnied in alarm.

"Sebastien, go in and tell them to come to the ice-house," Mme. Mauriac instructed.

"Yes ma'am."

The others, clinging together, blankets over their heads, made their way to the ice-house. While Phillip struggled to open the stubborn door, Sebastien joined them, panting from his efforts.

"Mist' Phillip," Sebastien said worriedly, "Caleb and Lewis, they say they wanna stay with the horses if you'all don' mind, Suh."

"The horses are frightened," Phillip said with understanding. "All right, Sebastien, let them stay."

Amelia kept her arms protectively about the diminutive Mme. Mauriac while Phillip

440

wrenched open the door.

"Let's push the hay on this side all the way to the back, Sebastien. Then there'll be enough room for all of us," Phillip said calmly. "The door will have to stay ajar to give us air."

Suzanne clung to a nearby chinaberry tree, stripped bare of its leaves by the force of the storm while her eyes searched anxiously for sight of Keith. *What was happening on the lake?*

"Amelia, help Mme. Mauriac into the ice-house," Phillip said after a few moments. "Walk carefully around to the left side. Suzanne — " He moved towards her, realizing she had not heard him in her concern for Keith. Close by there was a sharp, rending loudness as lightning struck a tree. "Suzanne!"

Twenty-seven

Suzanne felt herself pulled away from the chinaberry tree and hurled to the ground. She heard a painful outcry from Phillip. Dazed from the impact she managed to struggle to her feet.

"Phillip!"

A bough from the tall, moss-draped live oak that stood twenty feet away had been split by the lightning. Phillip lay beneath a segment of the heavy bough. He was unconscious, his arm outstretched at a strange angle.

"Sebastien!" she called urgently, dropping to her knees beside Phillip. With an effort she lifted the bough from Phillip, fought to hold it until Sebastien came forward to help her. Sebastien lifted the bough, cast it to one side.

"We gotta get him into the ice-house," Sebastien said fearfully.

"I'll help you." Suzanne was alarmed by Phillip's pallor. Blood was oozing from a cut on his forehead. "We can manage, Sebastien." *Where was Keith?*

Together Sebastien and Suzanne dragged Phillip into the shelter of the ice-house. Suzanne hovered over him, trying to determine the extent of his injuries. His arm was broken. The cut on his forehead needed attention.

"Suzanne, put some hay beneath his head," Mme. Mauriac said. "And cover him with a blanket against this cold."

Behind a protective blanket held by Amelia and Mme. Mauriac, Suzanne removed her petticoat and ripped it to bandage Phillip's forehead.

"The broken arm should have a splint." Suzanne's eyes searched the interior of the ice-house. "Sebastien, pull down one of those shelves there. Use the ice-saw to split it."

While Suzanne was tying the splint about his injured arm, Phillip stirred into consciousness.

"You all right?" He squinted at her in the dim light of the dank, cold ice-house.

"I'm fine," Suzanne soothed. "I wouldn't be if you had not pushed me out of the way of that bough."

"Lean closely. I want to tell you something."

Startled, Suzanne leaned forward, questions in her eyes.

"Keith doesn't see Manon anymore," Phillip whispered. "He's allowed her to stay on in the cottage because she lied to him. She told him she was terrified of the summer fever threats in New Orleans. But he hasn't seen her for weeks." Despite his pain he smiled triumphantly.

Silently Suzanne leaned forward to kiss him on one cheek.

"Thank you, Phillip. My dear, dear friend."

Awkwardly Phillip maneuvered into a semi-sitting position, wincing as he did so.

"I'll fix a sling for your arm." Suzanne took the remains of her petticoat and ripped from it a strip that could be utilized as a sling, all the while subconsciously asking herself, *Why is Keith not here?*

"Amelia, stop looking so frightened," Mme. Mauriac chided with rare irritation. "We'll be safe here till the storm's over. But where's Keith?"

"I'm here." Keith pushed the door wide, subjecting them to a rush of wind and rain. "Soaking wet but all in one piece." A small, stocky man, visibly shaken, followed Keith. An Irish setter waited uncertainly at the door.

"You don't mind if the dog comes in?" the man questioned politely.

"Bring him inside, please." Mme. Mauriac might have been inviting them into her drawing room. At a snap of the man's fingers the dog bounded inside, and his owner pulled the door into its previous position.

"Phillip, what happened to you?" Keith dropped to his haunches beside Phillip.

"I ran into a falling tree," Phillip said flippantly.

Quietly Suzanne explained.

"This is a day for heroics," their guest said with

the lilt of Scotland in his voice. "I was out on the lake when the storm came up. I tried to return to shore but the wind wouldn't allow this. The boat was in danger of capsizing. I tied a rope about MacAlpin's neck and tossed him into the lake. He swam to shore. The gentleman here — " He turned gratefully to Keith, "pulled me in. I owe you my life, Sir."

"The wind swept you far from your hotel." Keith was self-conscious at the display of gratitude. "When this is over, we'll take you there in the carriage."

"How long do you think it'll be before the storm is over?" Suzanne asked. "A doctor should set Phillip's arm properly."

"We'll have to settle in and wait," Keith said somberly. "I'm sorry, Mme. Mauriac. Half the roof has flown off the house and the gallery is a shambles."

"We are alive and well," Mme. Mauriac said with strength. "The house can be repaired."

"What about the barn?" Suzanne asked worriedly. "Caleb and Lewis are there with the horses."

"The barn was untouched when we came past," Keith said encouragingly.

He went to the other side of the ice-house, found two boxes on which Mme. Mauriac and Suzanne could sit. Amelia had already settled herself on a mound of hay. Mme. Mauriac reminisced about storms in other years. But all the while Suzanne's thought dwelt on what Mme.

Mauriac had revealed about Maman. She would bring Maman to Tintagel. All these years Maman had thought only of her; now she must think only of Maman. *How was she going to tell Keith what she must tell him? How was she going to survive without him?*

"This is not a hurricane," Mme. Mauriac said emphatically. "It is a bad storm. We have seen worse in Louisiana."

Earlier than they had dared to hope, the rain ceased to fall. A slight wind was blowing from the southeast, but the storm was past. Even as they emerged from the ice-house, a faint light broke through the grayness.

The ground beneath their feet was sodden and matted with the earlier avalanche of falling leaves. They walked cautiously over the broken boughs and twigs strewn about the earth. His dog at his heels, their guest took a hurried departure, after a reiteration of his gratitude for Keith's rescue efforts and an assurance he preferred to walk.

Keith kept a hand protectively at Suzanne's elbow. Her throat was tight with the knowledge that, despite the depth of her love for Keith, she meant to bring Maman to Tintagel. She painfully thrust aside the realization that the acknowledgment of Maman's identity would destroy her marriage.

"The barn's in fine shape," Phillip said with approval as they approached. The door was open, Lewis and Caleb peering out with wide grins.

"It weathered the storm better than the house," Mme. Mauriac said with ironic humor, her gaze moving from the barn to the battered house.

"Lewis, please bring the carriage out for Mr. Phillip," Suzanne instructed, grateful to evade briefly the inevitable confrontation with Keith. Lewis would travel with greater speed than Caleb. Phillip made a show of cheerfulness, but she could see by his pallor that he was in pain.

Keith turned to Mme. Mauriac with solicitude.

"You must change into dry clothing and we'll take you into New Orleans."

"I will change into dry clothing, yes," Mme. Mauriac said matter-of-factly, "but I'll remain here with Amelia and Sebastien."

"Mme. Mauriac, half the roof is off the house," Keith protested gently.

"That's why we have to stay. We'll try to protect those rooms the best we can. I would appreciate it if you would stop at Gilbert's office and ask his clerk to send two carpenters out here tomorrow morning. If you're going into the city," she amended questioningly.

"We must go into the city to return to Savage Oaks," Keith reminded. "We'll be happy to stop by the office."

"Thank you, Keith," Mme. Mauriac said gratefully. "And please tell Gilbert's clerk what must be done so he can have the carpenters bring out the necessary supplies."

"We'll be sure to see to it," Keith promised.

"Have Phillip travel alone so he can lie down in the carriage," Mme. Mauriac arranged. "Sebastien, go into the house and bring some pillows for Mr. Phillip. And take the blankets with you — "

"Yes, ma'am." Laden down with the damp blankets, Sebastien headed for the house, choosing his path cautiously over the sodden earth.

Her heart pounding. Suzanne waited for the carriages to be brought out. She searched her mind for the words that must be said, that would remove Keith forever from her life. She must be strong enough to see this through. She shivered, silently rehearsing the small, painful speech.

"You're cold, Suzanne." Keith pulled off his jacket and draped it about her shoulders. "Your boots are surely wet."

"No, they're not," she insisted. Only now did she realize she still wore her riding dress and boots. Keith looked upon her with such love, and on the ride into New Orleans she must kill that love forever.

Mme. Mauriac concentrated on seeing to Phillip's comfort, but Suzanne saw the deep compassion for her when their eyes met.

"We'll go directly to Mr. Mauriac's office," Keith told Mme. Mauriac when Caleb pulled up with the carriage. "If he's left for the day, I'll leave an explicit note."

"Thank you, Keith." She leaned forward to kiss Suzanne, pressed her hand reassuringly. But her eyes were troubled.

Lewis set off ahead of Caleb, the horses traveling at a steady gait despite the wetness of the earth. Caleb followed at a slower pace, distrusting the bad road.

"Keith, please tell Caleb to stop at the Mansion House before you go to Uncle Gilbert's office," Suzanne said slowly.

She had expected a shocked reaction from him, but without a word, Keith leaned out the window and gave Caleb instructions.

"Keith, I have to tell you — " But the words she rehearsed refused to come.

"Suzanne, I know." He reached for her hands, cold as ice in his. "Phillip discovered you had gone to the Mansion House — and why. We followed behind but not fast enough to be with you when — "

"You know about Maman?" she interrupted incredulously.

"Phillip told me," Keith said gently. "Your mother was worried because you had left in such a distraught state. Phillip was sure you would go to Mme. Mauriac."

"Keith, I never meant to bring disgrace to you — "

"Suzanne, I married *you*," he said forcefully. "I love you. Knowing about your mother changes nothing. Do you think so little of me," he scolded, "that you believed I would care what people might say? You're my wife, Suzanne."

"Keith, you don't understand," she said

urgently. "Maman is dying. I'm bringing her to Tintagel."

"You're bringing her to her home," Keith emphasized. "We'll go to her together."

"Keith, you want to go into government. How can you do that with a wife who — " She shook her head futilely.

"With a wife who is the daughter of Adrian Ramsay and the granddaughter of Judge Ramsay," Keith said strongly. "A wife who is beautiful, well-educated and intelligent. We may have some rough times, Suzanne, but we'll see them through together." His eyes held hers. "I won't let you go."

While they drove towards New Orleans, her head on his shoulder, Keith told Suzanne about the daguerreotype of them taken at their wedding, which Manon discovered in Yellowbird's bedroom, along with the ribbon-tied packet of letters Suzanne had written to Gilbert through the years. He talked about Jane's affection for Suzanne's father, the closeness of the two families.

The carriage pulled up before the Mansion House. Keith smiled encouragingly as he helped Suzanne down. Walking towards the door with Keith, her hand in his, she could feel Maman's grief when Papa died. Maman's will to raise her, at any cost to herself, as she would have been raised if Papa were alive. She would not allow Maman to refuse to come to Tintagel. This was what Papa would have wished.

Lloyd opened the door. His eyes widened in

astonishment at their appearance here again.

"Miss Yellowbird, she up in her rooms," he said respectfully. "She hasta rest."

"She'll wish to see us, Lloyd," Keith said quietly. "Please go up and ask if we may come upstairs for a few minutes."

"Yassir," Lloyd said uneasily and pulled the door wide to allow them to enter.

Suzanne and Keith waited in the foyer. He held her hand reassuringly in his. How could she have talked to Maman the way she did, Suzanne berated herself? How could she have been so insensitive?

Lloyd came down to the foyer.

"Miss Yellowbird say please to come upstairs."

They followed Lloyd up the two lofty flights. He opened the door to Yellowbird's private suite, and Suzanne and Keith walked inside.

Yellowbird stood at the fireplace of the small, charmingly furnished sitting room. Above the low mantel hung a gold-framed painting of a tiny, smiling girl. Papa's painting of her, Suzanne realized.

Yellowbird managed a tentative smile, but her eyes revealed her fear of fresh recriminations. Subconsciously the fingers of one hand embraced the ring she wore on the other.

"Maman," Suzanne whispered. "I said such terrible things. Can you ever forgive me?"

"Baby — " Yellowbird opened her arms to Suzanne. Tears spilled over unheeded. "My baby, my baby."

"I didn't know," Suzanne said, clinging to Maman. "Mme. Mauriac told me everything. I'll thank God every day of my life that at last I've found you."

"Mrs. Ramsay," Keith said with infinite respect, "Suzanne and I have come to take you to Tintagel."

Yellowbird's eyes clung disbelievingly to Keith's. Then she took a step back from Suzanne to seek confirmation in her daughter's eyes. Suzanne smiled tremulously, her face aglow with joy.

"Mrs. Ramsay, please call someone to pack for you. Suzanne and I have come to take you home," Keith repeated.

Yellowbird reached one hand out to Keith's while the other found Suzanne's.

"You two have given me the happiest day of my life." Her smile was radiant, her eyes luminous. "I dreamt of this moment, but I never truly believed it would happen. But I must stay here. It's better this way," she insisted with unexpected strength because she knew Suzanne was about to protest. Suzanne realized her mother refused to jeopardize the high respect with which the Savages were held in Louisiana. People would never forget that Yellowbird Shaw was the madam of the Mansion House. "I'm comfortable here in my old familiar rooms," Yellowbird continued with an air of conviction, "and you'll come to visit me often. Won't you?" she added softly.

"Every day," Suzanne promised. "I'll come to see you every day, Maman."

She would not allow herself to remember how numbered those days would be. They would enjoy every precious moment that remained for them. She had fulfilled the vow she made in the Cathedral of Notre-Dame. She had found Maman.